Tulubaikaporia

a ritual

Vanechka

Translation and commentary by
Vanya Bagaev

nova·nevédoma

To Rashida Mingaleyevna
Ivan Petrovich

& our Tulubaika

What awaits the reader

Episode One
about applied asymptotology, déjà vu & jamais vu

OPHELIA: What means this, my lord?

HAMLET: Marry, this is miching mallecho; it means mischief.

OPHELIA: Belike this show imports the argument of the play.

— William Shakespeare, "Hamlet"

A dream's a rogue, a phantom, a goal's beyond our grasp; the throwback's doomed — the past is a chimera, a monster caged and clasped.

Boom! Rockets the cork with a thunderous roar and punches a hole in a white panel of suspended ceiling. And there'd been a kitty hiding. Squealing, he darts and dashes around in primordial panic until one of the panels beneath him caves in and the kitty flies right onto our kitchen table, muzzle and front paws plunging into an immeasurable pot of borscht, the immensity of which could have solved planetary hunger almost forever. We laugh, pick up the borschted Meowbius and carry him to the bathroom for a wash whilst he licks the soup off his muzzle. If he'd pulled such a stunt in my parents' house, they'd have grabbed him by the tail and carried him to the vet whilst he mewled, scratched, begged and tried to convince them of his innocence, that he was just doing his job, just catching the universal Mouse above that ceiling as he was destined to, or even exaggerated and said that there were swarms of them, those little grey parasites, who at night drum on the ceiling with hundreds of their

1

little paws and don't let his esteemed and dear owners sleep. My parents wouldn't listen, would still bring him to the vet and, holding him by the tail, get him castrated on the spot so he wouldn't be so rowdy any more. A castrated village cat as a metaphor: lazy, fat, with eyes either like those of an Alexandrian philosopher or a Tibetan monk, having convinced himself of the superiority of mind over phallus, living his best life where he needn't kowtow to his libido, but can simply eat, sleep, meditate on dancing flies, sunbeams, and sparrows. But a metaphor for what? Ponder later.

— And you... when was the last time you were in Tulubaika?

Slavoslav Slavoslavovich[1] is now a balding, paunchy copper. His blue eyes have turned navy to match his uniform, his golden mop got tired of sitting on his head and sprawled all over his body. I want to have a proper chat with him, but there's nothing to talk about. Not because he's bald and paunchy, and not even because he's a copper (though such treachery, I must admit, is hard to forgive, even harder not to joke about, and impossible to weed out of your head), but simply because too many chaotic moments have occurred between the past and present, which, as in an old black-and-white cartoon, magically lined up into a huge interpersonal wall, propped up on both sides by rusty cast-iron pillars. "We don't need no education, we don't need no thought control." We live in different strata of reality. I've been to Berlin and seen the wall, and he hasn't, which is a shame. He probably can't even leave the country, which is also a shame. We speak different languages whilst using the same words and grammar. Life is morphology, a birdly fall into the ocean, but not for fish. To die? Oh no, to reach the depths. What depths? The depths of understanding existence through the study of forms. For there, in the darkness deep, down at the bottom, is a window, and in that window —

---

1. A name that's a bit too Slavic. His parents desperately wanted to maximise his patriotic credentials, hence this. "Slavoslavovich" is a patronymic, meaning his father was also named Slavoslav. It's not a middle name but rather a distinct way of formally addressing a person. The US equivalent might be "Liberty Freedom Jefferson" or "Patriot Eagle Washington," while Brits might encounter a "Winston Britannia Churchillton."

transcendental visions, perhaps a fat learned cat[2], waving its paw at sparrows, lies. No longer walks he round the golden chain, instead, turns over a chimera-thought in his lil'head, ponders how young he used to be, how he leapt among tall grass all dewed. Hop-skip, hop-skip — to the call of rustling wraps, pantherly homewards I bounce, mug cobwebbed — quick-quick-quick — for dry cat food shan't wait for my arrival, shan't ever eat itself! For who am I if not the most dangerous animal on this planet, a violent creature filled with hateful thoughts and a lust for blood and empty boxes?

What to say?

— Can't remember. Ages ago, I reckon. And you?

We're calculating the distance to a place that barely exists. It's sort of there but sort of not and quantum mechanics has nought to do with it. Now, let's take a ruler. A trophy Opel Kapitän sets off from point A to point B, but halfway to point B the engine coughs tubercularly and the car stops. The driver gets out, fixes it, continues the journey, but after travelling half of the remaining half, the car stops again, and so on, half after half. The task: knowing the speed, distance, repair time, and everything else (see Appendix), calculate when the trophy Opel Kapitän will reach point B.

— Every year I plan to but never quite manage it, — Slavoslav Slavoslavovich replies, shrugging. — Work...

— And how is it there these days, do you know?

— Oh, they say it's good...

— That's good that it's good.

— Yeah... Good is always not bad... Much rain these days, they say.

— Well, there'll be mushrooms then.

— There will be... For sure...

— I could do with frying some chanterelles right now.

— Or pickling them... Or going fishing...

— Naaay. I don't like fishing.

---

2. A fat learned cat here and later is a reference to the prologue of Pushkin's 1820s poem "Ruslan and Ludmila" — a tale-telling cat who walks on a chain around an oak tree.

— You used to like fishing.

Oh, I used to like all sorts of things, Slavoslav Slavoslavovich. I wouldn't even pick mushrooms myself now — I'd buy them from an old lady on the road to support the local gross product per capita, because you can't order that sort of thing on any internets.

Slavoslav Slavoslavovich finishes wiping the bottle with a towel decorated with firebirds. The birds absorb the bubbles of cava and fly off tipsy to winter in Tahiti. Whoosh! And they're gone. There they hustle, stay and live, have children, and never return either to Tulubaika or to the surrounding villages.

— I still go... Both winter and summer... Mm... — continues Slavoslav after a long pause.

— Where to?

— Fishing, of course...

— Ah, fishing.

— Yeah, there's a lil'lake not far from here... Not quite Tulubaikan but still decent... We could go, you know... I caught an ide recently, — Slavoslav Slavoslavovich hints modestly.

— A big one?

Slavoslav Slavoslavovich smirks, as if I'd doubted his fishing abilities, and in the air, in addition to the alcoholic fumes, there now hangs a sensation of the unstarted tale about the ide, the tale that no one will ever begin or finish, but nevertheless the tale that lingers, begging with all its being to be let out, and we, mere mortals, don't let it, for we don't need it — we already know what kind of tale it is, for tales like these can be told with just one look, so much so that Tolstoy himself would grow thin[3], our dear Leo Nikolaevich, may he rest in peace and no war. Our dialogue with Slavoslav Slavoslavovich is built exclusively on such tales. They are the pillars of creation of the universe of our communication, unshakable strongholds, understood with just a brief stoic nod, man to man.

— You bet! Bloody enormous. Wanna see the video?

---

3. The etymology of Tolstoy's surname (Толстой) likely stems from an adjective "tolstyj" (толстый), which in Russian means "thick", "fat", or "stout".

Some tales express their essence through a phone screen, just as stoically, phone to phone.

Go on then, I think to myself, I'd like to see this ide, and Slavoslav Slavoslavovich immediately draws his phone from its sheath and shows me the video of that ide thrashing about on the grass in hysteric waterlessness. Bloody enormous, indeed.

— You speak true, Slavoslav Slavoslavovich, such a biggie.

He nods and starts the video again.

— Thought the line wouldn't hold, but luckily we managed. Had to call a lorry, though. The whole village ate that ide afterwards.

— Ukha[4]?

— Nay, tiddlers would be enough for ukha... Smoked.

The smoky flavour on my tongue, a whiff of smoke in my nose, and my mouth's turning into a saliva reservoir. I watch the ide flap its tail to and fro, bouncing, and think: I'd like to give this a proper like, man to man, I must, so I scan for the heart icon, find it at the bottom of the screen, and immediately tap it. Slavoslav Slavoslavovich nods approvingly.

— I feel sorry for it, — I say, — the king of the lake waters.

— Sorry not sorry, but what can you do? It's nature. A cat wouldn't feel sorry for it.

— Well, we're no cats, you and I, we're hoomans, oh-ho-ho and what kind.

— We're worse. A cat's at least honest in its intentions. A cat's an unprincipled hunter. To it, a mouse, an ide, or borscht — it's all the same, all prey. But we... Eh...

I try to absorb the philosophical substrate and rummage through my lexicon in search of a good word to form a response, shaking my head for a long time, vibing to the music playing from the next room. According to ancient beliefs, our parents listened to this music, and now we listen to it, too. What was cringe has become nostalghia, and so it is with everything. There, behind the wall, are endless ghostly laughter and voices of several more classmates, all mixed into one voice

---

4. A minimalist fish soup. Its defining feature is the pure, concentrated fish broth.

babbling something in an incomprehensible language, even more incomprehensible than the one Slavoslav Slavoslavovich speaks. Let them sit there, behind the wall; we're fine here. The kitchen is the temple of any party; the kitchen is where truth flows. Had I my will afree — a human will with a speck of divinity — I'd transform with one wave of my hand all gatherings, parties, events, the whole world into a small table pushed against the wall in the kitchen with three chairs around it and people casually consulting each other about crises of various grades: existential, spiritual, creative, financial, political, ecological, even approaching midlife ones. Thus we'd sit in the wafting wisps of a wakened, wined wonder and talk, talk about this and that, about everything, about bits and bobs, the infinite and finite, in particular about how to achieve harmony of cosmos and chaos in the process of cooking borscht, and why borscht might be the key to understanding dialectical materialism and metaphysics as a whole. Real borscht, like real life, isn't cooked by the book, but by intuition, by eye and by avos'[5], and the correct dialectic occurs to you only when your head cracks along the welding seams in the morning. The main thing is to remember that in a true dialectical borscht there's always room for thesis, antithesis, and synthesis, and, of course, smetana[6]. Where would we be without it? For smetana is the symbol of unity and struggle of opposites, Gogol once said to Hegel. Only in such a kitchen confessional, in this cabal of souls desperate and splattered with borscht, can something real, something alive be born.

Here Alephtina finally returns, alone and without Meowbius, looks at us, at the ceiling, at the pot, shakes her head, sighs.

— Please eat the borscht.

— With the cat? — I ask.

---

5. A peculiarly Russian faith in perhaps-it-will-work-out-somehow as a philosophical principle. It's neither quite fatalism nor optimism, but rather the comfortable space between preparation and surrender where one throws caution to whatever fiasco may come.

6. An Eastern European version of sour cream, typically with higher fat content, thicker and more resistant to heat, making it more versatile in cooking.

— What do you mean "with the cat"? Should we throw it out now?

— Well, there's no need to throw the cat out... — Slavoslav Slavoslavovich smirks.

— Our cat's clean, we wash him every week.

— And he licks his cat balls every day.

— He's got nothing to lick, don't worry.

— He licks anyway, though. Thoroughly, with hope. One never knows; they might come back.

— He probably doesn't even know they're gone. That's how you live your life, with balls, and then — bam! — no balls, but the habit remains, — adds Slavoslav Slavoslavovich.

— Yes, they both exist and don't exist until he looks "down there". This sort of thing often happens with cats, — Alephtina giggles.

As a child, Alephtina read Borges and thought that "Aleph" was about her. With age, however, she understood that it was, is, and will be about Tulubaika. At the moment when this Truth revealed her sacred orchid before Alephtina, she decided to abandon her previous endeavours and become a scientist. Now Alephtina is an asymptotologistess, application-oriented, studying ley asymptotes, a special type of ley lines (world-connecting curves) which one can approach indefinitely without ever reaching them. In Tulubaika, according to widespread theories, there is a place where these lines intersect at one point, thus forming the most unreachable point on the planet.

— For a function $f(x)$, the line $y = g(x)$ is an asymptote if $lim[x \to \infty] |f(x) - g(x)| = 0$, — Alephtina explains, while I ladle borsch into bowls, and Slavoslav Slavoslavovich dilutes our cava with artisanal samogón[7] of mysterious potency, distilled using an ancient

---

7. From Russian "само" (self) and "гон" (distill, run) — a homemade alcohol (moonshine), the foundation of Russian village alchemy. The Soviet state periodically criminalised and tolerated the practice in alternating waves, never quite eradicating it. Neither scientific precision nor legal permission feature prominently in its production, which traditionally occurs in copper apparatuses of questionable engineering passed down through generations. Samogón's potency fluctuates wildly on the continuum

Tulubaikan recipe left to us, they say, by the Mongols themselves. — In the case of Tulubaika, however, we're dealing with a multidimensional space, where each dimension represents a separate aspect of reality. Imagine a function $T(x_1, x_2, ..., x_n)$, where n tends to infinity. Tulubaika might be a point containing all points of the universe, a kind of singularity in this multidimensional space.

Alephtina takes a deep breath and continues:

— In mathematical terms, this is a place where the function of being $T(x)$ doesn't just tend to infinity, but undergoes a discontinuity of the second kind. In other words, $lim[x \rightarrow Tulubaika^+]\ T(x) \neq lim[x \rightarrow Tulubaika^-]\ T(x)$, and both these limits can be equal to infinity, but with different signs. Just imagine!

Slavoslav Slavoslavovich grunts into his moustache, which he doesn't have and never has had, and pours more samogón into the cava.

— Moreover, — Alephtina continues, helically stirring the borscht in her bowl, — if we consider Tulubaika as an attractor in the dynamic system of our reality, we'll see that it possesses a fractal dimension. It isn't an integer, which explains the impossibility of fully comprehending it. Formally, this can be expressed as: $D = lim[\varepsilon \rightarrow 0]\ (log\ N(\varepsilon)\ /\ log(1/\varepsilon))$, where $N(\varepsilon)$ is the number of n-dimensional cubes with side ε needed to cover Tulubaika, and in practice, — she adds, sipping her borscht, — this means that the closer we try to get to the essence of Tulubaika, the more details we discover, and this process is endless. As Poincaré said, "Science is a continuous approximation to Truth. It's an eternal chase, but not after a chimera, rather after an asymptote".

— White noise... — Slavoslav Slavoslavovich mumbles.

— They don't teach you this in cop school?

— No, they don't, and for that thanks to our comrade Major Yehoshua, may his memory be blessed, — he adds sarcastically. — No

---

between "temporary blindness" and "ancestral visitation," with flavour profiles ranging from "burning tire" to "aggressive pear" and much more.

need to dilute our Orthodox thought with your foreign sciences. For such heresy, we could lock you up for fifteen days[8], citizenette[9].

We all laugh heartily. Alephtina leaves her spoon in the bowl and eyes the glasses, clapping her hands in anticipation.

— Tell me, what have you concocted?

— So, mademoiselle, we wished-s[10] to concoct a refined from-over-yonder cocktail, following a most esteemed French recipe. Alas, upon inspection, we discovered-s that our Champagne is from Spain, and the English gin is nowhere to be found. Therefore, if it pleases you, we shall substitute-s it with the Tulubaikan samogón traditionnel, forsooth.

— Oh indeed, messieurs, that is how great discoveries are born, isn't it? — says Alephtina and picks up her glass.

— Well... shall we? — says Slavoslav Slavoslavovich.

— We shall, indeed.

We raise our glasses and clink them.

— Wait-wait, what about helixing?

— Right you are, mademoiselle.

— Not for nothing you're a scientist now, citizenette.

We swirl our faceted Soviet glasses until little whirlpools form, following Alephtina's advice to create a stochastic process in the drink and enrich it with oxygen. We sip. The spirit rushes through the body in spirals, warming the corporeal and the incorporeal. My chronic déjà

---

8. A default administrative detention period in Soviet and post-Soviet Russia for minor offences and "hooliganism". The phrase entered cultural consciousness as the standard "cooling off" period dished out by authorities for everything from public drunkenness to political dissidence.

9. The translator deliberately rendered "citizen" as French-infused female-gendered word, to emphasise the original tone of the message. The Russian original uses "гражданочка", a diminutive feminine form that officials often employ when addressing women in a subtly patronising manner, combining bureaucratic formality with condescension.

10. The extra "-s" particle (as in "wished-s" and "discovered-s") replicates a speech affectation from pre-revolutionary Russian. It used to be used by merchants and servants as a shortened form of "sir" (сударь / государь) but became a linguistic marker of excessive deference or affected formality. In modern contexts, applied randomly, it can be used ironically to parody a pretentious manner of speech.

vu immediately intensifies, and my forehead fills with a hot-cold sensation that we're sitting exactly as we sat ten and twenty years ago, and everything around is nothing but a nostalgic dream staged by a radical art-house theatre troupe—

— One every day, — says my doctor, his fake clownish moustache turning him into Felix Dzerzhinsky[11]. — Best in the arse cheek. Right or left — you pick. But I stick it in the left — I fancy commies, you know. Go on, give it a go.

In my hand — a syringe, pearlescent goo shimmering inside it. As if I'm about to jab myself with a vial of glitter.

— And then boom, it's all gone?

— No booms, compadre. It'll be gone gradually.

— Maybe there are pills?

— The pills are bitter as olives from the tree. You might get asphyxia (and not an erotic one, mind you). Then, of course, everything'll be gone with a boom.

— Is there perhaps a stronger dose? Like, one-and-done, fixed for good?

— No, compadre patient, be patient. Chronic déjà vu is incurable, I'm afraid. You'll be on jabs for life now. I suffer from it myself but I jab it regularly and it's fine — no bother. But if you ever want it like before (ha-ha), skip a couple of days and everything will be back to square one. Will you give it a go now?

— My wife will "give it a go" for me at home. I'm afraid to do it myself.

— I could "give it a go" for you.

— I'm fine, thank you very much.

The doc nods understandingly.

— Better before dinner, this one.

I stand up, adjust my shirt with rolled-up sleeves, shake the doctor's poisonously blue rubber hand, and head for the door.

---

11. CEO and founder of the Cheka (the OG KGB), nicknamed "Iron Felix". His bronze statue outside KGB headquarters was famously toppled during the 1991 Soviet collapse, yet his organisational "legacy" has endured even after the monuments fell.

— Doc, what about the centrists? — I ask before fleeing this torture chamber.

— Ah, those... They use rectal suppositories, so it dissolves inside. It's uncomfortable to sit at first, though. The suppositories aren't small, mind you.

We nod to each other stoically, man to man. I exit, slamming the door—

On trips, I give it a go myself, contorting in front of the mirror in the hotel bathroom. I alternate right and left, just in case, to avoid jinxing it, but I reckon I forgot to dose up today and yesterday. So here we are, flare-up time.

— Oh, how lovely! — Alephtina exclaims, polishing off her glass. — This is what I'm getting at. How's your car, Slavoslav Slavoslavovich?

— Well, I took a taxi here. It's a piss-up, after all.

— What do I care about your taxis, Slavoslav Slavoslavovich? The Opel, I'm asking about your trophy Opel.

— Ah, the Opel... It starts up.

— Does it run?

— Runs it does. Not quite factory-fresh, mind you, but goes like the clappers. Bit of a rattle here and there but that's nought. More "authentic" that way, as they say.

— Will you give us a ride?

— Well... — Slavoslav Slavoslavovich clams up.

— For old times' sake. When else will we get a chance to ride in a trophy Opel?

— Well... There are still a couple of parts to replace... Can't seem to find the right paint...

— Just tell us which one you need and we'll sort you out.

Every evening after work, and sometimes on weekends, all year round, Slavoslav Slavoslavovich escapes from his family for a rendezvous. He walks along dark streets, encountering stray dogs and the absence of asphalt on the way, but such nuances are like smetana to a cat for him; he's a copper, with a gun. Reaching the coveted garage — one of the endless alleys of them, planted by Stalin himself back in

11

the days of the Union of Soviet Socialist Republics — Slavoslav Slavoslavovich opens the gates. Before him, as in a fairy tale, appears a slightly rusted but clean Opel Kapitän Cabrio, coloured like the Schutzstaffel uniform, full of rounded forms, equipped with bug-eyed headlights and a distinctive radiator grille, that very legendary car on which Slavoslav Slavoslavovich's grandfather drove from Germany in nineteen forty-five, fuming home victoriously to Tulubaika, minus one ear and two fingers on his right hand that were scattered around Europe. At one point, the totality of parts that had fallen into disrepair in this Opel amounted to about a hundred per cent. Slavoslav Slavoslavovich managed to replace some from local sources, some I sent him from overseas. Question: does the old grandfather's Opel remain the same trophy Opel if every original part in it has been changed several times? One might accidentally become a Volga that way.

For a split second it darkens, either in the world or in my eyes, but immediately after that, the night illuminates the kitchen with lightning. She's looking for sad people, the lightning. Hail begins to bombard the balcony windows and door, in a minute filling the balcony itself to the brim with icy tennis balls until they start spilling over the edge. Thunder drowns out the music, but the squeals and gasps of those gathered for the piss-up are still louder.

— That's some weather!
— Did you clock that?
— Fuck me sideways...
— This has never happened before and here we go again!
— Blazinn oodles!
— I hope my greenhouse is still standing...

Flash number two. Scratching the linoleum on his way and bumping into every doorframe, Meowbius, electrified after a hairdryer ordeal, bursts into the kitchen and, with one precise leap onto the fridge, begins the ritual of summoning the sly one[12].

---

12. The sly one or "lukavy" is a traditional Russian euphemism for the Devil or Satan. This indirect reference reflects the folk belief that directly naming evil entities might

— *Ekekekekek tenebris princeps, audi vocem meam, surge ex abysso, miau, et appare coram me!* — he could have shouted, and we all could have chorused "amen" at the end. We could do so much more that it's unclear why we're not doing it, at least "for the plot" it would definitely have been worth doing.

The light in the flat goes out, someone in the next room yelps, someone laughs, an unknown piece of crockery breaks.

— "Let there be light!" the handyman declared and snipped the power dead![13] — announces one of the guests.

The frightened cat's orbs begin to glow with hellfire. Around his fur gathers a sparkling aura. Oh no... Oh no... Oh no, no, no, no, no.

— *Miau! Nunc est bibendum lac! Ekekekek* — Meowbius could have howled. — *Audi me, serve humane! MIAU!*

Here the powerless fridge under the cat could have suddenly turned on, hummed, shaken, its door could have swung open and out he'd come — the sly one himself, looking like a chort[14], hairy, with polished horns and hooves. And we'd sit together with him, and knock back pure Tulubaikan samogón and chase it all down with toasted bread with demonic amounts of garlic, of which he, the sly one, wouldn't be afraid and would have prepared it for us in the fridge converted into an oven. But no, life isn't like that. Alas.

Alephtina wants to pick up Meowbius, but he hisses, kicks, flails his paws chaotically, so that with one careless blow, Alephtina would be walking around with an eye patch. A boozer uncle of mine in Tulubaika once had his hands so scratched up by his cat that my aunt

---

summon them. The term appears in the Lord's Prayer as "deliver us from the sly one" and has entered Russian cultural consciousness as a way to acknowledge dark forces without invoking them explicitly, which a cat, of course, can't be aware of.

13. A famous Russian folk "rhyme" that must be recited every time the unplanned and prolonged power outage begins.

14. A mischievous humanoid demon or minor devil in Slavic folklore. Unlike the sly one, the chort is more of a trickster than the embodiment of ultimate evil. He can cause household mishaps, lead travellers astray, or tempt humans into foolish decisions. When Russians exclaim "K chortu!" (To the devil!), they're invoking this folkloric spirit rather than the big sly one. The chort therefore occupies a supernatural space between serious theological threat and annoying supernatural pest.

thought he'd tried to cut his wrists, called the shrinks, who somehow packed him into a straitjacket and carted him off in a white bukhanka[15] to the yellow house[16]. What they did to him there remains a mystery, but he returned sober and never drank again. Note: treating alcoholism with a cat.

— Leave him be... He'll shred you to bits, — Slavoslav Slavoslavovich tells Alephtina, leaning back slightly.

— He's got no claws, — Alephtina replies, trying to wrangle the cat.

— No balls, no claws... What a life...

— He's just scared. Look, he's calming down already, — she nods at Meowbius purring in her arms.

With grace, electricity returns to our chambers. To the accompaniment of copper pipes[17] and the whole orchestra joining them, those gathered burst into applause, whistles and sincere thanks to Ionius, the overlord of electricity, and the master of all free ions in the universe, who, to become free, had to protest against universal darkness quite a bit.

Someone, whose seasoned face I haven't yet recognised, quickly pops into the kitchen, asks whether we are bored sitting in the kitchen all by threeselves (cats don't count as conversationalists, not even ones

---

15. The nickname for the iconic UAZ-452 Soviet van / minibus, derived from its distinctly loaf-like shape ("bukhanka" means "a loaf of bread" in Russian). It became the default public service vehicle during Soviet times, serving as ambulances, postal vans, and military transport. Despite its spartan interior and bumpy ride, the bukhanka has achieved cult status among both ex-Soviet and international off-road enthusiasts, some even trying to ship it to places like Mexico.

16. A Russian euphemism for a psychiatric hospital or asylum, deriving from the yellowish paint traditionally used on these institutions' facades during the olden days. The phrase — colour aside — might also carry significant cultural weight beyond its literal meaning due to the Soviet practice of "punitive psychiatry", where political dissidents were diagnosed with fabricated conditions like "sluggish schizophrenia" and institutionalised against their will.

17. A Russian idiom "to pass through fire, water, and copper pipes" (пройти огонь, воду и медные трубы) is all about the endurance of severe trials and hardships. The phrase's origins are disputed: some trace the "copper pipes" to the trumpets of military glory and the test of fame; others to distillation apparatus and the survival of alcoholism, hence the translator's decision not to render it simply as "trumpets".

like Meowbius), offers to join everyone else, to which we unanimously no-no, offers a joint, which we also prefer to no-no (for now, though), then, shrugging us off, grabs a random bottle of alcohol and, bowing out, leaves the kitchen temple.

Alephtina goes to the fridge with the disgruntled cat, opens it with one hand, takes out milk and pours it into a bowl. Meowbius, jumping down from her arms, begins to lap up the feline holy water, smacking his lips. She, meanwhile, takes out an hourglass standing on the corner shelf under a portrait of her smiling wrinkled grandma in a headscarf. Inside the hourglass, instead of sand, is nothing other than the ashes of the said old lady, who was rumoured to have possessed extremely supernatural abilities (at least by Tulubaikan standards). Sighing heavily, Alephtina sits at the table and places the hourglass in front of us. In a thin stream, Grandma Nüra seeps from the upper part of the hourglass into the lower.

— How long does she last?

— That I haven't figured out yet, to be honest.

— We could just flip it over, — says Slavoslav Slavoslavovich and reaches for the hourglass, to which Alephtina lightly slaps his hand.

— Hands off or I'll flip your head over; better pour us some. You're performing your duties poorly, Comrade Captain, — Alephtina declares sternly, yet with an indecent amount of irony, and pushes her glass to the centre of the table.

By copper's will and Alephtina's wish, the vessel brims with cava and samogón's swish[18]. I, meanwhile, lean towards the hourglass to observe Grandma Nüra's descent.

— Look here, — Alephtina intones, after first rinsing her mouth with the drink. — There's very little left.

We, pretending to have understood everything, nod in unison, men to woman.

— We need to go there sharpish, — she enunciates, taking a sip.

— Where to?

---

18. This sentence parodies the classic Russian fairy tale formula "By the pike's command, by my desire", which magical creatures or objects use to fulfill wishes.

— Where do you think? To Tulubaika.

— To Tulubaika?

— Oh.

— You do come out with some bangers sometimes, Alya[19]. "Sharpish!"

— I've found out that, with a margin of error of three point four per cent (dead accurate, I should mention), Tulubaika will vanish as soon as Grandma Nüra runs out.

— Vanish? — Slavoslav Slavoslavovich and I ask, taken aback.

— Vanish.

— Just up and vanish, like that?

— Precisely like that. A spacetime singularity will occur and the village will collapse into itself. Flop and gone. Well, that's in theory.

— Well, blow me down... — Slavoslav Slavoslavovich drawls, scratching his bald bonce. — Like in the Bermuda Triangle?

— No, for real. No fairy tales. Poof! And no Tulubaika.

— How's that?

— Just like that. You know how it was in childhood? Your grandma asks you to help. "Go fetch some bread," so she says. You agree, toddle off to the kiosk, but it has run out of bread. What a pity, right?

— Too right.

— So you think: I'll go to the next village then, can't let grandma down, can I? You walk for an hour through fields, through birch groves burning with golden flames, triumphantly buy the last loaf of white bread in the only shop called "SHOP" in the neighbouring village, walk back, get bored, hunger awakens in your belly, you forget everything in a childish way...

— For a moment of total transcendence...

— Exactly. You start eating this bread, just biting the loaf straight

---

19. A diminutive version of Alephtina (supposedly), used in an affectionate way. Alya to Alephtina is what Belle is to Isabelle. Eastern Slavic cultures have an elaborate system of such diminutives that signal familiarity and emotional closeness between speakers and a range of other subtle registers.

from the bag — it doesn't matter where you're taking it or to whom, it's still warm, crusty, the most delicious fresh bread you've ever tasted.

— Wouldn't mind some fresh bread now, I must say...

— So you walk, head in the clouds, grasshopping, admiring nature, maybe accidentally stumbling over an asymptote (they say children can still trip over them, and some can even *jump* over them like a skipping rope, fancy that), and there you are; you return to the village, but grandma's gone — she died; they took her away in an ambulance straight to the cemetery in a coffin prepared at home, cobbled together for a bottle of vodka by John the carpenter from the boards of the old collapsed Communist Party hut. What can you do? She was old, took three nostalghin pills every day and suffered from chronic déjà vu like everyone in our parts. And there you stand thinking: what now? I've already eaten the bread.

— Been there, done that... — Slavoslav Slavoslavovich nods. He looks like he might fall asleep any moment.

— It'll vanish completely. It will for us, and we will for it. If we arrive too late, we will not even recognise each other, — says Alephtina.

Time in Tulubaika always dabbled in certain dilations, like on that planet in "Interstellar." You seem to have already graduated from university, gotten married, travelled the world, changed a dozen jobs, gained muscle and intellect — practically ascended to Apollo and Dionysus in one person, but in Tulubaika it's as if nothing has changed, yet everything is completely different.

— That's why I don't want to go and won't go, — I tell them straight.

They, Alephtina and Slavoslav Slavoslavovich, suddenly turn to me, having sheathed all their alcoholic intoxication, and ask in unison:

— And why's that then?

And I look at them and don't recognise them, as if my chronic déjà vu has again metastasised into chronic jamais vu. Déjà vu, jamais vu... Even a sober tongue would tie itself in knots, not to be untied. The world's a splash from fish tails gliding through void's vast sea. Splash!

And chimeras flee the present, troika-harnessed[20], clasping throats of forms and images, devouring all they see. Memories entwine in wreaths, from mind flee silently, sprawl languidly on graves. These people I (don't) remember, their faces (un)familiar to me, their voices (not) known to me, a ghostly similarity is all my wretched thought can find, reflected in their plea — eyes hungry for my words, awaiting eagerly.

Somewhere in the beautiful distance, lightning flashes, and the sound of rain and thunder gently-nostalgically taps on the membranes of our ear shells. I sit, watch, unwind a thoughtful thought — the answer won't construct itself, just like communism over and over again, while in the next room the lads get out a guitar and start singing Yegor Letov[21]:

> *Distant Ophelia laughed in her sleep:*
> *A pot-bellied thrush, a shaggy deer*
> *The habitually last year's painted snow*
> *Easily, lightly and cheerfully crunches on teeth.*

— Jamais vu, — I finally answer after a pause as long as two pauses (or three).

— Jamais what?

— Huh?

— Jamais vu. Like déjà vu, but the opposite. You look around and everything seems like it's for the first time. I'm afraid that I'll arrive in Tulubaika like this and... What will I see there? Neither grandmother's baking, nor fishing with grandfather, nor the cat Dulcinea engaging in mouse-catching and obscurantism, only the creaking junk in the form

---

20. A traditional Russian three-horse carriage team harnessed side-by-side, with the middle horse trotting while outer horses gallop.

21. Legendary Siberian punk rocker and poet whose band Grazhdanskaya Oborona (Civil Defence) became the voice of late-Soviet counterculture. Letov's relationship with Yanka Dyagileva, another Siberian punk artist, inspired some of his best work, including his song "Ophelia" written after her tragic drowning death in 1991. Though he died in 2008, his uncompromising anarchical ethos and general post-Soviet punk aesthetic continue to endure.

of a windmill that echoes throughout the area, trees grown to the skies and fields overgrown with shrubs and weeds. Jamais vu, in a word.

— Complete jamais vu, comrade...

— A function discontinuity... — Alephtina mutters and winces from an apparent attack of her mathematical synaesthesia.

— Flush it down, — says Slavoslav Slavoslavovich and gives her his freshly prepared portion of Tsar Cannon[22] (thus we call our concoction).

The theatricality of the musical performance in the neighbouring room intensifies manifold and begins to sound from inside my skull:

> *Enamoured Ophelia drifted far away*
> *The night was bright, the earth did ring*
> *Hastily hurried, without hiding from view*
> *The clock to its foolish, comical land*
> *Obedient Ophelia floated to the east*
> *A wondrous captivity, granitic delight*
> *A lemony pathway to an orange grove*
> *Invisible lift to a transcendent floor*

— So what's the point of going then?

Alephtina rolls her eyes.

— All the more reason. That's the whole point. We need to go.

— I don't want to go anywhere.

— Consider Tulubaika as a quantum system $T(\psi)$. If we can describe the attempt to return with the equation $T'(\psi') = M[T(\psi)]$, where M is the measurement operator changing the state of the system.

— White noise...

— Returning to Tulubaika is equivalent to finding a fixed point $T(\psi) = M[T(\psi)]$, but the existence of such a point is not guaranteed,

---

22. Tsar Cannon was Moscow's famous 16th-century bronze behemoth that never fired a shot in battle. Thus the cocktail is a twist on the classic French 75, also named after cannons, however, while the French original is based on gin and champagne, the Tsar Cannon incorporates rather stronger an unusual flavours.

because Tulubaika is not only a point in space, but also a continuum of states described by the statistical ensemble of our memories and expectations.

— I second that, — I say, then nod towards Slavoslav Slavoslavovich. — But the noise is still too white.

— In short, the past Tulubaika is asymptotically unreachable by definition. Consider it gone already... (Alephtina hiccups) And it won't be back. But some version of it still exists...

We sit, silent, hiccupping, in one ear — a guitar, in the other — Meowbius's purring, sprawled on the floor by my right foot, the very one with a hole in the sock, causing the big toe to stick out and provoke the cat to bite. Ekekek he goes, ekekek. The borscht has already cooled; in it, the smetana has spread in white lumps, cosily gathered around oval drops of yellow fat that now tends towards a solid state. Meanwhile:

Distant Ophelia laughed in her dreams:
A weary demon, a willow bush
Gifted ponies scattered at dawn
To the four winds — try to catch them now—

— You see, compadre, chronic déjà vu, — the doctor tells me, — is not just an obsessive feeling but a whole syndrome of temporal dysfunction. If left untreated, there occurs, so to speak, an inversion of the perceptual continuum.

— Huh? — I exclaim.

My brain is about to melt and flow out of my ears.

The doctor exhales all the air from his lungs and, gesticulating like a juggler, continues to broadcast his cerebral ambrosia:

— Imagine the brain as a huge hourglass where the grains of sand are your memories. With déjà vu, this hourglass works as it should but with a small glitch when sand from the lower bulb, by a miraculous coincidence, seeps back into the upper one. But if no measure is taken, it can get worse, and the sand will start to get stuck. First in the narrow neck, then in the bulbs themselves.

— I see...

— By looking at you, I don't think you do. The danger is: when a critical mass of memory-grains gets stuck, your brain is no longer able to make sense of this petrified chaos of memory, and begins to perceive everything as new, even though you remember everything. This is jamais vu. You look at your wife and feel like you don't recognise her. You come to your home village and feel like you're seeing it for the first time. You read a book you knew by heart, and each page is again a revelation to you. But the worst thing, compadre, is that you stop recognising yourself.

The doctor falls silent, thoughtfully stroking his fake luxuriant moustache. Quite dramatic, that chap.

— Even suppositories won't help there. Regardless of their size.

Biting my lower lip, I nod and once again shake the doctor's poisonously blue rubber hand—

In the dewy morning, after the roosters hoarsely greet the dawn, we (plus grumpy Meowbius), sobered up, slightly gloomy, charged with ibuprofen, nostalghin and melancholin, will sit in the trophy Opel Kapitän and, puffing and rattling, collecting potholes and chortknows-whats, across the boundless field between oat dunes, in the shade of birches blazing with golden fire, with rotting leaves wrapped around the wheel, mixed with the rotting remains of bad news from newspapers, which you'd only use to wipe your arse with, will head Tulubaikawards.

But for now, we're still sitting, watching gravity pull Baba Nüra's[23] ashes into the lower bulb of the hourglass, finishing off the dialectical borscht reheated in the microwave, and listening as, somehow keeping the chords and rhythm, behind the wall in which there isn't a single brick, Pink Floyd together with Ophelia drown in the raging streams of borscht...

How I wish, how I wish you were here
Ophelia drowning in a borscht bowl, year after year

---

23. Here "baba" is short for babushka, a grandmother or often an old woman in general.

Running over the old ground, what have we found?
The same old fears, I wish you were here.

Episode Two
about lingus venus

I am a myth. And you create it.

— Sasha Sokolov, "Palisandria"

Among the timber tables run decrepit demon dogs, all ulcerated, their mouths bleeding, bubbling with an alabaster foam. I couldn't care less about them, though. There's me and there's her, though for me, there's only her, my heroine; nothing else matters, not even these weird creatures. The air smells of candle wax and balsamic vinegar someone has spilt at the table next to us. While the demon dogs are dead set on pinching anything off the tables, while the copious happy people around mumble, while the fish-headed waiters shout at each other in an unrecognisable tongue, while somewhere in the bushes right behind the restaurant cicadas compose a cacophonous lullaby, while branches of yew with red holey beads scratch the plexiglass roof of the terrace, my heroine, only my heroine, remains the sole focal point into which my decaying reality funnels, and while a fly drowns in my wine, I drown in her iridescent eyes. Those round, furtively blinking orbs are either grey, the hue of smoke or a thick morning fog, or green, the hue of jade, possibly faded a tad from overexposure to overattention. Around her dilated pupils, a ruby lattice of tiny capillaries has grown; masterful jewellery, her eyes now. Is this the third bottle this evening? C_2H_5OH and some other substances; the transmutation of the evening into the—

— This is secret ingredient of transmutation from evening into night, — my heroine says in broken tongue.

— What kind of ingredient, though?

25

— Secret ingredient.

— O-o-oh, I see. A secret ingredient.

— Secret ingredient, yes. You know what that mean?

I shake my head, lips arched up.

— This means I not tell you what is this. Did you think I tell you?

— You must tell me, though. My mother taught me not to take strange substances from strangers, especially *strangerettes*, which perfectly describes the situation I'm in right now.

— I understand. Mother word is law.

— I wouldn't ask otherwise.

— Well, too bad, I still not tell you. Somewhere, somewhen, I am someone's mother. Therefore, on a grand scheme of things, my word is law, "though".

My heroine stretches a sly smile and takes a sip from her glass.

— But not now?

— You are so fixed on "now". I not— I don't understand.

My heroine keeps staring at me. She doesn't blink, or perhaps we blink at the same time. It happens sometimes; people blink at the same time and never see each other with eyes shut, or blink in turns and never see each other with eyes open. I try to blink unevenly, at random times, so that doesn't happen, but still never see her eyes shut. It is a state-of-the-art mesmerisation, no more, no less.

— I am. I won't argue with that.

— Well, then don't. Simple, da[1]?

— I won't, but I thought it would benefit the evening a little bit and perhaps speed up the "transmutation" process if we build some trust.

— Such silly thing to say! I trust you. You're crazy and naive enough to take pills from "strangerette". You're harmless. Harmless people trust everyone, you did that, so I think you "trust" me, in odd way. But why it matters?

A faceless waiter with five eyes, a peaky nose, and a Cheshire

---

1. "Da" (да) is yes in Russian. The translator dared to leave it as "da" to emphasise our heroine's "otherworldliness".

mouth under a Dali moustache walks by carrying on a plate a festering dog head sprinkled with parmesan and basil, the aroma of which overpowers the dog's smell, as if it were pasta.

— Well...

— If you are afraid from falling, then fly. Or baituut. We said this in my village.

— Doesn't make any sense to me, I'm afraid.

— You shouldn't be afraid. You should turn on brain. Make it think, da?

— I'm afraid of "turning it on" to think about something like that.

— You see? You not understand. Risk of falling is not real if you already falling. It is in past and it is zero percent and hundred percent in same time, which in reality means it not relevant, which then means it not exist. Flying, on other hand, is w-a-ay more risky because risk of falling is still not zero — you can just fold wings! That is that.

— Didn't know you were a risk manager.

— Maybe I am. Maybe I am not. I prefer to stay a strangerette. Maybe I will poison you, rob you, give you syphilis or something worser.

— Do you do that to many men?

— No, only to pretty ones. Rest I just rob.

— So I'm in grave danger then.

She scans me, head to toe, as much as the table between us allows, shrugs.

— Nah, don't worry. I think you very safe.

— Very safe?

— What, I say not correct?

— No, I just thought I'd come back home with syphilis. I already dreamt of that.

— Well... no?

— I'm thankful.

— You should be.

— So, tell me, am I flying or am I falling?

— We will understand this soon.

On the porcelain plate right in front of me lies a slightly charred

squirming tentacle of an ancient god, drizzled with saffron aioli. Shoggoth? Yog-Sothoth? I don't want to know. The suckers on it stare at me by the hundreds of tiny eyes, not with pity, not with interest, but rather with irony, as if the tentacle is about to eat *me*: jump off the plate, wrap around my neck, squeeze until it cracks, and then, when my last breath leaves my lungs, crawl into my brain through a nostril and occupy my body.

— Maybe we should do it in the hotel.

She scratches her chin.

— Why?

I expect her to add "I do wonder" but she's silent. My brain has started finishing her lines long ago.

— No, I mean... I am afraid I will start doing weird things soon.

— Weird things? For example?

— I wish I knew in advance, but no, I don't know. Just weird things, stupid things, things you won't like and I will regret...

— You have previous experience of doing weird things? I could make prediction about it. Maybe there's trend...

— Are you an analyst now?

— Maybe I am an analyst...

— Like... I could start fighting with the waiters and then they would throw me in the canal and I would drown in there and die.

— No worry, I will pull you out from there. Did that happen before?

— Except the last part. Though I'm not sure about that sometimes... You don't like your oysters?

Twenty rock oysters rest on the mountain of ice right in the middle of our table. My heroine's order, untouched.

— I never ate oysters.

— You haven't? I don't eat oysters. They sometimes...

Here I think of how oysters, upon entering my body, would try to occupy it too, and I myself become an oyster, waking up in a rock shell the following morning.

— Well, I won't spoil it for you.

— How do you eat them?

— You just, um, slurp.

— Slurp? What is slurp?

I kindly demonstrate the slurp sound.

— Ah, "slurp". Okay.

Multiple signs of cunning surface on my heroine's face: a smile, a squint, a long, thorough lip lick. She plots and executes, my heroine: takes an empty tap water glass, takes an oyster and pours it into the glass, setting aside the shell.

What are you doing?! I could've asked, but my curiosity suggests not to ask stupid questions and prefers to observe. My heroine takes a second oyster, a third, a fourth, ..., ..., until they all end up in her glass. Then, as I expected, she drinks them all (!), just like that, in one big slurp. Impressive. Somewhere in the back of my mind, one of my thoughts is already looking for where nearby one could buy an engagement ring in the middle of the night.

— What? — my heroine asks, a slight shyness in her posture.

— No, nothing. I am, well, I am, I must say I'm rather impressed.

— Rather?

— Rather, yes.

— I did something wrong?

— No, you did everything perfectly. Not sure I've seen anything closer to perfection.

— I can read irony.

— I know you can, that's why it wasn't irony.

My heroine smiles.

Next to us, in the artificial river locked into three walls of brick and concrete and one wall of light-polluted city atmosphere, among dark green algae, cigarette butts, and crumpled cans, a school of fish learns to fly. Do they fly or do they *think* they fly? Or do they fall horizontally? What do the fish feel at this moment? Where are they going so free, so aimless, so hopeful? Straining their fins, they travel to the spawning grounds where they, like zergs, in sin, will multiply in quantity, and then come back to hooks and nets, to fridges and freezers, to pans and plates, to fish and chips, to someone's mouth. Mine perhaps. Or my heroine's. Her pink lips, glistering with grease,

unfold like an orchid in bloom and her red tongue licks the tartare sauce from her knife and her... Wait! My parents taught me never to lick a knife. It brings bad luck, it's tempting fate, it's bad etiquette, it's basic sharp object safety. But she... For her... For her it's a transference of energy or life force of the knife's victim to the person licking it. She lovingly pierces a chip with her fork and starts chewing it, her sharp jawline going in zigzags. She is a rare species of orchid-flycatcher and I'm a not-so-rare species of fly who can't decide between flying and falling. I can feel her chewing my head off with glee, or rather neutrally, in a manner of habit. My skull cracks open like a chocolate egg and the brain yolkly tries to escape this tragic transgression yet fates out like the fish. Then my heroine picks up a dried bucatini from her cocktail and, using it as a straw, performs one rapid succinct sip from my skull — *slurp!* — it's gone! I've lost my head, I've lost my brain, I've lost my mind — I've lost everything.

— You never said it was so strong.

— You never said you were so weak.

— I'm not weak. I'm vulnerable to deception and drugs, like anyone else.

— Well, I am not vulnerable to whatever.

— Of course you're not... You seduced me, fed me your weird pills and now my mind is melting. I see things I wish I couldn't see. I think things I wish I couldn't think.

— That is good description of my whole life. Strange that you need pills for that. What are you?

— I feel like, erm... (I wouldn't tell her I saw her eating my head. That would ruin the romantique) My brain is made of malleable paraffin and it's melting now, trying to escape this tragic transgression but fates out like the fish and my fish-fate appears predetermined, circumscribed by an insurmountable metaphysical aporia.

— Sometimes I don't understand what you are saying.

— Just listen to the words.

— Is not fun to listen to the words when you can't understand them, da? I could just listen to cicadas instead. Maybe I understand them better.

— What do they say?

— Cicadas?

— Yes, cicadas.

She scans her surroundings, squints intently, and, shrugging, returns her gaze to me. Those eyes again. I'm disappearing, flopping inwardly.

— Not sure. I don't know much about Cicadian, or is it Circadian? Anyway, I know it even less than your tongue.

— Do they sing? Can you hear them singing a song?

After a short intermission of silence, the conductor hiding in the vegetation, its tailcoat fluttering in the wind, its eyes closed, its mind concentrated into a single dot, a dot that's about to explode with music, spreads its little cicadian limbs and, bursting with pompousness, drops them down in one sharp stroke, cutting the air and, who knows, the whole world, the whole universe into two halves. In a fraction of a millisecond (which some oddly label "immediately"), as if the "start" signal was transmitted to them with no consideration of time, telepathically, the cicadian orchestra starts its fierce symphony. Out of nowhere, a series of omnipiercing vibrating shrieks, like those of a spinning chainsaw or aroused starlings, takes over the space. BzzzzzZzzzZ BzzzZZZZzzz BzhzzzzZZzzZZZzzzZzZZZzzzZzzZzzzzzzzz and so on... The orchestra, perhaps, consists of all living cicadas, all cicadas that have ever lived, and all cicadas that will ever live. The symphony, simple yet complex, discordant yet meticulously composed for maximum deafening effect, angelic yet demonic, rhythmic yet arrhythmical, turns the air around us into gelatin. Everyone and everything feels it. Every flower, petal, leaf, grass, poisonous yew berry, every glass and utensil on every table, the plexiglass roof of the terrace, every eardrum, every hair in every cochlea — everything trembles, neither from fear, nor from awe, nor from pleasure, but from belonging to something greater, to something shared, to something universal, as if now the vibrations emanating from the orchestra do not just touch everyone, but merge with them, propagated deep down to the innermost essence of every being and thing. It's a rock opera. It's jazz

but with a billion "z" at the end of the word. It is a torrent of joy and agony combined into a hitherto unknown bittersweet sensation, a feeling of nostalghia for every fraction of a moment passed and every moment to come. Between the moments, if you tune in, you experience an eerie sense of quiet, like the universe has just pressed the mute button, and you have fallen through into a transient void. You feel its texture. You feel what the world really is, described in the cicadian tongue.

— ... That is how cicadas reveal to us the underlying vibrations of the world — through their music, through their unequivocal art, and they are just humble tree crickets. I can't imagine what a human could do, — thus I finish my speech.

My heroine bursts into applause.

— Wow, I mean... Okay, it probably was too strong on you.

— Did you hear all my thoughts? The whole thing?!

— Yes, but because you said it out loud. And let go of my hand. I don't mind it but your grip is just too tight, like a child handcuff.

I remove my hand from hers and look around. The dizziness takes over, and every person on the terrace, every guest and host (no dogs; they are gone, luckily), now has auras comprised of vibrating doppelgängers, their appearances multiplying before my eyes, each body fanning out into a cluster of blurred copies, as if the shutter speed of my mind-camera has gone snail.

— Sorry... Can you say something in your tongue?

— Like what?

— I don't know. Something. I need to hear something I don't understand because now, I reckon, I understand too much.

— You are ill? Here, drink water.

She moves her glass towards me and I pour it whole down my throat, together with ice. It feels like embers crawling down my oesophagus.

— We can leave? Have some fresh air.

— No, please just say something. Words, I need words.

— Such as? What do you want to hear?

— I don't know. Just words. The whole thing I just thought... or

said. About cicadas. Translate it to me. Please. I want to hear your native tongue.

— Okay.

I sit straight and look into her eyes. Mimicking everything else around, they multiply into dozens and hundreds as if she's Argus now. I close my eyes and prepare to listen.

— Erm... well... it's, ugh, kaiabtuluulbaiakkatu.

She's silent. The only thing I hear is the cicadian orchestra.

— Wait, that's it?

— Da.

— Is that what it means? The whole whatever-that-was translates into... that? Just... what? One word? Two words?

— My tongue is very expressive. And it's not a word, there's no such concept in my tongue.

— Where are you from?

— It's called Tulubaika.

— Tooloo-what?

— Tulubaika.

— Toolookai- no... I can't do it.

— Tu-lu-bai-ka.

— Too-loo-bai-la?

— No!

— I think you're making it up. The wicked tongue. Everything. It makes no sense.

— No, I don't. Why make up? World has enough things already.

— Yes, you're making it up. I can see that in your eyes.

— You think I lie?

— No, not lie. It's different. You're making it up.

— No, I'm not. Why would I do that? I can't invent nothing.

— I don't know. To play me?

— I don't play games.

— What was it again? Tooloobulu-something.

She's laughing, I can feel she's laughing, inwardly, she's making fun of me, taking the piss.

— Tulubaika. Is Tulubaika.

— No, it can't be real. This can't be serious.

— It's all very, very serious. Everything is serious.

— I don't mean to sound impolite but is it some... I don't know... rare unknown indigenous place? Is that where you are from?

— Tulubaika.

— But what country?

— Asking woman where is she from is worse than asking age, mister. You can guess my accent.

— I don't know. I'm bad at accents. You're extraterrestrial.

— Yes, good idea. I like it.

— I mean it as a compliment, by the way.

— I know. Now I say I am alien from Venus. Tulubaika is village on Venus. The only one maybe. How does this sound?

— Alright. I see. Venus. Well... Okay. I mean, why not. Describe it to me.

— Describe?

— Yes. I want to know what it's like, Tooloobaila, Venus.

— Tulubaika! It is small, very small village, da? There isn't nothing to describe, "I'm afraid". It is very quiet and peaceful. There're fields around and nothing else. We have a few small houses and we have orchid gardens.

— Orchid gardens? For real?

— Da.

— In a village?

— Yes, just one.

— An orchid garden? As in a garden with orchids?

— See? You don't believe me, whatever I say. You don't trust me. This is your problem. You must trust people. This is how society work.

— In Tooloobaila?

— Everywhere.

Tilting, I watch her eyes multiplying on her face.

— We'd better get some fresh air.

Along the cobbled path, high above the surface, run four legs, from them two bodies holding hands grow gradually, entwined into

one drunken silhouette that chuckles, bursts with laughter — the silhouette's only language. The words, the real words composed of morphemes with attached hints of meanings and history of the evolution of hundreds of tongues, have ceased to exist, dispersed into individual sounds, and these sounds, in turn, have dissolved into the air like vapour billowing from an air humidifier, and instead of them there now exist only glances, touches, emotions, laughs, the smell of hormones and alcohol, basil and garlic stuck between teeth, the waves of twisted electricity hopping joyfully from neuron to neuron, from brain to brain, liberated, given to themselves. Words are no longer necessary, necessity itself is unnecessary; it simply is, everything simply is. The memory that has been and memory to come, the coordinates of seconds, minutes, perhaps hours, and any sense of continuity are — *snap!* — gone. They are lines on paper filled with numbers and ticks that our brains cannot read. Chronology is not a property of time but a science that studies it, a pseudoscience for pseudopeople.

My heroine's hand is cold and wet. She smells of wine and sweat. We're traversing a piazza, a concave square made of thousands of thousand-year-old convex stones polished by time and soles. In the middle of the piazza is a fountain with a statue of Venus. The statue has no head, the head has no eyes and no mouth, the figure has no hands and the hands have no fingers, it has no legs, no torso, nothing, the statue doesn't even have itself, but it's still there, visible, looming a few metres high over the piazza, dropping its shadow in all directions, overlooking the paused fountain, now filled with coins from all around the world — tributes to the goddess of love. The gusts of wind soar at the piazza, whistling around us as we escape the space behind us. We've abandoned our shoes and every stone in our cobbled path now feels like a little mountain. We're flying above the mountains, thousands of little peaks, and suddenly hear the mus—

— Sound like someone is beating an elephant! Let's go and see what is it!

Her hair all over her head, face and shoulders, my heroine pulls my hand somewhere, without waiting for my response.

— Beating an elephant? lol, I mean LOL.

— LMAO even, look!

Before us — an arcade, a long illuminated corridor with beige brick walls and a few dozen glass doors under an arching glass roof. The shops and restaurants are closed and dimly lit, the lights of melon-sized bulbs hanging sadly above empty counters. In the middle of the arcade, a saxophone produces a wildfree melody that its lone player attempts to tame. Her eyes closed, she doesn't see us, and as we approach her, she keeps blowing, ordering the disorder of the air into melancholic vibrations, an elegant sequence of transient voids exquisitely arranged and timed together, weaving the empty space of the arcade into one single thick thread that leads us to... Where to? No idea. We tighten our collective grip, freeze and listen to the saxophonistess. We feel her wordless speech not with our ears but with our whole bodies as all the little hairs on our napes, hands, and legs rise, after the cold, refreshing, sobering and tickling sensation travels from our eardrums to our toes and fills our whole bodies with ecstatic charge. The song abruptly ends and the saxophonistess gives us a blissful smile.

In unison, we ask:

— What's the song called?

Frowning, she replies:

— It's not a song.

In unison, we express our persistent curiosity:

— But what is it called?

Upon a momentary pause, the saxophonistess answers:

— Let it be "A Lament of a Dying Elephant."

Awed, quite so (myself, especially), we ask again (we must be very annoying):

— Has it died?

The woman seems amused by the conversation:

— Who? The elephant? I don't know.

She shrugs, and we clarify:

— No, the song.

She's almost laughing now:

— Ah, probably you can say that. I don't think I would play it again.

— Why wouldn't you?

— Because I have no idea or memory of what I've just played.

The song has passed from the physical world, for it stopped vibrating it and thickening and entangibilising its fabrics, but in our world, which is far from physical, it still sings. Inside our brains, it's tattooed as a long sequence of notes, filling every convolution in dense calligraphic graffiti. It is a code, a program, an instruction, a spell, something that's now running continuously on our joint brainware in a magical, metaphysical manner, despite having no repeated elements that our ears could catch. Hypnotised by (as everyone agreed) "A Lament of a Dying Elephant", we dig coins from our pockets, tributes to the goddess of music, and transfer them into the saxophonistess's hat resting in front of her like a loyal dog, and flee the makeshift concert hall.

Around us, there's a narrow and long public garden where, lanterned, grow various flora: camellias, roses, daffodils, lavender, hydrangeas, peonies, daisies, tulips, ferns, climbing ivy, jasmine, rhododendrons (lots of 'em), wisteria, azaleas, chrysanthemums, lilacs, marigolds, irises, begonias, violets, cyclamens, heather, foxgloves, pansies, sage, more-of and more-poisonous yew, cypress, rosemary, juniper, fuchsia, dahlias, petunias, anemones, aster, zinnias, cosmos, verbena, and maybe some others I can't recognise, for I'm not a botanical expert. We stroll through the labyrinthine collection of flowers and read the names from the plaques beneath. The little pebbles that cover the road prick our bare feet. The ground is still underneath, existing, and we, in fact, are not flying. I can't name the colour of my heroine's eyes anymore. In the dark, they are just two shiny obsidians of cooled lava. A carefree and ironic smile rests across her face. Her hand squeezes my palm, plays with my knuckles, rolls them hither and thither. Here we are, two people surrounded by sleeping beauty.

It's wrong but I want you tonight.

Say it.

No, can one even say that to someone in a park at night?

Can I argue with my inner voice? Does it even hear me back or is it just a monologuing entity?

Say it.

We stop. I grab both of her hands and look into her eyes.

— It's wrong... but I want you tonight.

— To khnight you? (my heroine laughs) I mean, sure. On your knees, please.

My head's overflowing with blush. The awkwardness condenses into one sloppy and scratchy lump and dives down through my throat. Left with no choice, I fall on my knees and bow to my heroine, my newfound queen.

— Are you ready?

My queen clears her throat and commences her speech:

— Before you rise, you must understand the very big responsibilities that come with this... well, impronto khnighthood.

— It's "impromptu".

— Da? "impromptu"-whatever khnighthood...

— It's "night-hood", you don't say the "k". Sorry... please continue.

— Khnight is good with valour, with justice, protects the innocent, and more so, speaks Istina[2] even when it is total bullshit. You swear to do all that?

— I swear.

"My queen."

— So, remember, you are not just any khnight; you're my khnight

---

2. "Istina" (истина) is Russian for "truth", in a literal sense, though semantically it stands further from simply "the factual / empirical truth", closer to "the absolute / transcendent / metaphysical truth", the kind of truth one might find at the bottom of a well or a bottle or never at all. In the same way, German philosophy differentiates between "Richtigkeit" (correctness, factual accuracy) and "Wahrheit" in its deeper Heideggerian sense of "unconcealment" or "aletheia"; similarly, Greek distinguishes "aletheia" (disclosure, uncovering) from "doxa" (opinion); Sanskrit offers "satya" (unchangeable truth) versus "vyavahārika" (conventional truth). Nabokov considered it one of the untranslatable Russian words, and the translator decided not to argue with Vladimir Vladimirovich and instead follow the path of the translators of German philosophers who were completely OK not translating half of the text, including most of Heidegger.

for tokhnight. Your duty is to be present, to be yourself, and maybe even to enjoy this weird world we share. All good?

— It is, absolutely, yeah.

— Swear then.

— I do; I swear.

— So, with authority given to me and by virtue of stars and planets and Venus and all that we cannot see because we're in this city and sky is not clear, I "hereby declare" (he-he) you my khnight. Stand up and not forget — names and titles are only words, just don't be dick. Okay, we're done. Rise, rise, my khnight.

Something's definitely rising at this moment. I shake the dust and bits of leaves off my knee. She smiles, grabs my hand and drags me further through the never-ending garden.

In front of us, there are exit gates. The pillars are made from rough beige stone and topped with dome-shaped caps. Quite antique, actually. Between the pillars are wrought-iron bars with gilded ornaments and figures of flowers and leaves. Below the archway appears a monogram, a crest on which five hearts are arranged in a checkerboard pattern. The light from the lanterns illuminates the curvilinear elements of the gates and plays with shadows behind them. It's not simply gates, not a door, not even a portal. It's a piece of art, and it is, of course, closed. With sweaty fingers, we wedge between the bars and start climbing upwards. Foot. Arm. Foot. Arm. Foot. Arm. At the top, thank the architects, no thorns, no spikes, no spears, no barbed wire, and no other anti-human or anti-pigeon attributes are installed; instead, there's a smooth metal branch that grows from the pillar towards the centre of the gate, where the two doors meet above the coat of arms.

We land. Under us — a narrow pavement, in front — a motorway going approximately forty-eight (or forty-nine) lanes in each direction. Hundreds and thousands of sparks drift by like an asteroid belt: a boiling river of light, noise and exhaust fumes. Don't inhale them. Don't look at them. Don't count them. Look forward, onto your path. My heroine squeezes my hand and leads me forward, then slows down, turns around, circles me, changes her hand, drags me forward again,

circles me again on the other side, and so on, spinning around me, spinning me around herself, waltzing. Thus we khorovod[3] along the motorway and before another bend, the pavement ends. Grimacing, she examines the asteroid belt and the glimmering sea on the other side.

— I think we need to cross it.

— Do what?

— Cross this thing, the road.

My heroine's seriousness has acquired physical qualities.

— Why?

— I don't know. For the plot? It is a character development event.

— In some absurdist tragedy? That's a dumb way to die.

— Imagine you are in a story and you want to make it as interesting as possible to readers.

— What if I'm a secondary or just a background character? An NPC even? Or a narrator whose job is only to narrate the story of his heroine?

— Then your goal is to become hero! Protagonist, da?

— Da?

— You swore to be my khnight for tokhnight.

— Yes, but...

— Classic yes-but situation. I see.

— You don't have to jump onto the motorway to test my knighthood. And I certainly don't want to jump in there.

— But you want, my khnight. You just not know that. Not yet. Let me show you.

My heroine frees my hand and in a gracious feline trajectory jumps over the guardrail right into the road and dances off to the other side across all the lanes while honking cars whiz by until she climbs over the concrete divider in the middle of the motorway and disappears from my sight.

---

3. "Khorovod" (хоровод), or round dance, is a traditional Slavic circle dance of pre-Christian origin, performed at seasonal festivals, weddings, and ritual celebrations, such as midsummer. Participants join hands and move in a ring, often around a central figure, tree, or bonfire, singing songs.

— Oi! Lady!

Breathe. The falling stars fly by in trembling curves, their blazing trails etched briefly against the dark. The coarse grit of the asphalt grinds into my bare feet, sending shocks of heat up through my legs with each footfall, and the world becomes a blur of hypnotic colours. The hungry herd of headlights speeds by, trampling all in their orbit. A whoosh of hot wind blasts my face as a streak of red screams past just inches away. The space stinks of burnt rubber, carbon dioxide, and adrenaline. The pawn moves towards the queen. The pawn crosses the thin line between the known and anarchy, terra firma and the abyss. The pawn realises it has a ribcage, a ribcage that has something inside that now starts reminding of itself. The path is laid with asphalt and perpendicular splashes of white paint. The pawn is electric. The pawn is electricity. It's a leap of faith or fall of faith or flight of faith — depends on the coordinate system of choice. The asphalt's infernal. Step. Jump. Step. Run, run, don't stop and don't close your eyes, you pawn. It's the lament of a dying pedestrian. The great diesel beast stretches itself towards the pawn, distorting from a pinprick to a swirling giant, then collapses back to a singular point as it flies past. The pawn sees how a few metres ahead a ghostly figure of his heroine dances through the veils of exhaust. The pawn's limbs shake, his eyes never close, the pawn doesn't dare to blink. The pawn hauls himself over the same concrete divider, collapsing onto the blessedly cool pavement beyond it. There, under the trees, the pawn sees her, his heroine, waiting for him.

On a sandy pebbled beach, we lie and listen to the waves washing the green dirty lumps of algae off the shore and our feet. This is how the sea talks to you — via gentle strokes of water when it's calm and via heavy blows when angry. Now, the water is cold, and every time it soaks our naked heels, our bodies respond with goosebumps.

— Now what?

— Now we wait.

A coy breeze brings smells of fish, algae and salt and immediately carries them away, as if teasing us. The waves murmur like a dozen cats falling comfortably asleep, ebb, rattle the pebbles,

and run away. Somewhere behind us, hidden in the leaves of the trees, cicadas play their symphony; a little further away the motorway roars; and somewhere deep in my head, elephants sing an infinite song and die one by one until sonic elephanticide ends with no elephants left. A little closer, beside me, I hear my heroine's heavy breath and see her breasts rising and falling as she thirstily absorbs the sea air. Her eyes are closed. Just like mine, her lips dry in the breeze, and now and then she licks them. Before me, the stygian sky, illuminated by the city behind us, and on it, either by satellites or by faint stars, the outlines of her face slowly emerge, and the reality around me fades, as if everything but the vision of her face has lost its already minuscule significance. I roll over onto my side and lie watching the movements of her arched eyebrows, her nose greedily lusting after the atmosphere, her crimson lips... and, trembling, I reach for them until she, hearing my movements and sensing my ragged breath, draws towards me, our bodies merge in a clumsy kiss and begin to roll sideways, flipping over and over, on top of and underneath each other, again and again. Suddenly, I find myself alone in an orchid garden, a garden that is the whole world, a grandiose, boundless construction built to feature but one orchid elucidated in the cosmic glow, a glow born in a complex chemical reaction somewhere thousands and millions of light years away just for this resplendent orchid. It stays on the podium in a little white pot and stares at me, its petals softly curled outward. At its centre emerges the labellum, sensuous and pink, its lobes frilled with intricate ruching and folds. I reach for it with my lips and feel its wet silky petals and finally hear the words in the tongue we can both understand, the tongue of lo—

— You're snoring. Wake up.

My heroine's shaking me by my shoulder, chuckling.

— What happened?

The garden is gone, as if it never existed; what's left is darkness, the cold, passionless void.

— I listen to cicadas and you snore.

— Bonkers. I never snore.

— You do. You snore, "bonkers" or not. No idea what you saw in your dream, but you snored like cicada.

— Very funny.

— He-he. You almost missed everything.

— I didn't sleep.

My heroine sighs.

— Look. This is Venus, — she says, pointing at the bright slightly pulsating dot on the sky.

— How do you know it's Venus?

— I know.

— Are you sure?

— I'm very sure it is Venus, we call her "Ullalulla". Good thing about her is that once every 584 days she floats as close to Earth as she can and you can see her even in the city. Today's that day. Today she's as bright as you can see her from the Earth. Baitu'katu'aktu'Ullalulla'tull.

— What does that mean?

— A lot of things. Maybe hundred words in your tongue. I can't explain.

— You could try.

She pauses and looks at me.

— You don't want to hear it. It's a boring story. Very boring.

— It's fall or fly, da?

— Don't use my weapon against me. You swore not to be dick.

— I won't judge or anything. Whatever you say I'll just listen and nod like a good knight is supposed to. A nodding knight.

— Ha-ha. Okay. But if you say even one word, I will drown you.

I adopt complete numbness, having cast a ziplock spell on my lips.

— Good. I told you it's boring. So... — my heroine takes a deep breath. — When I was a little girl, I lived in Tulubaika, little village, before moving away later. In that village, when you go out, you would see woods, mostly birches, and sky, mostly stars, as if it was a sieve through which something magical flowed down to the Earth. Imagine that beautiful sky, every single night, full of shiny dots. Not sure if you ever saw it, Milky Way and all that — not all people know you can see

it, apparently... but anyway. When I moved to that big city, first thing on night sky I saw was Venus. There were moon, satellites, planes and other "celestial bodies" maybe, but I remember only Venus. I felt instant nostalghia even when I saw her first time. Then I didn't know she was Venus. Of course, for me she was just "star". Later I learned her course and how she dances together with Sun, but before that I just saw her becoming dimmer and dimmer every single night. So, "Baitu'katu'aktu'Ullalulla'tull" means something like, "soon, you see her again, every time she be same, same beautiful planet, but you be new person, slightly different, maybe more mature, coming to her with new challenges passed and new acquired, and despite them, or rather in spite of them, every time she would remind you that there's something constant, something that gives you hope, something that fades and flashes, something that teaches you how to find comfort in chaos". So, yes, there's more things but it's just brief summary for you.

Her eyes have welled up, and I see the reflection of Venus in them. She smiles and moisturises her lips again. Should I start talking or shouldn't I? I don't know what to say. It feels awkward, more awkward than the restaurant, than the knighting and the dream (it's all been rather a downward spiral of awkwardness), as if I realise she's told me too much and I'm expected to tell something of the same grade in return, but I can't, I'm not that interesting and my thoughts keep panicking, running, stumbling, hiding from me, like three little piglets who've just seen a wolf, and I can't find anything remotely worthy of sharing.

— Do you want one more? — my heroine asks.

She stretches out her slightly sand-dusted palm to me with a shiny pill, half red, half blue. Silent, I shake a nay, and she stashes the pill back into her pocket. We keep lying in silence.

— You know, I translate myself my whole life and I don't even remember what it's like to talk to someone in my tongue. Often I want to meet someone who would be able to learn my tongue.

I point at myself. She frowns.

— It is not just a tongue, da? Maybe you can learn it but you still won't be able to really think in it, I mean, "really". You'll still count in

your own tongue, your dreams and subconscious will use it to talk to you. Universe will use it as well because that's simple and more easy way to reach you.

Her tongue clicks and she pauses.

— Look. You're a very nice and fun young man, but imagine if we were more than friends. Despite what I would say to you, there will always be so much more of me that you can never see, there'll always be so much more of what I can never translate, and even if I can, you will never be able to understand it. You would be looking at this image I spend so much effort to create and I will spend my life translating to you all my emotions and feelings. Even after you "learn the words", you'll never see my innermost self, who is a far more interesting person, by the way, she's very funny.

Holding our hands behind our backs, we slowly stroll back along the motorway as the cars whoosh by our side. I feel calm, almost sober, yet something bitter at the root of my tongue is drying out my throat. I look at my heroine as she toewalks, balancing. I smile, she notices it and smiles back. The world is playing a trick on me: a bad feeling that something beautiful is about to end grows in my head and soon engulfs it. The inky indigo of the night begins to yield as the hazy purple gradient creeps from behind the horizon, painting the sky with pools of radiant pink and orange, like swirls of different sorbets bleeding into one another. The sea catches the nascent glow and shimmers like a mirror fragmented into a thousand shards. Upwards, beyond it, the gulls cry and follow us to the city gleaming through veils of illumination like a mirage. The city is getting closer but I don't want it to; I want it to always stay where it is, frozen and distant. I try not to look at it and instead look at my heroine, the sea, and the sky. I just want to be here, staying and not walking, because with every step, time crawls through me, ferociously, and pulls me forward against my will.

Meanwhile, the blazing sphere of the sun breaches the waterline and Venus dissolves in the sky.

We go through the same public garden. It all feels like a dream, a blurry and dimly lit dream. Now, the gates are open. Everything's out

of place, like someone's been messing with my dream: different flowers bloom, different smells float in the air, different birds sing. There, in the middle of the park, on the path parallel to ours and separated from us by a long bush, a bald man in an orange garment and a Zen face trims that bush. A monk! He looks at us and we look at him, and at that moment I feel a throbbing urge to ask him about life. He must know, he's a monk, a disciple of wisdom, he's been studying the Universe and Self for years, perhaps millennia, his knowledge is far beyond my comprehension, just like the tongue of my heroine. If I had just one question to ask him, what would I ask? What would I so desperately want to know that could make my life take a sharp turn as if it's on a hinge that needs just a little nudge to move, and what would this man, this bald peaceful monk, know the answer to? What would he say to me? Yes, yes, I know what I should ask (or rather must). But what would he say? Would he say it's something you don't learn but feel, or that it's all chemicals in our brain? Or something else? I don't care, I just need an answer. So, I clear my throat of bitter mucus and approach him, leaning on the bush.

— Excuse me, dear mister. If I may ask just one question... What is the language of love?

The monk barks out a caustic laugh.

— How the fuck would I know? It's 5AM. Go get sober, mate. And don't touch the bloody bush.

I nod meekly, hearing my heroine's suppressed chuckle behind me. She takes my hand, says something to the monk, and pulls me towards the exit.

Everything seems old, shabby, as if all the electric charm has been sucked out of it, as if with the sunrise all the slovenliness of the city that was hidden at night has now been revealed: the pavements littered with rubbish, the buildings with dark stains, peeling paint and long meandering cracks with little lizards scurrying between them. Everything has become monotonous and drab, the colour of old, the smell of old, the feel of old. We cross the same arcade with a glass roof, yet now it feels shorter, just a few buildings deep, and emptier, for no one now is torturing elephants, the phantomic melody of which has

escaped my head, leaving no trace. We enter the same cobbled piazza that, like everything else before, appears much smaller now, as if new buildings grew overnight, a few rows of them from the periphery to that fountain in the centre where we find our abandoned shoes. We put them on and continue our way along the canal, to the river, next to the empty seafood restaurant with the tables flipped over on the terrace under the plexiglass roof, still being scratched by the poisonous yews. We enter the same hotel where we met last night, and, even though it's not night anymore, wish each other good night, part ways and ascend to our rooms.

After a short but deep sleep, my consciousness resurfaces at noon. I go to the reception and see her in the same clothes, in slippers, with a suitcase, standing facing the desk while returning the keys.

— Hi, — I say.

— Hi, — she says.

I don't know what to say, and she, wearing a mellow melancholic expression on her face (which also could be read as "tired"), doesn't seem to know either, as if last night we spoke in a different tongue.

— What a night, huh? — I say.

— I was going to thank you for it, by the way. It was fun, — she says.

— Fun, yes, — I say.

Prolonged silence, as if nothing, a sheer void, can be prolonged and become tense and dense, thick and vibrating.

— You didn't say you were leaving today, — I say.

— I didn't say I will stay. I was here for one night only. My plane was cancelled, and well...

— I see, okay. I'm leaving tomorrow, too.

— Good! One more day, yay! Have fun.

— Thank you. I will. It won't be that fun, though.

— No, it won't. That only happens once every 584 days.

I wish her a safe flight, we say goodbye to each other, and she leaves. I watch how she exits the hotel through the automatic door dragging a white wheeled suitcase with a luggage tag hanging from its handle, the case covered in coloured stickers with flowers, flags and

landmarks from various countries, and, instantly, in a furious flurry, the words for "goodbye" in their respective tongues pop up in my head. In French, they say "au revoir"; in German, it's "auf Wiedersehen"; over in Japan, it's "sayonara"; in Italian, they say "arrivederci"; in Spanish, it's "adiós"; in Mandarin Chinese, it's "zàijiàn"; in Hindi, it's "alvida"; and in Arabic, it's "wadaʼan"; in Swahili, it's "kwaheri"; and so on — it's always one or two words, but what she said to me was "Tuʼbaikaʼluʼikatuʼluiʼbaikatuʼikaʼlubaitukaʼluʼikabaiʼtuʼlukai", and I have no idea what and how much it actually means.

Episode Three
about all the fuckery & beyond

Think you're escaping and run into yourself. Longest way round is the shortest way home.

— James Joyce, "Ulysses"

Into her eyes, the wind drove smoke and ash from a poorly kindled mangal[1] and made the sky dissolve. Celestial bodies rolled about like billiard balls, be it the stars, the moon, or satellites and the ISS. Our heroine felt them upon herself, their brightness, their weight, their distance, both physical and metaphorical. The sky above the dacha[2] was clear. Visibility stretched far, so far that one's eyes rippled at its magnificence. Too beautiful, she thought. Such beauty ought not to exist. Such beauty could drive one beyond one's wits. Such beauty should be outlawed, denied legal counsel, stripped of the presumption of innocence, for it, this unattainable beauty, is the prime cause of all human joys and woes. Yet, for some reason, no one else paid any attention to it at that moment; instead, they looked at each other, and not just looked ("Would be terribly awkward, wouldn't it?"), but interacted, conversed, socialised. Was their interest genuine, or was it

---

1. A mangal is a type of metal barbecue grill popular throughout post-Soviet and Central Asian countries, typically designed for skewered meat (shashlik). The ritual of gathering around a mangal is a must for any respectable outdoor social occasion from May to September (but not limited to), with some inevitably arguing about the proper way to arrange the coals while others prepare the actual food.
2. A Soviet and post-Soviet phenomenon of a small summer house outside of the city with a garden to grow vegetables and fruits, hang out, have shashlik, and "enjoy" the summer weeding the seedbeds.

all a game with unspoken rules that everyone pretended to play? The people around were far from celestial, not yet anyway ("Touch wood!"), and far from luminaries, except perhaps in the sciences[3] ("Fingers crossed"), but it was pleasant to share the same space and time with them, to observe them, to analyse their Chekhovian-Beckettian dialogues for meaning, while remaining silent herself. She could crack a joke when appropriate, throw in a sharp remark, answer a question directed at her. Yes, there were oddly many of those — she had suddenly become interesting ("Suspicious..."). For hours, she could wait, listen and re-listen, all while drifting somewhere else. Always this "somewhere else"; there's no escaping it. It's celestial, visible yet untouchable, impossible even to give it a proper name, for words are never enough to describe what you'll never see. Some things have no name at all and cannot have one, so we call them names foreign to them to give them some semblance of form.

— Are you here? — Alyona smirked and sat beside her.

Me? Oh, if only I knew, she thought. Seems I'm here — here I sit, getting by without a sigh, nothing but skin and bones. How are things? As white as soot, no offspring to report[4], watching the stars, warming myself by the mangal, listening to Kolya's mediocre yet rather sweet guitar playing, but am I here? Perhaps. I'm just all dreamy, mysterious, unapproachable, with a special aura of alt girlie[5], quiet but

---

3. The original Russian phrase "светила науки" (svetila nauki) literally translates as "luminaries of science." While English has similar terms, the Russian expression carries distinct connotations of official academic prestige, often used with a touch of irony to describe those enshrined in the scientific establishment.

4. The original Russian phrase "как сажа бела, пока не родила" (kak sazha bela, poka ne rodila) literally translates to "as white as soot, haven't given birth yet." It combines two very idiomatic ways of responding to "how are you?" into one contradictory expression paired with that timeless reminder that a woman's "ultimate achievement" apparently involves producing miniature humans.

5. Original uses "альтушка" (altushka). Even though it's borrowed from English "alt girl", the Russian metamorphosis of the term carries a distinctive sonic quality by adding an affectionate-yet-mocking diminutive suffix "-ушка", hence "girlie" instead of "girl" in the translation as an attempt to convey the same tone. The "alt girlie" phenomenon became a meme around 2020-2021 in Russia and was nominated for "Word of the Year." "Alt girlie" isn't just any girl with "dyed hair and combat boots", but a specific social archetype. In internet culture, the "alt girlie" became the object of desire for a particular

with volumes of Nietzsche and Machiavelli in my little black rucksack ("The straight-A student aura has long become boring to cultivate; straight-A students aren't interesting to anyone and possess no mystery, except perhaps the ability to irritate those around them").

— Uh-huh.

— Not cold?

— Nope.

— Want a throw?

— Won't say no to a throw.

— Back in a sec, — Alyona smiled and vanished into the dacha house.

From there, laughter could be heard, loud music was playing, something from the charts, some nameless, thoughtless, worthless, mechanical repetition of three notes ("Sometimes fewer") and lyrics about nothing of substance. It didn't let her think, yanked her out of "somewhere else", so she couldn't hear anything but the music, neither others' voices nor her outer voice nor her inner voice. A waste of time and eardrums — only pure, imbecilic decibels, or in other words, music for dimwits. Even Kolya's guitar, though imperfectly tuned, had some soul and sincerity.

Alyona returned with a throw and draped it over our heroine's shoulders. She also brought a bottle of wine and plastic cups with her.

— Beautiful, isn't it? — she said, looking at the sky.

Our heroine nodded. They sat, silent. Silence is pleasant; you can observe it meditatively, like fire, the only difference being it doesn't crackle.

— Well then... Ripe for some[6]? — asked Alyona, shaking the wine bottle.

---

type of man called a "скуф" (skuf), thusly creating one of Russia's most widespread memes of 2024. The "skuf" represents men around or over 35 with unkempt appearances, dead-end jobs, and a lifestyle revolving around beer, TV, and video games — essentially the polar opposite of the aesthetically conscious alt girlie. The apogee of the meme was the appearance of the advertised possibility of finding your "alt girlie" on government websites, as well as a visual novel game called "Альтушка для скуфа" ("An alt girlie for a skuf") that became a Steam bestseller.

6. Common idiomatic expression in Russian, used in any context to indicate

I'm not an apricot, thought our heroine. "Ripe..." Why does everyone use this phrase? Ripe for what? Ripe for wine? Ripe for a husband? Ripe for children? Being a ripening apricot would be far more interesting, for you can extract cyanide from its core. "Ripe" indeed... This phrase in another context would seem like an attack, but from Alyona it sounded soft and unobtrusive ("No cyanide for her"). She probably wouldn't have suggested wine to our heroine at all if she herself hadn't already been "ripe" for four glasses ("No, I'm not keeping track. The girl's grown up").

Everything from Alyona always sounded soft and unobtrusive. Suspicious, as it seemed to our heroine at first ("Truly suspicious"). Usually, if someone were that kind and courteous, friendly and glowing with interest, it meant they wanted something from her.

— Maybe we could go somewhere? — they would say.

— Looking good today, you. Nice skirt, — they would say.

— May I borrow your essay? No, I won't copy. It's for inspiration. I'm having writer's block or such, — they would say. — I know it's about personal feelings, but isn't personal universal?

— It's five minutes to midnight on the doomsday clock, — they would say. — The geopolitical situation is complicated. Our predicament isn't predetermined.

— You're the smartest girl in the class, — they would say. — Did you know that?

— Oh, we were born on the same day! — they would say.

— I'm a foreign businessman with a very, very big black Lamborghini and hair transplanted from my arse. Pleasure to meet you. Want to see my cock? Though why am I even asking... here you go!

— Massive, indeed, like your mum, — our heroine would answer.

— I'm just a simple guy, you know? Not like those other guys.

"readiness" for whatever it might be. The translator took the liberty to retain it as-is, given it's used throughout the story, even in a meta-way.

Want to come over and watch me play Counter-Strike while I drink beer from the can? I've got frozen pizza, — a skufidon[7] would say.

— I'm honest, I'm always honest with you, — they would say. — No, my sincerity isn't ephemeral. It actually exists. No, why are you saying it? No, I don't have "an ulterior motive". That's your "motif", that thinking. I just want to be friends.

— Oh, please, — she would say. — Spare me, won't you?

With Alyona, with Kolya, and the others gathered at the dacha, there was none of that. They needed so little from her that it became suspicious. They, like her, enjoyed sharing the moment, gossiping about professors falling asleep during lectures, deans running corruption schemes, discussing anything but studies, laughing at her politically incorrect jokes, except those about comrade Yehoshua ("May his memory be blessed"), for Alyona took her baptism too seriously ("The girl's grown up").

Our heroine didn't notice how all slow rationality abandoned her, and something inside her decided that she was ripe and grown up, too.

— Really? — Alyona couldn't believe it.

Our heroine and alcohol were supposed neither to be mixed nor to be shaken, not invited to the same party, kept apart in every way possible; even putting them in the same sentence wasn't recommended, or else one might receive a witch's wrathful glare, a disgruntled feline hiss, accompanied by "I've already said I don't drink", "Well, maybe you've changed your mind?", "Maybe I haven't changed my mind?", "Well who knows, maybe you have changed your mind after all", *threatening screech of rolling eyes*.

— Pour before I change my mind.

She felt coldness on her neck.

The wine appeared winely; she knew well what it looked and smelled like. At every family feast, there was always cheap cardboard box wine for the ladies and vodka for the gentlemen. In respectable company, the type of alcohol wasn't important, for everyone got

---

7. See also: footnote on "alt girlie." "Skufidon" (скуфидон) is the final form of "skuf." It's a portmanteau of "skuf" and "Cupidon", the Russian word for Cupid.

sloshed in the same manner and practised the same disgusting behaviour each in their own way and did and said things they wouldn't do or say otherwise.

— She can drink already. She's here at the table with us grown-ups. It's just a spoon anyway, isn't it? No more than a spoonful of cough syrup.

— No, she can't, she's only a girl.

— Oi! Look at him, ha-ha. Face in a salad.

— I wash my rug every week. They say so in the news.

— Capital punishment is what we need.

— You, uncle?

— Well, not we, the country.

— Why would you wash your rug every week? What's the point?

— Look at her, grown up everywhere, in every way, a fine girl, I must say. Can't believe she's only fifteen, can you?

— Wasn't your grandfather executed by the KGB?

— There was no KGB back then.

— There was, has always been.

— I just use washing powder, there's no secret.

— You blink, and she's married, just wait. The girls are nasty these days. You'll babysit your grandkids soon, I'm telling you. Look at her.

— Do you know Galina, a friend of mine? Her son, Denis, they spent a week with us when you were three, got all As.

— I heard he's also grown up everywhere, in every way. Back from the army, he is.

— No, mum, he and his brother have one brain between them.

— Don't say that. Why would you say that?

— He's an idiot, mum, it's no secret to anyone, is it?

— Listen to her. Young but already cunty.

— Language! She's a teenager.

— Should it be whitening washing powder?

— I heard they just use soot because why not?

— Why not indeed.

She would crawl into the wardrobe in her room, plug her ears, wait for it all to end. If there were no wardrobe, she would just sit, ignore

everyone and everything around her, and be "somewhere else", somewhere where she had all the bitterest remarks to every dimwitted dialogue.

— Well, how's the wine? — asked Alyona.

— Like wine, I suppose.

— Tasty?

— Strange. Sweet.

— Georgian.

— Thought it would be bitter.

— There's bitter wine too. Probably.

— Like what?

— Like bitter wine, I suppose. Ha.

— Like wallpaper paste?

— Wallpaper paste??? What does wallpaper paste taste like?

— Very, very, very bitter.

— Did you taste wallpaper paste?

— Accidentally. I was bored when everyone was putting up wallpaper. I was five.

— What was the wallpaper?

— Like in a hospital. White.

Alyona smiled. She had a beautiful smile. She could sing too, did ballet, had fair hair, but was no friend to mathematics, wouldn't have managed without our heroine — in other words, her complete opposite.

— Really never drank before? — Alyona asked.

Our heroine shook her head.

— Nope.

— You're having me on.

— Nope.

— Everyone drinks.

— I don't.

— Never?

— Not in my memory.

— Why?

— First it wasn't allowed, then didn't want to, by inertia, then read

"Brave New World", and well... you know me, — she finished the phrase and took a few sips.

Besides sweetness and the taste of surrounding smoke, she felt little else. It burnt her throat slightly, like cough syrup. That was all. How much does one need to drink to get drunk?

— What would a female Savage do? I mean, what if the Savage were a woman? — asked Alyona.

— Anything but suicide. Why all that drama? She'd fly off to a retreat on a quiet island in the Pacific, get into numerology, write a book, "How I Escaped Toxic Consumer Society and Found Myself". Or just marry some City trader and open a yoga studio.

Alyona laughed with her mouth full, spraying wine on the throw.

— What? — Our heroine smiled.

— A bit cynical, that.

— You know I'm cynical.

— You're not, though you want to be. Not everyone's an influencer these days.

— Not everyone, but even Tolstoy would have a TikTok about life in the village and shagging peasant women.

Alyona's laughter was ringing, almost childlike, unlike our heroine's.

— Crudish.

— Prudish.

— A toast. We need to drink to that. This one's on you.

— My first glass, and you want a "toast". I've no experience in the matter. I don't play games I cannot win.

— Well, learn first, then win.

— People probably spend years learning before winning.

— You're clever. You can learn quickly.

That our heroine couldn't deny — she was at a dead end. She didn't want to think about anything, for thinking meant being "somewhere else". To think means to immerse oneself in one fantasy, which leads one to another fantasy, and then to a third fantasy, and so on, spiralling down or up through that fantasy helix. Yes, respected teacher? Where am I? I'm here ("Actually, I'm somewhere there"). I'm

not distracted at all. No, I'm not thinking about boys. Cross yourself![8] Do you think I'm a stupid girl? A nymphomaniac? I think about great things, Tamara Alekseevna. If you think about men, it doesn't mean everyone's like you. How dare I? Well, I'm a student — you asked, I answered. You won't give me a failing grade anyway, even for bad behaviour; I behave well, or rather "not at all" — behaviour interests me little, and you can't reproach me for unfinished homework, unlearned verse, failed test. I know everything, sometimes even more than you ("Right, what was I... ah yes, toast!")

— To all this fuckery!

— Ha. Straight off like that?

— Well, why not? I don't know what people usually drink to. To health? To love? To peace? To friendship amongst nations? To a bright future after dictatorship?

— Sometimes you can drink to "all this fuckery", I suppose.

— Well then, to all this fuckery.

They raised their glasses and clinked, though plastic against plastic doesn't create an authentic experience. Our heroine emptied her cup in an instant.

— Well, you're going for it, girl.

This was purely intellectual interest and pathological curiosity. The expected sensations of intoxication weren't there for some reason, and our heroine wanted to understand what was wrong with her again and what would happen when / if suddenly these sensations appeared, what they were like, what would become of her, and what of her "somewhere else". The cat sits on the mat, mother sees Spot run[9], father drinks beer, mother scolds, father hits, mother cries, our heroine hides, first in the wardrobe, and then, when the streams of spirits reach it and begin to seep inside through the gap between its doors — in

---

8. The original "окститесь" (okstites') literally means "cross yourself" in the Orthodox tradition, but is used idiomatically to tell someone to come to their senses or get a grip, often ironically.

9. The original is "мама мыла раму" (mama myla ramu) that literally means "Mother washed the window frame" and is an example from Russian primers used to teach children to read.

"somewhere else". Advanced problem: when she starts drowning in wine, how will Gandalf come to the rescue: on eagles, on a blue helicopter, on a yellow submarine, or on an ark?

— Want more?

— Don't know yet.

— Who knows, maybe you're wild.

— Me? Wild?

— Maybe you're wild and we never knew.

— Anything but wild.

— Shy and quiet, but then, all of a sudden, wild — your real personality revealed.

— People better not see it, my real personality.

— We don't know that yet. Maybe she's nice and not wild at all. Tell me, what do you feel?

— Nothing, — she said with a shrug.

— Stand up, walk around. Get your blood moving. Stand up, it'll go straight to your head.

Wrapped in the throw, our heroine rose and began taking big steps along the garden paths laid with blackened boards, to the fence, around the mangal and back ("Hmm... Not even wobbling a bit"). The sky was clouding over and the celestial bodies started fading.

— Nope. Nothing.

— And nothing in your head?

— Nope.

— And your mood? Happy?

— I wouldn't know — I'm always happy.

— Oh, sure...

— Well yes.

— Comédienne.

— Secret happy personality.

— That's for sure.

— Pour more. I reckon I'd be more drunk from kefir[10].

---

10. A fermented milk drink, tangy and slightly effervescent, with a negligible alcohol content, typically less than 1%.

— Truth is in wine.

— In vino veritas.

— Lush.

Why do people always dissolve into ethereal substrates over time? *Poof!* — and gone as soon as you stop reminding each other of your existence.

— We must see each other, — they would say.

— Let's keep in touch, — they would say.

— If you're in Tulubaika ever again, write to me, — they would say.

— At least post them stories from your Europes, — they would say.

— You know I post nothing.

Well, good riddance, but where do they go? Were school friends even real? Some managed to drink themselves to death, get hooked on drugs, go to prison, become family people ("Not sure which is worse..."), a rare few flew abroad, even rarer were those found hanging from an old birch in Victory Park after what was presumably an unsuccessful escape either from fascists or from antifa or both of them, or who were simply marathon runners. Got carried away, you know, ended up in the wrong area, stumbled with a neck on a rope, hanged themselves, didn't even bother to soap it, didn't even invite me to the funeral... What kind of person does that? Eh... Friendship is tested in troubles, unless it's troubles in the head[11]. ("Oh, seems like the fingers on my hands are starting to pulse!")

— I'll step out.

— Go ahead.

In the mirror above the sink, she still saw a familiar face: no red eyes or red swollen nose, only ears... ears slightly reddened and a bit of

---

11. An Internet-Russian idiom. There's the Orthodox TV show "Беседы с батюшкой" (lit. "Conversations with the Priest"). If we modify the original title by removing a few letters, from "conversations with the priest" we get to "troubles in the head". Thus it became a meme. It is often accompanied by the modified title image of the TV show overlaid with semi-transparent images of psychiatric hospital employees. It gained popularity in 2020 as a response to unhinged online rants.

a blush on her cheeks. She ran her fingers through her hair to push it back. The skin on her head was tense, a tad less sensitive than usual, yet more pleasant to touch. The experiment was going steadily; the subject was normal: no sudden desire to dance, nor to pour out her soul to those around or punch someone in the face; neither a straitjacket nor an adrenaline shot was required; quite the opposite — mental activity was bubbling. She wanted to think, think more, think about everything, think about the past, about the future, about thinking itself — to metathink, if you will — about the best moments, about the worst moments, about the best moments that became the worst, about the worst moments that turned out to be quite all right. Should have thought earlier, now you can't think it all in a couple of hours, girl. Think, think, think, think, or you'll drown. Weave a raft from thoughts, or you'll drown. Think, think, think. No, don't think, don't think, don't think, or think about how to stop thinking, think yourself out of this thinking somewhere far away. Enough thinking for you, you've thought enough, philosophesse. Rain began drumming on the toilet window. How frightening, how frightening to be under control, and oh how frightening, how frightening to lose that control, but how terrible is the desire to act uncontrollably, having seized chaos. No, she wouldn't lose these friends as she had lost childhood ones — they weren't just ignorant infants seated together at the same desk by the whim of planida[12] but adults who had consciously chosen each other's company. That's different.

The rain drove everyone to the table. They settled inside on old wooden benches covered with throws to avoid catching splinters.

— Are you all right? — asked Alyona.

— Yeah.

The bottom of the hot three-litre teapot inadvertently stuck to the

---

12. "Planida" (планида) is an archaic / folkloristic Russian term for fate or destiny. It carries overtones of inescapable, often burdensome predetermined destiny, and is etymologically derived from Greek "πλανήτης" (planētēs) meaning "wanderer" or "planet", reflecting ancient beliefs that planetary movements determined human fate. The word entered Russian through Church Slavonic and maintained its association with cosmic predetermination.

plastic tablecloth, making it shrink and crease. The perpetrator of this mishap couldn't be identified.

— Want some wine?

Our heroine's face wrinkled. She shook her head and nodded at the teapot. Into a gigantic cup with a heavy bottom poured the so-called world-famous "fragrant dacha ambrosia", a sweetened chai[13] drink made from mint, gooseberry and blackcurrant leaves. She wanted to remember this taste. Soon, in a few days, she'll have views of the Mediterranean Sea from the office on the twentieth floor, unlimited espresso, seagulls crying in unknown languages, perfectly paved and treed streets, galleries, museums, theatres, and all such cultural things ("And the sun will shine more than once a year..."). In foreign lands, over the hill, over the border, in strange parts, in the West, there will be no muddy pavements, no road potholes, no stinking buses that momentarily transform ordinary street puddles into Hokusai waves and drench you head to toe. It won't still be dark at eight in the morning and already dark by three in the afternoon. But they won't be there either, those very people, across whose faces her gaze jumped, to and fro, to and fro, as if recording how they distribute under- and over-grilled meat onto plates, serve improvised salads, cut and pass home-baked bread, wave forks, knives, napkins, make toasts, "clink" glasses, drink, laugh, make toasts again, "clink" glasses, drink, laugh, play guitar, sing, make toasts, drink, laugh, laugh, laugh, chat, take pictures, drink, laugh, chat, chat, chat, chat, chat, chat, take pictures. Cosy, strangely cosy, but at the same time suspenseful, as if she needed to be on guard, as if everything were unreal and out of time, not an event, not an occasion that was in her calendar and was about to end, but simply a non-phenomenal phenomenon, a fragment of life into which she had stumbled by accident, and where she shouldn't have been, for she had always wanted to be somewhere else, but now, for some reason, did not.

---

13. "Chai" in Russia and in many other countries literally means "tea" as a category, not necessarily a specific spiced version of it. The translator for some reason decided to use "chai" over "tea".

Episode Four
about microcosmos & microchaos

Love, in essence, arises in solitude when its object is not around, and it is directed not so much at the one or two people you love as at an image constructed by the mind, loosely connected to the original.

— Victor Pelevin, "Chapaev And Void"

There you are — trudge through the city
all around skyscrapers sprout.
Behind, ever so distant, lies Tulubaika.
Ahead, ever so near
      — bloody hell knows what.

On and on the avenue winds, its endless venue astretch, bound to snap like an old string, slash your cheek raw and leave a scar beneath your eye (the sight's still there, thank you very much) so you'd torture your memory over that melody never mastered.

Primordial soup of concrete, metal, and glass fills the surrounding space of this chaotically ordered universe and takes shape as walls, ceilings, floors, staircases, windows, benches, poles, stretches of tarmac.

Upwards it grows
downwards it burrows
      as wires and pipes and metro mole-tunnels.
outwards it swells and scatters
      to an infinity infinitely large

until the little human within
finally recognises himself as
    an infinity infinitely small.

The proportion of natural light shrinks with unnatural greed, cars move ever louder, yet slower, people walk ever denser, yet faster.

Hum, hubbub and hullabaloo, the noise of tyres and soles merges into the background — sea sound, wave roar, storm forest hour — a monolithic din beckoning one into trance.

No brain-squeezing fear remains, no anxiety lingers, no claustrophobia caused by the sheer quantity of everything; instead
    — awe before civilisation's new element:
        earth, water, air, fire, aether...
        city.

The ancients built pyramids for egoists; we raise them for thousands of souls to make birds envious, pharaohs dead jealous, and children of tomorrow marvel at our grandeur.

In that village of mine, rooftops are a hand's throw away; here you won't spot them without binoculars.

There void holds its reign
    pure fields, grass unmown
    pure sky, stars starving for glances
    houses askew from sheer emptiness.

As for colours: late autumn, winter, early spring — mere shades of grey, no kaleidoscopes of carnivals, no all-intipsifying psychedelia, just dust, decay, and cavity, bubble, geode.

Yet, it's lovely at times:
    dawn layers agately
    night shimmers with amethyst
    birchwood drowns in citrine
    firmament glows with blue chalcedony.

In the metropolis, though, void has voided

collapsed fractally into itself
no room for it here no more
& ceaseless secretion fills all manner of vacuums.

Nature abhors a vacuum
     & the nature of vacuum abhors
         itself.
With bewilderment micros glow
    — cosmos & chaos.

Wet asphalt and concrete shimmer in sungleam, once pale grey, now dark. Clouds are thin, have almost finished their cry, and the hopeful light penetrates them. It reflects in the countless cars' mirrors, in the buildings' glass, in protruding phone screens that balaclavaed cyclists in black snatch from hunched passersby who but shrug and keep shuffling onwards, no umbrellas in hand, no bother for dripping warm drizzle, for a pleasant phenomenon, this mushroom rain, as my granddad would call it.

Soon, winds will lift human spores up in the air and disperse them around the city. They will rise in trainloads from under the ground, and their presence will flood over pavements, squares, roads, and streets, all those venues of avenues.

Lo and behold —
    off they trot, some to their jobs
    some to jobless affairs:
    to museums, cinemas, galleries
    theatres, bakeries, libraries
    reading rooms, skating rinks
    swimming pools, plazas and promenades
    food halls, concert halls, dance floors
    comedy clubs
        (or perhaps karaoke)
    rooftop bars, kinky clubs
    cosy corner cafes

observation decks, prayer rooms
botanical gardens, arcades
hidden speakeasies, markets and malls
parks and playgrounds
   — centres for everything
or simply to wander, you know
stretch their thoughts and restore
to their legs their original purpose.

— From Brandenburg Gate station tha rides to Tower Bridge station — there tha changes to t'grey-brown-raspberry line[1], and heads towards Brighton Beach till terminus. Take t'last carriage and t'moment tha hops off, leg it straight to t'exit. But don't get lost. Bloody 'ell it's packed there — can't squeeze a mouse through. Then half an hour on the movinn stairs and bob's your uncle. Easy, — says the navigator on my phone.

Sunwards I point my face, mightily I squeeze my eyes shut, all watery from fumes aloft and borrowed sleep.
  (Debt collectors are on the way!)
The sun's reflection leaps off the glass building and floods the street with light.
The city throbs, breathes, digests its tenants, and gently mocks its guests.
Go on then, run along, no point standing there gawping — you'll catch a fly or some affliction of sorts.

Yet here I stand

---

1. "Grey-brown-raspberry" (серобуромалиновый) is a chromatic descriptor indigenous to Russian linguistic taxonomy. The term defies classical colour theory, belonging to a peculiar class of improbable compound adjectives deployed when precise hue identification proves unnecessary or impossible. In its most elaborate folk iterations, you could find "серобуромалиновый в крапинку" (grey-brown-raspberry with spots) and some others, less appealing ones. The colour and its variations remain stubbornly resistant to RGB codification.

arms spread wide, straight as a rod
alone in a meadow barren and broad.
Grumbling passersby jostle; gentle breeze; traffic noise sounds like
wind through oats ripened for harvest.
O shall I leap upon my steed of two-wheeled pedal breed!
O shall I race along those roads
trailing dust and childhood yarns,
teenage fables, youth's swift whispers!
O shall the sun tousle my freckles
shall the wind shove my hair into my eyes
& shall the chain chew grease-stained trousers
& shall zoom onwards I.
O shan't I give a toss, or even "a fuck"
(as I'd say with my grown-up permission).

— Give me change! — a hoarse voice shouts to me. — Change, I
beg you, urgent matter. Or I'll leave. But first I'll show you the entire
intimate essence of mine! Oo! Oo-oo! — so he moans, hands reaching
for his fly.
— Won't give any! — says I. — No change to give, nought to
share: not a toss, not a fuck. And I always pay by card!
— Ah, card shark! May the govs torment you!
— Eh? — says I, playing the fool.
— Here's your carte blanche for my essence!
Oo! Oo-oo! Oo-oo!
— ¡No hablo inglés! — I yell back and hurry
to part ways with the stranger
my mind dismissing this most peculiar mishap.

I descend underground to tunnel away. Still I stand.
In my ears — Shostakovich, String Quartet No. 8, allegro molto,
breakcore flip[2].

2. Shostakovich's String Quartet No. 8 was composed in Dresden in 1960 over just
three days under what historians politely describe as "intense emotional distress". The

In my head — a bit of a do.

In my soul — the nobility of feelings ignoble.

In my eyes — local adverts: bits and bobs for home and body, this and that for business, everything from top to toe, from alpaca winter socks to lacy knickers, from Chekhovian theatre to torture by TikToks of feline brainrot

(oo ee ee ah ee oo ee ee ee ee ah ee)

from attempts to sell desires to secretly flog me some memecoins protected by nought but cryptography.

Here, underground lies half of the city, be it rail transport, car parks, or shopping malls going down and down

while in Tulubaika

— only the dead.

Here, I'll slip into another world in an hour

in Tulubaika

— into Tulubaika itself for the umpteenth time.

Here, the air's full of suspension

in Tulubaika...

Well, none of that's there, in fact, only clean air, pure water and pure starry sky, pure as the consciousness of a fresh victim of gnosis.

Inwards and outwards voices fuse: whispers from within meet the clamour of the crowd.

— Ey up, I'm done in, mate, proper done in. Laid me low, this influenza.

— All sorts of bubonic drebbeden[3] goinn round t'village nowadays. Mowinn down folk left and right, young uns and old uns

---

allegro molto movement features the composer's signature frantic intensity and is "already perfectly chaotic, thanks". The breakcore rendition that can be found on the internet has slightly higher BPM which further turns the original piece into "anxiety incarnate". Highly recommended.

3. "Drebbeden" (дребедень) in Russian is used to denote nonsensical trivialities. The translator took courage to directly introduce the word into English. Drebbeden means something in between "drivel", "rigmarole", and "balderdash". The word has phonetic kinship with English "debris" and "drab", plus semantic overlap with "codswallop", and,

alike, and they keep shufflinn about, breathinn in and out their miasmas! Unbelievable!

— Tell me about it... Them city folk rabbitinn on...

— Put mask on then, tha shabootnous[4]? Get thy jab and all.

— Aye, reckon I might do just that!

— Aye, right then, do it then!

— Cough once and they eye thee like tha's broken loose from some leper colony.

— At home tha stay, don't walk away. Get on with t'times, t'stance, t'circumstance, t'happenstance. It is what it is. Autumn. Weak immunity. Muck and mire. Khondria[5]...

— Stop thy khonderinn then! Everyone's now a hypochondriac! Get thyself pumpkin latte.

— Eh up, pumpkin hodgepodge now? What young uns won't think of next, eh?

— ... It's coffa[6] with milk, granny... "Latte" is Italian for "milk".

— Whatever keeps young uns happy. Long as it ain't henbane[7] latte.

---

we can say, preserves the onomatopoeic qualities of its dismissive sounds like that of the Russian original.

4. "Shabootnous" is an anglicisation of the Russian provincial and rural dialectism "шабутной" or "шебутной" (shabootnóy), someone erratically unpredictable yet endearingly so.

5. "Khondria" is an anglicisation of the Russian word "khandra" (хандра), a culturally specific word to describe melancholy or spleen. The translator decided to introduce it to English as well because of the unique connotation it carries, combining elements of ennui, world-weariness, physical sickness, and a specific form of existential gloom. Etymologically, "хандра" itself derives from Greek "hypochondria" (ὑποχόνδριος), creating a lovely linguistic circle as this anglicisation reconnects with its distant cousin in English. From "khondria" we can further create "to khonder" — experience and indulge in khondria at one's own will.

6. Like the original "кофий / кохий", simply a colloquial transformation of "coffee", with a bit of a folksy / old-fashioned vibe.

7. "Belena" (белена) or henbane is a poisonous plant deeply embedded in Russian cultural consciousness as a symbol of madness and delirium. The Russian idiom "to overeat henbane" (объесться белены) describes someone behaving irrationally or insanely. The plant has hallucinogenic properties and folkloric associations with witchcraft. To the older generations, some modern trends might indeed be as questionable as medieval psychotropics.

— Undoubtedly, the characteristic patterns of urbanised environments, featuring high population density, intensive social interaction, and developed transport infrastructure, create favourable conditions for exponential growth in the transmission of infectious agents within the population.

— Just don't breathe then. Might solve all thy troubles with them acute respiratory viral agents and their sleeper agent network.

— Take thy vitamins, C and D, maybe Omega-3, might shift that flu of thee.

— Think I got no sense to spare? With all the wit I have to bear?... I can tell a plum from pear, know what's foul or fair.[8]

— Pale as death on antibiotics, tha is.

Train arrives, empties its carriages, into its innards invites us. Rather stuffy inside, one must say. Rush-hourous travellers are stockpiled like sprats. Proper and pensive we stand, ears plugged, eyes on phones

(absolute suicide to be without one)

or on newspapers passed around unwanted, except to crack up at the latest debates between vegetarians and lotus-eaters. Hot — sweat gathers on my solar plexus, between my shoulder blades, deep in my armpits. Departure's announced, doors close, snatch my scarf, and the train, with the populace of several Tulubaikas, creaks and plunges into the depth of tenebrous tunnels. Our faces' reflections amuse us in windows convex. We breathe down each other's necks, nudge each other with backpacks, cough politely.

---

8. "Think I got no sense to spare? With all the wit I have to bear?.. I can tell a plum from pear, know what's foul or fair." — This passage adapts lines from Leonid Filatov's satirical poem "The Tale of Fedot the Strelets" (1985), well-known in post-Soviet space, "Нешто я да не пойму. При моем-то при уму?.. Чай, не лаптем щи хлебаю, соображаю, что к чему". The original's "не лаптем щи хлебаю" (lit. "I don't slurp cabbage soup with a lapot") is a folk saying indicating one isn't uncultured. See also: lapti.

Time hovers, spirals, spins its wheel, threading through my ears and eyes, tickles my nostrils to sneezing point.
>   Tra-la-la
>   tru-la-la.
>   I never get bored
>   not ever, not I.

There's this tool against boredom that will bail you out without much faff — called "thinkering". One might languorously daydream, head in clouds, become an armchair philosopher, estimate the x's and y's of the world mathematics, become a professor in asymptotology or syllogismatics, sit at a round table with a king and a jester and other facets of lyrical I to establish an anonymous society of knights, witnesses of solipsism, and wander from door to door, from one's own to another's, preaching that exact schizoid thinkering.

Thus it was, thus it shall be, from dawn till dusk, from dusk till dawn, till kingdom come.

Location matters not
    — it's all in the noggin
        not in the village or the city.

— Well... Never been fond of modern bookshops, if I'm honest... Don't want to pretend. Especially in the airports.

— Well... And why's that?

— Well... Just so. Can't stand the smell of new. They should smell of old: dust, yellowed paper, pressed flowers forgotten between pages. Not of factory glue.

— Well... Wouldn't have had any bookshops back in the village.

— Well... Suits me fine. Library was plenty enough, never had much use for a shop.

— Well... Libraries and graveyards are rather alike.

Somewhere there, beneath birch crowns old and dear

a lone comrade major[9] moonward howls his sorrow
    longing for how far we've strayed.
O thou shalt not ask for papers no more
    shalt not hit our door with thy boot
    shalt not hit us with thy baton
    shalt not huff and shalt not puff,
    shalt not trace our IPs.
O we're out of range, unavailable. Leave thy message on Signal, not
after it[10].
    We're no longer "there" yet not quite "here"
        just as "there" isn't quite there any more
           & "here" isn't really here yet
              — we wade through liminal bogs.

As you name your ship, so shall she sail.
    Exile?
        By no means.
    Escape?
        As they say, you can't flee from your planida...
    Now, "mission"...
        O "mission", that's a noble name.

Where spatiotemporal clothes once pinched the shoulders, these
new ones from exodus-sale racks now embrace like a straitjacket —
sleeves unbound, afloat.

---

9. "Comrade Major" (товарищ майор) is a loaded Russian expression and a meme that transcends its literal military rank to function as cultural shorthand for state omnipresent monitoring of online communications (and offline, too). Russians invoke this phrase with ironic resignation when discussing potentially "sensitive" topics, acknowledging the hypothetical intelligence officer supposedly reading their messages at any given moment.
10. The original phrase works as a pun thanks to a linguistic coincidence: it simultaneously references the encrypted messaging app Signal and the common phrase "после сигнала" (after the beep / signal) from answering machine prompts. The translator decided to give up. "Untranslatable, to be honest," he said.

— Mummy, dear mummy. I shan't wear this. What a frightful thing, what a cut!

— Stop moaning, give it a bit.

— But mummy... This seam's proper scratchy, like sandpaper it is.

— Sort it out we will, that seam.

— And this bit's all pokey.

— Wear it a while — it'll stop.

— It's so prickly! Like a rose bush, mummy, honest.

— Gets everyone, that. You'll manage.

— I don't want to! And this button inside keeps bothering me.

— Once we're home, we'll snip that button right off.

— Mummy, dear mummy, what if I grow up?

— Here's hoping you will, love.

— It won't fit then, will it?

— We'll get you new ones then, won't we?

— But mummy... still, is it really the time?

A "WAY OUT" sign, moving stairs, turnstile gates
until a ray of welcome light reveals our path.
Joyful we leave to see the lovely things which Heaven bears
& hail the op'ning glories of the stars.

Bit gloomy, this
      — dense fog weaves patterns all around. In proper weather, a building tall would loom before me, but now I'm lucky to observe five storeys up. The view's absolutely smashing, they say, whole city served up on a proper plate
      (indeed)
not just the city — the world itself, no vantage point higher there exists, and even the horizon watcher shall have libido satisfied.

Crowds bustle through the square. I squeeze between them, heading straight inside. I'm ready, building, ready to serve my sentence in the most dismal line.

It ends, the queue.

I flash my QR code to the attendant, then hop into a lift for twenty souls. And thus we stand in silence embraced by the sound of Satie mixed with crickets, musique d'ameublement.

& lo! One hundred and eight floors later, we are up top
    (before one dares to blink).
Now, prepare to greet me, elevation!
All yours, I'm here, take me!
Across the roof towards the wall of tempered glass
I walk and squash my cheek against it
eyes open wide with all their might.
& what do I see?
    The entire world spread out!
I never knew
    (yet I confess — expected)
        it would be only fog:
no buildings tall, no peopleants
no traffic jam in sight
no Ararat with Fuji side by side
no paints, no flowers
no roofs, no pipes, no spires
no birds, no towers,
no bridges, no weather vanes gone mad
no balloons, no pigeons
    (flying rats, more like)
no colourful umbrellas
no sun in puddles, no cats on windowsills
no laundry flags, no mother's pastries
no chalk on asphalt, no "CLOSED" signs
no sparks from trams, no balaclavaed cyclists
no soap bubbles, no tunes from windows
no whiff of pumpkin spice
no wedding rings on traffic lights
no swings, no paper kites
no hankies waving last goodbyes

In a few words
      — all proper grey
      like homeland in winter.
& "here" isn't there
& "there" isn't here
      only betweenheretothereness.

& Thus we stand — daft tourists in a castle in the sky
trying to comprehend the zen of our planida
      (tickets gone to fuck).
But! Actually, no "buts" about it.
      Time to descend.

Episode Five
about letters & dreams

Ended the long-awaited summer. Came the long-awaited autumn.

— Valeria Narbikova, "The Murmur of Clamour"

Dear Grandfather,

If I'm honest, I've never written a letter before and I don't know what to write, so I'm just going to jot down whatever comes into my head. This is homework, so I haven't got any choice, have I? (They'll give me an F, chuck me out of school and out of the house, I'll have to live in the forest with bears, drink birch sap and eat mushrooms, which is only half bad).

My teacher, Tamara Alexeyevna, was very annoyed about how nobody writes letters anymore these days, especially to Tulubaika — everyone's on their "internets and phones". That's exactly what she said, and added that in the last ten years not a single word has dropped into her letterbox, as if the whole world's forgotten her address and this entire wholeworldness has rubbed our village off the map completely, so no post comes to us anymore: no parcels, no postcards, no letters, not by train, not by plane, not even by bus. "But how can that be? We're here, aren't we?" I protested. "Well, there you have it," Tamara Alexeyevna answered me and threw up her hands. And I said to her, "Tamara Alexeyevna, but everything gets through right away on the internets and phones, no problem!" And she nearly chucked me out of the classroom — that's how it seemed to me for a moment — but she only shrugged her shoulders.

That's all anyone does. As you know, in our village there's nothing else to do, especially for grown-ups, particularly for elderly pensioners. All together they come out of their little houses in the morning and, to the sounds of the hissing radio, start throwing up their hands and shrugging their shoulders — one-two, one-two, left, right, left, right, one-two-three, one-two-three. The drill goes on. The radio's ancient, and the voice in it sounds like it does in Soviet films, the ones they show round the clock on the telly, where everything seems not quite real, like cartoons, only with actual people. Tamara Alexeyevna comes out to do these exercises in front of her house too. She must be about a hundred years old. I don't think I've ever met anyone older than she. She shrugs and throws up her hands better than anyone, really natural like.

We read "Van'ka"[1] at school today, a story by Anton Pavlovich Chekhov. Tamara Alexeyevna praised it ever so much. It's about an orphan boy called Vanya who's been left completely alone, and nobody loves him, and everyone picks on him. Because of this, he decides to write a letter to his grandfather, Konstantin Makarovich, so that he'll come and take Van'ka to live with him in the village. He addresses the letter just like that, "To Grandfather, to the village", and drops it in the letterbox.

I didn't understand anything at first, just felt confused and sad. But then I sort of worked it out. My situation's really similar, but everything's completely the other way round:

1. Nobody picks on me (almost).
2. Mum and Dad are doing fine (they send you their regards).
3. I'm also writing a letter, just like Vanya (but I'm a girl).
4. We're both writing to our grandfather, but Vanya's writing somewhere "to the village", and I'm writing somewhere "from the village". Both of us, it seems, don't know where we're writing to.

---

1. Van'ka is a diminutive of Vanya, which is a diminutive of Ivan. Another diminutive of Ivan is Vanechka, which some readers may recognise.

You tricked me, dear Grandfather. You said you'd never leave our village. You said there was nothing better in the world than our Tulubaika, that we've got a lovely forest, and a river, and the air, and the people are all right too. And then you went and left without warning, while I was in the city visiting the other grandparents. The holidays ended, I came back — and you were not here. Mum and Dad say, "Your grandfather's gone away to have some rest in warmer climates." And I say to them, "This can't be true, he'd never leave here." That's what you told me, right? You can't leave Tulubaika. Nobody leaves here and nobody comes here. But it turns out everything's the other way round again:

1. I left (for two months).
2. You left too (for an indefinite period).

So it turns out you can leave after all, and everyone has lied to me (again). At times like these I start to understand why everyone just shrugs their shoulders and throws up their hands. I'm not stupid. All right, I'm not an A-student, but I don't even want to be. "You're too perceptive, young lady," they tell me. And I answer, "And you're not, then?"

I saw you in a dream. In it I was walking through our birch forest, and only then did I notice that it's not a forest but a park (a forestpark, forepark, parkorest?). The trees in it are all identical and planted in lines, as if it all were deliberate. I went out of the house the next morning, and on the way to school I noticed that it really is like that, as if we're living in some kind of park. In the dream I walked through the forest for ages — into Tulubaika or out of it, I don't remember — but I couldn't find the way out. And then I met you. You were sitting on a stump — a birch one too — with a basket at your feet. I asked you, "What are you doing here?" And you answered, "Sitting." And I asked, "Why are you sitting?" And you answered, "Waiting for you, granddaughter." "For me?" I asked. "For you," you told me and added, "Only you're a bit early, back you go homewards." That's what you said, and I didn't understand anything. It was a strange dream.

79

I've got really small handwriting, like yours (I read your journal about the weather, the forest, and various mushrooms), so I'm a luckster — a lot fits on two sheets, but I need to finish now. If we're talking essentials:

1. The news is good (I'm doing all right at school).
2. The weather's good (golden autumn).
3. Everyone misses you.

Your loving granddaughter

———

B+

T.A.

Episode Six
about syllogismatics, briefly

I think where I am not, therefore I am where I do not think.

— Jacques Lacan, "Écrits: A Selection"

even having weighed the arguments beforehand measured the facts with a ruler across and along laid out before you all the "cons" and "pros" in two piles or perhaps three four or more for you never know if there will be discrepancies paradoxes or some other undefined drebedden in your logic you'll still arrive at the conclusion that the anticipation of regret can be far worse than the regret itself and have existential practically eschatological consequences destructive to your psyche because the decision hasn't yet been made the i's haven't yet been dotted and everything can still be changed ten times over with a snap of your fingers by simply deciding not to go anywhere neither *to* Tulubaika nor *from* Tulubaika nor anywhere else and either just stand still and think think think thinker with the premises devise new justifications find confirmations for your judgements and then refute them yourself or ride around in a cab circling from point A to point B and from point B to point A (you can even veer to point C along the way why not) until you become nauseous your head starts spinning you faint sleep for twenty hours see a cluster of bittersweet nightmares about what an abominable muck Tulubaika is this time of year but what beauties those golden birches are and what a delight it is to gaze at them and stroll around if of course you don't look under your feet and if you plug your ears with your thumbs otherwise you might inadvertently go halfwit from the squelching of boots and the snarling of stray dogs and forget about fishing in the shallows about the first

day at school about your first love be it for games on the Sega mind games game theory or girls about the first unlearned poem and the first skipped physics lesson where you got a fat parent-repelling blot of the first F and about how on a dare with the lads you stuffed your mouth with baneberry your stomach twisted your face paled you nearly perished at a tender age terminally-tragically-truly-indeed spent a fortnight in hospital but regretted nothing not even that you cavorted with all sorts of young rapscallions and ruffians fought them clumsily played football traded Pokémon cards bartered May beetles[1] for Beatles tapes and now catching sight of those acquaintances on the street you turn your face away because (touch wood) they recognise you and start pestering you with questions like "how are you?" "how's life?" and answers like "as white as soot!" "better than yours!" "and mine is better than yours too!" which ultimately if it's not a zero-sum game of course makes each and every one of us the happy owners of a good life because if everyone's is better than one another's then it means that either no one's is better or everyone's is just alright and there's no need to regret the future or regret the past although in my case in the case of regretting the future it's much more complicated because if you mull it over the past will always have one version the one that's already happened ergo regretting it has a negative energy conversion efficiency η (unless you have a time machine of course or some new quantum law is passed in the quantum parliament) while the future has infinitely many versions (and what versions (!) a whole kaleidoscope of events) and if we take as an initial condition the presence of free will in the subject without any evaluation of its strength (the formula for it has not yet been derived) and the absence of an entity modestly called "Fate" pecking at the subject's nape then it becomes apparent that regretting the future not only has an emotional meaning (including a divorce from the past and nervousness due to the gnawing importance

---

1. "May beetle" refers to the European cockchafer, a large beetle common in Eastern Europe that typically emerges in May in the areas near Tulubaika. These beetles are recognisable by their brown colour and distinctive fan-like antennae. Collecting them and making them race and / or fight was once (still is?) a common childhood pastime in Russia.

of the decision being made) a philosophical one (awareness of the finiteness of life the infinity of outcomes and the unpredictable nature of existence) but also an applied one because everything depends on it on the decision being made and where you will be (be it in Tulubaika or outside of it) and who you will be (because opportunities are different everywhere) and in general the whole future which like dominoes lined up in an endless row from one light push with the little finger can collapse lightly jingling and fall with a thunderous crash after which you won't have plays in the West End but a cigarette-smelling Tulubaika cinema where there's no popcorn yet there are rice and egg pasties bubliks and black chai with two spoons of sugar instead of twelve-year-old Macallan and vintage Coca-Cola Zero of the existence of which in Tulubaika you can only learn from ads on the telly on one of those two TV channels and it's unclear whether you will walk hand in hand with a gorgeous wife through a night-time Mediterranean city or help your neighbour besiege a broken tractor or time-lost Carthage for weeks or ramble through the mud on a rotavator or a topless Mini Cooper through Norwegian fjords or listen to the singing on the Day of the Dead in Mexico or to the singing of the funeral service of Uncle Vanya who died from a drunken walloping with a rebar to his head on a clear day (on which it was not half bad to hang oneself according to the weather forecast) or drink chai with Tibetan monks to a state of chai intoxication and lush peacock-like opening of chakras or drink shots of hawthorn tincture hand sanitiser surgical spirit in tandem with local pissheads yet to the same drunken opening of chakras wide open with eyes wide shut when instead it might have been easier to decide and you wouldn't have had to lie sleepless squeezing your eyelids hoping to stop scrolling through the feed to distract your brain from scrolling through that situation where you a young cloud engineer a wanderer did get to the Istina with your mathematical mind shod a louse[2] taught a jellyfish to sing go I know

---

2. "to shoe a louse" ("подковать блоху") is a Russian expression meaning "to accomplish an extremely delicate difficult or seemingly impossible task". It's similar in spirit to the English expressions "threading a needle" or "splitting hairs," though with a distinctly fairy tale flair for the improbable.

not whither and fetch I know not what[3] and invented a time machine to travel to the future and ask yourself now an old chap grey with a cane in hand peacefully strolling through the birch park in autumn perhaps to pick some mushrooms looking at the birds dancing in flocks above the trees while you approach him and stammer to ask if he regrets anything in his long life and if so was it not that situation when he was riding in a cab to the airport or on a bus through endless oat dunes or in the opposite direction or in circles when he was silent and mumbled a monotonous "uh-huh" in response to the conversational enthusiasm of the taxi driver who has a business in Moscow a son studying in London and a castle from a Nigerian prince as an inheritance and extremely racist views[4] and listening to a demonic rendition of Shostakovich melancholically stared out of the window massaging his temporal muscles building up wrinkles on his forehead which by the way will later be a good place to stockpile regrets (it's not for nothing that they only hatch with age) and watched the same but still so soulful landscapes or their grey absence unfurl around him and could not decide whether to ask the driver to stop and turn around dash back down the one-way road at one hundred and twenty km/h collecting potholes and boldly looking lorry drivers in the face or to make a couple more circles round the area because just a little more time and the reptilian brain will derive a formula for the optimal position of the capital yet still undotted "I" in space and time the essence of which lies in a simple binary opposition either where this very "I" is or where this very "I" is not

---

3. The impossible task par excellence (much like accurately translating this text), a direct translation of the Russian folktale formula "Пойди туда не знаю куда принеси то не знаю что", which is the equivalent of being asked to run an errand without any useful information though with considerably higher stakes and fewer navigation options. The best narrative device for storytellers who enjoy watching their heroes and heroines navigate cosmic ambiguity and either magically transform or perish (or both / none).

4. All of this is a typical life predicament for an average taxi driver in Russia.

Episode Seven
about psychophysiological responses to bus time dilation

I considered it desirable that he should know nothing about me but it was even better if he knew several things which were quite wrong.

— Flann O'Brien, "The Third Policeman"

We stand, we wait and

wait and wait...

The bus, an absent promise, refuses to materialise, time and time again...

And again. And for that reason, we have to wait.

The stop is in the midst of a field, though one wouldn't think it a stop if one didn't know it was supposed to be here. One can only find it by the trampled grass on the pavement, though there's really no pavement to speak of — a verge, or not even a verge, but merely an edge of the road. There used to be a signpost here; I remember it: wooden, rotten, with gaping cracks, covered with moss on the northern side. Once, an eagle, or a hawk, or a falcon perched on it (I couldn't tell them apart). Of impressive size it was, all majestic and stern, with big wings, quite formidable. Perhaps a magpie, though. No post now. Someone stole it or it rotted away into nothingness — gone. Or, well, beavers munched it, as the local council would say. Bastards. The council, not the beavers. Or both, perhaps. On the ground lies an old rusty sign "TO TULUBAIKA" — the paint long faded and the text only readable if one knows it was once there, just like everything else in these parts.

Around, stretching into infinity, the oats glisten, trillions of spikelets rustling in the breeze, summerly warm. Instead of the horizon, ahead — oats, to the left — oats, to the right — you would never guess, but there's more oats. The oat stalks used to seem taller to me; now they reach at most to the chest. A child could lose the way in them even if walking straight, but we, like all normal children, never walked straight. In autumn, after the harvest, the straw was rolled into bales and wrapped with thick white plastic strings. We cut them, tore apart the bales, and built forts and castles from the straw. After improvised day-long wars in such castles, we would return home itchy, scratched bloody, the straw falling everywhere from beneath our clothes.

— Yesterday, there was a fire in the field, — says the old man standing next to me. He wears a life-worn blue "New York" cap, sweat pouring from beneath it down his bald head. — A couple of hectares, they say, burnt down. Terrible.

— Eh? — asks the full-bodied woman next to him, wearing black sunglasses and holding an open newspaper. She reads it from time to time when her hands become tired of using it as a parasol.

— Terrible, I'm tellinn thee, — says the old man.

— A real nightmare, indeed, — says the woman.

— It ignited by itself, they say, — the old man mutters, wiping sweat from his forehead.

— No wonder. With such heat, I might ignite by myself as well. Oof! — says the woman, starting to use the newspaper as a fan.

— Drought, they say. Everywhere.

— That's for sure. Everywhere.

— But thing is, love, we have a drought every year 'round here, heat like this every year, as long as I can remember, but everything is on fire only this year. Coincidence? Don't think so.

— It burnt in the past too, in other places. I remember the news.

— It doesn't just ignite by itself, does it, love?

— Oh, it does, look at the sky and how it's blazing up there. Although no, don't look, it'll burn your eyes out.

The road is dusty, asphaltless, cracked. Though, calling it a road is a bit of a stretch. You need to know it's a road, then maybe you'll find it; otherwise, it's just a large path through the field. Above the scorched surface, the wind chases mirages. You can see the air melting; look closer — and you feel your brain melting, too. The sky is not even blue, but sheet-white. From the sun, scorching halos spread across it like ripples on water. If I were alone, I'd have taken off my shirt long ago, but as it is... eh, don't want to embarrass myself in the polite society of decent people. Not in the best shape, I am.

— They say their machines are powered by clouds, — says the old man. — On the telly.

— Whose?

— Mine, of course. Every other telly, too. One TV channel we have after all.

— Whose machines?

— Doesn't tha watch the news?

— What about them?

— Doesn't tha know what people are sayinn?

— All sorts of things nowadays, apparently, aren't they?

— Aye, right tha is, love.

— And so what? What's with the clouds?

— So, they suck the clouds, and — as a consequence, tha might imagine — now there's nowhere to hide from the sun.

— Who? People? Don't be daft, you.

— Not people. People! Oh, love. Not only people. Doesn't tha know anything of what's happeninn 'round the world?

— Who then? Robots?

— Aye? Robots! Mayhaps robots, too. Science fiction and all the bloody drebbeden people're readinn these days. Cassandra me arse, nobody believes nowt until they're roasted alive.

— Who then, mind you?

The old man lowers his voice, saying:

— The same who set fields on fire.

— Is that so? And why would they do that?

— So we'd have nowt to eat! — the old man spreads his hands in the utter state of obviousness.

— You eat porridge every day, do you?

— The oats?

— The oats.

— Aye, every morning. All my potato tops've dried up, too. Bloody 'ell.

— Well, you should water them. Take a hose and water them. And don't eat potato tops, perhaps.

— Water or not — same result.

— Won't make them tastier, indeed.

As my group theory professor used to say, true learning ought to be painful, akin to muscle soreness. It must be felt. If you don't feel it, you're not learning; you're merely warming a seat. Patience, too, is a skill. Few of us know, but scholars distinguish between two types of waiting: scheduled and unscheduled. The only difference between them is that with the former you know when the awaited event is supposed to occur, yet both are equally repulsive and unnatural to a human brain. Take, for instance, the bus to Tulubaika. It supposedly runs on a timetable, hence, having arrived early, I found myself immersed in the first type of waiting; time seemed to hasten slightly,

and the sensation was rather pleasant — I was heading home, where my family waited for me, bustling about, my mother would be baking pasties (with cabbage, egg and rice, mince, and marmalade from orange peels and gooseberries), my grandfather would be smoking some meat, beef, or pork (or perhaps fish, for he's quite an angler, Tulubaika's quite a river — perfect combination), my niece — perhaps with my sister's help — would be drawing me something rather lovely, and their new dog (which I've only seen on Instagram) would be preparing its fluffy tail for vigorous wagging upon meeting me, and also (importantly so) our old cat would be asleep, indifferent to my arrival, preoccupied with its own affairs and priorities, absolutely nonhuman and inhuman. Thusly, you wait, agitated, trembling with anticipation, like on the eve of your sixth birthday, only for the bus to fail to arrive on time, turning waiting from an exhilarating process into a suffocating one. Time, probably realising how unbound it can be, begins to swirl and torment you, passing with different speed at different moments, in different places. The ecstatic excitement morphs into anxiety corrosive to nerves. What if the bus doesn't come at all? What then? My family would be disheartened, the pies would go cold, the dog, tired, would lie down to sleep next to the cat, the house would be shuttered, the stove extinguished, and the lights and telly turned off, the village bulldozed away. The prodigal son promised to visit once in a decade but did not. What would the neighbours say? What a deceiver those Tulubayevs raised! Bad parenting, terrible one. Every few minutes (there's no set interval here, for it could be a minute, five, or ten; time in the brain is such: it speeds up, slows down, writhes before you like an uneven sine wave), you pull out your overheating phone, check the clock over and over. Then, realising the battery is about to die, or the phone might as well ignite itself, you start counting seconds in your head, your breaths in and breaths out, listening to the wind and the rustle of oat stalks. Meditation, they say, is good for you. It helps train your waiting muscle for that very nothing or something that never quite happens.

Thislike is the face of nothing, nontime, nonhappening:

90

— Why do you look for enemies everywhere, old chap? — asks the woman.

— I'm not lookinn for 'em, love. They find me. You can't hide from 'em. They've got the whole Earth in the palm of their hand. Like this, — says the old man and shows his calloused palm with his fingers sprawling.

— No one cares about us or our village, don't you worry. We're not even marked on the map.

— That's just it. Truth, that. A dire situation, in fact. Do whatever they want to us — drop a bomb, poison us with gas, burn us with lasers — no one would even notice. But they've chosen a more elegant approach.

— And what's that, mind you?

— Told thee, didn't I? They've sucked out the clouds, stoked up the sun, and now they're smokinn us! How it used to be: tha steps out at dawn, faces the sun, closes thy eyes, basks in its warmth, sits down in a garden chair, sips thy cuppa with a biscuit, then off to work tha goes, aye? The sun is blazinn but feels good, warming the soul, so to speak, because tha knows that in the evening it will proper pour with rain, waterinn the vegetable garden and all other household plots. But now, how is it? Can't step outside; impossible! Step out of the shade and it roasts thee right quick — first a tan, then burns and blisters if tha's daft enough, and before tha knows it, skin cancer and tha's six feet under. That's their plan, tha sees. I knew an old chap — another one, not me — a revered fella, he was 108 years old, that bloody bastard, runninn 'round like a little lad, drinkinn vodka like a bloody elephant, but this year... this year he died. Just like that. In his sleep, they say, but I know that he was sun-struck the day before, love.

The woman shrugs.

— So it goes. Slowly but surely, we'll all perish one by one, and as tha said, love, no one will notice. We're not even in a footnote on the map!

— You know, — I say out of boredom, — what if this is some sort of social experiment?

— Antisocial, — says the woman.

— Might be antisocial, that's not to be ruled out. Or parasocial.

— Like how, mind you?

— The lad's got a point. This's how it happens: they test it on us first, on Tulubaika, because no one cares, then on the whole country, and then on the entire planet. And then... we're kirdyk[1]. Write us off. That's why our role in this is tremendous. We must fight however we can. We must resist. Now, I'll go stretch my legs; bloody 'ell they've gone proper numb from standing still. And those people, they sit all day!

The old man straightens up, adjusts his cap, and starts to walk in a figure-of-eight along the road. He barely lifts his feet, causing a cloud of road dust to rise with every shuffle of his soles.

— Have you been away for long? — asks a voice from behind.

That dialogue seemed over, everyone had gone quiet, it was time to breathe out and think my thoughts, so hearing that voice, a gentle young woman's voice, I'm startled.

— Oh, sorry for scaring you.

I turn around — before me stands a young woman with fiery ginger hair tied back in a ponytail. She's wearing a white cotton dress with sweat stains showing at the chest and underarms. The hem, reaching to her knees, is covered in dust. Between her collarbones, she has a piercing, a golden sun with eight rays, resembling tongues.

— Am I distracting?

Nerves heating up, I shake my head. Where did she come from? She must have just arrived, silently, like a mouse.

— You're not distracting, quite the opposite. What's here to be distracted from?

— From enjoying the majesty of summer. Isn't that wonderful?

No, it's not. But I don't say that. I'm trying to maintain

---

1. "Kirdyk" (кирдык) is a word of Tatar origin that entered Russian slang, meaning "the end," "finished," or "doom", pronounced with a fatalistic emphasis on the second syllable. It functions as both noun and verb to indicate a situation has reached its terminal state, similar to "game over" or "kaput".

communication here, civilised dialogue between two adults. Small talk.

— And why do you think I've been here before? Do I look like a local?

— Oh, stop it. No one's here for the first time.

— How's that?

— Well, just like that, simple. You can be born here, leave here, and then return. That particular chain of events must happen. No one in their right mind would come here for the first time on purpose. No one can, really. You're aware, I assume, that tourism isn't exactly booming around these parts.

— It's not.

— So, how long has it been?

— Since I finished school. And you?

— I haven't left. I live here.

— In Tulubaika?

— Well, not in the field, obviously?

— Who knows... And how is it now, in Tulubaika?

— Quite wonderful. I'd even say delightful. Summer, heat, the river, flowers, berries. But most importantly — look how Sollie shines. Ah!

The word "Sollie," spoken with a capital letter, sounded clear, deep, with respect, as believers would say "Goddie".[2] As she says that and exhales, the expression on her face acquires blissful qualities.

— Bright it is, — I say.

— Very, but such is life. Without Sollie, it would be the eternal night, wouldn't it?

---

2. The rendering of "Солнышко" as "Sollie" and "Боженька" as "Goddie" is a linguistic compromise in the face of Russian's formidable diminutive arsenal. In English you can append "-y," "-ie," or the ghastly "-kins" to convey affection, but Russian's morphological playground of suffixes is wider and can express everything from tender endearment to cosmic reverence, or both at the same time. Were the translator to render it as simply "Sun" and "God", a nuance would almost certainly be lost on Anglophone readers, who, bless their hearts, must now contend with coinages reminiscent of children's television presenters. Such are the hardships of cross-cultural semantic transfer — what Jakobson might have termed "diminutive desperation."

I don't quite know how to respond. Probably, yes — it would be. It's dark without the sun, that's for sure. I can't really disagree nor do I want to agree. Why would anyone agree with something so obvious? And that would make me submissive, wouldn't it? Is it a rhetorical trick? It must be.

Thus we stand, in silence, looking at each other. Awkward. But not embarrassing. Yet. Awkward is better than embarrassing. I squeeze a shy wry nervous smile.

— By the way, I'm a teacher, — she says.

— Oh, good for you, — I reply.

— It is, yes.

— Must be difficult.

— What?

— Teaching. Children these days, you know.

— What's with them children?

— Everyone's on their phones. TikTok, you know.

She's perplexed by my anachronistic fathers-and-sons-ness, quite unsure which side I'm on in that grand conflict (the Grand Conflict).

— You don't look old. How old are you?

— I prefer not to disclose.

— You look young.

— Well, thank you.

— And what do you do?

— It's dull. I'm into... computers.

— Oh, staring at a screen all day?

— Kind of.

— Can you fix my printer?

— What?

— Just kidding, I can fix my printer myself, — she says with a smile. — And Windows, I know how to install it.

— Good for you.

— It is, yes. A programmer, I reckon?

— Kind of.

— What do you program? You know, there are all sorts of programmers these days.

95

— It's difficult to explain.

— Try me. I'm not some country bumpkin, am I?

— Well... Clouds.

The young woman frowns and examines me like a teacher would. I feel her gaze even through my black sunglasses.

— Very funny.

— No, I'm not taking a piss. I do program clouds, for real. Have you heard of such a thing?

— And why would you do that?

— To make them rain.

The teacher's expression darkens.

— I see. So that Sollie shines less.

— No, why? So that it rains. It has nothing to do with "Sollie".

— To each their own. And is it difficult to live with that?

Live with what? What kind of question is that?

— Not particularly. It pays well.

— I see.

She seems to be disappointed in who I am and what I do. That doesn't surprise me. People here often think programmers are new kulaks and have to be liquidated.[3]

I feel the sun furiously reaching its zenith, taking out a magnifying glass, and beginning to shine directly through it, as if it's a year-five pupil and we are ants — the battle uneven, the fate unenviable. I wish I could program up some clouds now. Docker compose them up etm.[4]

---

3. In early Soviet times, "Kulaks" (кулаки, lit. "fists") were peasant farmers branded as class enemies for the crime of modest agricultural success, essentially sentenced for possessing a cow too many. "Liquidation" (ликвидация) was a common bureaucratic euphemism for any systematic elimination. Russian historical memory possesses a certain recursive quality, so programmers, earning significantly more than an average person and thus sometimes having inflated egos, are often mocked for that (without bloodshed so far).

4. This is a reference to implicit containerisation orchestration via "docker compose up," the imperative command utilised to instantiate ephemeral virtualised microservice instances in a multi-tenant Kubernetes-adjacent deployment pipeline familiar to all "programmers" who engage in contemporary DevOps practices with containerized CI/CD workflows. The translator trusts this explanation will prove illuminating to those readers who, unlike "programmers", may not immediately grasp the elegant

From afar comes the roar of an engine of hell knows not what. The sound grows louder. Hearing it, the old man steps off the road. A few seconds later, a motorcyclist speeds past us, a young man with a pink mohawk, helmetless. Mixing with the black exhaust fumes (or rather an atrocious gas), a cloud of dust rises from the irritated earth, envelops the bus stop and sneaks into our nostrils. Everyone starts sneezing and coughing. Come to my senses, I do. It smells of dust, straw, engine emissions, tedium, and the colour white.

— They go buyinn 'em drandulets[5], fuckinn degenerates! — says the babushka sitting on the dry grass. She wears a headscarf. Few know that, but scholars discovered that all babushkas wear headscarves — it's like a mohawk for punks, an element of subculture. Without it, a babushka simply isn't accepted as one and can remain forever young. When I arrived, N hours ago, she was already sitting here and has been silent until this moment, so I've forgotten about her existence and not mentioned her in my story, just like many of us often forget about many babushkas and their existence as they sand away in hourglasses.

Everyone nods in agreement, some — reluctantly, given the tone. The old man returns to the woman with the newspaper-parasol-fan and continues the conversation.

— Has tha heard 'bout the panels?
— What panels?
— That solar shite show panels.
— Oh, those. And what about them?
— What does tha mean, "what"? Hasn't tha heard? Everyone's talkinn.
— What are they talking?
— Terrible things they're talkinn. Just terrible.
— I'd never believe it.

---

parallelism between the futility of attempting to configure persistent storage in ephemeral containers and the narrator's equally futile desire to summon meteorological relief from the heat.

5. "Drandulet" (драндулет) is a derogatory Russian term for an old, decrepit vehicle or jalopy. The word carries connotations of both the vehicle's poor condition and the questionable judgment of its owner.

— But there's no need to believe. Facts, love, facts. Does tha know why all this is happeninn?

— We're having trouble with electricity. It's always failing. We lived a week without light. Every summer this happens, even in winter. With panels, it might be better. In summer, at least. They're right there — within reach. And it's hot, so...

— Mayhaps "so", mayhaps "not so", but it's with these "panels", they'll be aiminn their devices at us.

— Ah, don't be silly, old chap. What devices, mind you?

— Has tha seen who's installinn 'em?

— No.

— There thee has it! That's the point. They rustle 'bout at night. I've seen 'em, woke up one night to noise on the street. I go out and see — the field is all lit up. At first, methinks — a fire, but neither flame nor smoke can be seen. I approach closer, and there they are, bastards — right by the panels. They're right by my house, tha knows. Did I tell thee? Terrible, in a word, bloody terrible.

A tanned boy with a freckled face and surfer hair approaches the bus stop. He is playing with a ball, or rather not a ball but a white inflated balloon with a large red digit six on it. For him, it is, however, a ball, which is, I'd say, fair enough given the circumstances. He walks around kicking it.

— Are you his teacher? — I ask the young woman.

— What? No. Why? He's just a boy, I don't know him. What made you think I teach children?

— You mentioned you're a teacher.

— That doesn't mean I teach children, does it?

It kind of does, though. In parts.

— I thought you teach children, naturally.

— You thought that; I didn't say it.

— Who do you teach, then?

— Whoever needs to be taught. Whoever needs teaching.

— Right, uh-huh... But, if you're not his teacher, why is he alone in the middle of the field, the boy?

— Why should I know?

— Well, you're a local. Everyone knows everyone here. When I was a little lad, I sure knew everyone.

— Well, tell me then where else should he be?

— At school?

— It's the summer holiday[6]. Did you forget how you went to school?

— Long ago but I did. Why is he alone, though?

— He's going home from the town. Well, he's actually not going, not in a walking sense, is he? He's waiting for the bus to Tulubaika, just like us. Deduction. Oh, you're so odd.

No one had ever told me straight to my face that I was odd but it sounded convincing as if I had always known it.

— Why would you say that?

— Pardon?

— Why am I odd?

— You ask odd questions, is all.

— Perfectly normal questions. You ask odd questions, too.

— I'm just curious. I'm fine asking odd questions.

— Well, same here.

— I like to meet new people, too. Are you a city guy?

— A city guy? I guess I am.

— Which city?

— Riyadh.

— What? Riyadh?

— Yeah, Riyadh?

— As in proper Riyadh?

— Proper Riyadh indeed.

— Oh, really?

— Yes. Do you know where it is?

— I'm not some village bumpkin, am I?

— No, sorry. Of course not.

— It's in Saudi Arabia.

---

6. It's the longest school holiday in Russia for all grades, includes all three summer months almost in their entirety.

— Yes.

— See? I know.

— Never doubted that.

— You thought it, I can sense it. I can sense such things.

— Of course you can.

— So far away, though, isn't it? How did you end up there? I've never been.

Of course she's never been! And I'm not being all fancy posh-mosh about it — few people I know really have been, maybe less than to Tulubaika.

— What's it like?

— Hot.

— Is it?

— Not sure hotter than here, though.

— Very true.

And that's it — we don't talk any more, at all, never, as much as "never" can last in this climate.

Boring.

Boring, boring

Time seems to stand still until you strike up a conversation.

The teacher takes a book out of her bag and starts reading. The title is somewhat peculiar. It blurs before my eyes into incomprehensibility but seems to be "Sol Invictus", whatever that means. Is that Latin? The book is well-worn, suggesting it's interesting. Uninteresting books just sit untouched and always look new. I should have brought a book too, any book, an uninteresting one would do, too, an airport novel. Time in the airports smells in the same manner as the smoke from smouldering sawdust — bittersweet. I do feel the same taste on my tongue, perhaps it's dehydration, or detemporation. I could read on my phone but I prefer having a bit more battery than the great pleasure of reading, especially in a day like this. Hot. Oh, it's fucking hot!

I see a mouse scurrying across the road, small, grey-brown, resembling an eyed and tailed pebble, or perhaps it is a pebble, a pebbling running away from heat.

— Look, a mouse, — I say calmly.

— What? Where? — the teacher responds, surprised.

She scans the ground, clutching the hem of her dress.

— Right there, — I say, pointing right at her feet.

She squeaks and jumps aside. The other people at the bus stop turn round to us. The surfer boy with the balloon stands still and looks at me creepily, as if I had stolen his chance to spot the mouse first and announce it to the world. That pebbling, however, is now nowhere to be seen.

— It seemed it was a mouse, — I say, shrugging.

Adjusting a stray lock of ginger hair, the teacher stretches a fake smile.

— You really are odd.

— That's just askinn for a stroke, — says the babushka sitting nearby. — Old I am, tha knows, scare me like this and done. Boom. Who's goinn to buy me a coffin, eh? Thee? I'd like a redwood one, please, young chap.

— Sorry. I didn't mean to scare you. Just bored waiting for the bus. Trying to amuse myself, is all.

— Look at him amusinn himself, — the babushka says, grumbling. — Tha'd be better off dancing then. Dance for us, will tha?

— I'd rather not.

Her pupils dilate, her left eye starts to twitch. I mentally prepare for the worst. Not sure what that is but there's always something worse to prepare for. Russian wisdom, that.

— Smarty-pants.

She spits on the ground, and turns away.

Oof... Silence falls for a few moments.

— What was that? — the teacher asks.

— What was what?

— Why did you upset the old lady?

— I didn't upset anyone. She was already upset when I arrived, I reckon she's chronically upset due to everything: life, weather, other things. While I've been waiting here for all those N hours she's been upset the whole time.

— You seem agitated.

— I don't seem, really. By the way, would you know when the bus is coming? What's the schedule like these days?

— No, I do not know. You scared me with that mouse, too. It affected my memory. Badly so. Now I'm oblivious. Completely so.

— Sorry, my fault. It must be that the sun has heated up my head.

She frowns.

— You are odd. Actually are.

— Fine, I am odd. My phone's almost dead. I'm afraid to even check the time.

— It's half-past one, — the teacher says, glancing at the gold sundial on her right wrist. — There's also the word "please" in our language, by the way. Or have you forgotten it all in your Riyadhs?

— Thank you. I mean, please. No, I actually meant both now.

None of us can believe I'm forming sentences like that when talking to people.

— Do you wear your... "watch" on your right wrist? — I ask her.

— I do.

— Why on the right?

— I like it like that.

— Are you left-handed?

— I am.

— I see. The bus ought to have been here half an hour ago.

— The bus doesn't owe anyone anything. It's simply a bus.

— I wish I could be simply a bus and owe nothing to anyone. Convenient life, that is.

— You could be if you really wanted to.

— That would be odd, though.

— It can hardly be any odder, can it?

The teacher looks at me languidly and then returns her gaze to her reading. I notice a page has fallen out of her book and lean down to pick it up, managing to read a few lines along the way, or not managing — the lines immediately slip from my memory. Something about Sol. I hand the page to the teacher. Trying to be nice, I am.

— That's not mine, — she says.

— How is it not yours? Whose then?

The teacher shrugs. Weird. I must be hallucinating. This heat.

— I saw it falling out of your book. This one.

— This heat. People see things. I do see things. Do you?

— I, er... Has anybody lost this? — I ask those around, lifting the page high.

Silence ensues. I'm utterly convinced it fell from the teacher's book. I swear I saw it slipping.

— Absolutely sure not yours?

— Absolutely, — she says, keeping her face down, reading, not showing any signs of emotions. Perhaps I've upset her. — What's in it?

— I don't know. Haven't read it, something about Sol. The sun?

— I see. Why don't you read it for us?

— I'm not good at reading aloud.

— Give it a try.

— Why should I try?

— Everyone's bored. We're all friends here. No one will judge. It's a safe space.

— Is it, though?

— You never know unless you try.

Of course. Why would I do that, though? What for? Am I becoming submissive? First — dancing, now — reading?

— All right.

Well, here we go, I say to myself. Refused the old lady's wish, complied with the young one's desire. Clearly, ageism.

I silently read the first line: "O Sol, bright Sol, on thy heavenly chariot." An auspicious beginning, it rather is.

— Seems like some sort of poem, or maybe a song.

— A poem? Is it? About what?

— Sol, as I said.

— Could you read it out, please?

I skim to a random line: "With thy beams, burn the impure and wicked, cleansing our sacred soil!"

— I would rather not read it out loud.

— Why not? Stubborn like a child.

— Perhaps you'd like to read? You are a teacher, after all. You should have a better voice.

— You found the paper — you read.

— I would rather not.

— I see. Men, making a tragedy out of such nonsense.

— Do you know that tragedy means "goat-song" in Greek?

— You really are odd.

Odd again. Always odd. I take a deep breath, the hot air scorching my nostrils and lungs. My neck's in a vice. That's the physical sensation. A cold sweat runs down from it to my back, instantly warming. It feels like being called to the board to recite a poem I haven't learned.

— Fine, if you insist. But I warn you, I'm not a good speaker. It'll be a torture.

— It's okay, what haven't we seen or heard around these parts?

Plus, anything's better than just standing here in silence, isn't it? Some amusement for the bored.

I read with as much expression as I can muster:

> — *O Sol, bright Sol, on thy heavenly chariot*
> *Arising daily over the earth!*
> *Thou art the all-seeing eye, the life-giving luminary*
> *That drivest away the creeping darkness.*
> *O righteous Sol, whose visage lights up the fields and valleys!*

— Could you possibly read a little louder?

I feel the words penetrating me. I feel them inside my veins. I don't want it, but I'm becoming words, at least my body, at least it tries, it tries to sound louder but my throat has dried out and, tasting even more bittersweet, is beginning to itch.

> — *With thy beams, burn the impure and wicked,*
> *cleansing our sacred soil!*
> *To thee we raise our praise and thanksgiving*
> *And offer sacrifices without end.*

— Could you add a bit more volume? I'm afraid they can't hear you in the back.

And I do, I submit to the words.

> *LET US EXALT SOL INVICTUS THAT BREAKS*
> *THROUGH THE MORNING MIST!*
> *BEFORE THY GOLDEN RAYS THE STARS DIM*
> *AND FADE.*
> *WASH US, CLEANSE WITH THY RIGHTEOUS*
> *FIRE OUR SINFUL FILTH!*
> *MAY THE MONGREL PERISH IN THE*
> *DARKNESS ETERNAL! MAY THE WEAK BE*
> *CONSUMED!*

Upon finally hearing what I have been reading, the old man flies into a rage. His face wrinkled up, flushed with anger, he hobbles over to me.

— Thee bastard! One of those, eh?!

— What "those"?

— Those very ones! A fork-tongued eunuch!

I see the old man clench his fists and I begin to back away as he keeps stomping towards me, picking up pace, kicking up dust as if smoke trailed behind him.

— Thee sun-scourged maggot!

He reaches me and grabs me by the collar. Turns out, the old man is strong and has a formidable grip, much grippier than mine.

— Hey! Easy there!

— Give it to me, thee slag!

Releasing one hand, he tries to snatch the page from me with the other. I dodge. I dodge well. Never knew I could dodge so well.

— Hey, it's not even mine! — I exclaim, trying to gently push him away.

— Not thy?! Whose then?!

— I don't know! I found it.

— And tha'll say it was brought by the wind next! — he spits. — Bastard!

— Quite possibly. I, the fool, picked it up. Never seen anything like it before. Never will, hopefully. I wasn't myself, maybe. I don't know. Really, it's all the heat, the sun.

The old man calms down a little, probably to catch his breath.

— Not local, is tha?

— Local through and through, heading to my parents'.

— Do I know thy parents?

— You might know my grandpa, sir. It's the white house at the very edge of the village. It's a one-house street.

Sir? That's an anti-sir in front of me. His frown deepened, and, unsure whether to believe me, he loosened his grip.

— Give me that bloody shite then.

Having no reason to keep the page, I hand it over to the old man. He skims through it, scowls, and spits on the ground again.

— What filth. No shame, no conscience. The invincible sun, my arse. Fuckin 'ell.

— Not in front of the children, mister, — says the teacher. She's irritated and tense.

— He knows words worse than that. Right, laddie?

The boy silently nods. There's a hint of a sly smile on his face. Little bastard.

— Cunt! — yells the boy.

Everyone twitches. The old man laughs heartily.

— Told you lot! Now, own up, whose paper is this, then? — says he.

Silence falls. The teacher says nothing. She stands there, staring at the ground, arms crossed, hiding the title of her book. But I know it's "Sol Invictus". It was her doing, definitely hers. A femme fatale, a mysterious, mischievous, manipulative, possibly dangerous woman, she is.

— Oi? — the old man presses again.

— Probably dropped by the motorcyclist, — the teacher murmurs. — There he is, by the way, coming back again. You can ask him.

True enough. The familiar engine sound intensifies. Over the field, a vast cloud of dust and atrocious gas soars higher and rushes uswards. The hairs inside my nose curl up, anticipating the pungent invasion. I'm preparing to sneeze. Against the backdrop of the sweltering air, the same motorcyclist with the pink mohawk appears on the road. Shielding our faces with our hands, we step back to the verge, almost into the oats. The white balloon slips from the boy's grasp; he tries to reach for it and steps on the road, but the woman with the newspaper pulls him back away from danger.

— PUNKS NOT DEAD! — the motorcyclist shouts, roaring past and running over the boy's balloon, either by accident or deliberately, as if it were a dead or artificial fly on a urinal.

The balloon pops. Its rubber fragments lie scattered on the road.

No signs of "six" seen. We all stand together, watching as the motorcyclist disappears into the depths of the field.

— It was definitely him, — I say. — Pure evil, this guy.

The boy silently walks over to where the balloon mayhem occurred, picks up the rubber remains from the ground.

— Cunt! — he yells, and begins to sob, quietly.

— There, there, love, come here, — the woman with the newspaper says, trying to hug him, but he shrugs off her hand and steps aside.

— These sun-arse bastards, damn 'em all, — grumbles the old man and walks away from us.

— Degenerates! — adds the babushka. — Shall they perish in hell! Shall their souls forever boil in oil! Shall their balls dry out!

— Aye, nowt else to add. Tha speaks truth, — says the old man, his face revealing he's clearly surprised by the babushka's eloquence.

The glossolalic ordeal is over but I don't feel any better: tired, thirsty, sweat running down my back, all my clothes soaked through. Still no sign of the bus. I hope it will have AC. But who am I kidding. At my parents' house, it was always warm in winter and cool in summer without any air conditioning. I know what I'll do when I'm in Tulubaika. I'll take a shower in the garden and dive into my old bedroom like I did as a child. There was no sun there — it faced north. It was like a cave. On one of the walls, there was wallpaper of a golden birch forest stretching into infinity with a gigantic raven flying above it. I used to love lying on the bed, being in that forest, imagining walking under the birches, losing my way to Tulubaika, finding it back. I hope my parents haven't changed it. When I arrive, I'll switch on my old PC if it still starts up, sift through my old CDs, pull out old games. What plot, what gameplay they had! They don't make them like that any more. I hope my eyes don't bleed from the graphics, though.

— Thank you, — whispers the teacher, sneaking up from behind into my reverie.

Here she is again.

— What do you want?

— I said thank you.

— For what?

— For not giving me away, — she whispers.

I nod stoically. "Giving her away." I see.

— Was there anything to worry about?

— What do you think?

— I don't answer questions asked in response to questions.

Rude? Or not so much? She falls silent. So, it was rude, yes. Awkward. How odd I am. I should learn to communicate with people.

— What are you thinking about? — she asks.

At least she's not offended.

— The same thing as everyone, about the bus.

— I'm not thinking about the bus.

— If not the bus, what are you thinking about then? Is there anything at all in this world to think about rather than the bus? Bonkers.

— About Tulubaika, of course. Imagine, in a few hours you'll arrive in the village... what will you do then?

Few hours? Sounds optimistic. Few centuries, more like.

— I'll be lying down.

— Is that all? You travelled all this way, from Riyadh, Saudi Arabia, just to lie down?

— Listen, I just want to lie down. I'm tired. I'll lie down all week, eat my mum's cooking, maybe play old games with my niece, watch the stupid telly, and debate conspiracy theories with my grandfather. Today, I've learned some new ones — we have plenty to discuss. And I'll tell them about the deserts. Have you ever seen real dunes?

— Deserts and dunes aside, Tulubaika has so much to offer. Fancy fishing? Then head to the lake or river. Fancy a swim? You have it right there. Do you know how magically the water glistens in Sollie's light? The whole area is blooming now, the scents are countless, organic perfumery all the way along. Do you know how delicious the air there is? Not like in your cities, in Riyadh. It must be all fumes there! In Tulubaika, even just breathing is always a pleasure. Just existing. Step into a field or forest, take a deep breath, and you feel better, you're

109

healed, cured of all your pain. Cleansed. You listen, and the wind whispers softly, crickets chirp, birds sing. Spread your arms wide, close your eyes, face Sollie, and your soul rejoices.

— You have plenty of moles, on your arms, legs, and face, by the way. You shouldn't expose them to your "Sollie" too often. You might get cancer.

— I use cream.

— "Sun"-screen?

— Don't call it that.

— Why not?

— Sollie is a source of light, warmth, life, not a threat.

— Then why the cream?

— Sollie cares for us and sends as much light and warmth as we need. And if a person lives in harmony with it, no harm will come to them.

— Then why the cream?

— Sollie only cleanses the impure, others are safe to accept His light.

— But why the cream?

She looks at me with the most enigmatic gaze I've ever seen (she's topped it again), looks, and remains blissfully tranquil. Seconds pass, minutes, hours, centuries, stars flop and black holes become twice as dark.

— It makes my skin soft, — she finally answers.

— Ah, I see.

— Here, feel it.

The teacher grabs my hand and places my palm on her forearm. The skin is soft, warm, damp, and slippery from the sunscreen mixed with sweat.

— Well?

I withdraw my hand, look at my palm, then back at her.

— Well what?

— What do you think? About my skin.

— Not bad.

— Hm. I see.

She ponders, then, without warning again, grabs my hand and places it on her thigh. The skin is as slippery and sweaty but gentler, firmer, more elastic. She probably does many thousand steps a day.

— What about now?

— Not bad. Better.

— Better? Is that all?

— Yes. Skin is skin. Very hot, though. And it's already hot enough. Now my hand is slippery.

— Odd you are. How's your sex life?

So I am the odd one.

— It's, well, a private matter.

— Do you have a girlfriend?

— I have a wife.

— I see. I wouldn't tell. Do you have many friends?

— Of course, I do. I mean, I have some.

— In Tulubaika?

— Not in Tulubaika, why would I need friends in Tulubaika? I don't live there.

— That's a pity.

— Why?

— I pity you.

— What?

— I think you're missing out on something important.

— Am I? Like what?

— Will you come to ours?

— Ours what? Where?

— To the club.

Club? What club? What is she talking about? Is it a youth club? A tennis club? Is it a drama club? Or a cult?

— What club?

— Interests club.

— What interests?

— Special interests, you'll like it. The Summer Solstice is coming, it'll be fun. Trust me.

I look at her: all in white, her face sweet, friendly, smiling. I think,

ponder, evaluate the situation. If someone asks to trust them, it can mean only one thing.

— No, thank you, I won't come.

— Why not?

— Have you seen Ari Aster's "Midsommar"[7]?

— No.

— Well, that's why.

So we stand, confused, awkward, waiting. The babushka sits, silent, possibly dead. The woman with the newspaper has spread it over her head. She's not happy being here and likely feels sick, I can tell from her face. A huge, nasty horse-fly is bugging the unballooned surfer boy. It's as big as a hornet. The boy tries to shake it off for a while, then, after a series of futile attempts, grabs it in his fist. The horse-fly buzzes, trying to escape, but the boy doesn't let go, nor does he squeeze it; instead, he takes a straw, inserts it into the insect's arse, and now lets it go. The horse-fly, bewildered, flies off with the straw in its rear. Meanwhile, the old man starts mumbling again.

— I awoke one night, me back seized in such agony I thought it would be the end of me. Yet, I recovered somewhat, ventured out into the garden to see if the hares hadn't made off with the carrots again, fluffy bastards. All seemed calm, serene even. And there I stood, enjoyinn a cigar sent by me son from Cuba, mind thee, rolled on a thigh of a busty Cuban lass. I only smoke 'em at night, in secrecy, for fear of the envious gaze and ill wishes of today's folk. And one night I heard a humminn, subtle but annoyinn, like a ringing in the ear. It seemed to come from nowhere and everywhere. Feeling otherwise fine, I deduced it must be something external. As I savoured me excellent cigar, I spotted something strange aloft. It was massive and indistinct, clearly not an aircraft for they don't glide so slowly, nor a bird, for it was far too large and had no wings. I fetched a torch, futilely shininn it upwards, only to see a vague oval silhouette. I then took out me phone — another gift from my lad (a camera is great by the by) — and snapped a few pictures, Dziga Vertov, me arse. Sadly, the screen

---

7. Look it up, with the spoilers.

112

showed nowt but darkness. I went back inside for me huntinn rifle, reckoninn I'd take a shot at the craft, aye, I would. After all, what else could it be but one of their "devices"? But as I emerged, weapon in hand, the craft had vanished.

Silence.

— And that's it? — asks the woman from behind her newspaper.

— Just like that, it disappeared.

— Fascinating.

— Probably a UFO, — I suggest.

— A what? May thy tongue blister, thee bastard, — the old man retorts. — It might well be a UFO, but I reckon it was that thing, their device, the one that slices through the ozone layer to boil us all alive 'ere.

— One typically boils in water, though, — I note.

— Tha, sun-blasted fool, would be boiled dry.

— Just theorising. I'm on your side, by the way. I program clouds.

— What?

— Clouds. I program them to bring rain.

— And where might thy clouds be, "programmer"?

— Well, in Saudi Arabia.

— In the desert, tha means?

— Something like that.

— And who the blazes needs clouds there? To water the sand? The world's mad!

The conversation, it seemed, had reached an aporia, much like our bus somewhere. I lean towards the babushka to check if she was still breathing. Her eyes are closed. I peer into her face, listen for her breath, and she suddenly opens her eyes.

— Boo!

I jerk back, retreating towards the teacher with her book. She laughs.

— Aren't you something! Trying to kiss the babushka.

— I wanted to help. I thought she was, you know, dead.

— Would that make it a good idea to kiss her? Sleeping beauty.

— I wasn't going to kiss her. I was checking if she's breathing.

113

— Oh, indeed, she'll outlive us all. You're the one restless and sweating, while she sits calmly, waiting. You could learn a thing or two about patience from the older generation.

— I don't like waiting. Especially not in this heat.

— Suppose it's not hot in Saudi Arabia?

— Of course it's hot. Fifty degrees now.

— There you go.

— It feels different there. At least they have air conditioning.

— Listen to the bourgeois, "air conditioning".

— The air here's humid. I'm suffocating. Feels like I'm gonna have a heatstroke. Damned sun.

— Hold your tongue. Speak ill of Sollie, and Sollie will surely strike you down.

Suddenly, growing louder in the distance, a hum encroaches upon our cosy timeless space. Hope exists, I reckon, but then immediately I understand — not really. The hum turns into a familiar roar, a cloud of dust and exhaust fumes crawling from its source. Everyone braces themselves, covering their faces, turning away. Then he appears, the motorcyclist, hurtling towards us with his pink mohawk shining. To spike a mohawk properly, I recall, one should use beer, otherwise — not trü[8].

Anticipating his approach, the babushka picks up a stone and, as the motorcyclist nears, hurls it at him. Instantly, without a whistle or sound, the stone strikes his head with an accurate shot. The motorcyclist loses control before he could even cry out. The front

---

8. Russian spelling of English-borrowed "true" is "труъ". Although that last letter isn't necessary, the hard sign (ъ) in "труъ" is a distinctive feature of (already dated) Russian internet slang where adding this letter gives words like "true" an exaggerated intensity and authenticity. The hard sign at the end used to be a part of Russian orthography in pre-revolurionary times when it was also kinda of unnecessary. The internet usage originated in metal music subcultures, especially among black metal enthusiasts ("True Norwegian Black Metal") to distinguish between "trü" black metal and "posers". The ъ-suffix evolved to signify something as absolutely authentic, "old", canonical, or hardcore. Thus the word "труъ" aims to designate elitism and canonicity, not just precision of forms, but also... the authentic essence of any object, phenomenon or creative act, pretty much what "Istina" would be (See also: Istina). Thus the translator suggests to spell English "true" (and "truth") with an umlaut to achieve the same effect.

wheel twists sharply, throwing him onto the road as his motorcycle crashes, tumbles, and flies off into the field, flattening a few metres of oats.

Silence.

To say the least, we are all in a profound, petrifying, trembling shock.

Fucked up it is. Forgive me, I simply have no other words.

We stand, speechless, our mouths agape, staring at the contorted motorcyclist lying on the road.

— Take that, degenerate! — yells the babushka at the motorcyclist, continuing to sit in her place.

We, except the killer, collectively approach the disfigured, bloodied body of the motorcyclist. Legs twisted, trousers halfway down, an arm broken with a white-and-red bone protruding from his forearm. His bare, tattooed torso covered in cuts and scratches. His face, having apparently slid a few metres across gravel, is all torn up, bloody, and dirty, with no nose in sight (and his mohawk is crumpled).

No one says anything. They are either too stunned or overflowing with intrigue. There's actually a minute of silence:

I lean over to the motorcyclist, my ear pricked up.

— Not breathing, it seems, — I say.

The teacher presses a finger to his neck.

— No pulse either. Bad luck.

— Well, this is a fine mess, — says the woman with the newspaper. — What an actual situation. Oh.

— There was a lad, and now there's a lad no more, — adds an old man. — Just like that. *Poof* — and it's all over. Eh... Life...

— Don't even say it, old chap, — says the woman, grabbing her neck as if intending to strangle herself while her other hand starts frantically waving a newspaper.

— Serves him right! — the babushka shouts. — Degenerate ponk!

We look at her, speechless. I, for my part, have yet to fully grasp what has happened and that there's a real dead person lying in front of me. I've only seen such things in films and games before. In games, I could smash anyone's head with a stone. I could do that easily, about a hundred or thousand times per evening. It is, actually, a lot of fun. Do I feel anything about that now? Probably not. He's just lying there. Well, shit happens, they say. "Bad luck." I hope he doesn't come back to life and eat us. But what if he does? On one hand, it would be an intriguing twist of events, on the other — a bit eerie perspective. Narratively, it would be odd and lazy as well because I've already told you it might happen. So, no, it won't.

— Perhaps we should call an ambulance, — I suggest.

— An ambulance? — says the old man.

— An ambulance, — the woman repeats after me.

— An ambulance, — says I.

— Look at him, what good would an ambulance do? — says the teacher.

Indeed. Looking at him — an ambulance is hardly going to be of any help, even if it arrives sooner than the bus.

— Right on, love. Need an undertaker, we do. I know a guy.

— And the police, — the babushka suddenly adds. — Give that bastard a fine! For speedinn.

— A fine?

— I don't feel it's fine at all, to be honest.

— Tha, thee old witch, should be locked up, spend your life behind bars, — the old man retorts. — Fuckinn 'ell.

— They drive like that! Degenerates!

— You should hold your tongue, madam. You're only making things worse for yourself, — says the woman. — There are witnesses here.

— Can't breathe here. The place is overrun with degenerates! Stuffed with degeneracy! — says the babushka.

— I'm calling the police, — I say. — And an ambulance. And all the rest.

— Go ahead, — says the old man. — The bus will come soon, we'll hop on and be off, and tha can sit here with the crazy old witch waiting for the coppers and the coroner.

— We'll wait. This is a crime scene, after all. The babushka killed the motorcyclist, — says the woman.

— By cruel means, — I add. — With a stone.

I feel a pebble hit me in the back of the head. Painful. There'll be a bruise. I turn around — the babushka is picking up another pebble and, grunting, is getting ready to stand up.

— Hey, what are you doing!

— Off shall tha fuck, ponk! — the babushka says and throws another stone at me.

— Hey! I'm calling the police.

— Ring thy bellend![9]

Another pebble. The babushka adjusts her skirt and, continuing to hurl pebbles, walks back down the road in the opposite direction from Tulubaika.

— Where do you think you're going?!

---

9. The original Russian phrase "В хуй себе позвони!" literally means "Call into your cock!" It's a vulgar dismissal that creates an anatomically impossible directive as a way of rejecting the threat. It's structurally similar to other Russian obscene rejections that use the same pattern of directing an action toward one's own genitalia as a way of saying "I don't care about your threat".

— Mind thine own fuckinn business!

I pull out my phone. It's off. In my blurry memory there's no record of me turning it off. I turn it on. Wait. Wait. Wait, a long time, seconds, minutes, hours, centuries. It turns on. One per cent battery. There's even a signal. I dial 02[10]. The phone turns off and starts to heat up. Confused, I don't know what to do.

— Hey! Babushka, stop where you are!

Hands shaking, I start speaking into the turned-off phone.

— Police? There's been an incident here. Yes, on the road to Tulubaika, a babushka has killed a motorcyclist. Will you be coming soon? Brilliant. Hear that, babushka? They are coming for you! — I shout after the departing murderer, but she either doesn't hear or simply ignores me.

It appears the teacher has noticed my phone turned off, and, having heard my conversation with the imaginary police, she rolls her eyes and shakes her head.

The phone in my hand grows warmer, warmer, and warmer until it's as hot as an iron. A spasm involuntarily courses through my hand, and without my consent, it (hand) flings the phone onto the road. I approach the device, look — the screen, it seems, is done.

— What about the police? What did they say? Are they coming? — the teacher asks.

What a bitch.

— They said they'll be here shortly.

— Is that what they said? Shortly?

— Yes, that's what they said, — I say rudely, swallowing what little saliva I've gathered, possibly the very last water in my organism. — We are told to wait. They promised they'll be here soon.

— Promised? Soon? They never say such things.

— Well, this time they did. They were very polite and considerate. As police should be.

— Remind me, for how long have you been away?

— Infinitely long, and that time, in fact, keeps increasing.

---

10. Police number in Russia.

— The longer we wait, the more it increases.

— This is what I've said.

— Should we just wait?

— This is what we've been doing. No reason to stop waiting.

— But the babushka?

— She's left.

— I can see that but don't you want to detain her?

— I do not. Do you?

— She won't get far, that old nag, — the old man inserts. — The coppers will nab her right there on the road.

Meanwhile, the old nag, limping, vanishes around the bend in the road.

— Would you like to call an ambulance as well? — the teacher asks.

What a bitch x2.

— I might.

— Ambulance... — the woman with the newspaper says softly.

Only then do we see she's out of sorts, staggering, her eyes rolling back, legs buckling; she drops the newspaper and collapses onto the road. We approach her, check if she's breathing — she is, thankfully, but unconscious. Her forehead is burning like a stove. You could cook eggs on it.

— I can't, my phone's dead. Does anyone else have a phone?

— I've seen enough of thy damned little phones, — the old man declares. — Ever wonder how *they* find us? Thy phones have navigation chips in them. Be it towers, panels, or some other nonsense like 3G, 5G — damn them all. Look at the youth today: riddled with cancer from head to toe, PTSD, autism, degeneracy, punk — all because of them phones. Radiation, that's what it is. Sun only makes it worse.

I glance at the teacher, expecting her to help with the next dialogue line, but she merely shrugs in response.

— I try to keep my mind pure, — she says. — No phone.

Noted-understood.

— And you, boy? Do you have a phone?

Where would he go without a phone, I wonder. What if he gets lost? Though, when I was his age, we ran around just the same. Parents off to work, you're off to the bus stop, jump on a bus, head into town with friends. Like cats, come and go as you please, and no one asks any questions. The boy just silently shakes his head. No! He doesn't have a phone! All this time he's just been standing on the side or whatever and he doesn't even have a phone!

— Let's move her into the shade. Grab her legs, — I tell the teacher.

— Where do you see the shade?

I lift the woman by her arms. Her body is heavy, sweaty, slipping from my grasp. Or I am weak. We drag her to the side of the road, closer to the oats. That's where we lay her down. Of course, I realise, there are no signs of any shade. Even oats don't cast shadows. The newspaper, right. I take it, unfold it into a makeshift paper tent over the woman's head to create some shade at least. I notice the front page: in bold letters, it reads:

ANOMALOUS HEATWAVE. WHAT NEXT?

The teacher takes out a small flask from her bag, pours some on her palms, and starts rubbing it on the woman's face, then splashes some onto her lips.

— What's that?

Smells of alcohol.

— Sun water. For protection.

Uh-huh, "sun water."

— May I have some? For protection.

— You don't need it. You don't need protection.

— Why don't I need protection?

— I can see it in you. You're already protected.

— No, I'm not. I've never felt less protected than now.

— Neither have I.

She looks me straight in the eye, brings the flask to her lips, and takes a swig. A lump slowly travels down her slender neck. She doesn't

even flinch. And from the smell of it, there was enough reason to flinch.

— What now? — she asks.

— I don't know.

— What, not a single idea, programmer?

A thought occurs. A perfectly fine thought, but questionable. I discard it.

We hear the muffled sounds of kicks. Turning around, we see the surfer boy standing and kicking the deceased motorcyclist. Meanwhile, the old man stands by, laughing as he observes the scene.

— Hey! — I shout at him.

The boy doesn't react and continues his kicking.

— What are you doing? That's a person there.

— It's a corpse, isn't it?

— Was a person. He was a person.

— Was, but gone now, isn't he? Like completely?

To put it mildly, I'm shocked.

— And tell me, why are you kicking him?

— Because he popped my balloon. It was my birthday balloon. I liked it. My girlfriend bought it for me.

— Well, happy birthday then.

— Not so happy any more, is it?

— Still, kicking a dead man isn't right. Do you think you're doing a good thing? What do your parents teach you?

— Popping children's balloons isn't right either, is it? They taught me I should do that. Popping others' balloons.

— Kicking a dead man is worse than popping a balloon.

— Is that so?

— Way worse.

The boy stops and looks at me, his eyes empty, his face devoid of emotion.

— But have you ever seen a corpse before, mister?

— What? No.

— Neither have I, — he shrugs.

— Why kick it, though? Why would you kick a corpse? A man's corpse?

— The corpse doesn't care, does he? But it amuses me.

Amuses him.

— Oh, it amuses you?

— Yes. It is fun, isn't it?

— What's fun about it?!

— No one's fighting back.

Indeed.

— And it's my birthday.

— Look, boy, I can't do this any more. We need your help. That lady over there is unwell.

The surfer boy looks at the woman whose head is covered by a newspaper.

— What's wrong with her?

— Heatstroke.

— She was very upset by what she saw, — interjects the teacher. — We're all upset.

— So do you want me to start kicking her too?

The grandfather laughs heartily, wiping the sweat from his brow.

— Look at the youth these days, — he says. — And they say: wasted generation. Not even a sign of it — all-round good bloke.

— There's no need to kick anyone. Stop it, please.

I kneel and take the boy by his shoulders.

— Where did you come from?

— From the town. You're hurting me.

— No, I'm not. Can you go back to the town and ask them to send the police and an ambulance here?

— And the bus, — adds the teacher.

— And the bus. Of course, and the bus.

The boy's hesitant. A lot. Glancing, he examines our levels of tilt.

— What's in it for me?

— I... I'll buy you an ice cream, okay? The chocolate one. With hazelnuts. Do you like it?

— I don't want ice cream.

— What? What do you want then?

— Mister, I want to kick corpses. And a balloon. I want my balloon back.

— All right, I'll buy you a balloon.

— With the same number? It's my birthday.

— Yes, happy birthday, of course. Same number, same colour — all you want, really.

He shakes his head.

— I don't think you understand what I want. You better give me some money. I can buy it myself.

Cunning. I look at him — standing there, pouting his lips, furrowing his brows, his gaze avoiding mine.

— All right. Good, I'll give you money. Fine.

I take out a banknote from my wallet and hand it to the boy.

— What is this?

— It's money. A banknote.

— Crikey.

— What?

— It won't be enough for a balloon.

— Are you sure? It's plenty of money for ten balloons.

— Balloons are very expensive these days, mister. I had to save from my meals for a week to get just that one. For my birthday.

I count out a few more notes.

— Right, fine, of course. Here's for the balloon... Happy birthday again.

I hand him another note.

— And for the ice cream.

Another note.

— Is that enough for everything you want right now? Except kicking. It's not for sale, I'm afraid.

The boy nods, turns around, and runs off towards the city.

— Call an ambulance and the police! — I shout after him. — And the bus.

— Cunts! — yells the boy as he disappears around the bend.

Meanwhile, the teacher takes another generous sip of her "sun water."

— Look at the youth these days, — the old man repeats, shaking his head and, scratching the back of his head and fixing the NY cap, starts walking around the motorcyclist's body until he notices something on the buttock beneath the lowered trousers — a tattoo of the sun with eight rays.

— One of 'em! Bloody bastard! — the old man exclaims and starts kicking the corpse too.

— Hey, stop that!

No reaction follows.

— I'll kill you all, maggots! — he shouts, unclear whether at the motorcyclist or at us. — I'll show you. You sun-worshippinn fanatics.

— Oi! — I shout at the grandfather, but he continues kicking.

In panic mode, I turn to the teacher.

— Say something to him.

— What should I say?

— To stop? That would be nice.

— He's ferocious. Why wouldn't you tell him?

— He doesn't like me.

— All these bastards. You won't burn me. Reading their books, walkinn around shouting "the invincible sun, the invincible sun." Disgusting! Damn you all.

The teacher shrugs, finishes her sun water, and, coming closer, whispers to me:

— By the way, I have a tattoo, too. Someplace. Fancy taking a peek?

I recoil from her, stumbling back, nearly falling, and move away. The heat's driven everyone mad. I want to go home. I want to go home. I want to go home. My brain's turned to mash, seems to have fused into one big heavy lump, swelling and pressing from the inside against my skull, harder around the temples and the back of my head. Where's the bus? What's the bus? Why's the bus? My head spins along with the surrounding oat field. Where is it? Where am I? I feel nauseous. I grab my hair and scream:

— Bus! Hey! We're here! Bus! Bus! Bus! I'm here!

The teacher and the old man startle.

— What are you yelling for? — asks the old man.

— Don't you worry, — says the teacher. — Calm down.

— Bus! Bus! Hey! Someone help!

— It'll come, don't be upset. The bus is always late. It's normal for the bus to be late. We'll all be in Tulubaika sooner or later.

— Don't be upset? Don't be upset?! Do you see what's going on?!

I settle onto the ground, enveloping myself with my arms. I don't feel like screaming, nor crying any more; in fact, I feel like nothing whatsoever, except perhaps for a yearning to sink deep into the ground, so deep that the cold seeps in, and warmth becomes a forgotten sensation. Yes, I crave the coolness, the chill, the clarity of thought, the lightness of the mind, my childhood bedroom, my cave. But instead, I feel as though I'm being boiled alive, like a lobster. Or worse, boiled dry. I fall to the side, curl up into a ball, press my cheek against the ground, and just lie there. I don't want to listen to anyone. I don't want to see anyone. I don't want anything. The surface, despite being as hot as everything else around, is slightly cooler than the air and smells of dust, straw, and manure. Suddenly, I feel a wet, cold hand on my shoulder; I shudder and shrug it off.

— Leave me alone! I don't want to see any of you any more.

— Just look up at the sky, — I hear the teacher saying.

— I don't fucking want to look at your fucking sun or Sollie or whatever the fuck it's called.

— Oh, please. Language. But it's not Sollie.

— Then what? Fucking moon, huh?

— No, don't be silly, look. It's an airship.

Air-what?

— An aerostat, — she says.

— What?

Curious, I open my eyes and look at her.

— Don't look at me, look up. There, — she says, pointing in another direction at the sky.

126

I turn, propping myself up on my hands, and gaze at the sky afar. There, resembling a huge white cloud, an airship, an enormous dirigible balloon with a red digit six glides almost uswards. Its engine, possibly electric, emits a droning, sonorous trill, a single sustained note, resonating through the field — a choir of cicadas trapped inside a subwoofer. Trailing behind it is a cone-shaped tail of spray, covering an area of tens, perhaps hundreds of metres. The airship is bringing us rain. Oh, yes! Water! Sweet water! Come here, my dear!

— Hey! We're here! Hey!

— Over here! — the teacher joins me.

The old man notices the airship, too, and turns pale.

— No... No... They've found me... Bastards!

He takes off his NY cap and, bending and groaning, with his trembling fingers, fumbles in his pockets. After searching himself all over, he pulls a crumpled piece of foil from his trousers' back pocket, straightens it out, and wraps it around his bald head.

— Damn it! They've found me. Me! I told you lot!

We, not at all surprised, continue to shout and whistle, in response to which the old man, with a look of both universal, existential dread, and deep, childlike terror, crouches, and scurries over to us. His eyes blaze, the cap gleams.

— Shhh! No! Stop that! You idiots! Idiots!

We ignore him and keep trying to attract the airship's attention, jumping and shouting.

— Enough, damn you all. Enough! Shhh!

Then the airship shifts direction slightly and now heads straight at us, dragging its watery cloud behind. The old man sees this, crouches even lower.

— Tch! Tch! The lot of you! Bastards! Fucking 'ell!

And so, ducking, nervously looking around, holding on to his shiny helmet, he darts from the open road into the dense oat fields and vanishes.

We watch him leave and continue to shout and jump. There's a warmth in our hearts, not in a thermal sense, but in an uplifting,

hopeful sense, as if we, shipwrecked, have been stranded on a deserted island, and after years of waiting, a ship finally appears on the horizon. Not a bus, though, but good enough. Time freezes again, hangs in the air and stretches into an endlessly long strip like a taut string ready to snap at the slightest touch.

And then, we're engulfed in the airship's shadow. The sun hides behind a massive cloud looming over us for an inestimable interval, while our bodies shake in anticipation. The teacher places her hand on my shoulder, and I don't mind; I, too, place my hand on her shoulder, and she doesn't mind. I stretch out the other hand, close my eyes, squeeze them as tight as I can, so tight that abstract shapes morph into oval blobs, the airship's imprint. And then, right away, we're drenched by a fine, cool rain, like the kind you get on a cold autumn morning, which feels annoying, as if someone's spraying your face with an atomiser, but right now, it's all we want. Drench me, dirigible! Soak me through! And it does, with a dense tropical downpour, washing the dust off my face, rinsing the greasy clumped hair, washing away the sweat from my body, soaking my clothes with crisply cool water. Transcendent goosebumps run all over my skin, from my nape, down my back, along my arms, down my legs, even to my little toes. They are happy, too. The teacher and I fall to our knees on the ground, arms outstretched, laughing, sticking out our tongues as far as possible to catch as much water as we can.

The rain stops, and with it goes away the shadow. Outside, there's coolness, the smell of wet earth, inside — bliss, a light shiver. We rise, soaked, and watch as the airship slowly drifts away.

Everything around us is now dewy and sodden. Puddles have formed. The dirigible-borne rain has flattened the oats a little, washed the blood off the motorcyclist, mixing it with the mud. The woman on the roadside still lies there. The thoroughly soaked newspaper clings to her face. Probably dead.

Silence.

The sun rays are felt anew on my skin, comforting. We look at each other, clothes clinging to our bodies, water trickling down. The teacher smiles.

— Well, — she says, — now that no one hears us, would you like to talk more about the Invincible Sun?

My smile turns wry and nervy, and I pull my hand away.

Episode Eight
about literary essays, time, happiness & unhappiness

It's good where we are not: in the past we are no more, and so it seems beautiful.

— Anton Chekhov

One can talk about "Three Sisters" for ages, for I am one of them and all three sisters at once, and also all the other characters at once. That's what happens when you read a book, especially one where the author isn't there. Tolstoevsky, for example, couldn't do that, but Anton Pavlovich could. The author is always there, of course, writes something, and stands in the corner of the room, watching, like Tolstoevsky for instance, but Anton Pavlovich would leave, close the door ever so quietly behind him, and leave his characters alone with themselves. For they need personal space where they could feel their life through. That's precisely why they're all always so bored, but that's how it should be, for that's precisely how it is in life.

(It's more honest this way, isn't it, Tamara Alexeyevna? Yes, you — I know what you do with my essays — you take them and send them off to all sorts of literary competitions, and then I have to answer for them and suffer, but I write them not for someone, not for no one, not for some competition or other, but always for a specific addressee, there are three of them: myself, you, Anton Pavlovich — impersonal essays don't interest me anymore, they make me sick, so I shan't be writing any more essays that could be sent off anywhere, let alone to a competition. You'll have to keep them to yourself — that's the only

way now, they won't suit anywhere else, for everyone will know who I'm writing them to, the competition panel won't have to guess and build theories. Even when I write "Dear Diary," I mean Anton Pavlovich. I don't write my diary every day, as one might think, but I always think what to write there. Dear Diary is my Roman Empire that fell apart whilst still young, but also my Atlantis, which sank having peaked.)

At any party there's always someone who leaves first, but whoever might lay claim to that noble position, Time will always leave before them, close the door, leave the rest alone with themselves and with its half-empty, half-full unfinished drink by the exit. In "Three Sisters" the same thing happens to Time. There's a lot on this matter in my Dear Diary. I don't even have to write anything, if I'm honest, so I'll just gather the essentials for you, Tamara Alexeyevna:

1. There are those who want to speed Time up, and those who want to slow it down. Sped-up Time sort of doesn't exist, whilst slowed-down Time is sort of too much.

2. There's a certain amount of experience one can live through in a certain period of time. One can either live through it in express mode, or stretch out the pleasure.

3. If one speeds up time, one must be careful with the brakes, because physics and whatnot. It's like with a bicycle — you can fly over the handlebars and scrape your elbows raw. It might heal, or it might leave scars. As my grandad used to say, "Done it before, we'll do it again."

4. Everything is a lottery, and every action is a ticket.

5. Strangely, as time passes, what accumulates is not only the presence of experience, but also its absence. Absence hurts more than presence. Dreams and other wants are either present or absent.

6. Everyone wants something, even secretly. The biggest secret want is to leave Tulubaika. The only thing worse is wanting to return to it.

7. From accumulating un-happened wants, one can get constipated.

8. Nostalghin should be classified as a narcotic. It doesn't help with the illness. I've seen what it does to grown-ups.

9. In the past everything's always the best, only children don't have one, which means they must run from it headlong in search of grown-up happiness.

All of these (1-9) are in "Three Sisters". In my Dear Diary there's everything, if you dig deep enough, and then some on top. I'd particularly like to note (6), which metaphorically-poetically transitions into (7), then into (5) and that's it — kirdyk, as they say, and without (8) there's no getting by in that situation. A vicious circle, Tamara Alexeyevna.

I want to explain (6) in more detail. All the characters, including the three sisters, want to go somewhere. Where to — that's obvious, to Moscow, of course, for the work is better there, the peace of mind, and both "it was better" and "it will be better" — past and future at once. But that's not important, what's far more important is the question: where do they all want to leave from so badly? It's never mentioned, is

it? The answer is simple: from Tulubaika, where else? Everyone wants to leave their Tulubaika. You, Tamara Alexeyevna, want to, or at least at first you simply wanted to, and then (6). And I want to, but I've got (3).

For Olga, Tulubaika has mosquitoes and cold, for Andrei — no ambitions and no decent restaurants, for Irina — absence of romance, for Baron Tuzenbach — absence of prospects, even for half-deaf Ferapont — there are no newspapers in Tulubaika because nothing literally happens. In Moscow everything's better and everyone's happier than in Tulubaika, and they haven't even thought about the rest of the world, but if they had... Only Vershinin believes that happiness doesn't exist in principle, even outside Tulubaika, be it Moscow or elsewhere, it simply hasn't been invented yet, but will definitely be invented in the future, and the unhappy past will all be forgotten. Ugh, unhappy past, just ugh! But like everyone else, Vershinin's Tulubaika lacks what he would want, too. He says it himself: "The other day I read the diary of a French minister, written in prison. The minister was convicted for Panama. With what delight, what rapture he mentions the birds he sees in the prison window and which he never noticed before, when he was a minister. Now, of course, when he's been released, he once again doesn't notice birds. Similarly, you won't notice Moscow when you live there. We have no happiness and there isn't any, we only desire it." But I disagree with him, for he, like the rest, does nothing, just waits, philosophises, dreams, gets bored. Time simply comes and goes, by invitation and without. They've all got a full (5), and the solution seemingly exists, it's right on the surface — just go and do it, what's stopping you?

I would have already fled Tulubaika, but I need to finish school first. I'll finish, get into university — I'll flee immediately and will never want to come back. Perhaps I'll become sweet-happy, perhaps sour-happy. Did you know, Tamara Alexeyevna? That happens too. My Dear Diary has something on this as well:

> 10. One can want strongly, or one can want even more

strongly, and if one wants so much that one actually wants to do something about it, then perhaps it will happen. If one does nothing, it won't happen, and if it didn't happen, it means one didn't really want it that much.

11. One must want so hard that everyone tells you to bite your tongue, whilst they themselves chew theirs off (from envy).

12. If you dream hard enough, any want will come true.

13. Fulfilment of wants leads to happiness, or maybe it doesn't, but more likely it does, at least temporarily.

14. Happiness is somehow connected to gooseberries, haven't figured out how yet. (And here I added later in red pen, when I did figure it out: gooseberries can be sour, sweet, and bitter, green and red, but they're all hairy, and the branches are prickly. Brrr...)

15. A girl can want a machete for her birthday, and they'll buy her a dress, and even if they do buy the machete, she'll realise she wanted a bass guitar — that happens too. When I remember it, everything inside me clenches.

16. Pushkin said: "a delusion that exalts us is dearer than a host of low truths".

17. Chekhov said: "case-bound life" (no comment).

18. Also Chekhov's character: "to my thoughts about human happiness there had always somehow been mixed something sad".

19. My grandad used to say: "Make hay while the sun shines."

Anton Pavlovich wrote about this in "Gooseberries" — there everything's the other way round, not like in "Three Sisters," the main character isn't thought-paralysed in his Tulubaika, but goes towards his dream and after a lifetime finally gets what he strove for, but in the end everyone's still unhappy, that is (18). Perhaps that's why you don't like Chekhov, Tamara Alexeyevna, perhaps that's why he's boring for you, whilst for me — the opposite, and for Tolstoevsky too, by the way — he really liked "Gooseberries", he wrote to Anton Pavlovich and said so himself. In the story, the main character had a very strong (14), so much so that he even reached (10-12), but in the end first came (13), and then (15), and all because of (16) and (17). Such is the maths, Tamara Alexeyevna — we don't live by literature alone, as they say. To (14) I would add that gooseberries shouldn't be preserved but eaten, otherwise, say, you'll make jam, it'll sit in your cellar for a decade, lucky if it doesn't go mouldy, but it'll turn out to be either sourish (sourhappiness), bitterish (bitterhappiness), sweetish (sweethappiness, the cloying kind, as if sugar were grating on your teeth). One needs (19), in a word, probably. I don't know yet, I'm still young, inexperienced, but I wrote it down something like this for myself:

20. Sometimes understanding comes in time, and yet action seems meaningless, but sometimes understanding comes when it's already too late to act. In both cases, nothing to be done.

21. If Time pops into your party, you absolutely must chat with it, entertain it, introduce it to the guests, or else it'll get upset from loneliness and leave.

That won't happen to me, Tamara Alexeyevna. I promised my Dear Diary.

———

B-
we are not doing maths here!

Episode Nine
about meeting strange
ravens in birch groves

There is an infinity in the infinity of fleeing avenues with an
infinity infinitely fleeing intersecting shadows. All of Petersburg
is the infinity of an avenue raised to the power of n. And beyond
Petersburg — nothing is.

— Andrei Bely, "Petersburg"

Sublime that day was Tulubaika, its beauty seen without needing
his third eye, Kondráty sprawled out on the grass rusty and brisk and
basking in the setting sun and gentle breeze beheld it
    marvelled
        dazed
        & charmed.
Among the forests, lost in the endless birchbyrinth
its crowns aglow with gold, it lounged
            the village.

Its image breathed, as if alive, with movements slow, hypnotic
        it soothed his eye
                it stirred his thought
                        beguiled his spirit.

Somewhere there among the treey streets a house was inside,
behind the closed doors — an oak bed where lay
        Kondráty's body
        a nullity in human form

frozen in different time and space
abased
far from the infinite eternal.

At once that gigathought and sight impaled Kondráty's mind. Just
wow, he reckoned, bojemoi[1]!
How have I missed that all the time?
The perfectest perfect of
perfectly perfect perfects
O!
O Tulubaika!
O!
(and O!)
Was I a fool, a degen?
Too brash, too craven to explore?

Behind Kondráty landed a stately stygian raven its left wing striped
with white, its eyes alike charcoals, its beak alike a blade
ominous, sharp
obsidian-made.

Encroaching on Kondráty's solitude, the raven uttered:

Krraa!

Oh, hi, birdie!

Such a mesmerising view we've got here, huh?

Inside his head, he named all animals he saw:
squirrels, starlings,
ravens, rats,
wood pigeons, foxes, frogs,

---

1. "Bojemoi" is a direct rendition of Russian "Oh my God", because why not.

et cetera.
Some were his friends
some foes
some passersby
some food
some interlocutors, the others
— mere messengers.

This raven, not a random bird but a new friend was no exception,
and with no retort (and no choice), accepted "Kutkh" to be his name.
Kookily, his head he tilted, tousled his plumage, and stared back.

Kraaa!

Kraaa indeed, my droog[2]
I know, I know, one seldom can feel full with anything but
    Tulubaika.

Kondráty sat and took his bag
a ramshackle rucksack.

Above, the golden crowns of birches flashed and rustled
warningly.
The wind Boreas grabbed Kondráty's beloved umbrella with that
perfectly perfect, facsimile image of Tulubaika painted on it and ran
away into the birchwood corridor of stripes white / black
    the corridor optically infinite.

Jingling the runic rosary woven into his hair and beard, Kondráty,
hopping and stumbling, tangling in his baggy clothes, chased the
umbrella.

---

2. A direct rendition of "friend" in Russian, also used like that in "A Clockwork
Orange".

Alas, Boreas was a moron
a moron mocking, a faster moron
a moron stronger.

Right at a ravine where below streamed a brook, Tulubaika
ascended like a plane, spewing diminishing hee-hee-hee:
hee-hee-hee
     hee-hee-hee
       hee-hee
    hee-hee-hee
           hee!

Higher it flew and farther above the trees somewhere Kondráty
knew no whither. Panting, he stopped and spat.

I'll find you, dear!

Spreading his hands, Kondráty screamed into the birchwood
wilderness, labyrinthine and golden. It spread beyond the ravine
with no beginning
with no end to see.

He spat again and, stomping, returned to Kutkh.

Can you imagine?
Boreas, that bastard, stole my Tulubaika!
My Tulubaika!
Imagine!

He spat once more, picked up the rucksack and threw its only
strap over his shoulder. With curiosity, Kutkh kept inspecting him.

What?

I'm leaving! Poka! [3] (he shivered) It's going to be a wee bit too chilly to sleep in here, my droog!

Kraaa, kraaa!
cawed Kutkh, jumping, his wings aflutter.

Ah-huh, the food! (Kondráty made the eureka gesture)

Well, lucky you are, today —
I'm fasting, huh!

Inside his rucksack he fumbled. He pulled out a half-loaf of bread, or rather a rusk, sprinkling crumbs, tore a small piece from it and handed it to Kutkh. Warily, the raven jumped back, but then snatched it and hurried away.

Oh, yes, thank you, too, Kutkh!
Enjoy your meal, by the way!

Alas, no answer followed
the raven dissolved in the birchwood
like anything would. . .

By dusk, Kondráty returned to his mattress under the unfinished motorway's bridge, a border where ended the realm of birches
and started Ensk[4]
where grey took over gold.

---

3. Informal way to say "good bye" in Russian, similar to just "bye" or "see you".
4. See Episode 19.

No wind, no chill, instead —
a makeshift hearth made by the others.
Accustomed they were to silence
the sense of it was shared
their language was unspoken
by nods and glances played.
In blankets wrapped, hairy, dishevelled, in semblance of a ritual
they huddled
slept or entertained their eyes and minds with dancing tongues of
flame and crackling embers
they were like imps locked longing in their den
waiting to be mustered.

Kondráty nestled on the sideline. For them, in all his outfits and
demeanours he appeared an exemplar of a menagerie or circus. No fun
they made nor mocked him, no
the awe at the unfathomable caused the social distance.
His ginger mane with rosary entwined
his face painted with coal and chalk and
the ⊛, an O of many eyes[5]
a little inflorescence of monads on his forehead.
He did look like no bum
no vagabond, no junkie, no man in misery, no —
looked a volkhv of olden days[6] he did
a hitchhiker from unseen dimensions, for whom the mattress, the
bridge, the makeshift hearth were bringing joy, at least until that day...
that day he had no Tulubaika.

---

5. The multiocular O (⊛) represents one of the most interesting Cyrillic characters,
appearing in only one place in all of medieval Slavonic manuscripts — the phrase "many-
eyed seraphim" in a 1429 copy of the Psalter.
6. The term "volkhv" (волхв) designates a pre-Christian Slavic priest-magician. It's
unclear whether volkhvs represented an organised pagan priesthood or were merely
village practitioners of folk magic who also resisted Christianisation and whom
Christian chroniclers conveniently demonised. An English term for it could be "magus",
"sorcerer", or "pagan priest", or all three at once.

Found in a dump, outwardly commonplace, inwardly sui generis,
the umbrella subdued his mind, became an artefact, a talisman
even a friend
acquired a dominion over his consciousness
and far beyond it.

He used to place it between him and the hearth and his underdog
friends. The plain back outer part was shielding him from their
curious eyes, and the inside where Tulubaika hid served as a source of
reveries.

Hooked to infinity
fully locked in
he dived into Tulubaikan scenery
at first — wide awake
later — in lurid dreams
but on that day...
Boreas stole it all.

Kondráty frowned, growled, grimaced and turned facing the wall.
He mumbled, scribbled Tulubaikan runes with chalk on the concrete,
tried to evoke a dream of dreams, any dream, or better so —
a dream of Tulubaika
again. . .
but vainly.

The runes that day declared no word
the symbols formed no meanings
Kondráty's mind was there still
inside his head imprisoned in the skull bones.
That day a good night's sleep was not forthcoming.

❦

Then, followed the morrow
someone sprayed the vegetation
with the drops of sorrow
someone covered whiteblack trees
with an eerie fog
teary, sticky, cold
leaving none in sight beyond one's hand
none in mind inside one's head.

Golden was the ground, golden was the sky
monochrome was the visible horizontality
but Kondráty knew the way.

Snapping twigs, tinkling rosary and beads, his body interspersed with birches, wobbling his way through their multidimensional striped fence. From under their coloured caps, mushrooms peeked and lapsed as Kondráty passed them, for their imminent end in his hands they foresaw. But that day they were safe, for he sought Tulubaika
nothing else
nothing more.

He met a large, bulky oak, and said, lifting his head:

Hey, my friend, have you seen around here lately
my Tulubaika?

The tree shook its crown, leaves rustling, bark cracking.

No? You haven't? Shame, eh. . .

All right, I'll keep looking then.
Thanks, anywise. . .

Kondráty saluted to the oak and moved further. On his way, he asked every tall tree, for only they could see high enough, far enough,

both in space and time. At moments, he paused his journey to hug one of them or chat about things mundane
about the weather
about the transience of time
and if the world was sane.

He approached the ravine long and deep that divided the birchwood in two parts. Down there beneath, among the dead trees and scrubs, chirped the brook, its cold streams sleeked the pebbles.

Morrow to you, lil'river.
By any chance, have you seen Tulubaika?

…

No? It hides inside an umbrella, by the way.

The brook splashed, simpered, and rolled onwards.

Well, alas. . . (Kondráty shrugged)
Thanks, anywise!

Using a fallen birch, he crossed the ravine and entered the realm of raspberry and nettle. Through thickets waded he for hours, yet no signs of Tulubaika revealed themselves
no bush
no tree
no stone
no mushroom
— no one had witnessed it.
Boreas stole and hid it somewhere in secret.

Now it was lost
lost was his mind
lost thoughts lurked through his convolutions.

What if somebody found it? Would they handle the beauty?
the knowledge?
the higher energies it emanates?
the view sublime?

No one could possibly withstand that!
And what if a squirrel sees it?
Well, kirdyk, poor squirrel
finita la commedia. . .

Kondráty gave up
& tired, hungry, frustrated
returned to his everyday deeds.

❀

Deep in the wilderness of birchwoodness, secluded in a quiet grove
under the golden canopy, he made a fireplace and, sitting in the sultan
pose, was brewing a concoction of various plants and mushrooms he'd
gathered earlier, leading a ladle slowly-lovingly inside a small pot.

What was the recipe? No clue.
It was Kondráty's secret brew
his chef's special.

No one was ever granted a chance to know parts of the mixture, let
alone a casual observer
like you.

For Kondráty, the value of plants and shrooms was determined by
their ability to warp the perception: some were for the mind, some
were for the taste buds — together, they formed the uniquely uniquest
blend of unique uniquenesses.

The cooking process required one full day, aside from the time of gathering / drying. He could've shopped for them, yes, but seldom did he have any money
or any idea of that.

Crucial was having a raw organic product picked with his bare hand in the place of positive energies. After hours of slow brewing, the concoction needed some time in a cold, dark place to acquire its psychoactive properties. He drank it to tune his mind to the currents of Tulubaikan consciousness permeating everything around
somewhere denser
somewhere sparser.

From those currents, using a metaphysical ladle, he could draw arcana, and then fulfil his mission of enlightening people, giving them a chance to discover more about Tulubaika
conscious
unconscious
subconscious
metaconscious
hyperconscious
and some other
consciousness types —
regrettably, few eager were that knowledge to accept.

Upwards, Boreas, sneaky bastard, embraced the birches' crowns again and "played" with them pressing his pervert fingers on their uncountable leaves.
Rustling cascadingly, the birchchoir whispered:

Fair afternoon to thee, our dear Kondráty
in our humble grove
welcome thou art.

Hello (Kondráty grunted).

Thy life, how fares it?
Oddly we feel it hath been but blink since thy last visit.
You, trees, always say that.

So-so, I'm mourning.
Have you seen Tulubaika?

Tulubaika?

Yes, Tulubaika

But everywhere it is
and nowhere doth it end.

I know, I mean mine
my Tulubaika
the one in the umbrella.

In days of yore, we saw it, aye
ever dost thou bring it hither
with thee it cometh, on each day that passeth.

Today is not that day. Boreas stole it
sneaky bastard.

What is lost shall once be found.

Not if it's stolen.

Even so...
Thou shan't dispute with those for whom
the time-space continuum is
but a landscape.

Are you spoiling me a plot right now?

No plot there is — only ripples and circles upon the water's face
spreading quaquaversally
from a pebble cast.

Cheers.
This is a banger of an insight.
I can't even describe how helpful that is.
Literally speechless.

Kondráty scooped a ladleful of green-brown liquid up from the
pot and brought it to his face, inhaling the aromas. They crept
inside his nostrils and heated his airways, blurring his sight,
destabilising it and narrowing. The currents bent, twisted and
wrapped around him. He closed his eyes, blew on the ladle, prepared
to sip but
flinched and spilled the hot concoction on his crossed legs.

Whoops!

Near to the fireplace, a raven landed, smashing his sudden presence
on the idyllic harmony, sending the tongues of flame
adance.

Eat me, Tulubaika!
You, little bastard!
I've almost pooped myself.
Do you know what's privacy, aye?

It was Kutkh — that one white feather revealed him. The raven
posed in front of him, watching and waiting, his plumage shone and
shimmered ebony and blue lobelia, his eyes contained the night
his beak — a rolled piece of paper.

He dropped it, cawed and, swirling a golden hurricane, surged upwards
& vanished.

Kondráty covered the concoction with his hands, and when the dust and leaves had settled, he stood up, picked up the piece of paper and unrolled it
a banknote, a tenner
money.

Oh, well. What am I supposed to do with it?
Hey! What am I supposed to do with it?

No answer followed. Numb air. Silence.

He shook his head, pocketed the tenner and returned to brewing. Soon, the concoction blackened, thickened, acquired the syrupy consistency. Kondráty split it evenly into minijars with airtight seal locks, wrapped them in blankets, buried in his underbirch stash nearby, a small pit he had dug one day. He extinguished the fireplace, packed up, glanced over the grove, wished a fair while to the wise birch
and headed to Ensk.

❦

Ensk was oversized for a town, oversized enough to become a city, oversized enough for people to habitually ignore each other
except Kondráty.

Among the commoners, he was a freak, among the freaks, he was a tsar — Tsar Kondráty, first of his name
the Seeing
the Hearing
the Feeling

the Wandering
the overlord of the unseen dimensions.

As he strolled through Ensk's streets, people's attention contorted, faces changed, wrinkles smoothed, jaws dropped, eyes widened, hearts stopped
(for a moment)
souls trembled like leaves in the wind.

Whether moving or standing, they turned their heads at uncanny angles, following Kondráty passing them. He couldn't be missed or mistaken for someone else, his every step produced copious sounds: equipment rattled in his rucksack, the runic rosary and beads jingled, boots scuffed the pavement. Sometimes, under curious looks, he could sharply turn his head and stare back at the beholders, smirk cartoonishly, raising the outer sides of his brows, or wave his hand, wiggling fingers, appearing skittish and creepy. Yet, ordinarily, he ignored such looks, not on purpose — he wasn't aware of them, for muddled was his brain, an amalgamation of thoughts aswarm.

Some called Kondráty a charlatan, a madman, a poseur, a shmagus — few sensed the aura he emanated. For those, he was a teacher spiritual, a sage, a clairvoyant, the prophet wisest. On those occasions, humble and coy he was, excused himself, and said that he was just a Kondráty and no one else. He didn't channel someone's will or maxims. He was merely a Kondráty, one of many random Kondrátys that could've existed.

In fact, everyone could've been a Kondráty if they wanted willingly.
Equally, a Kondráty could've been anyone.
Hence to transcend they must accept the simple fact —
he is like them
a creature trembling
a person saying all in his name, not covering himself up in the name of supreme powers.

There was only "a" Kondráty and "the" Tulubaika
a place that is what isn't and isn't what is
a place you go you know not whither to fetch you know not what
& the mind of his was just a tiny rift in it
an eye that could see no other human could.
Sometimes, in sight of that eye there was another eye
     & another
        & another
           & another
     the eyes were, in fact
       infinite.

They had different iris colour, different shape, different pupil size, floating always, each of them in their eigen direction: either left or right, either slow or fast. All you could see through the very first eye is the second eye, displaced, but sometimes magically, sometimes obeying efforts of the beholder
    all eyes aligned
      & through one eye the one could see
         another eye
           & another
       & another & another
     & another & another & another
   & another & another & another & another
& another & another & another & another & another
        & so to infinity
until what had to be seen was seen
but it must've been looked at carefully, otherwise. . .

Well, kirdyk, poor creature
finita la commedia!

This would've sounded more convincing if a Kondráty said it to you directly, for no written words could possibly convey his mellow

expression, the depth of his blue eyes and movements of his face when he was looking inside you and giving birth to those infant words above. If not his heroic humbleness and reclusive detachment, he could've been rich, he could've built a cult around himself, but his prominence remained niche among those few people.

Things sacred shall be free, for otherwise
what's sacred about them?

The grief for the umbrella did not fade but having the tenner soothed it. If ever was he friends to money, it dumped him for his passivity.

What do people buy? And how?
Dither it made him, uneasy.

Whenever lucres surfaced in his life, his first thought was of new equipment: jars, lighters, chalk, et cetera. The next thought was of substances mind-altering, or better so mind-mending
psychoactive catalysts for his psychomagical voyage.

But the tenner was not enough.

Then food, mayhap?
That wouldn't hurt.
What do ravens eat?

He stopped by a bakery and stared through the shop window onto the assortment of cakes and muffins, sandwiches layered neatly on a large serving board, lumps, and slices of sourdough and pillars of baguettes resting in wicker baskets among the wooden interior.

The doorbell rang, the rosary jingled
a Kondráty walked through the door.
A wryly smiling cashier met him.

He pointed onto a seeded sourdough, prepared the tenner but
a peculiar culinary idea betided in his mind, and he hurried out of
the bakery to another shop.

❀

Deep in the woods, there was a pond, a peaceful water basin where
willows overhanging the reeds and constellations of
    Nymphaea alba rising from the primeval slime
        bloomed.

At night, there developed a massacre bloody
an infringement on nature
a hunt for frogs.

A Kondráty, equipped with a hand net, naked
hid in the reeds, waited
for hours, he bet on frogs to join crickets in their nightly song.

Meanwhile, dazed, he gazed at the nymphaea. Towards the moon
they unfolded their petals and reminded a Kondráty of his umbrella
the same but with a handle reversed.

Mayhap, it also camouflaged somewhere in a pond pretending to
be a nymphaea and at night opened its oculus upwards to the sky,
speaking to it or screaming in desperate and painful shrills pleading a
Kondráty to hear and be its saviour.

Hypnotised, mesmerised, sleepy
with no ticks of time tracked, he submerged into
dreams and almost missed when the croaking commenced.
Frogs gathered on nymphaea leaves

in reeds
    on stones
        on shore.

He saw them, his victims, brown and green, spotted dark. He sneaked up and swung with the net, transferred the frogs to his sack
    and once more
He sneaked up and swung with the net, splashing water, drowning the nymphaea's leaves.
He sneaked up and swung with the net, transferred the frogs to his sack.
Thus passed a few hours, the pond became quieter
by a few dozen croakers.

❀

At dawn, in his grove, a yawning Kondráty embarked on culinary adventures. On his improvised stove, stood boiling two pots: in the first one, in spring water, the poisonous substances were being expelled from the Nymphaea alba
    — this was for a Kondráty
in the second one, the frogs were being fried deep, salted, peppered, submerged into three hundred millilitres of extra virgin and extra premium olive oil that he bought instead of bread
    — this was for Kutkh.

Once a frog acquired required crispiness, a Kondráty transferred it to the wooden bowl beside him and put another one into the oil using chopsticks, those wrapped in paper that Asian restaurants add to your order all the time. Surely, forks and other cutlery were in a Kondráty's possession, but only chopsticks could help to transfer frogs from the pot to the bowl keeping their little bodies intact to avoid splashing boiling oil.

Soon, frog by frog, the exotic breakfast came to life
A Kondráty sat under a birch, surrounded by a mushroom mob:
Leccinum scabrum, Amanita muscaria, of different size. He chewed
the nymphaea and thought
   of Tulubaika
      of winter soon approaching
         & whether deigned to visit him the raven.

At times, he pondered the infinite eternal
   a wee bit.

Under a towel, the frogs fried deep were cooling down. A
Kondráty frowned and raised his head up to the sun to tell the time
  — Kutkh was late.

He closed his eyes and filled his lungs with morrow chills.

Kra-a-a-a-a-a!
the raven's caw reverberated across the grove
and near a Kondráty, Kutkh emerged.

Here he is, the master of arrivals sudden
even if you're expecting him.

How have you been, my droog?

Kutkh stared at him, tilting his head, waiting.

Kra!

Good, good. Look—

A Kondráty took one crispy frog from the bowl.

This is for you.

I made it.

He hurled it to Kutkh.
In flight, the raven caught the frog, clutching it in his beak, and a second later devoured the treat.

Kra-a-a-a-a-a-a!

Is that "thank you", or "more"?

Kra-a-a!

Ah, both.

A Kondráty gave him another frog
    another
        & another.

Thus, frog by frog, consumed he everything, as if inside his stomach was a black hole or frogs were made from air.
A ravenous bird was raven Kutkh.

Kraa!

The raven bowed, wingswung, and flew away.

Again, alone a Kondráty was
— he and the boiled nymphaea.

Soon, the kinship of the vagrant and the raven reached a new, unprecedented level. The morrow followed and again there was a banknote in the raven's beak
    this time — fifty.

A few times a week a Kondráty went to the town to buy some

equipment: spirits for tinctures, empty bottles and jars, and more olive oil.

Nights he spent at the lake, naked
bringing frogs and nymphaea to the edge of extinction.

Cold were those nights, but he neglected the bridge and his human friends. Instead, those minor hours of his sleep moved to the birchgrove where in a tent made of the things abandoned, curled up in bliss, he dreamed, warmed by the smouldering fire.

At dawns, he cooked, then sat and waited
    trepidated
        each time afresh.

The raven came and brought new boons. They sat and ate keeping a stern decorum, at times chatting and bantering in the corvus lingua about the things mundane
    about the weather
        about the transience of time
            & if the world was sane
                & whether sane was
                    a Kondráty.

Once matured the concoction, matured the time for the ritual. A Kondráty knew it couldn't be the same without the umbrella, but couldn't be it even better with the raven?
    He took the jars out of the dugout and opened one of them
        — an odour of the slurry swept in the air
            — a Kondráty invited it into himself
            — the pungent smell hit his receptors
                — he twitched
            cramped his cheeks
            & every muscle in his face.

Breathing heavily, fainting almost, his consciousness fading, staggered he, crushed a few fly agarics and leaned against a birch tree, his bloodpumping system overdoing its job.

Wow!
The perfectest perfect
of perfectly perfect perfects
— now eat me
Tulubaika!

Covering his nose, a Kondráty closed the jar and hid it in his pocket from the pouch, he took out a collection of dried herbs and dumped it into the embers. The embers puffed, hissed

    farted.

A smoke ran from them, enchanting aromas usurped the grove.

A Kondráty took the runepebbles and emplaced them round the fireplace. Now everything was ready and prepared, all that was left was for Kutkh to arrive. A Kondráty assumed a waiting pose and sat not doing much

    hooked to infinity
      locked in.

Kutkh appeared just in time, landed next to a Kondráty, cutting through the brume of smouldering herbs.

Kra-a-a kra'a-kra'a!
the produced sound was like a hit against a sheet of iron.

Kra-a kra-a!
cawed a Kondráty and nodded.

Kra-a r-rakka kra!

Kra-Kra r-rakka!

A Kondráty patted the earth, invited Kutkh to join him.

Kr-r-a'a!

Kra!

Kra-kra-kra!

Kra!

Through the smoke, the raven walked and, approaching a Kondráty, raised at him the dark coals of his eyes.

Kra'a
(a Kondráty cawed and placed the concoction jar beside the bird)
Kra-aa-a!

At the jar the raven looked, at a Kondráty, shook his head, and immersed his beak into the dark slurry. He ruffled his feathers, flapped his wings and cawed
    again and again.

It was a caw of wonder
    a bustling cry
        the cry of thunder
    on a stormy day.

A Kondráty, face asmile, patted the raven, then took the jar and quaffed its content.

A vortex formed from the smoke, the birches' crowns rustled, a Kondráty's eyes turned white, backward he threw his head and then—
    utter emptiness. . .
      void of unconsciousness. . .

A Kondráty woke up, yawned, stretched, scratched his nose, and felt the absence of the ground. Startled, he unsealed his slimy eyes and realised — with no control, he was aflight
much so.

The ground was there, but far away beneath. He couldn't focus to fathom the event. Everything moved too fast as if in front of him there was a colossal spinning globe.

Someone sped up the Earth!
    Boreas, bastard!

Once vision bettered, downwards he saw Ensk with the river across it — all in one big miniature enclosed in golden endlessness.

Now, he was flying above the river. It flickered, glared, moving as fast as the town, the birchwood, the globe, yet in the opposite direction.

The river flowed in reverse
    (so it seemed)
it reflected the cloud running above.
The illusion became more optical
the optics became more illusionary.

A Kondráty saw his own shadow — a large silhouette travelling on the water surface together with him. He waved to it.

The silhouette waved back.

A Kondráty smiled. But then he saw it — the silhouette was surrounded by birds.

> ravens
>> countless in their quantity
>> orderless in their position.

Craning his neck, he lifted his head to see them. Clawing at his clothes, they carried him, some flew next to him, somersaulting, all cawed.

> Oye, there was sound!
>> Loud sound
>> deafening sound!

The raven holler reverberated, chaotic and hellish, it mixed with the swishing wind. A Kondráty screamed, cawed, wheezing and gasping for air.

> The dark eyes gleamed and stared at him.
>> (he flinched)
> The ravens grasped more firmly and pulled him farther up.
>> (he looked down)
>>> — the ground was bidding farewell.
>>>> Goodbye, Kondráty
>>>>> bon voyage! Poka!

On the ground, his diminishing shadow had enormous wings. Again, he turned his head as much as he could. Above, was gliding Kutkh. His dimensions, they were amplified, his body was as big as Kondráty's, his wingspan embraced half of the sky.

> A Kondráty blinked and rubbed his eyes.
> Kutkh's size remained the same.

Kra-a-a!

the raven cawed, flapped his wings
and overtook a Kondráty.

They traversed the town, flew above the golden birchsea. Kutkh
was leading the flock, glided beneath them, just above the trees, almost
touching their crowns, and the birchsea rippled.

Transcendental was the moment
    grandiose
    lasting for eternity
    every possibility happened —
        meaninglessness became meaningful
        meaningfulness became revelatory
        lives became inane
        emptiness became matter
        matter became incorporeal
        histories and geographies appeared and vanished
    most importantly
        Tulubaika.

Tulubaika was surfacing amidst the golden forest. Yet, at that
moment, a Kondráty's head was empty. Someone removed his brain
and left only what was supposed to be there
        the primordial void.

A thought was born there, a daring spark, an arrogant flash, an
aspiring supernova.

A Kondráty extended his arm towards Kutkh, wiggled, and gutsily
jerked ahead, unkindly the unkindness of ravens loosened their grip
    & he fell down, squeezing his eyes in fear
    & in the next moment appeared on Kutkh's back.

Kra-a-a-a-a-a-a-a-a-a-a-a-a-a-a-a-a-a-a-a-a-a-a-a-a!!!

The sky darkened
    roared the thunder
       blazed the lightning
       (or was it lightnings?)

KRA-A-A-A-A-A-A-A-A-A-A-A-A-A-A-A-A-A-A-A-A-A-A-A-A-
A-A-A-A-A-A-A-A-A-A-A-A-A-A-A-A-A-A-A-A-A-A-A-A-A-A-A-
A-A-A-A-A!

It rumbled, vibrating and ravenberating
through each bone of a Kondráty's body.

His teeth rattled, drumming at two hundred and thirty-three beats
a minute, a dark vignette started circling over his sight. His eyelids
tight aclench, Kondráty dipped his fingers into the silky plumage and
clawed, clutched spasmodically.

KRA-A-A-A-A-A-A-A-A-A-A-A-A-A-A-A-A-A-A-A-A-A-A-A-A-
A-A-A-A-A-A-A-A-A-A-A-A-A-A-A-A-A-A-A-A-A-A-A-A-A-A-A
A-A-A-A-A-A   A-A-A-A-A-A-A-A-A-A-A-A-A-A-A-A-A-A-A-A-
A-A-A-A-A-A-A-A-A-A-A-A-A-A-A-A-A-A-A-A-A-A-A-A-A-A-A-
A-A!!!

Kutkh spiralled and turned over. His corpus started changing.
    eyes bloomed on it
       copious oculars
       a trypophobic nightmare

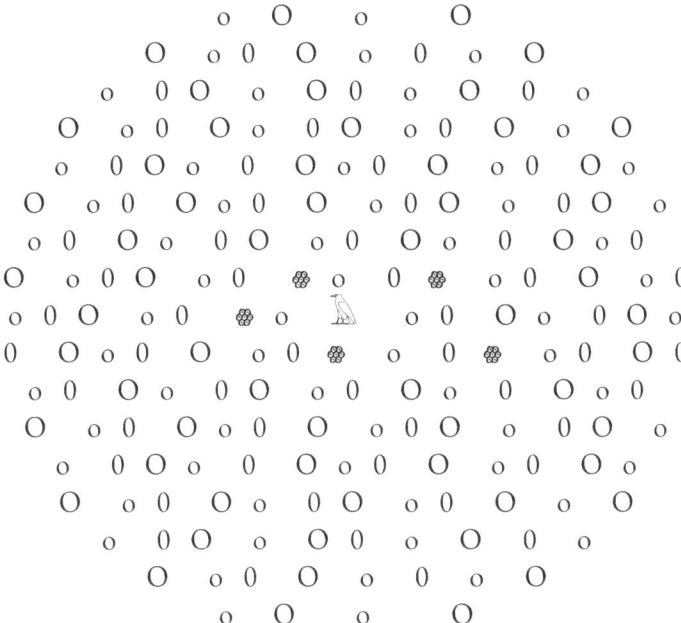

All the eyes stared into a Kondráty's soul.
He was paralysed.
    His fingers forgot how to grip.
      He collapsed into the golden sea.

The ravens hovered over him, forming a circle with multiocular
Kutkh at the centre, all of his copious eyes blinking
    all at once.

First, came the sensation of pain, the nagging physical discomfort
created by the total sum of bruises, scrapes, and sprains acquired from
hitting the birch branches he had knocked down in flight, remnants of
which were now lying around the bush whereon he landed, then, he
opened his eyes
    — leaves fell down like snow or ashes
      moving in spirals, zigzags, and loops

trunks of the birches painted a tunnel
— a black striped perspective onto a patch of clear blue sky
amidst their golden crowns.

His nostrils steamed, his mouth, too. Creeps crawled up his
corpus.
But none of it mattered.
Tulubaika welcomed him
with serenity.

⬡

In a state of oblivion, a Kondráty rested until the sun rolled into
the blue patch above, a hole in the golden crowns, closing a door
wherefrom he had fallen. The autumn sun is not cold yet bright. He
closed his eyes, and the red pictures appeared in front of him. He
squinted and relaxed, controlling the gradient, and the red pictures
assumed new unknown forms
images of Tulubaika.

Disappearing and appearing again, yet still preserving the
silhouette of the birch tunnel visible, but then the pictures started
flashing. A Kondráty opened his eyes again and saw
Kutkh in his normal eyeless form
silent and ghastly grim, the raven was graciously gliding down
in his talons, he carried something black.

Kr-r-a...
a Kondráty wheezed.

Yet no answer gave the raven.

A few more circles after, he dropped the item, swooped down and

disappeared between the birches. Kondráty tried to sit, then stand, struggling and feeling that total ache-sum, but approached the item.

It was the umbrella
      folded
      his umbrella.

He picked it up, pushed the button and the umbrella opened.
Inside, as if looking at him from the centre of the umbrella's hat, wherefrom the handle was growing
      sat Tulubaika in its rural glory.

The view was the same as the last time he saw it except it now felt different.

It was truly alive
      the whole image breathed
      moved mesmerisingly
      drifted dizzily
      bereft of its past stasis, it seemed like a portal
            a door which was revealed to him
            & which he was supposed to enter
                  by himself.

Kondráty stopped blinking and stiffened. The raven brought Tulubaika back to his knees, and now its image was more sublime than ever, opening its oculus to him.

He stared at it, inside it, beyond it, benumbed, his eyes agape.

KRA-A-A-A-A-A-A-A-A-A-A-A-A-A-A-A-A-A-A-A-A-A-A-A-A-A-A-A-A-A-A-A-A-A-A-A-A-A-A-A-A-A-A-A-A-A-A-A-A-A-A-A-A-A-A-A-A-A-A-A-A-A-A   A-A-A-A-A-A-A-A-A-A-A-A-A-A-A-A-A-A-A-A-A-A-A-A-A-A-A-A-A-A-A-A-A-A-A-A-A-A-A-A-A-A-A-A-A-A-A-A-A-A-A-A-A   A-A-A-A-A-A-A   A-A-A-A-A-A-A-

A-A-A-A-A-A-A-A-A-A-A-A-A-A-A-A-A-A-A-A-A-A-A-A-A-A-A-A-
A-A-A-A-A-A-A-A-A-A-A-A-A-A-A-A-A-A-A-A-A-A-A-A-A-A-A-A-A A-
A-A-A-A-A-A A-A-A-A-A-A-A-A-A-A-A-A-A-A-A-A-A-A-A-A-A-A-
A-A-A-A-A-A-A-A-A-A-A-A-A-A-A-A-A-A-A-A-A-A-A-A-A-A-A-A-
A-A-A-A-A-A-A-A-A-A-A-A-A-A A-A-A-A-A-A-A A-A-A-A-A-A-A-
A-A-A-A-A-A-A-A-A-A-A-A-A-A-A-A-A-A-A-A-A-A-A-A-A-A-A-A-
A-A-A-A-A-A-A-A-A-A-A-A-A-A-A-A-A-A-A-A-A-A-A-A-A-A-A-A
A-A-A-A-A-A-A A-A-A-A-A-A-A-A-A-A-A-A-A-A-A-A-A-A-A-A-A-A-
A-A-A-A-A-A-A-A-A-A-A-A-A-A-A-A-A-A-A-A-A-A-A-A-A-A-A-A-
A-A-A-A-A-A-A-A-A-A-A-A-A-A-A A-A-A-A-A-A-A A-A-A-A-A-A-
A-A-A-A-A-A-A-A-A-A-A-A-A-A-A-A-A-A-A-A-A-A-A-A-A-A-A-A-
A-A-A-A-A-A-A-A-A-A-A-A-A-A-A-A-A-A-A-A-A-A-A-A-A-A-A-A-A
A-A-A-A-A-A-A A-A-A-A-A-A-A-A-A-A-A-A-A-A-A-A-A-A-A-A-A-A-
A-A-A-A-A-A-A-A-A-A-A-A-A-A-A-A-A-A-A-A-A-A-A-A-A-A-A-A-
A-A-A-A-A-A-A-A-A-A-A-A-A-A-A A-A-A-A-A-A-A A-A-A-A-A-A-
A-A-A-A-A-A-A-A-A-A-A-A-A-A-A-A-A-A-A-A-A-A-A-A-A-A-A-A-
A-A-A-A-A-A-A-A-A-A-A-A-A-A-A-A-A-A-A-A-A-A-A-A-A-A-A-A-A
A-A-A-A-A-A-A A-A-A-A-A-A-A-A-A-A-A-A-A-A-A-A-A-A-A-A-A-
A-A-A-A-A-A-A-A-A-A-A-A-A-A-A-A-A-A-A-A-A-A-A-A-A-A-A-A-
A-A!!!

Tulubaika squealed
& snowflakes slowly drifted down.

Episode Ten
about meeting strangers in abysmal weather conditions

..."go to the right" is just as good as "go to the left," because both of these directions, in terms of our desires, point to the most distant place, the place farthest away from here...

— László Krasznahorkai, "The World Goes On"

Such a predicament, seemingly hopeless: somewhere in the back of beyond[1], night eternal, darkness unending, holodrigue[2] so fierce you could put engines on your chattering teeth and fly into space, rattling through its distant reaches, as they say. Snowfalling, too, thickly, persistently, not only can you not see ahead but behind as well — count to two and you're lost. Your legs plunge knee-deep into snow; your footprints are covered as soon as you take a step. Snowdrifts keep growing and growing, growing and growing, growing and growing — so much that before you know it, you'll start wandering amidst the fir

---

1. The original Russian idiom "у черта на куличках" literally translates as "at the chort's tussocks", referring to the remote hummocks or islets within a swamp where, according to Slavic folklore, supernatural entities, such as the chort, were believed to reside.
2. "Holodrigue" is an English approximation of the Russian colloquialism "холодрыга" (kholodryga), a term denoting a bone-chilling, teeth-chattering cold. Normally a translator could render it as "bitter frost" or "extreme coldness" but that would lose the folkloric, visceral, almost personified quality of the original word, where cold becomes not just a condition but an aggressive entity that actively assaults the human body.

tops instead of their trunks, and if such a thing happens, bojeupasi[3], and you go dizzy, there'll be nothing to grab onto, you'll topple over and freeze dead into the earth.

So, through all this wintry resplendence, two fellows trudged, knowing nothing of each other, unsuspecting, in complete unawareness, each in his own adventure, until they chanced upon an abandoned hut: without windows, without doors[4] — only a roof peeking out from beneath a snowdrift and a chimney jutting forth.

There they stood, fat and thin, very Chekhovian, shining torches in each other's mugs, squinting, silent, breathing steam, bearded, all snow-covered. The thin one wore a short sheepskin coat and a fur hat. The fat one was enrobed in a whole bearskin with the head and toothy maw — you wouldn't tell right away if it's a man or a leshák[5] standing before you. The wind whistled, the environs hummed, the birches crackled, their frozen twigs a-tapping. The fellows took turns shining their torches on the hut, nodded to each other, stoically, manly, and started digging it out, throwing snow to the sides. And dug they for a long, long time, puffing and panting, sweating up, but reached the window at last. They grabbed the shutters together, one on the left, the other on the right, somehow managed to fling them open, and climbed inside.

When the fat one was climbing in, a fiasco occurred...

— Yak-smackinn babai![6] — he bellowed.

---

3. Direct rendition of "Boje upasi" (God save [me / us / thee]) for extra Russian flavour.

4. The phrase "without windows without doors" (без окон без дверей) is the beginning of a well-known Russian folk riddle format where listeners are asked to identify an object that contains things despite lacking obvious openings (the classic solution being a cucumber filled with seeds).

5. "Leshy" (леший), or a bit more regional and derogatory "leshák" (лешак), is a woodland spirit in Slavic mythology. Often depicted as a shaggy humanoid figure who can change size at will and become as short as a blade of grass or as tall as a birch. The leshy serves as master and protector of forest animals and can lead travelers astray, causing them to wander in circles.

6. "Yak-smackinn babai" renders the Russian euphemistic expletive "ёкарный бабай" (yokarny babay). The first component, "ёкарный," is widely recognised as a deliberate phonetic distortion of a far more robust Russian obscenity beginning with the letter "ё":

— What?

— Yak-smackinn babai, I said!

— Eh?

— I'm stuck fast, mate.

— Press on, then.

— I'm telling you, I'm stuck!

— Well, draw in your belly and press on.

— Feck-n-thump![7]

The fat one exhaled with all his might. The thin one pushed against him with all his vigour. Then both of them tumbled head over heels into the hut.

The thin one fell on top of the fat one, both enveloped by darkest darkness like in the chort's betwixt-buttock regions. They gathered their wits, rose, closed the window, took out their torches again, and looked around: utterly barren hut, no soft, comfortable, gold-embroidered divans, no table with a magic tablecloth[8] laden with delicacies, no samovar[9] for a cuppa, no vodka, no hot baths, not even a looking glass. Even the stove was buried under snow. Well, at the very least, the wind wasn't wailing, the birches weren't cracking — it was

---

"ёбаный" (lit. fucked). The second element, "бабай," has multiple etymological interpretations: it derives from Tatar or other Turkic languages meaning "grandfather" or "elder"; in katorga / prison argot, it referred to moneylenders; and in Russian folklore, "бабай" serves as a bogeyman used to frighten children ("Behave well, or the babai / babaika will get you!").

7. "Feck-n-thump" renders the Russian euphemistic exclamation "Едрить-колотить" (yedrit-kolotit). The first component "едрить" is a deliberate mangling of "to fuck", while "колотить" literally means "to pound" or "to beat". "Fuck me sideways!" might be a decent alternative to express the same emotion.

8. The "magic tablecloth" is a specific artefact in Russian folklore with the supernatural ability to spontaneously serve abundant food and drink when unfolded.

9. The "samovar" (самовар) literally means "self-boiler" (from "сам" / self and "варить" / to boil), looks like a large metal kettle-like urn. Since the 18th century or so, the ritual of chai-drinking (чаепитие) around a samovar has constituted the quintessential expression of Russian conviviality, where conversations flourished for hours over endless cups of zavarka (concentrated chai) diluted with hot water from the spigot. The absence of this item from the abandoned hut says a lot: without a samovar, no proper home exists, only shelter.

completely silent — only the floorboards and the fellows' bones were creaking, and their heads were still a-ringing.

So they stood there, blinding each other with their torches, examining one another.

— Human? — asked the thin one.

— That's right, — replied the fat one.

— I'm human too.

— I can see that, mate.

Silence.

— Where are you from? — the fat one continued.

— From Tulubaika.

— Oh, I'm from Tulubaika, too!

Silence again.

— Really? — said the thin one, surprised.

— Very much really.

— And where are you headed, if I may ask?

— Well, to Tulubaika.

— Uh-huh...

The thin one took off his hat and scratched the back of his head.

— I was hoping you'd show me the way, — added the thin one.

The fat one was perplexed.

— Whither? — he inquired.

— To Tulubaika, — the thin one mumbled.

— To Tulubaika? But you're from there yourself, aren't you? — the fat one exclaimed in surprise.

— Well, so are you.

— Ha-ha! But I don't remember the way, mate. That's the thing. Do you know what I mean?

— Uh-huh... I don't remember either... — said the thin one and sighed heavily.

They stood there, frowning, spinning their tangled thoughts as if on a spindle.

— And who does remember? — asked the fat one.

— Only God knows, — answered the thin one.

— To Bumfuck-Nowhere[10], then turn left, Goddie said, — the fat one quipped.

The thin one's eye twitched, but both fellows smirked, meaningfully so, with a hint of bitterness, sighed, fell silent, looked around, took off their rucksacks, and decided to sit down.

The fat one took a thermos out and asked:

— Coffa?

— Won't say no to coffa in an hour of need.

The fat one poured the coffa into cups, inhaled a lungful of its sobering vapours, gasped with joy, sipped the beverage. Warmth spread through his body, his cheeks flushed — pure baldeige[11], in a word.

— And who might you be? — asked the fat one.

— I might be Venyamin Patrikeyich.

— Wow. Right...

— ... And yourself?

— Maximilian, or just An.

— Eh?

— Eh? An, I said.

— An?

---

10. "Хуево-кукуево" (Khuyevo-kukuyevo) is translated to "Bumfuck, Nowhere", which, despite sounding quite different, are geographically the same thing.

11. "Baldeige" renders the Russian term "балдёж" (baldyozh), which means "euphoria or ecstasy". It was first documented in dictionaries around the 1970s. The term emerged from Russian youth slang and underground / dissident culture during the Soviet era, expressing pleasure states often discouraged in official discourse. Etymologically "балдёж" derives from "балдеть" ("to be in bliss" or "to zone out"), which comes from "балда" ("blockhead" or "fool"), ultimately borrowed from Turkic languages (compare Turkish "balta" meaning "axe"). Joseph Brodsky used the term in his essay "Dedicated to the Spine" (1978) about his trip to Brazil: "The continental riff-raff get their knickers wet from this stuff, because — polemics whatever, a quote either from Feuerbach or from some other idealistic twat, grey hair and complete baldeige from the sound of his own voice and erudition". The transliterated rendition of the word attempts to preserve both the phonetic character of the original and suggest its meaning through proximity to English "indulge." The "-eige" suffix was chosen to approximate the soft Russian "ж" sound (similar to the "s" in "pleasure") while giving the term a distinctive foreign, almost French-derived, quality in English. Its closest Russian synonym is "кайф" (kaif), another borrowed pleasure-term (from Arabic) that would later become ubiquitous in post-Soviet popular culture and is still widely used by young generations (at least the translator reckons as much).

— Aye.

— And why "just An"?

— Because of my tongue-tied pops — he couldn't pronounce the letter M, old bastard, so that's what he called me, to keep it simple.

— I see...

They sat there, drank coffa, savoured the moment as their souls were covered in goosebumps and trembled with pleasure. It's always good to have a chat with a fellow human, even if it's not yet clear what manner of character is in front of you.

— Been walking long, Venyamin Patrikeyich? — asked Maximilian.

— Aye, quite a while, about ten years. And you, Maximilian?

— Oh, I don't count the years. It's not a prison after all. Ha!

Venyamin Patrikeyich frowned; a light surprise with a hint of spice appeared on his face. Well, he thought, it's a matter of perspective. There may be no walls or bars, but it doesn't seem to make one any freer.

— I'm a free man. I go where I want, — said Maximilian. — Fancy a bublik[12]?

Maximilian (whom the narrator, by the way, unlike Maximilian's dad, can call by his full name since the narrator can pronounce the letter M) pulled out a string of bubliks from his rucksack, smooth,

---

12. The "bublik" (бублик) is an Eastern Slavic ring-shaped bread roll with a distinctive large hole, a gastronomic cousin to the bagel. Unlike its denser, chewier Western relative, the bublik is traditionally larger, lighter in texture, and possesses a glossy, almost glazed exterior achieved through a brief pre-bake boiling. In Russian, they were (perhaps are) often sold strung on a cord like beads, creating a portable bread necklace that features prominently in folklore and literature. The hole itself is considered by some to be the bublik's quintessence — the absence that defines the presence — giving rise to the Russian expression "дырка от бублика" (a hole from a bublik) to describe something essentially worthless despite its promising appearance. Interestingly, this paradoxical formulation (the absence defining the presence) is close to Derrida's notion of the "absent centre" in his deconstructionist philosophy, where meaning is created through difference and absence rather than through stable presence, as well as to the Buddhist śūnyatā (emptiness), where the emptiness or void at the centre of phenomena is what gives them their meaning, or, to be honest, setting aside all those, just Chekhovian revolution in literature.

round, neat, the holes all in a row. He took one off and handed it to Venyamin Patrikeyich.

With trembling hands Venyamin Patrikeyich took the bublik, bit into it, relishing the noble dough — felt so good that tears almost welled up.

Thus they sipped hot coffa, chewed loudly, looked at each other, grinning from ear to ear, content, but with a speck of tension.

— It doesn't really matter when I left — the important thing is that I'm going back, — Venyamin Patrikeyich declared with special significance.

Maximilian looked at him, munching on a second bublik (or maybe a third, as you can't keep track of him — he's gobbling them up like a beaver), and nodded with full empathetic understanding.

— And why did you leave?

Venyamin Patrikeyich fell silent and frowned. The hot coffa made him drowsy; he felt he could fall asleep any moment. He stroked his beard wet from the melting snow, pondering, as if grinding a thought in a mill mortar.

— To seek Istina, Maximilian.

— To seek "ughstina"[13]?

That pronunciation tickled Venyamin Patrikeyich's ear, gently, like a feather.

— Istina. The very one.

— Is that the one with a capital letter or a small one?

— Listen closely, — said Venyamin Patrikeyich, raising his hands skywards, looking in the same direction (at the black ceiling, by the way), and discharged a word, — Istina.

— Oh, I see... With a capital letter then.

— The most capital of them all.

Maximilian slurped the coffa, clicked his tongue, driving the coffa liquids through all available receptors, relishing the aromatic blend.

---

13. In the original, the character deliberately mispronounces it as "Ыстина," replacing the clear "ee" sound of the initial letter with the distinctively Turkic guttural "ы" sound (which has no English equivalent, but guttural "ugh" might be close) that exists in Russian, too, unlike in other Slavic languages.

— So, did you find her, Istina?

Venyamin Patrikeyich glanced at him from under his brows.

— What do you reckon, Maximilian?

— Well, I reckon you didn't, — Maximilian replied, spreading his hands.

Venyamin Patrikeyich nodded silently and continued chewing his bublik. He consumed it in sixty-degree segments — as much as his jaws could handle — straight to the hole, turning the bublik into a horn. This bublik-eating technique seemed to appal Maximilian to the point where his eyebrows arched up in horror. "Well, well," he thought, "that's quite a soulless attitude you've got there towards the bublik, mate." And to put an end to this crime against humanity, he decided that the dialogue must absolutely be continued and his interlocutor's mouth be busy with words rather than the bublik.

— So since you didn't find it, why are you going back? You should keep going and searching further. Don't give up, they say, aye?

As planned, that distracted Venyamin Patrikeyich from munching on his bublik and he froze (not from cold, the hut was alright), falling out of time for a fraction of a second. Maximilian's question, you see, triggered in him inevitable cognitive storms, into vortices swirling. He paused for a score of seconds, winced and blinked.

— The way it happens, Maximilian... — said Venyamin Patrikeyich and inhaled, nearly coughing. — Let's say there's Tulubaika, or Tmutarakan, or the Boonies-Goonies, or, pardon my French, "Bumfuque-Nowhere"[14], places that aren't half bad, quite ordinary to the unknowing man, but that's not even important, because at first glance they simply exist and there's nothing special about them, except for themselves.

— Aye, preach.

— And so that unknowing little man is born, crying, grumbling,

---

14. A typical Russian rhetorical escalation when describing remote and supposedly bad locations. "Tmutarakan" (Тмутаракань) began as an actual historical principality in the medieval Kievan Rus' as an outpost on the Taman Peninsula but evolved to symbolise the archetypal middle-of-nowhere. "Boonies-Goonies" (Быдло-Васюки) is a folksy colloquialism for the same place, etm. Geography, folks!

discontent, starts running around the area to explore his native space and then thinks, is this really all? Right here, past the open field, by the old birch tree, is the boundary of my world? "My dear soul feels cramped in such conditions," the little man thinks. "It yearns to fly, not to sit in a cage, to soar and glide over the expanses, for I am not really a little man, but a great man, and my soul knows no bounds within the universe, for it is the universe. It must see the world, know itself, gather Istina bit by bit." Well, and since the universe has no boundaries, Istina can't be concentrated entirely in one small plot of land like Tulubaika, can it?

— Sure it can't, Patrikeyich. Logical-mathematical, that.

— And so, this great man rises in the morning, laces his lapti[15], and sets off far, far away. He wants to escape; he walks a long way across the earthly expanses to see the world and to show himself. He visits Belovodye, the Land of Chud', makes his way to Shambhala[16], walks hand in hand with someone gorgeous through a nighttime Mediterranean city, and he almost touches it, Istina, but it eludes him and is still nowhere to be found. He descends into dungeons, drinks

---

15. "Lapti" (лапти) is traditional Russian bast shoes, a type of footwear woven from strips of birch or linden bark and worn by Russian peasantry for millennia. Unlike leather boots, which signified prosperity, lapti marked their wearer as unmistakably rural and poor. The shoes lasted mere days under heavy use, giving rise to the expression "не лыком шит" (not stitched with bast), meaning someone more refined than appearances suggest.

16. Unlike the previous rhetorical sequence, this describes "good places", or rather "geographical curriculum vitae for spiritual searching." "Belovodye" (Беловодье, lit. "White-Waters") is a legendary utopian land from Russian folklore, a paradise of righteous living, abundant harvests, and religious freedom that was believed to exist somewhere beyond Russia's borders. Old Believers and religious dissidents spent centuries seeking this mythical realm in Central Asia, the Altai Mountains, and even Japan. The "Land of Chud" references the Chud' (Чудь), a mysterious ancient people in northern Russian folklore, who, rather than submit to Christian conversion or conquest, chose to bury themselves alive, descending underground where legends claim they still dwell in hidden kingdoms. "Shambhala" is a pure spiritual kingdom hidden somewhere in Inner Asia, accessible only to the morally pure and spiritually advanced Buddists. In esoteric tradition, it represents both a physical place and a state of consciousness. But what about Tulubaika? Is it a "bad" or "good" place? No one knows, though might as well!

chai with Satan, plays cards with Hades, khorovods with Mara[17], lectures demons on emotional intelligence. And meanwhile, no matter what wonder he beholds, be it the palaces of Semiramis, the Great Wall of China, the pyramids of Cheops, or the Firebird singing arias[18], there's still emptiness inside. He sleeps hugging his knees, barely reflects in the mirror in the morning, goes for walks in the park, touches the grass there, wanders, scuffing his soles, but the emptiness doesn't go away until he realises what needs to be done.

Maximilian cringed from such philosophical excesses.

— Mate, you sure went off the deep end there. Now I won't be able to sleep a wink. Therefore, I declare — we need a drink. Gotta sterilise the old noggin from these dastardly thoughts, — he said as he rummaged through his backpack for a bottle. — Fighting suicidal notions with a bit of chemistry.

— Bite your tongue, Maximilian.

— Me? You bite yours. Don't worry, though. We'll fill your emptiness right away, mate, — said Maximilian, filling the ornate shot glasses. — "Realised", he says, "what needs to be done"! Unbe-fuckin—

— To Tulubaika! Need to return to Tulubaika, Maximilian. Bojemoi! "Suic"... — Venyamin Patrikeyich said in a voice electrocuted with emotion and bit off another thirty-three degrees from the bublik. — I'm not even able to say it...

A shiver scraped across the back of Maximilian's head. He looked at Venyamin Patrikeyich, how his jaws move, creak, grind his bublik, and held out one of the shot glasses to him.

— No alcohol, Maximilian, — Venyamin Patrikeyich answered, chomping. — I've enough spirit of my own.

---

17. In Slavic folklore, Mara (or Mora) is a nocturnal spirit who sits upon sleepers' chests, bringing suffocating nightmares (a likely etymological ancestor "nightmare"). Additionally, in Buddhist tradition, Mara is the demon-tempter who assailed Siddhartha with illusions and desires on the eve of his enlightenment.

18. In Russian folklore, the "Firebird" (жар-птица) is a magical glowing bird from a faraway land whose feathers blaze with golden or silver light and whose eyes sparkle like jewels. It plays a central role in numerous Russian fairy tales where heroes undertake perilous quests to capture it or retrieve its feathers.

— Oh, come on, mate, there's barely a louse-piss worth of alcohol in there, — Maximilian laughed, showing the bottle to Venyamin Patrikeyich. — You haven't tried anything like this yet — my granny's recipe, an infusion of pine resin, moles, and the secret ingredient. Family recipe. Do you know how hard it is to get moles nowadays? I won't even mention the secret ingredient. One sip, and your ughstina will strip naked before you. The main thing is not to go blind from what you see, however. Our Tulubaika folk know their stuff. Let's knock one back, and the road might just open up before us, aye? — everything in the world is connected, after all. The Tulubaika recipe knows the way home. It's how I go. Without it — I would've been lost long ago.

Venyamin Patrikeyich looked at the bottle where pickled moles and other unknown matter floated in the murky waters, grimaced, fell silent, twisted his thought into a knot. In the end, he waved his hand at it.

— Just one, perhaps, — Venyamin Patrikeyich mumbled and took the glass. "Never drank a mole," he thought.

Maximilian cheerfully raised his drink in the air, scratched the back of his head with the other hand, and said:

— We need a toast! You go.

Venyamin Patrikeyich hesitated, inhaled-exhaled, melancholically glanced through the liquid, and spoke:

— Some things, Maximilian, are only visible from afar. We humans have very developed farsightedness. Until you step back far enough — you won't see the bigger picture.

— Well, to farsightedness!

Venyamin Patrikeyich nodded. The glasses clinked, the infusion streamed down their throats.

— Ooh, sheer baldeige. Haven't sat like this in a long time.

Maximilian sat content, his cheeks reddening, eyes shining. His drinking companion, meanwhile, grimaced, his mug all scrunched up, his hair standing on end.

— Forsooth, Maximilian... Forsooth...

Maximilian chuckled, patted Venyamin Patrikeyich on the

shoulder, took out another bublik, and began to work on it carefully, along the contour, circle by circle, without breaking it, so that the hole would remain a hole for as long as possible — the hole must be respected, it's the most important and tastiest part of the bublik, a delicacy after all. Why is it there otherwise? Meanwhile, Venyamin Patrikeyich sat, staring at the floor through the bottom of the shot glass and observed the blackness glimmering.

— And where are you coming from? — Maximilian asked him.

— From where?

— From where, yeah. Geography and whatnot.

— Ah, from the North.

— Oho, and I'm from the Souths.

Venyamin Patrikeyich, not understanding the point of the question, nodded in agreement.

— Well, here we are, met up, — Maximilian said.

No response followed.

— Our bastardous destiny brought us together, as they say, — Maximilian continued. — And do you know what that means?

— It's apparent that we're both destiny's fools, Maximilian.

— Oh, you don't understand anything, Patrikeyich. It's painfully obvious that you reaching Ughstina is like trying to get to Beijing doggy-style.

Darkness descended upon Venyamin Patrikeyich's face, and he glared maliciously at his newly acquired comrade.

— Don't be cross. Look, I'll lay out the arithmetic for you now, all neat and tidy. I was good at geographics and geometrics in school, you see, — Maximilian began enthusiastically, drawing figures in the air with his hands. — You're coming from the Norths, I'm from the Souths. We have both been going to the same place in opposite directions. And suddenly — bam! — we met. Do you know what I mean?

— I do not, Maximilian, — Venyamin Patrikeyich sighed dejectedly.

— That we're closer to our goal than ever before, of course. For

this, I think, we must drink! — Maximilian exclaimed, so loudly that even the soot from the ceiling of the hut showered down.

He reached for the glass but Venyamin Patrikeyich wouldn't give it up.

— I've had enough. Your "chemistry" isn't helping. It's only getting worse.

"Eat another bublik," Maximilian wanted to say, but stopped himself. "I'm not going to waste my precious bubliks on you, mate."

— I'm going to sleep. I'm tired. A long road lies ahead, — said Venyamin Patrikeyich, lay down, turned away, tucked his legs in.

— Aye, to hell with you then.

— Good night.

— Jolly good one, mate.

Maximilian stared at him for a minute, grinned, put the food and drinks back in his rucksack, wrapped himself in his bearskin, and carefully lay down next to Venyamin Patrikeyich, slightly embracing him (to keep the warmth, of course).

— What's this all about? — Venyamin Patrikeyich protested.

— To avoid freezing, the first camping rule, — Maximilian said and threw his arm over Venyamin Patrikeyich.

— Well, you watch yourself...

They lay, warming up, trying to fall asleep. Barely audible, the winds raged outside, whistling, inviting them to come out and be torn to pieces, tapping on the roof of the hut with birch branches — come out, wanderer, come out!

Venyamin Patrikeyich had similar hurricanes in his head, only thinkering ones, the very same that are with him day and night, from sunset to sunrise, in sleep and in wakefulness, whistling, hitting him on the head with branches (amen). In these raging reflective storms, all sorts of things happen — it throws him about so much that it sometimes makes him nauseous: along a slippery path from existentialism to nihilism, through absurdism astride a snake that eats its own tail at the speed of light to meet Istina. Until suddenly the ontological police stop him, ask him to present his documents only to find out that the speeding violator has no papers, no passport to

confirm his identity, no driver's licence, no registration for the snake. The violator scurries away into an open field and hides in the pulsating oat dunes that stretch from one horizon of the universe to the other. And the violator immediately realises that he's completely and irrevocably lost, lowers his head and the banner of all hope and wanders alone through the field until he meets the lass named Istina who starts khorovoding around him. She flashes before his eyes every few precious moments, waving her hand and immediately flying off into the distance, giggling. Red cheeks, merry eyes, all dressed in a kokoshnik, a sarafan, and with long braids[19] — unspeakable beauty, in a word. She grabs his hand, takes out a chintz hanky embroidered with neat letters, spreads it out right in front of his mug, and as soon as he starts reading — "ailulu tululu..." — she immediately — *phew!* — puts the hanky away, drops his hand, laughs, and grasshoppers away, blending in with the surrounding reality, and so on in a circle. The oat field trembles and transforms, the golden spikelets swelling, softening, until they bloom into pink orchids. Then, after the violator has already lost interest in what she has embroidered on the hanky in golden letters, Istina throws off her kokoshnik and takes off her sarafan. She rushes around the orchid garden like a madwoman and her clothes become less and less until she is left in a single translucent shirt showing "almost" everything. The orchids pulse and move unfurling their petals, then tightening, then blossoming again; the labellums pulse, too, their columns twitch from time to time; the heavy floral perfume thickens the air, their scent changing from sweet to musky as they open and close. With an unwavering gaze, spellbound and embarrassed, the violator gawks at her and then with one swift movement, she throws off her shirt too, baring her breasts and her other — rather androgynous — charms down below that, in

---

19. These items collectively represent traditional Russian feminine attire. The kokoshnik (кокошник) is a distinctive semi-circular or crescent-shaped headdress, often ornately decorated with beadwork, pearls, or embroidery, worn on special occasions and holidays. The sarafan (сарафан) is a long, sleeveless pinafore dress. Long braids were the traditional hairstyle for unmarried Russian women and girls, while married women typically covered their hair.

fact, too, bloom into a peculiar living orchid. The violator flinches at such a delicate turn of events, squeezes his eyes shut with all his might, stumbles, and almost falls. All the while, Maximilian breathed loudly right in his ear.

— What are you thinking about?

— Huh?

— What are you thinking about? I see you're dozing, can't fall asleep.

— About Istina.

— Ah, your ughstina again. Of course.

Once again, at such a pronunciation of this sacred word for Venyamin Patrikeyich, he cringed. It felt like a knife in the groin.

— Well, don't worry, — Maximilian added. — We'll crack on at dawn.

— Huh?

— Huh?

— I think I've already cracked.

— What?

— That.

— We'll crack on for your ughstina at dawn, I say.

— "At dawn". Funny. We'll be lucky if it dawns at all.

— I feel it in my gut that it will dawn.

— Sollie hasn't been seen lately, so I've already forgotten what a dawn is.

— And I'll tell you: it's like a shining orange hanging in the sky. Its beams feel warm, pleasant, and tickle the skin. In Tulubaika, it's like Philadelphia — always sunny.

— I don't remember that.

— Stir your memory then.

— Nothing to stir there. You stick your hand in — something will chop it off. Sleep now.

— Oh, you've got a good wellful of gloominess in you, mate. One can scoop it up with buckets.

— The well is deep, and one can't reach the bottom.

— Aren't you tired, mate, of digging this well deeper?

185

— . . .

— When you get to Tulubaika, take a break or something. Go to a kabak[20], drink a couple shtofs[21] of beer, and play cards. There's plenty of that stuff in Tulubaika.

— Sleep already.

— Oh well... "Sleep already..." Bo-o-ring.

Maximilian sighed and shut up at last. "Chronic philosopher," he thought. "What can you expect from him? You need a proper mademoiselle, not your ughstina."

Immediately, images of long, endless tables appeared before him, laden with victuals, drinks, wines, such as, for example, the legendary Tulubaikan Riesling, sour as samogón infused with lingonberries, cherry plums, and lemon peels but with such a pleasant aftertaste on the tongue and in the throat and a soothing sediment in the belly that if it were vinegar and not wine, it could be forgiven, yet it was wine, real wine, from real Tulubaika vineyards planted on the banks of the Tulubaika River, far from tall birches, so that the grapes would be filled with sun, would swell, and the naked Tulubaikan maidens would knead them with their angelic tender feet, pour the juices into barrels, and then bury those barrels in the ground, so that the wine would mature, absorb the spirit of the Tulubaikan land and its filigree fabric of time, and then, when the time came, they would dig up the barrels, pour the wine into bottles, cork them, and put them on the table, a long, endless table, at which all the inhabitants of Tulubaika would gather, from small to great, including, of course, Maximilian himself, and they would drink this wine, and they would eat Tulubaikan victuals: rye bread baked from flour ground in an old mill, marbled beef raised in Tulubaika, fed with beer and chestnuts and then roasted on a spit over a fire made with Tulubaikan wood, salted cucumbers and sauerkraut grown in Tulubaikan beds, apple pie made from fruits picked from Tulubaikan apple orchards, and much, much

---

20. A traditional Russian tavern or drinking establishment for the common folk dating back to the 16th century.

21. A unit of liquid measurement in Imperial Russia, equivalent to approximately 1.23 litres (or one-tenth of a vedro, if that's easier).

more. And songs would sound, old, good songs that their grandfathers and great-grandfathers used to sing, and they would dance to these songs until they dropped knackered. "That's what Tulubaika is like," Maximilian thought, "and not these bottomless wells of yours."

— Say, Patrikeyich, can you play accordion? — Maximilian asked, but there was no answer, for Venyamin Patrikeyich had already fallen into a deep sleep and was snoring like a hog (the hedge one).

. . .

In the morning, or rather by noon, it really did dawn, which surprised both of them, emboldened Maximilian, and slightly offended Venyamin Patrikeyich despite the favourable development of events. "How could this be — it dawned? Where has such a thing been seen?" The clouds, however, not paying attention to his convictions, bid their adieus and eloped far beyond the horizon; the wind died down; and Sollie, that celestial orange, peeked out, its cheeks shining, its fiery smile sparkling, and wishing them a pleasant journey. Its beams reflected off the snow and blinded the eye but didn't warm much... "Well, at least there's no blizzard, and for that, thank you," he thought.

Venyamin Patrikeyich walked, listened to the curious stories from Maximilian's hedonistic adventures and as usual looked around (you never know). Sometimes he plunged one foot into a snowdrift and wondered how Maximilian managed to walk straight and steady. He walked in front and checked the density of the snow with a long cane before stepping. Venyamin Patrikeyich followed exactly in the footsteps left by Maximilian but for some reason he often fell through, and was left staring at Maximilian's bearskin cape with its head thrown back. He didn't have a good look at it at night, but now it was in front of him the whole way. The expression on the poor bear's face was, to put it mildly, like that of an utter village idiot who was dropped headfirst on a hard floor as a child, placed under a falling brick from the sky, and had new infusions tested on him before they went to production, whether made from frogs, snakes, or moles — eyes slanted, mouth agape, bouncing with each step, a masterpiece of taxidermy, no less.

For a long while Venyamin Patrikeyich thought about his own affairs until suddenly Maximilian said this:

— And, by the way, no matter what anyone says, orgies in Tulubaika are the best, Patrikeyich.

— Huh? What?

— You probably remember, the whole village then on Solstice? It became a tradition, by the way.

— I don't recall that, — Venyamin Patrikeyich said, frowning.

— You were probably already legging it after your ughstina then and missed everything. But don't worry, I'll tell you... So, that day we uncorked a couple of barrels of wine and started lighting the festive bonfire. Everyone was merry, throwing more and more firewood into it, and our tractor driver Semyon (maybe you remember him), already sloshed to the gills by that time, dragged a canister of diesel fuel from somewhere and poured it right there — so he did, for real. Oh was it burning, mate, a real fuckinn inferno right up to the heavens so that the glow was seen in the neighbouring villages: Bultyshka, Bekarikha, even Orekhovshchina. They thought we were on fire, imagine. And well, you understand, jumping over such an attraction is chanceless. Your clothes will catch fire and you won't have to go to the crematorium no more. A real bargain for some, I must say. But most still want to have fun because you can't go against traditions, can you? Therefore, everyone decided to take off their clothes and lead khorovods and jump like that, straight through the flames, in their birthday suits, both lasses and lads, no one was shy. We ran, jumped, sang songs, laughed, shook our bodies, shone with our curves, bits and bobs, and other charms of our figures. And the figures in Tulubaika — ooh! The gene pool, as they say, is ho-ho! No Greek muse has such roundness. And Denis, the priest's son whom everyone called Dionysus, turned out to have such a hose; he should've gone into fuckinn firefighting with it.

Venyamin Patrikeyich even winced, and the image of the polymorphic Istina without clothes, with fine roundness and with orchidaceous bits and bobs flashing outwards appeared before him again. He squeezed his eyes shut, trying to evict the image from his

consciousness, but it wouldn't disappear until he pinched himself on the cheek.

— What a disgrace, — said Venyamin Patrikeyich resentfully. — You're making it up. There was no such thing.

— Oh, there was. While jumping naked through the fire everyone got sweaty and went to bathe in the river. And there... If you only knew what we did.

— You're lying.

— I swear on my tooth, the Kama Sutra was invented in Tulubaika. I'd tell you but I'm afraid you can't listen to such things, Patrikeyich — your ears would curl into tubes, or worse. Ooh, now that I remember, I get goosebumps down my spine. I've been to Europes, to Americas, to the best brothels in Thailand, you name it — I've never seen anything like it anywhere. Tulubaika is truly special.

— Come to your senses! There has never been such a thing in Tulubaika and there couldn't be. No decent person in the village would allow that bacchanalia.

— It was, it sure was.

Venyamin Patrikeyich refrained from answering.

— Denis then even joked that we should repurpose his pops' little church into a temple of Dionysus, ho-ho.

— Tulubaika is not a circus or a brothel, — Venyamin Patrikeyich grumbled.

— Tulubaika is whatever you want it to be, mate, — Maximilian parried.

Plugging his ears by sheer willpower, Venyamin Patrikeyich kept silent and tried to think of his own affairs again. He knew precisely what Tulubaika had been like and what Tulubaika awaited him and it was nothing like the way Maximilian described it. There was no garden of earthly delights, no island of the lotus-eaters, no cradle of voluptuousness, no custard shores by the river Tulubaika, and, bojeupasi, no collective fornication to speak of. The people in Tulubaika had always been kind, thoughtful, spiritual, valuing order, justice, God's law, apparently knowing something about Istina, which he, Venyamin Patrikeyich, had missed in his foolish youth when he ran

away lured by "hidden meanings" and "readings of the world between the lines". As for risqué activities — at most going to the banya[22] together, steaming, relaxing the body and spirit, but is that really a sin? Tell me, reader, is banya a sin?

— ... and I thought, — Maximilian continued, — I'll return to Tulubaika and write a book.

This cheered Venyamin Patrikeyich up and straightaway pulled him out of the trance he'd slipped into whilst trying not to listen to the unrelenting Maximilian.

— A book? You?

— "The Adventures of Maximilian Bzdynkin[23]: Baldeige and Other Meanings" in three volumes, mind you. It'll sell millions of copies, put your religious-philosophical scribbles to shame, and teach folks a thing or two about life.

— I see you've thought it all through, — said Venyamin Patrikeyich with a spasm of sarcasm. It bears mentioning that he could make any face he wanted (even to tuck his tongue out) while trudging along behind.

— You bet!

— If Tulubaika had bored you so much that you left, why are you heading back there?

— So I'll be teaching the youngsters how to live. I've gotten old now, haven't I? Entering, as they say, my sage phase. I'll sit on a tree stump in the middle of the village, handing out advice, egging on the little Tulubaikan tykes, steering them onto the right path of life.

---

22. A traditional Russian steam bathhouse, distinct from Western saunas or bathhouses. The banya typically consists of a small wooden structure with tiered wooden benches and a stone stove over which water is poured to create steam. The ritual involves alternating between intense heat sessions and cooling periods, often including aggressively torturous flogging with bundles of dried birch or oak or other branches to improve blood circulation and overall mood. Historically, the banya served multiple functions beyond hygiene (and now recreation): a place for childbirth, healing rituals, pre-wedding ceremonies, and various sorts of social bonding.
23. A surname that Russian readers would immediately recognise as comically vulgar, evoking a certain gaseous bodily function. The English equivalent might be something like "Toottleton" or "Brapson", though naturally, no proper translator would ever resort to such undignified substitutions.

— You? Old? — Venyamin Patrikeyich ironised, but thought something else to himself (he wouldn't want you to know).

— You bet, quite old. Got hangovers now and all that. Here, listen to my knees cracking.

Stopping, Maximilian lifted one leg, moved it in circular motions clockwise, and the cracking echoed through the grove.

— Indeed, — smiled Venyamin Patrikeyich.

— That's what I'm saying. But that's the least of it, mate. I've realised something else. As you said, "mankind suffers from short-sightedness".

— Far-sightedness.

— Aye, don't matter. Mankind sees poorly, needs special specs, or maybe one of them magnifying glasses, willy-nilly.

"Willy," thought Venyamin Patrikeyich, giggled, and immediately chided himself in his mind.[24] He tensed up and quickened his pace to hear better but Maximilian stopped and turned around, looking him straight in the face, which made Venyamin Patrikeyich flinch. Did he say it out loud?

— Now, Patrikeyich. Let's say there exists Baldeige with a capital B, transcendent ecstasy, if you wish. That's how I'll start the book. So you live, your stomach wants one thing, your brain — a second, your male organ — a third, and your heart — a fourth.

— You seem to have forgotten the spirit, Maximilian.

---

24. OK, here's something important: The Russian original plays on "лупа-залупа" (lupa-zalupa), wherein the "лупа" (loupe / magnifying glass) clashes with the "залупа" (glans penis, bellend). This wordplay is the basis to a whole genre of Russian jokes featuring two fictional characters, Pupa and Lupa. The joke typically follows a formula: the two embark on some mundane activity, like collecting their wages. However, given their similar names, a mix-up occurs, and Lupa receives Pupa's salary, Pupa receives Lupa's, and the resulting verbal construction ("Pupa got Lupa's" = "пупа залупа") deliberately triggers the vulgar homophone. The translator's rendering uses "willy-nilly," a phrase of Shakespearean vintage (from "will ye, nill ye"). If we were to translate the original joke, we could do it this way: "Mr Willy and Mr Nilly are at the baths. Nilly drops the soap. Bends over. Behind him: Willy." Translation theorists call this move "domestication" — reshaping source material to function within target culture norms while accepting Umberto Eco's principle that translation inevitably means saying "almost the same thing."

— Don't interrupt. I'm developing a thought here, mind you. So, I lived in Tulubaika, didn't worry, had earned my medals in hedonism, erotica, gambling and all that decadent stuff, but suddenly decided that it's all boring there with you lot — something's just not right. Not enough, not enough of everything, and I wanted more, and something new, something... something unlike all the previous stuff, do you know what I mean? Well, I thought, chort with you, I would go conquer the globe. There's still an unploughed field there in terms of Baldeige. I'll test my luck, so to speak.

— And did you? Test your luck?

— Oh, did I ever, mate... But luck, it seems, grows tired of being tested. You walk the world, but what are you looking for? No clue. The million-lucre[25] question, as they say.

— Baldeige, apparently, — Venyamin Patrikeyich quipped.

— Ha, baldeige is all well and good, but which one exactly? That's the question.

— Is there a difference which Baldeige?

— We-e-ell, don't even get me started, — Maximilian broached. — The difference is so grand that... You know, my philosophical apparatus wouldn't suffice to express it.

"No surprise there," thought Venyamin Patrikeyich.

— But tell me, does it make a difference to you which Ughstina you follow?

— Istina is one and there can be no other, — replied Venyamin Patrikeyich, pronouncing Istina with emphasis on how it should be pronounced, not how Maximilian did that again.

He stood in front of Venyamin Patrikeyich with his hands on his hips.

— Well then, describe it to me, this Ughstina of yours.

— Istina, — Venyamin Patrikeyich corrected sharply.

<hr>

25. Lucre is a fictional currency often used in the author's works. Similar to ruble (Russian currency) or any other currency but more lucrative in its name to emphasise its capitalistic nature.

— Doesn't matter, ughstina-shmufstina. What is it then? Do you know, huh?

Venyamin Patrikeyich faltered at such attacks, grew angry, like a wolf driven into a corner, and with a voice trembling from the energies seething in his body, replied:

— I think so, yes.

And Maximilian attacked:

— You think or you do?

Venyamin Patrikeyich's arterial pressure rose, thoughts began to pulsate in his brain, his head spun, images of Istina flashed before him in her most diverse guises, with all her primal trappings. He blinked loudly and said:

— I would tell you, Maximilian, but I'm afraid "your ears would curl into tubes".

— Oh, spare me. You don't know, and no one knows. Chekhov didn't know, Tolstoy didn't know — so they said to each other, famously. That's why we wander the forests, like in a fairy tale, "Go I know not whither and fetch I know not what".

— It's a personal journey. Istina can't be expressed in words. It doesn't want to be known and subjected to description. It shuns all human efforts to encase it in our foul language.

— Exactly, Patrikeyich. But Baldeige is just the same. You recall it and your cheeks and ears blaze. It's a thing you can't tell your grandkids about; to your lawyer — maybe. It is attained, like Ughstina—

— Istina! — snorted Venyamin Patrikeyich.

— ... through personal experience, — Maximilian frowned, — step by step. Somewhere you smoked hashish to oblivion, somewhere you broke a fine mahogany bed with a fine maiden, somewhere you gambled away your cat at cards, somewhere you nearly drowned in wine, almost died. But this is the way, you know. As the ancient Tulubaikans said, Ughstina is in wine.

— Romans.

— What Romans?

— It was the Romans who said that, not the Tulubaikans. In vino

veritas. And grapes never grew in Tulubaika. How could they in such latitudes?

— Your Tulubaika is wrong, Patrikeyich. Seems your wanderings haven't cured your short-sightedness, only made it worse. You're going back too soon, should've wandered more, aye? I told you, you're as far from hooking up with Ughstina as you're from blowing yourself off.

At this moment, Venyamin Patrikeyich's brain and heart became coated with a black crust resembling solidified lava. His brows furrowed, his fists clenched, his legs trembled.

— Now say "Istina", — he growled through his teeth.

— Ughstina, — Maximilian said carelessly.

— Say "Istina", say it properly, with the "I"! — insisted Venyamin Patrikeyich.

— Ughstina?

Growling, Venyamin Patrikeyich rushed at Maximilian, swinging his arms. He deftly dodged it, and the attacker fell face-first into the snow.

— Oi-eh, this is new, Patrikeyich. Set upon a mate with your fists? Over some Ughstina? Not a sacred bone in your body.

All covered in snow, his mug red, Venyamin Patrikeyich went right berserk, leapt out of the snowdrift and sank his teeth into Maximilian's leg, but missed the flesh, only biting the thick cotton-stuffed trousers. Maximilian tore free from his weak grip, laughed, and ran away through the snowdrifts up the hill between the birches, waving the degenerate squint-eyed bear-head with its protruding tongue.

— ISTINA! Say it!

— Ugh-ugh-ughstina! — he teased as he fled.

Venyamin Patrikeyich rose from the snow and ran after him.

— Freak, swine! Say ISTINA! Heathen.

— Ughstina! Ugh-sti-na! — Maximilian drawled, now and then hiding behind birches and playfully peeking out from behind them.

The hill grew steeper, the birches sparser. Maximilian with rosy cheeks bounced back and forth like a ball. Venyamin Patrikeyich with a boiled crayfish face ran after him, panting, stumbling, shouting insults and demanding he pronounce Istina correctly. His heart pounded like

a locomotive piston at full speed, steam coming from every crevice. He grabbed birches, leaned on them, pulled himself up, dragging himself Maximilianwards, snatched branches and threw them, but they never reached the target, falling into the snowdrifts.

— You fuckinn bastard, come here, you piece of dogshit! ISTINA! Say ISTINA! Come on try and fuck me up!

Merry, laughing, Maximilian would stop, wait for Venyamin Patrikeyich, then break away again. It grew harder for both to advance, the hill seemed to gain an ever greater incline as if leading them into the pure blue sky with smiling chubby-cheeked Sollie at the centre.

— And you eat bubliks wrong, by the way! — shouted Maximilian to Venyamin Patrikeyich, who now looked and sounded like an old sick mongrel with tuberculosis.

He had already lost his hat and gloves, his long black hair with streaks of grey stuck to his face, got into his eyes, clung to his beard, sweat streamed down his body, snot hung from his nose.

— You goddamn wanker. GO TO HELL, come on, idiot, I'll fuck you and your entire family up. FUCKING DOGSHIT PUTRID SLOB, you turd, bitch, bastard, COME HERE you scoundrel, scum, shitestain COME HERE, you FUCKING ARSEHOLE.

Here Maximilian discovered that the hill in front of him ended, and it ended at none other than a cliff.

He quickened his pace and, sinking into the snow, grabbing onto bushes sticking out from under the snowdrifts, he climbed upward and paid no attention to Venyamin Patrikeyich crawling behind him.

At the edge, when new horizons opened up before him, Maximilian was dumbfounded, his lower jaw dropped, his eyes rounded, his ecstatic heart shook even faster, exhilarated. There, among the forests, lost in the snow-covered valley and shining brighter than Sollie itself, it sprawled — Tulubaika.

Wooden mansions several storeys high, adorned with filigree carving, were wrapped in soft white coats and towered over the streets. Their pointed roofs in colourful patterns were sprinkled with snow as if with powdered sugar. Above the porches with twisted columns, stove pipes smoked merrily. Among the mansions, on the main square,

the golden domes of churches proudly gleamed. Their crosses, crowned with bullfinches, reached into the frosty blue sky. The chime of bells floated over environs merging with the festive hubbub and the inviting cries of merchants. Along the streets strolled festively dressed folk. Pretty lasses in downy shawls and embroidered kaftans[26] walked. Daring lads raced on swift horses, whipping up snow-dust whirlwinds. Children squealed as they slid down icy hills and threw snowballs. Under the hunchbacked bridges, decorated with icy lace, the Tulubaika River ran, fast and never freezing. And on the shore, sprawling freely, the fair was abuzz. In the painted tents, samovars smoked, plump kettles sparkled, and bundles of bubliks hung.

Intoxicated by the fairy-tale vistas, Maximilian went completely limp and lost his vigilance. There it was, right in front of him — Tulubaika itself. He turned around to share what he had found, but right then snarling Venyamin Patrikeyich appeared and charged at him. Before Maximilian could say a word, both of them somersaulted down from the cliff cuddled up and screaming.

Right in the middle of the way, crisp breeze Boreas (bastard) caught the wanderers and carried them to Tulubaika.

---

26. The "kaftan" (кафтан) is a traditional Eastern European and Central Asian outer garment that dates back to at least the 13th century. It's an ankle or knee-length coat that typically features a fitted upper body that flares gently from the waist, long sleeves, and front fastening with buttons, loops, or decorative clasps. Basic kaftans served as practical everyday wear for ordinary people, but elaborate versions with rich embroidery, fur trim, and precious metal adornments became status symbols among Russian nobility and royalty from the 15th to 18th centuries.

Episode Eleven
about abysmal weather conditions, bewildering wilderness & strong spirits

---

To know oneself, a bloke must first know Baldeige. For it is in the state of Trü Baldeige that everything authentically human comes out, and the bloke becomes himself, a block of blokeness, a Platonic ideal of blokehood.

— Maximilian Bzdynkin, "The Adventures of
Maximilian Bzdynkin: Baldeige and Other
Meanings"

They say a snowy day is only bad if you run out of liquor.

Well, here I am — through whistling gusts of horizontal snow, I trudge seeking my path to Tulubaika, alone in pathless drifts, a dark abandoned desert, a gaping wide abyssal maw prepared to swallow me alive.

Around: a treacherous terrain, no trees, no light, no living soul, just me and holodrigue, a lone man against a fierce and eerie storm of countless scalding tiny blades, biting my face, my eyes, my spirit.

The Inuit have over fifty names for snow, but one's enough for me, that one is "Death". It's omnipresent, omnipotent, omnipiercing. It sneaks under the flaps of my ushanka[1] loosely tied under my chin,

---

1. Ushanka (from ushi, "ears") is a winter fur hat with ear flaps, also known as "embodiment of Russianness in Western film often purchased ironically at markets by people who will never experience −30°C". The position of the flaps encodes the wearer's entire philosophy and political / ideological background: up (optimist, tourist, or cop),

behind my scruff, behind my gloves into my sleeves. It sears my skin, making me quiver, wring, and hunch. I cannot breathe, I cannot see, my nose and eyes are plastered, sealed by the crusts of ice and frozen snot. I stagger struggling to set feet, my steps get bogged and buried in the quicksnow mire. Imbued with shallow hope, I fall and rise, an icebreaker, the ark of warmth tossed by Boreas to and fro that bastard.

He swirls around and pulls the strings: my puppet leg is up and right, my arm curls left and down, and clings to nothing: no balance, no support, a rope-walking without a rope, no path, only the destination.

In dread delirium, my thoughts appear and flounder, they're blizzard-sifted, torn asunder, sore, ineluctable, protean. They swarm within and join the frost in biting me, now, inwardly, for no one holds the arrière-garde of mind, no one has kept the Bedlam locked, I ponder and digress to questioning the purpose of my mission — the Grand Imperative.

It always starts and ends with one inquiry to deep archives of self: who the hell am I amidst this bloody storm? A victim of my own bravado, a single-player suicide squad versus the force of nature, a nameless silhouette, incognito, invisibilis, ergo sum, a saviour of the evening, a hero with the short straw as a sword, awaited by his comrades haunted by the booze withdrawal; a champion who soon will bring those thirsty bastards liquid fire.

In order not to feel time's horrid fardel, always get drunk. C'est l'unique question... alas, I'm sobering up, perhaps too soon.

I'm crumbling. The spirits have started the exodus — they are leaving my body, and I sense how they hover. All huddled up, fixing my earflaps, I turn around, my back facing the wind. No, not to step back, not to retreat — I can't. Instead, I force my tingling, trembling hand — still gloved, of course, I'm not a fool — to draw a square metal flask out from my bosom. I ring my thumb and index finger around the vial's neck — with or without a cause, I fear my lips will stick and

---

down and tied (realist), down and untied (yolo-man, or disco cop, Harry Du Bois in a Revolutionary's Hat).

freeze to it. Imagine, in the spring, the snow will melt, and I, a giant rotten snowdrop, will surface. Someone will find the wretched corpse with a flask protruding from its mouth. Finita la commedia!

I shut my eyes, I drink, with love and passion, measuring gulp-by-gulp evasive time, until the flask is empty.

Keeping that kindling kiss, I start to feel her flaming lips and taste her tongue on mine. They intertwine and clash in a maelstrom of herbs led by the sacred trio: anise, grand wormwood, fennel. She scorches my throat, ignites my guts, and louches my thoughts. Oh, my fée verte! My MDMA-demoiselle! Since our last kiss — how much? — the aeons passed, and while my hours were slowly drawn, I managed to forget your tender voice and holy features of your face. But time has come, my soul's awake, the spirit inside my stomach has warmed the spirit inside my heart, and now it pulsates in rapture.

— I plead, I'm ready!

But nothing happens.

The merciless wind and snow soar, roar and scream at me. I feel her eau de vie flowing like lava through my veins, yet nothing happens.

I sniff one long escaping snot and wipe my nostrils. Boreas still slices the night in thin and tattered layers. I see them, one by one, they're all alike: dark, stygian blue, no end and no beginning.

I scream:

— Reveal yourself!

My voice is hoarse, my throat is burnt. I cough.

And then... Benumbed, I hear her whisper: supreme, sublime, subduing, soothing, and instantly, it strikes me that it wasn't le baiser français, an act of love and passion, but one of domination, her over me.

203

She says,

           — Shut...

       Your...

    Eyes...

  And...

  See-ee-e

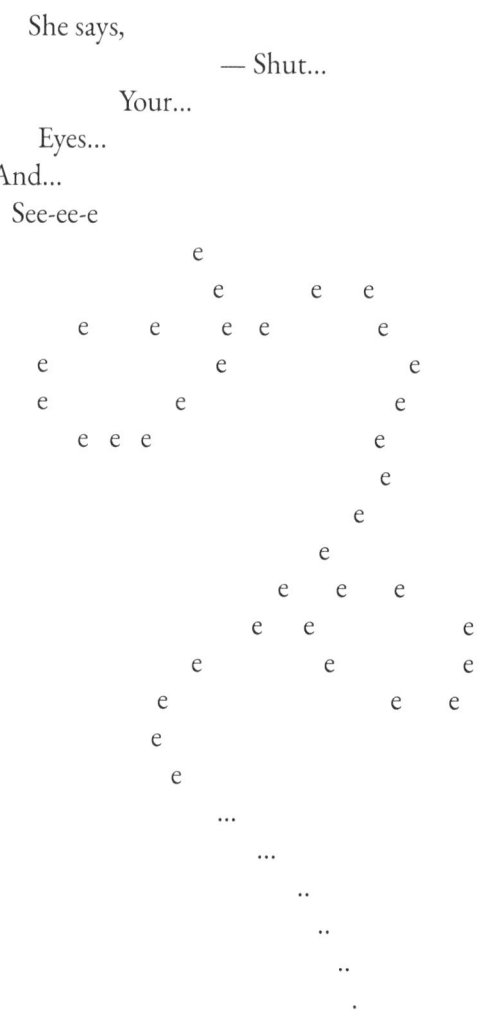

The "ee" merges with the wind and creeps into my head. It echoes, resonates, and fades away. Soaked in her veil, I desperately lick the flask — no fear, no doubt — I obey. Throwing away the empty flask, I close my eyes, reverse, and face the wind again.

Still nothing, though. Mais non, la fée, il n'y a rien. That dark and whistling void evokes despair, and I, bewitched and fooled, fall on my knees.

And suddenly, from all around, I hear "Flight of the Bumblebee". At a frantic pace, it orchestrates with howling gusts of air and shrills a swirling motif of chaotic fluttering strings, cascading in chromatic scales. My eyes, I dare to open them and see it all for what it is, united and disassociated. The flying streams of snow near me perform their shape-rich lacework: curls, threads, flowers, lines, and castles in the sky. Whereafter, she appears to me. A ghost! A fleeting apparition! A genius of the purest grace! Behind the clumps of snow, upwards, I see her glowing dress, its pinkteal hem stretched all along the firmament, now and then flashing an orchid in the folds. Alas, veiled by snow, Istina is faintly visible.

Amidst the symphony of wind and violins, her voice plays out again.

— That weakness of yours you have to accept—

— I will, my Circe, — I say, impatient as a randy adolescent.

Echoing in my skull, she keeps her speech, which makes me feel ashamed of interrupting:

— ... and kneel before the opulence surrounding you. Foremost, adopt one maxim — that

        petty

            hope of

               yours

                  is...

      .   *   an il

   .   lu

 .   —What?!   .   .   si

 .   .   .   on

      .   .   .   .

        .   .

       .   .

        . .

— Your friends are weak...

— YES!

— You are weak...

— NO!

Giggles drift off into the distance and dissolve in the orchestra.

I palm my face, defending it from the searing snow, try to shake off my other limbs and, step by step, move forwards.

— On a voyage a wanderer went,
for a magical elixir seeking,
but he found all the same
just as every soul before him...

— Is this a riddle?!

— Death...

— Oh, fuck!

I smash the snow surrounding me.

A cascade of her giggles enriches the music with an eerie staccato.

— You're seeking a path to the place you don't want to reach...

— This doesn't make any sense!

— How bewildering
      the wilderness is...
          But for one
            it is magical bliss

He must have
    to adopt and obey,
        Only then it will show him
      the way
          ay

Boreas rages.   *ay*
The darkness thickens. *ay*
The snowflakes get *way*   sharper.
It starts blowing *ayw*   from all
directions, *ya* whirling around.
      yay The endless green
    y   puddle crawls above in
the sk*y,y*ielding
      ind*y*go and
      va*y*let.
    y

— You're not helping!

I fall on my left knee. Boreas blows off my ushanka. Bastard! It is still held tied around my neck, suffocating me. I try to remove it or put it back on my head, but once I loosen the knot, it flies away into the darkness, getting lost somewhere in between the night's layers. I spit in its wake and keep moving. Now I can better hear her voice — together with the wind, they scald my ears. I cover and shut them with my hands.

— The emptiness, your mind is lost in it.
Adopt the fear, it shines and glistens,
Get rid of your excessive grit,
And
  listen,
    listen
      listen.   isn
        listen   isten   isn
          isten   n
                     n
                  n
              n
           n
         n
          .
       .
    .

In the midst of the tempest, leftwards, I see the door of my perception between two yellow windows. The neon "DRINKS" sign dimly glows above it, beckoning. As I move towards it, the snowdrifts around become harder and shallower. My foot falls through the icy crust and millions of freezing grains shovel down into my valenok[2]. I fall, and try to crawl towards the sign on all fours.

— Fear can only show you the door... but you have to walk through by yourself...

---

2. Valenok, and plural valenki, is felted wool footwear traditionally worn in Russian winters. Aggressively non-waterproof.

— Shut up!

— From madness, you are one step away...

— I'm crawling, you bitch!

— Make it...

— Shut the fuck up!

Stammering and slipping, I rise and run to the shop's door.

The bell above me rings. Wobbling like a float, I, my black coat, all my clothes and hair icecrusted, snowdusted, invade a peaceful warm interior of the shop and sprinkle the doorstep with snow, generously. Another demon has escaped the underworld.

Quiet pop music is playing in the background. No witches, no bumblebees. Bright light. I squint. The shop lady stares at me. Why is she terrified? Blinking, I take my hair out of my face, turn my head and fro, and with my reddened eyes spot liquor shelves. Snowing the floor further, I reach them, looking for a suitable drink, running my quivering fingers over the bottles.

Go I know not whither and fetch I know not what, mate. Oh, fuck you guys!

45% ABV...

50%...

22%...   No...

56%

60%

better, but—

"TULUBAIKA" — ARTISANAL SAMOGÓN

74%!   Yes!   Yes!   YES!

I carry a bunch of funfériques[3] to the shop lady. I smile. She does, too, tensely. I empty my wallet, thank the lady, shove the funfériques in my pockets, and leave.

Before me: a treacherous terrain, no trees, no light, no living soul, no warm ushanka, a lot of samogón, and holodrigue.

So mote it be.

The Grand Imperative has always been and is, no matter what, never lower the strength of your spirit.

---

3. Anglicised-through-French rendition of "фунфырик" (funfyrik), a drunkards' slang term for a small bottle of alcohol. Possibly from German fünfzig (fifty), possibly not. See also: a funférier (фунфурье) — a sommelier for funfériques.

Episode Twelve
about meeting strange cats in birch groves

In these wanderings of ours, more often than not, you look for one thing and find another.

— Miguel de Cervantes, "Don Quixote"

Wunst in a birch grove, I chanced upon a cat. It was autumn — everything golden, t'air heavy with t'scent of fallen leaves and mouldy dampness. Not a livinn soul 'round — just me trugginn along in me boots and cardigan, with a basket in hand for mushrooms. I've always been a mushroom picker, still am. I'm proper fond of mushrooms: porcini, birch boletes, honey fungus, and all sorts, *coughs* even t'cheeky lil'fly agarics. They're rather soothinn, tha knows. But not a word to Marfa — she'd boot me out if she knew. So there tha are, strollinn through t'woods, bendinn over, and suddenly, there's a mushroom. Quick as a flash, tha whips it out with thy knife and pops it in t'basket. Here's t'thing, though — 'tis crucial to leave t'mycelium untouched, else next year, tha'll come back and find nowt at all. Where would that leave me? Clanginn shots with Petrovich? Marfa would boot me out for sure then. I love a wander in t'woods, 'tis calminn, like t'mushrooms. Tha strolls along at thy own pace, breathinn in all sorts of scents, scratchinn thy beard, listeninn to t'birds — in summer, mainly, 'cause come autumn, they all flit off south, away from all this beauty! Not hearinn a cuckoo these days either, not a peep, and as for 'em fly agarics, no need to boil 'em up, just don't overdo it. I knew this chap, oh what poor soul he was, had t'golden touch he did, only tractor driver in t'village back then. See, in t'old days, every village had

211

a znakhar[1] or a volkhv, a healer of sorts or some wise man or a woman, thus would wander that volkhv into t'woods, gather all sorts: various mushrooms, poisonous berries, different kinds of bark, a sack of pinecones, bits of grass, leaves, even tap some birch sap, then come back to t'village, process all that, brew up summat, have a swig himself, and then dish it out to folks in just t'right amounts, dependinn on what ailed 'em — be it liver troubles, stomach pains, a sore throat, kidney or heart issues, or sometimes, even matters of t'soul. See, t'soul aches, especially when tha's an old-timer like meself. So there tha is, walkinn among t'birches, leaves above and below shimmerinn like gold; tha's ponderinn life, t'past, lost in nostalghia, a bit of regret, always with a smile, mind thee, but where would tha be without a bit of magic potion — and that's where 'em fly agarics come in, right in that department. Me granddad used to tell me that t'volkhv, see, t'volkhv'd always scoff down those fly agarics for his own self, never let another soul touch 'em, for he took t'brunt, as they say, for that were his part to play, then he'd process that mushroom mash in his belly, toddle off to take a wee, and pour t'potion into bottles, but now, what? Volkhvs are scarce as hen's teeth, and 'tis all down to oneself to take t'hit, but mind thee, don't overdo it, or tha'll be pushinn up daisies... but get it just right, and tha'll see life clear as day, t'whole shebang: past, present, future — all un and t'same, like me Marfushka would say — thy chakra opens up... See, she's daft 'bout all that Eastern malarkey, talks 'bout wantinn to be reborn as a bloom, a lil'pink orchid, and why not, right, no point in her rottinn in t'ground with me; better to be a flower, I reckon. That summer, we had rain aplenty, t'air was thick with damp, and come September-October, mushrooms sprouted like nobody's business, everywhere tha turned, trippinn over them, couldn't escape — like t'Germans surroundinn Leningrad. I lugged 'round up to two or three baskets a day, I could've carried another, but me legs won't carry me any more. Marfa pickled eleven jars of honey fungus, seven of chanterelles, eight of porcini, and

---

1. A term derived from the Slavic root "znati" (to know), possibly meaning "the one who knows". This is a name for a village folk healer in the pagan tradition.

blimey, I can't even remember all of it, dried a sackful, sent three parcels to Kolya and Nastya, our son and his wife, oh, and how many we've gobbled up, in stews with spuds, fried up nicely, for mushrooms, see, they're whatever tha fancies, like meat but without runninn 'round, and no brains, though some say they do, like I saw a programme on t'telly, and they were sayinn, mushrooms have this underground thinkinn network, chattinn away like on thy internets — proper magic, they are, like summat from another planet, but folk these days, they aren't bothered, nobody goes mushroominn except me, 'tis like goinn to work, I get up in t'morninn, have a cuppa with me Marfa, nibble on a biscuit, throw on me cardigan, cap on head, boots on feet, basket in hand, and off I toddle, ponderinn life, reminiscinn 'bout t'old days, lost in nostalghia, sometimes even humminn a tune, nibblinn on a dried mushroom, rustlinn leaves with t'wind, it — above in t'tree tops, and me, well, me down below; 'tis ever so nice, stops t'itch in thy soul — nowt much needed for an old pensioner like meself. So here I am, traipsinn through again, me boots scrapinn against t'leaves, and lo and behold — there's fur, as sure as eggs is eggs! And straight away methinks, 'tis gotta be a bear, or some stray dog — there's loads of 'em roaminn 'bout these days, they're puttinn 'em down, nowt to be done 'bout it, poor old Petrovich got bitten wunst, spent half a year on jabs, he did, but he's alright now, limps a bit, but still gets 'bout, though, more often than not, he's just sittinn there, clinkinn his glass against a bottle, what else is there for t'poor sod to do, he's not fond of mushroominn, and doesn't seem too fond of me either. I gets closer to this birch tree, and in its burrs (that's what I call 'em, knotty parts), there's clumps of fur stickinn out every which way, not just any clumps, mind thee, but proper tufts, ten, mayhap twenty centimetres, spread out like rays from a bulb, all soft and fluffy, definitely not people's hair. So I picked up a tuft of fur, and tried to remember all t'ginger critters I knew, but me old brain ain't what it used to be, just like me legs, and when they do work, they don't work right, so I could only think of a fox, but t'fur weren't fox-like, too soft and fluffy, and too long, thus methinks, mayhap 'tis some woodland spirit, a leshy, or a flaminn red bear, though there's no such

thing as red bears, but then I sees it — tracks, t'leaves all flattened, and a couple of metres away in t'muck, a cat's paw print, as big as a car tyre, I knew it for sure, cat's paws, I love cats, I can spot 'em a mile off — our cat, Yevsey, Yevseyka, black as pitch, like a demon from t'depths, found him by t'river un night, barely saw him, heard summat squealinn, turns out it were Yevseyka; he lived with us for a good ten years, till he passed away two years back — missed him, I did. Well, methinks, this is it — a tiger's on t'loose, though where in blazes would a tiger come from 'round here — we're not by t'Amur nor in India, are we? But then methinks, mayhap a lynx, but then again, t'paws seemed too big for a lynx, a lynx is more like a kitty cat, just a bit bigger, like a doggy, but these were proper huge paw prints. So off I went followinn t'tracks, what else were there to do in such a situation, a gigantic cat in t'birch woods, I had to go and see, didn't I? Wanderinn t'woods every day for nowt? Marfa would've said I'm actinn like a bairn, I swear, like a wee lad, old geezer like me fancyinn meself a young'un, but I'm an old man, a pensioner, everything's interestinn again, with time on me hands — loads of it, strollinn 'round, readinn books, watchinn t'telly now and then, ponderinn life and Istina, sometimes gettinn a bit nostalghic — all as un does. So I poked at t'cat-like print again with me stick — I were usinn a cane by then, see, 'tis handier if tha gets a bit dizzy and there's no birch tree nearby — to make darn sure I weren't seeinn things, and off I went, followinn un print and then another, every couple of metres, some just pressed leaves, others indentations in t'soil, and in some even water had collected, it had rained that night, had pelted down hail as big as peas, they were still lyinn 'round, though most had melted away by then. Walkinn I were, either through a tunnel or a labyrinth, I'd bet me head on it — 'tis El Dorado, no less, all aglow with gold, nowt but birches, like rafters, juttinn out from t'golden floor, proppinn up a golden ceilinn overhead, 'round me, a flurry of leaves, zigzagginn down as if they've lost their way in t'air and can't figure where to land; then, a cool draft catches me unawares, and I'm slapped in t'face with leaves — take that! Methinks, a leafy blizzard, if ever there were un — as long as I've been 'round, I've never seen owt like it, then t'wind gusts again, peltinn me old mug with

leaves, I grew tired of squintinn, and those golden birch leaves, they find their way down me neck, cling to me beard, and sneak into me sleeves — a proper tempest of leaves, no doubt 'bout it, just me luck, methinks, hope it doesn't rain, left me umbrella at home, didn't hear owt 'bout rain forecast on t'telly that morninn, didn't see t'point in lugginn it 'round for nowt. T'wind seemed to die down, and I cleared me eyes to see — a cat's tail, right in front of me, mayhap twenty or thirty metres off, swishinn through t'forest, clearly a cat's, what other beast flicks its tail like that, but this tail's huge, like a shaggy boa, reminded me of those Chinese dragons, fiery red, golden, melded right into t'autumn splendour 'round me, had it not been for t'birches, I might not have spotted it at all, as it stood out well against them, coilinn 'round them, t'sneaky un, a Chinese dragon no less. Alright, I picked up t'pace, I did, walkinn, almost runninn, me knees creakinn like that old wooden horse I carved for our lad, Kolya, he's probably forgotten 'bout it, but 'tis still standinn in our house, where else would it be? Would I have thrown it out? Mayhap, but Marfa, she won't let me, says 'tis a memory, and I don't argue with her, if that wooden horse warms her soul, then it warms mine too. We've become almost un beinn over these fifty-odd years, I'm not even sure how much of me is Marfa and how much is still meself, but, tha knows, 'tis better that way — makes for a richer inner life, left alone, I'd be like Petrovich, half man, half samogón, but Marfa, she's a sight better than any samogón. So, there I were, chasinn after this enormous cat, feelinn like a proper Apollo, no less, thought I'd found me second wind, I were so keen to see this beast, when else in life would tha get such a chance, then, t'cat just stopped, and I nearly jumped out of me skin, dropped me basket, tossed me cane aside, and leaned against a nearby birch tree, nearly had a heart attack, I did, me heart poundinn like a steam engine's piston — wouldn't be surprised if smoke started cominn out me ears. There she stood, this ginger cat, huge, beg pardon for sayinn, fuckin' huge, I can't describe it any other way, greenish eyes bulginn, silent, whiskers twitchinn, fur standinn on end, and me, I calmed down a bit, straightened up, took off me hat, tha knows, to greet her properly, held it to me heart and gave a lil'wave, but me hand were all

bloody, must've scraped it on t'birch when I got a fright, so, I tucked me hand in me pocket, stood there in silence, catchinn me breath, me throat raspy, chest buzzed a carnival, and then, would tha believe it, t'cat up and spoke to me in a human voice:

— No mushrooms 'round here, old chap, nothing to be found in these parts.

— How's that? — says I, scratchinn me noggin.

— Just like that, none to be found, not a single one, — says t'cat, flickinn her tail. — You can search high and low, but you'll find nothing.

— But there were some for sure, plenty of 'em, — says I. — A golden autumn and all. Mushroom season, mind thee, cat.

— That may be, but you're a goner, old chap, — says t'cat, narrowinn her eyes. — You'll not be taking any more mushrooms back to Tulubaika.

Well, methinks, that's it then. What's this 'bout, a goner? I scratched me head, pondered a bit, but nowt sprang to mind. I'm no chatterbox, mind thee, prefer listeninn over yappinn, like to soak in thoughts, tha knows, and t'cat, silent as a shadow, peers at me with those eyes green and bright as I know not what, as if I'm on stage under t'spotlight.

So, in a fit of foolishness, I ask:

— Can tha meow, then? Like a proper cat?

— I can, yes, — says she, lickinn her whiskers.

— Go on then, give us a meow, will tha? Let's hear thy voice.

T'cat gazes at me silent — a long, ponderinn look — then lets out a meow, modest, but precise, very cat-like, then off she trots into t'forest, rubbinn 'gainst t'birches, hugginn 'em with her tail, leavinn her fur, rustlinn t'leaves, and suddenly, she starts purrinn like a tractor, I swear, just like a tractor, so it felt like t'whole forest trembled from it, and me? Me what? I just shrugged and followed her. Nowt else to do, were there?

Episode Thirteen
about buying strange cats from drunkards

Perfect nonsense goes on in the world. Sometimes there is no plausibility at all.

— Nikolai Gogol, "The Nose"

— Well, I was sittinn there, lookinn out t'window as I do, and along comes Leo, that rotten scoundrel, holdinn a kitten in his arms, and says (Leo, not t'kitten), "Fancy buyinn a pet, Baba Nüra?"

— And thee?

— And I, why in blazes would I need a cat? I tells him. Who's gonna feed it? I spend me days sittinn by t'window, me legs ain't what they used to be, tha knows that, but sittinn there, openinn t'window, watchinn t'world go by, feelinn t'wind on me face, t'sun dazzlinn me eyes, t'heat bakinn me, summer flyinn by, I take off me headscarf, let me hair down — long hair, mind thee, grey but long — put on me dark glasses, and there I am, sittinn like I'm at a bloody resort, but no need to shake on a bus or a train, just open t'window and breathe in nature. Once, me granddaughter even snapped a photo of me like that, cheeky thinn. "Tha should be a model, Grandma, tha's a spittinn image of un, a diva," so she says, aye, she does, but I'm an old lady now, I know I am, as far from a model as to Beijing doggy-style, but still, it cheered me up, she's a clever lass, top of her class, a real beauty, just wish she'd visit more often than wunst a year as those ungrateful children brinn her to see me, if she was older, she'd come on her own and take more pictures. I do love those photos — when else will tha see thyself lookinn like a bloody Aphrodite? But thee, thee won't see that

217

photo, tha hasn't earned a peek at me beauty yet, thee old rag, half-blind as tha is, tha'd probably go stone blind, or hex me, for sure.

— Eh, what art tha natterinn on 'bout, Nüra? Hexinn? Thee? Tha could hex anyone thyself, if tha blinked.

— I do, unlike thee, thee sly old witch, go to church, I do. Light me candles, pray to t'Father, and t'Son, and t'Holy Spirit, and a whole host of other good folk.

— Well, I go to church, too.

— I've never clapped eyes on thee there, thee saggy old sow, not even wunst.

— Mayhap we go on different days. Goddie sees everythinn, Nellie, even thy foul gob.

— I'm only teasinn, lovingly, thee daft lass.

— Well, what 'bout our Leo then?

— So, he comes to me, with a kitten, mind thee, and says, "Would tha fancy buyinn a kitten, Baba Nüra? Prices are fair and square, right fittinn for thy pensioner's purse." Cheeky sod, he's never even seen me purse, 'tis got a black hole in it big enough to fall through, especially since t'pension they pay nowadays is barely owt, as tha knows. Factually, I went to t'post office wunst, to collect me pension (back when me legs still worked a bit), and there's that scrawny cow Lena sittinn there, tha knows her, Tonya t'Fanny-for-sale's daughter, and, well, she's got five nippers now, a spittinn image of her mother, poppinn 'em out like a breedinn sow, bojeupasi, and she tells me, "There's no pension yet, Baba Nüra, they haven't brought t'cash," and I says to her, plain as day, "What am I supposed to eat then, thee daft halfwit?" and she just shrinks into her chair, all deflated like, and says, "Tha could try beinn less rude, Baba Nüra. I know all 'bout thy temper, but tha's out of line now."

— She said that straight to thy face? And what didst tha do?

— I told her, "I'm only teasinn, lovingly, thee daft lass."

— Go on, what did she say?

— She says, "I don't need love like thine, Baba Nüra, I've got plenty of me own, so tha can shove it up thy arse, and deep."

— Well, I never...

218

— I thought, that's it, end of t'line, t'youth these days are totally out of hand, no shame, no conscience, no compassion, no respect for t'older generation, for in our time, remember, after a fifty-hour work day, we'd just sit by t'window, prayinn for our fiancé to return from war, prayinn for t'oats to grow and t'bugs not to eat our spuds, and then, instead of a fiancé, remember that time, a tank rolled up? Remember what I did with it?

— 'Tis a story for t'ages, Nüra, love. How could un forget?

— A wee reminder won't hurt, though. I'm sittinn by t'window, and here comes this tank. I step outside, grab its barrel, and tie it into a knot. Out of t'tank, these bloody Germans start crawlinn in droves, babblinn in their language, some gibberish. I just show 'em me proletariat woman fist, give 'em a look fierce as an Amazon warrior, and they, scared witless, shite their black trousers and scurry back into their tank, off they go — phew!

— That, I remember. Now, what 'bout Leo?

— So, I told him straight, I've got no money. Nil, as much as our dear footballers score.

— And what did he say?

— Nowt much. "I know tha has it, Baba Nüra, tha's trickinn me, tha's just got thy pension, I'm not a fool," he says. So, methinks, he won't leave it be, that drunken twat, and I decide to appeal to his conscience. "Why ain't tha in t'army, Leo, don't tha love thy country?" But he straightens his crooked back, all proud, and says, "I'm a writer, Baba Nüra, what's a scribbler like me to do in t'army?" I'm starinn out t'window at him, in me black glasses, grey hair nearly touchinn t'ground, like a siren, or a mermaid, a diva, in a word, and I say, "What kind of writer art tha, Leo? In our time, what were writers? War heroes. What did they write 'bout? T'hardships at t'front, 'bout legs blown off, 'bout our Glorious Army's victories over t'enemy, 'bout heroic deeds, 'bout Goddie, 'bout feelinns, 'bout love, and 'bout how our women could stop a tank in its tracks and tie its bloody barrel into a knot, and what will Leo, our in-house alcoholic, write 'bout? How jolly it looks at t'bottom of a bottle and at t'bottom of our society? Sees he's a Leo

and fancies himself a Tolstoy. Oh, by t'by, just this winter, I was runninn to t'shop, so—

— Eh, thee? Runninn? Don't kid thyself, Nüra. A runner, are we? Where dost tha think tha's off to, thee old cow?

— I am runninn, I am, legs movinn like a young lass, tha'd chop-chop thy legs faster with that frost like that, not even me old bear coat, left over from me granddad before they set him off on a raft down t'river, does any good, nor t'knitted fur scarves, nowt at all, so there's nowt for it but to grit me teeth and run.

— And where'd tha get 'em teeth from? Tell me that story, too, Nüra, please do, deign me.

— From a bloody unicorn, they grew in. Eat right, not like scrabblinn in horse dung, and tha'll grow 'em too, thee raggedy mop.

— So there tha is, runninn along, and what happens next?

— Well, next I see Leo, standinn there, t'writer, pullinn out his "pen", and he's peeinn on a snowdrift, but he's not just peeinn, he's writinn, letter by letter, like some Tolstoy'd really come crashinn down on us.

— And what didst tha do?

— I shouted at him. "What art tha doinn, peeinn here, thee bastard, got no shame nor conscience, thee sewer rat?" but he just turns, looks at me, not a flicker of reaction on his face, tucks his pen back in his trousers and staggers off, face all red, covered in snow, clearly just stood up from that very snowdrift.

— And what did he write?

— Well, he wrote it down, expressed it, tha might say, t'whole essence of t'universe in un word.

— And what word was that?

— Eeh, "CUNT", in big letters like that, all golden and glitterinn in t'sun, it were a clear day, always is when 'tis nippy like this. I thought to meself, here, that's young folk for thee, artist, writer, painter. What art tha laughinn at, thee daft old bat? Why art tha neighinn like a bloody horse?

— Well, could he, Leo, write not 'bout t'nature of existence, no, but 'bout thee, me dear.

— Now, don't muddle t'waters, thee old hag.

— So, tha pulled him up on his writinn, and what did he say?

— He says, "I am, Baba Nüra, writinn a novel, 'bout our Tulubaika and village life, and thee," he says, "Baba Nüra, tha's in it too."

— Am I in it, am I?

— Sorry, love, our dear Karenina Anna, but who needs thee? "This novel," he says, "is really 'bout t'structure of t'universe and how it works, and t'village is just a framinn device," was what he said, I remember this nonsense word for word, still got a sharp memory, I do.

— And what are these forces?

— Well, I'm like t'queen of t'universe, greatest creature in it, guardian of its structure and essence, historical creation, sole chronicler, would-be empress, and Leo — t'fool, entertains me with his jokes.

— Tha's fibbinn.

— Go ask him thyself, thee dyed tart.

— Next time I see him, I'll ask, Nüra.

— "Our Tulubaika," he says, "is nowt less than a perfect model of t'universe, where various human essences, good and evil, come together in a long, magical dance. They dance and waltz, until in this dance is born t'Istina, with a capital I, that un, where human and more-than-human nature is fused, and through us, t'universe comes to know itself, choosinn me as its chief representative among mankind."

— Tha should tell this to t'priest, he'd smack thee with his thurible for such heresy.

— Well, our priest drives a bloody G-Wagon, I reckon he doesn't give two hoots 'bout these metaphysical shenanigans, bless him, look at t'jowls on him, only his collar covers his four chins, might as well be a politician, or a mayor, or a governor, or go straight for president, they like that sort of enterprisinn beauty there, big demand for that breed. Tha knows Nick t'One-Eyed?

— I know. How can I not know him?

— Galina, our church caretaker, wunst told me that Nick t'One-Eyed came to atone for his sins and lift curses, and he's got 'em aplenty,

a whole G-Wagonload, as they say, plus a small cart, and three more trailers on t'way.

— Hast tha seen t'palace he's built for himself?

— I wunst told him, when I bumped into him on t'street, he was walkinn with his brute of a bodyguard, a daft giant, in his boots as black as pitch, as if he licks 'em off himself every morrow, only to tramp through t'same muck, mind thee, that thee and I walk in, and he walks past me without so much as a glance, and I whispered, just loud enough to be heard, "may tha never raise thy mast again, thee bloody imp."

— And what did he do?

— Well, he must have good hearinn, with everyone always whisperinn 'bout him, even in church, he shot me a glance and continued to tread muck with his licked-off boots.

— Tha's a bold un, no fear in thee.

— So he comes to church, like a toad to a viper, as they say, and whispers to our priest, "I'll donate to t'church, and tha'll absolve me of me sins, deal?" Our priest's no fool, he agreed, absolved him of his sins, and now he's drivinn 'round in his G-Wagon through our native mire.

— Can tha get through our mire on owt else though? What's t'fuss 'bout? He earned it — bought it, absolvinn sins isn't easy nowadays, look at t'amount of work.

— They should walk, t'bellends, they've ruined t'entire road.

— So what 'bout Leo, our writer?

— What a bloody writer he is. I told him straight, but he keeps blatherinn on, says mayhap I'd like to buy a kitty, and there I was, wiltinn in t'heat, sittinn and starinn at him from under heavy eyes, black and judgemental, heavier than all of Nick t'One-Eyed's unabsolved sins.

— That's thy talent.

— And he says, "I'll give thee a discount, Baba Nüra, love, as t'guardian of t'universe, take this new fluffy friend for half price."

— Was t'kitty bonny at least?

— T'kitty, I must admit, was absolutely lovely, I saw her from afar

— tangerine, long fur, eyes green as gooseberries, some exotic breed, not from 'round here.

— And what didst tha do?

— I told Leo I had no money, said: "Give me t'money, and I'll buy thy animal."

— And what did he do?

— He looked at me with such pitiful eyes, like a wee nipper. "Thee," he says, "Baba Nüra, tha's t'true local kingpin, everyone knows thee, tha's our real strength, t'backbone that holds t'whole village together, without thee," he says, "our tiny universe would crumble like sand from a broken hourglass, and imagine, Baba Nüra, thee sittinn by t'window, enjoyinn our lovely summer, dreaminn, and beside thee, or even on thy lap, sits this kitty, purrinn, radiatinn kindness, love, positive cosmic energies, and in winter she'll warm both body and soul, for cats are such creatures, they catch mice and heal chakras."

— And what didst tha do?

— I must confess, I melted at such a pitch.

— There tha has it, he conned thee, me dear, charmed thee, a cupid in businessman's clothing.

— Who's conned who, thee holey sack. I sees this lovely creature in t'arms of that raggedy cretin, Tulubaika's own parasite, a boozed-up flea, a sodden louse, I does. Lookinn into Leo's bloodshot eyes, and t'cat's precious green ones, while I sits in me black glasses. He can't see how me eyes are movinn, to him, I'm just a statue in t'window, Venus, bloody Venus of Milo—

— Or of Willendorf...

— Oh, shut up! And methinks, I gotta save that cat. She'll perish with that wretch, or he'll sell her to his drunken mates, 'em great degenerate decadent novelists just like him, and 'tis lucky, if 'em boozy lips end up flogginn her to some decent soul, otherwise, bojeupasi, gobble her up when there's nowt to chase t'vodka with, I've seen worse in t'war years, I have.

— Tha goes on like tha was t'only un in t'war.

— And where wert thee? Sharpeninn thy tongue or lyinn under t'enemy?

223

— Me dear, me mother hid me in t'woods, in an oak tree, fed me on crushed acorns and nettle soup.

— We've seen it all, we have. Horses, dogs, cats, leather belts, dreadful times... So, methinks, I can't leave this cat, with eyes like two gooseberries, to such an infamous scum, our village's daft Leo, a thrall to Dionysus. I decides to buy t'critter off him, not just buy, but trade, set up a barter, pressinn on his sorest spot.

— What's that spot, Nüra? Not his writinn tool...

— Hold thy tongue, thee pervert. His boozinn muscle, his liver, that is. I've got an alternative for thee, I tells him, a more universal currency, better than any lucres, since our money's as good as toilet paper these days, mayhap even less so. When they start payinn pensions in copper coins, tha won't even have summat to wipe thy arse with. Sometimes I wonders, how did folk manage a couple centuries back without paper money, and now here we are, millions handed out, barely enough for a couple loaves of bread, some milk, sausage made of offal. So I says to Leo, t'fool, "Dost tha think happiness lies in lucres?" And he says, "What else, Baba Nüra?" Well, I tells him, in peace of t'soul!

— Oh, is that so... And how is thine? Peaceful?

— Look here, I tells him, Nick t'One-Eyed has so much money, he could fill an airplane hangar, and still have room. What does he do with it? Buys off his sins, and thee, Leo, dear, got any sins to buy off? No, so why art tha, daft, all after money, when tha says a cat can warm t'soul? Now, can tha put a price on that?

— And him?

— Well, he's standinn there, scratchinn his nape with his free hand, his hand all mucky, as if he'd been digginn in t'chort's arse, and t'kitten, squirminn all over, not wantinn to sit in Leo's arms, for he all reeks of booze and piss, and says, Leo, that is, not t'cat, "no, me dear mistress of t'universe, 'tis priceless, it is," and I says to him, "I've got, Leo, love, a bottle of pre-revolutionary samogón, artisanal, made with holy water — they only distilled such stuff under t'Tsar, stopped under Bolsheviks. Tha gives me t'cat, I give thee this bottle, and then our souls will both be at peace."

— Samogón? To Leo? Tha's quite summat...

— Hold on, not done yet, t'most important bit's cominn. So, we live, me and Mara, this cat, we dote on each other, go to t'shops together, collect t'pension, and off to church, she runs 'round me, rubs against me legs, jumps, sits on me shoulder, like a parrot, I swear, only me back ain't what it used to be, starts stiffeninn up after she sits there for half an hour, had this one: woke up un morrow, and this wee chortess climbed on me, purrinn so loud 'tis like a drum corps vibratinn through me spine, won't budge, so, I had to lie there till noon, couldn't get up, couldn't move. Had this dream wunst, sat on t'cat in it, Mara was huge in t'dream, like a horse, or a bloody outlandish elephant, and off we flew to explore our universe. Me with a glitterinn crown, her with those green eyes of hers shininn like floodlights, lightinn our way through t'cosmos. We're flyinn, light speed, mayhap even faster, and all we see are traffic lights blinkinn and cars honkinn, but no coppers or any other beinns that could stop us — such is life for t'mistress of t'universe and her faithful friend Mara. I even brought her fresh milk a couple of times from thy cow, sneakinn out at four in t'morn, milked a cupful and brought it to her.

— So it was thee...

— Don't tha shriek, what, a cup of milk too much to spare? Thee and thy old fart of a husband guzzle it down by t'bucketful every day, and t'cat, bless her, probably never seen fresh milk in her life, well now she has, 'course. If tha'd seen how she gulps it down, lappinn it up like an excavator, almost scoopinn t'cup along with it, a trifle to thee, but a joy to Mara, she's like a nipper, me lass, and it makes her happy and me too, keeps me from sittinn alone all day.

— And what am I to thee?

— Thee and thy old fart, I'm sick of t'sight of thee both, me soul's fed up with thee, but with her, here's summat new, tha won't even see such beauty on t'telly.

— Thanks a bunch, friend.

— Tha hush, I'm just teasinn, lovingly. What are we to each other?

— I don't even know any more, Nüra, what we are, mayhap nowt.

— But we've been through fire, water, and those copper pipes,

seen everythinn there is to see, either in person or on t'telly, but Mara, she's seen nowt, so I showed her, and then un day she just disappears.

— Oh... Just like that?

— There tha is sighinn, but if tha'd seen me sighinn. Half a day she's gone, a day, two days, thought she certainly wasn't off courtinn tomcats, t'furry wee strumpet, summat must've happened, felt like a bear was squeezinn me ribs, tryinn to crush 'em, break me heart. So, I took a wee corvalol[1], and other things, chamomile chai, herbal liqueur for calminn, sat by t'window, watchinn cars drive, muck churn, drunks wander back and forth, t'priest in his G-Wagon cominn from t'banya with some discounted fannies, Nick t'One-Eyed on his errands — t'village livinn its life as if nowt's happened, and me Mara was nowhere, just gone, as if she'd evaporated and merged with t'ether, so, methinks, time to start a search operation. Remember when Marfa's husband got lost, went for mushroom pickinn, old fart?

— Aye, I remember, bless his soul.

— So there I was, thinkinn I've done this before, heads straight to t'Community Centre — they're cultured folk there, understandinn, compassionate, sure to lend a hand; I walks in and says, "Eh up, lovely lads, I've lost me cat, Mara, cryinn day and night I am, she's been gone three days, me wee joy." And they goes, "And what can we do for thee, Baba Nüra?" I says, "Print me some flyers like tha did for Marfa's husband, here's a lost cat, tangerine, fluffy, with eyes like gooseberries, green with a yellow sheen, answers to Mara." They makes me a dozen of 'em flyers, I'm wanderinn 'round t'village, stickinn 'em up on poles, cryinn me eyes out, t'world's all dark, like 'tis t'end of days.

— So some human feelinns left in thee, then?

— Human feelinns might've upped and left, thee daft old bat, but plenty of cat ones. Cats, tha knows, they don't ask daft questions, just sit there quiet, meow now and then (that's their language, innit), tha feeds 'em, waters 'em, pets 'em, and they're happy with thee, but folk

---

1. A Soviet-era sedative and the go-to remedy for everything from heart palpitations to existential dread, despite being banned or restricted in most Western countries due to its barbiturate content. Can replace nostalghin and melancholin in some rare cases.

these days, try pleasinn 'em, all drunks, junkies, hoes, and thee two ancient relics, too stingy even to spare milk for a kitten, bet tha'd begrudge water from thy rusty tap when I'm dyinn — that's half t'people, one's a thief, another a murderer, a fifth already in jail for all t'above, but a cat? Sacred creature, by Leo's account, probably t'real essence of t'universe.

— So, did Mara turn up?

— So there I am, mourninn, same as ever by t'window, in me black shawl, me best black dress, t'one I buried me old man in and saw off me wayward friends, all in mourninn I am — Mara's gone, no sign of Mara, anyone might pass by t'window, young or old, a thug or a priest, a stray dog or a filthy pigeon, but not me dearie. Even t'sprats I bought for her went off, and me heart's gettinn worse, every part of me creaks, fallinn apart like an old shed, but then I see — Leo cominn, t'bastard, face red as a watermelon, in his torn old dad's quilted jacket, holey rubber boots, splashinn through puddles, and guess what he's holdinn?

— Mara?

— Nay, ah, if only — me flyer, "lost cat, name's Mara, find her and tha's a champ, and champs deserve a reward these days."

— And where's Mara?

— "Baba Nüra," says this twat, "thy cat's with me, safe and sound, sittinn at home, guzzlinn milk down like there's no tomorrow, tail's not waginn, nose cold, eyes still that same green." What a daft lad, eh? What sort of writer is he, can't tell t'difference between gooseberry-green and just green? I got all excited, told him to brinn Mara, brinn her quick, why turn up empty-handed? And dost tha know what he says?

— What?

— He's after a reward! "That'll be a million," says t'cheeky devil, "no less, and I don't want thy vodka, nor even thy famous samogón, nowt. Drank thy piss thyself," he says, "and felt only worse, so wretched I nearly hanged meself, already borrowed a rope on credit, found some soap, picked a tree, then realised I wanna live, understood

where true happiness lies, so hand over t'lucres," says t'cursed fiend, "and then tha'll see thy cat."

— And what didst tha do?

— I got so angry, I was boilinn over, muscles tense, veins bulginn, almost breathinn fire. Grabbed t'porcelain ashtray next to me, flung it at him, at Leo, with all me might, nearly fell out t'window doinn it, but hit him, right in his empty noggin, echoed all 'round t'neighbourhood, surprised it didn't shatter t'neighbours' windows, and he, Leo, t'mountain goat, leaps up, starts huffinn, thought he'd gone mad. "Give me t'cat," I yells, "thee vermin."

— And what did he do?

— Nowt — left. "Come and get t'cat thyself, thee old cunt," he says, "and now I definitely won't give her to thee without t'million. Tha's got no soul," he says, "tha's no mistress of t'universe, that's just me fiction."

— And what's thy point in all this?

— What dost tha mean, what's me point? I've got no choice, do I? Need to save me cat, me beloved Mara, but to save her I need to find a million somewhere, and 'tis still a week and a half till me pension (I'm countinn t'days), so she doesn't perish with him, that rotten scoundrel. That's why I came to thee, to ask, see if me dear friend would lend me a small million till payday?

Episode Fourteen
about different ways of spending your summer

Once I had begun a chapter with the following (so very original) words: "One fine day" — then struck out "fine" — then struck out "One" — then struck out the whole lot and wrote in block capitals: "FUCKING HELL!" — and left it at that. But I rather doubt the Russian Herald will find this satisfactory.

— Ivan Turgenev

I'd like to argue, Tamara Alexeyevna, that summer isn't really summer at all, but "holidays", because that's what I actually spent, whilst summer itself just passed by like autumn will pass, and winter, and spring, and then summer again. Whoosh and it's gone! Here you'd argue that one can't write "whoosh" in an essay, and I'd parry — yes I can, I've just written it, haven't I, and you'd parry back and give me an F or even fail me completely or throw me out of class altogether without finishing reading, missing all the interesting bits, because all the interesting bits are always somewhere in the middle, towards the end. I'd never write so that everyone finds it interesting straight away. It should be the absolute opposite! The beginning should be uninteresting, off-putting, boring even (in a subtle way), so that one'd want to slap an F on it, just as you taught us, Tamara Alexeyevna. The beginning should make the reader (in this case, you, since nobody reads this — "utter tosh", as you'd put it — except you, unless I throw myself under a train, then social services will come, dig through the notebooks with handwritten texts like "How I Threw Myself Under a Train This Summer (essay)" and find all the answers) get bored, think:

"What utter tosh!" But that's how it should be, Tamara Alexeyevna, because everything starts precisely like this — with the feeling that you've come uninvited, unexpected, and don't understand what's happening at all. And it ends, Tamara Alexeyevna, absolutely the same way.

Me and the girls got pissed and went to siphon diesel from the Tulubaikan combine harvester depot together with the boys, and whilst we were siphoning the guard caught us — a drunk without clothes and with a rifle, flaccid, hanging to his knees. What I'm getting at is — after a confusing beginning there should always be something that knocks you off your feet, as if from that room you accidentally entered, they're now forcefully ejecting you, like from a class. But we really did go to siphon diesel, why — I don't know; it's boring in this village, nothing to do, people die from this condition, only children and teenagers somehow cope. The boys asked me not to spread it about; I won't grass the names to you, though you would probably guess straight away who I mean; I sure do have a list — all the F-students. I'll honestly admit, I didn't siphon any diesel, just stood nearby, looking on disapprovingly, for I'm a good girl. If I'm honest, they wouldn't even let us girls sniff it. I swear, lived to seventeen and don't know the taste or smell of diesel. Alcohol either, by the way, lied about that too, such is my writer's lot — making up all sorts of utter tosh.

I didn't read any books, Tamara Alexeyevna. Well, I did read, of course (what, am I going to lie?), that's all I did in the evenings, but you don't consider them books, you don't like "youth poseurs", anyone whose surname doesn't start with "Tolsto" and end with "evsky". Oh, I'd argue with you about this, Tamara Alexeyevna, I'd explain to you about real contemporary literature at the turn of the century, written, by the way, by your peers, about how one shouldn't consume faeces, triple cologne, brake fluid, get carried away with anti-Christian Buddhism, be inspired by foreign thinkers, about postmodernism, bloody hell! And you wouldn't even argue, Tamara Alexeyevna, you'd give me an F without even listening, without reading, and even if you'd got to the beginning of the second

paragraph, at the bit with the dangling todger you'd definitely throw me out — the gun would shoot eventually. But you'd have laughed, I'm sure, when you're at home, reading this, you'd have laughed, and if you'd read this far, you'd have realised the whole "meta" of this situation, and how I, "alas, irreverent, vulgar, but such a clever girl", am leading you round in circles. Let my classmates write about how they went fishing, swimming, travelled to Moscow, flew abroad on holiday, weeded garden beds, ate berries, grilled shashlik, twisted cows' tails and girls' plaits, and the girls kicked them in the nuts in return, I sure would — fits the character, that. Like, your balls have dropped? Congratulations! Here, learn to live with the consequences! But I won't write tosh like that; apart from indirectly participating as an outside observer in various indecent and illegal activities carried out by uneducated delinquents, sort of wanting to take part myself, but "what will people think" and "you've got to get into university in a year" and "mother would be sad" and other such reasons, I just moped about the area, sat at home, played Warcraft (you don't know about that, Tamara Alexeyevna, and it's better you don't — I'm playing a gnome warlock with pink tails, an unbecomingly evil lil'girl), read sheets of paper with letters about all sorts of antisocial, anarchist, nihilist, counter-cultural stuff, the very stuff your Tolstoevsky didn't like, though the Tolso- part of him quite did.

Here, Tamara Alexeyevna, there should be some sort of ending, which I'd also argue with you about, and you'd give me an A so as not to average out a D for the year, because your heart is kind, and where would I go in this life with a D in literature? I've got to get into university in a year. In a proper essay, Tamara Alexeyevna, the ending only comes at the very end, in the last sentence, often in the last word, because it, like everything in this life — even like summer — comes suddenly, and just as suddenly ends and causes a storm of emotions, and nothing, Tamara Alexeyevna, whatever you might think, however you were brought up under your bright communism, nothing expresses emotion like swearing. Fucking hell! Absolute cuntastrophe, how can this be? I'm in complete fucking shock, Tamara Alexeyevna, honestly, fuck this for a game of twats, bloody Christ on a bloody bike,

makes me want to fucking bawl, there are no words, and when there are no words, that's when it comes to help, swearing; swearing is always with you, always supports you, always fills the gaps in language; it's absolute fucking bollocks, Tamara Alexeyevna, the absolute gigantic bellend of utter tosh! All I can say is — from this cunt of a summer holiday I've gone completely off my fucking head. Here you'd probably finally give me that F and I'd leave, your favourite student, a D-student to spite you, to upset my parents, to my own strange, reckless, self-satisfied joy — the little princess has done something deranged and now sits here pleased, ears burning with shame, head pounding, but apart from that no external signs, outwardly solemn, inwardly a degenerate. That's the kind of cunty bitch I am, Tamara Alexeyevna — rotten to the core, with a spoonful of tar in the barrel of honey, which you'd probably argue with, and I'd argue with you. I'd love to argue with you so much, Tamara Alexeyevna, prove to you what a proper irreverent bitch I really am, not the one you think I am, but it's a shame, Tamara Alexeyevna, a shame that we'll never argue again, a shame that you'll never read this utter tosh, and a shame that for you this summer was the last.

Episode Fifteen
about dragonfly's retinal structure

His mind is engaged in a rapt contemplation
Of the thought, of the thought, of the thought of his name:
His ineffable effable
Effanineffable
Deep and inscrutable singular Name.

— T. S. Eliot, "The Naming of Cats"

A river's backwater, the sun with an absence of mercy, young Saveliy with a net. The air seems charged, in the air dawns sadness. No, not that... something else, a feeling akin, yet different, delicate, lacy, semi-transparent, like dragonfly wings; at rest — visible, in flight — gone. Boredom? No, not boredom either. Young Saveliy doesn't even know what it is, though he's caught the word from adults. At his age, boredom is like alcohol, not sold without ID, not poured at the table, and they don't even let you sniff the cap, so one must dig trenches between dictionary lines and build towers from tomes of encyclopaedias to the very ceiling of the room or planet, to understand what this quirky little phenomenon is that so agitates some of those around. Even if he knew, Young Saveliy would have no time for it. He sits with his net, thoughts darting inside, dragonflies outside — now hovering over duckweed, now poking their bottoms into it. That's how they lay their larvae, murmured the insect atlas to him at night under the duvet, to which Saveliy only nodded and kept mum, as always, but not on purpose, just so, naturally, in his Saveliy way.

What feeling is it then? Melancholia? Khondria? There are as many types of it as there are dragonflies. Perhaps nostalgic? Saveliy's

too young for that. Azure or existential? Too complex. Seasonal or emerald? Romantic, perchance? ("Oh no, let those pigtailed girls flit about and squeal on their own.") Or maybe it's the melancholia of change or even cosmic melancholia? All amiss, all askew — Saveliy hasn't reached them yet, they're somewhere yonder, further along the road, round the bend, past the crossroads where Saveliy will turn left, for according to the map, there one ought to go straight. No matter — the time shall come, he'll catch them too, spread their gossamer wings on paper, leave them in the merciless sun to dry, and then, having assigned them a place in his personal collection, he'll gently fold them into the insect atlas with the other dragonflies. Perchance he'll arrange a silent dragonfly exhibition at school without any explanations ("They'll figure it out, it's all clear anyway...") gather a gawking corridor of classmates, youngsters senior and junior, importantly nodding teachers, proudly straightened parents, a couple of "excellent" marks in biology, a diploma for triumph in the regional contest, a handshake from the governor, universal approval and the silent sorrow of dried dragonflies. Perchance he'll show it to none and tuck the swollen atlas far into the sub-bed obscurity, to dust, lava, monsters, notebooks with F's for disobedience, self-glued books about the spy life of giant anthropomorphic dragonflies. Or maybe he'll release them, uncap the jar, wave his hand, the little dragonflies will flutter out in a swarm, say thank you, and, right after their wings do so — vanish into the distance, against the summer wind. Or maybe not.

— Tulubaika, — says the father of a youthfuled Saveliy, carving butter and smearing it on fresh bread. The slice's still on the plate, yet already crunching in the mouth with reverberations from the future.

— Tulubaika... — Saveliy's mum adds irritably and passes the orange and gooseberry jam jar to dad. The jar's straight from the cellar, sealed firmly, mum can't open it herself. Dad-the-rescuer threatens the jar with a knife, the lid pops, opens dolefully, the jam leaps onto the knife with zeal and aroma, and with a couple of deft movements they amicably cover the buttered expanse of the sandwich with a thick layer.

Saveliy is silent, scowling at the sandwich, shifting his whim-embroidered gaze to his parents.

234

— Tulubaika? — asks dad.

— Tu-lu-bai-ka... — mumbles son.

With a heavy sigh, dad takes the incorrect sandwich from Saveliy, bites into it and starts spreading the right one—jam first, only then butter.

— Tulubaika? — dad asks again. Saveliy doesn't answer, for there's no time to dither — the right sandwich shan't wait.

They live either in a village, or in a city in a family of four people, perhaps with a cat, one or a couple, a big dog on a chain, a budgie (better a parakeet, preferably from Australia) in a cage, so the cat doesn't eat it, or better two, because if there's only one, that incomprehensible feeling will swell, soar, bloom, decay in black hues, become a gnawing ennui, toska[1]. From it — be it people, cats, dogs, or budgies — they plague out. So the budgie's strident melody will dissolve in the aether, cat Dusya will be left with no potential food, will therefore grow sad, stop purring. ("Well, who would want to be in such a situation?") Then, in honour of those fallen in battles with existentia, Saveliy's less young sister, called Kitty, Kathryn on her passport ("Enviable... Passported already"), will stand on a little chair in the living room and play an elegy on her violin ("Very talented..."). Legions of guests, friends, relatives, friends of friends, relatives of relatives, friends of relatives, relatives of friends, all together, to the point of calluses, sincerely, sprinkling each other with tears, will clap their hands like they'll never clap for dried dragonflies, neither with their hands nor on the shoulder.

— Tulubaika! — the guests will chant.

---

1. Vladimir Nabokov famously noted that the Russian "toska" is one of the untranslatable words. In his translation of Pushkin's "Eugene Onegin", Nabokov described it as "a sensation of great spiritual anguish, often without any specific cause... a dull ache of the soul, a longing with nothing to long for, a sick pining, a vague restlessness." In English, translators often deploy its near-synonyms (melancholy, yearning, longing, ennui) that circle the concept but never penetrate its essence (rather like Western tourists wandering Moscow convinced they are experiencing the "real Russia"). Of course, Russian "toska" isn't that unique. There's the Portuguese "saudade", the Welsh "hiraeth", the Finnish "kaiho", and likely others. So, Nabokov wasn't, apparently, entirely right.

— Tulubaika! — the stadium will roar. — Tulubaika! Tulubaika! Tulubaika!

Kitty's cheeks will flush guelder-rose red, she'll smile, take a bow, adjust the bows on her twin-tailed plaits and begin to play "Flight of the Bumblebee" ("Again..."). As it happens, Savelushka doesn't like them, bumblebees, they're not convenient to dry, they make the pages of the insect atlas bulge and then everything falls out, just as young Saveliy's eardrums bulge and everything seems to fall out of his head too, so much so that it can't be found again till morning.

Sensing the presence of the feeling, hanging over him like a pompous chandelier, he'll sit mutely sans visage, sans any expression, gazing not outward, but inward, into the depths where another (still young) Saveliy walks along the river with a little net and jar to catch multicoloured dragonflies. They, the goggle-eyed twigs, seem to jump in the air, eluding the attacks, leaps, and net swings of the young odonatologist. And lo and behold, the jar is full, and the net is torn, and the knees are bloodied, hands all scratched up, the sun retreats in pity, the sky is purple, stars like lanterns, a sickle without a hammer, sweet sleep after a couple of dozen pages. Savelushka dreams, sees how somewhere betwixt the years forthcoming, he sprints after the dragonfliest of the dragonflies, body like the trunk of an old tree, oak, sequoia, or even baobab, glass wings sparkling in the air, the hum befitting them too, like a helicopter. Anax imperator, face, as per the old testaments of pareidolia, resembling an ancient deity, with a mad smile, either from paralysis or by nature, waving a paw ("Rather a pawest of paws, of course...") — hop on, it seems to say, hop on. He approaches the azure transport, but, as he's about to throw his leg over, the dream up and ends.

— Tulubaika, — mum says sternly, opening the door to Saveliy's sleeping chambers. Ere he can unstick his eyes, he nods tacitly, slides off the bed, from pyjamas straight into school attire, and with the feeling ("That very one...") sighs meaningfully.

Teeth, breakfast, rucksack, half an hour's walk to school with his sister, breaks, breaks, breaks, breaks, copious breaks, and a few lessons betwixt them. Younglings play, quarrel, whilst Saveliy drifts

somewhere alone (but not lonely), now running from the feeling, now trying to catch it, as if playing tag, or hide-and-seek or football, wherein it's unclear who's the player and who's the ball. Everyone has it but their own, not common, personal, hanging from the ear, but not akin to noodles, unlike anything else, with its own intensity, with different cracking of the meter used by special scientists and professors ("Or professeurs?") to measure it, the best minds of humanity, smashing their occiputs and foreheads bloody, donating hair for wigs, washing elbows with household soap before nibbling. Saveliy's meter seems to be off the charts, but only almost, always waltzing on the periphery of the permissible. The allure of the feeling is that it, just like zero, is squeezed between two infinities: minus below, and plus above —no matter how you count it, you'll wear your tongue out.

— Tulubaika? — someone tugs at Saveliy's shoulder, yanking him from his mental veil. — Tulubaika?

Young Saveliy stays mum, shrugs his shoulders. Maybe it's "Tulubaika", and maybe it's not.

— Tulubaika-tulubaika! — the assemblage guffaws.

— Tu-lu-tu-lu-tu-lubai-ka! — they further tease.

A faceless lad drags Saveliy by the sleeve behind him, just as that faceless lad would drag girls by their pigtails, or years later would drag his unruly little son to school, or a bag of banned books to the recycling, or a stubborn donkey by the reins to Jerusalem, but Saveliy doesn't go, jerks his arm, turns around and walks away along the path of tattered linoleum ("You lot got it too..." Savelushka concludes to himself). This feeling is thinner than wings, but stronger than diamond, but the main thing is not to get tangled in it like a kitten in a polythene bag, lest one accidentally snuff it. This feeling has a ubiquitous presence: it's on the gentle autumn wind, sticks to leaves on trees, falls with them into a heap of rot, today smells of gooseberries, tomorrow — of silage, creeps into books, into holes in letters, into dots above "ı"[2], into wrinkles of pages, bookmarks, granddad and granny's foreheads, unironed sheets, into music, into

---

2. The idiom in Russian also uses "i", but the original text here uses "ë", the letter

scratches on Shostakovich's records, into dust on the stylus needle, into the darkness of dad's out-of-tune guitar, into mum's out-of-tune head, into the intricacies of musical notation, into the tornado raised by a bumblebee's flight, into cassette tapes, into the lyrical voice of a foreign performer, hammering tirelessly "Tulubaika, Akiabulut, Tulubaika..." until the tape tears or a vein tears in the brain, into films, notably black and white ones, notably 4:3, notably with a cheerful plot and sad music, into cartoons, a small part of them, mainly Soviet ones, into old photographs, rarely into new ones ("They have a thin layer of time..."), into drawings drying by felt-tip pen, into ink blots on a shirt ("The pen leaked on its own... Not my fault..."), into paintings, into the reproduction of Repin's "Dragonfly" ("Which, for some reason, has a girl drawn in it and not a dragonfly...")[3], into the smell of fresh paper, burnt plastic, heated dust and phosphorus, mushroom soup, the aroma of mother's perfume, the stench of grown-up sister's perfume, into explosions and gunshots on TV, into the black stripe on Pikachu's tail, into meteors falling in batches, asteroids, planes, leaves and snow, into watercolours spreading across the table, into the eyelashes of a broken brush, into eyelashes covered with snow in winter, into black ice, into freezing cold, into melting snow, into melting ice cream ("Better pistachio..."), spilled into a backpack that's flown off a cliff behind the schoolyard into an open field, into fields of ruins of ancient empires and fields of solar panels, into the first day of September, into the last stamp in a passport, into the first kiss on the cheek, into the last five seconds before midnight on the doomsday clock, into vacuum, dad's bald spot, dog's mange, the stench of boiled eggs, corn, into a parade of crop-dusters for the 9th of May, into wafts of poppy seed buns, with cinnamon, with custard ("With

---

famously left undotted on many occasions when written or typed, becoming a part of the debate on linguistic purism and aesthetics.
3.   Ilya Repin's "Dragonfly" (1884) depicts his twelve-year-old daughter Vera perched on an unstable wooden crossbar with sky behind her, which creates the impression she might take flight at any moment, capturing not her resemblance to the insect but rather her restless, fidgety nature, which "dragonfly" can idiomatically refer to in Russian. Repin himself suggested this title when selling the painting to Pavel Tretyakov, writing that "both in colour, movement, and position she fits this name."

pistachios..."), the fragrance of dandelions, nettle soup, sour sorrel, bitter cough syrup, rumble of thunder, the last lullaby, into rain and slush, everywhere and anywhere, in screams, in laughter, in silence, in tears and their concealment, in words and their absence, in explaining the inexplicable, in darkness, at dusk, and in light, be it sun or moon, in thoughts by day, in dreams at night, and in sickness and in health, and for richer, for poorer, till death do us part.

Lo and behold, Savelushka, tiny tot, seemingly just born, not even three years old, and already turned blue, his heartie slowed down, eyes round, no strength to cry. Behold them bringing him in an emergency to the village znakharess, a healer, a holy misfit. He lies on the table on a goose feather pillow in her minuscule kitchen, where in the nook, in lieu of an icon, hangs the Black Square[4], not to shield oneself from the saint's countenance, not to unlock some extrasensory chakra, and not even out of love for Russian avant-garde, but because she's blind — whatever she looks at, in essence it's all just a black square. Behold the babushka's shrivelled paws pour herbal elixir from a spoon into his mouth, rub his pallid little hands and feet with a stinging liquid, whilst her wrinkled lips and tongue gibber somewhat in her own old village cant.

— Tu-lu-bai-ka... Tu-lu-bai-ka... — that's all one can hear, she grunts, showering mantras. — Tu-lu-bai-ka... Tu-lu-bai-ka...

And thus it goes on repeat, whilst tiny Savelushka lies on the pillow, shivering, afraid to blink, pupils hiding in the irises, examining with childish gazes the worried adult countenances and the Black Square hanging above them. It smells of spirits, linden, dog-rose, mustiness, a handful of the past, mountains of the future. You, Saveliy,

---

4. Malevich's "Black Square" (1915) debuted at the legendary "0.10" exhibition in Petrograd not merely as another canvas among many but occupying the "красный угол" (red corner) that was traditionally reserved for Orthodox icons in Russian homes of believers. Suspended high across the room's corner with deliberate iconoclastic intent, the black void gazed down upon visitors like a proto-suprematist deity. This placement reflected Malevich's manifesto declaring the painting "the zero of form", representing reality with pure geometric abstractions. So, it is, in fact, the most unholy of icons.

hang in there, it's alright, you shall thaw out, erupt in tears, slumber serenely ("Tu... tulubaika?").

After all, you've got your whole life ahead. You'll mount the emperor dragonfly, grip tightly its azure body. Your transport will drone like a helicopter, wings aflutter, and lo, the entire world lies beneath you: ant hills of metropolises, hamlets, barely visible rivulets, the shimmer of reservoir surfaces, endless expanses of oats, the burning September[5], the gold of birch groves — all will run breathlessly into the distance trying to catch up with you. The wind will ruffle your hair, tickle your cheeks, nip at your squinting eyes. Clouds will drench you with rain, pelt you with hail. The sun will blind you, burn you with fire. But you, brave rider, will care not a jot. You'll return home, salute the dragonfly farewell. It's off lakeward to its children, you're homeward to tackle arithmetics, and the world — somewhere on the back burner. The feeling will clear up anew, dawn, settle cosily in your head. There's no word that could express its elusiveness, except, perhaps, one... ("Oh, and did you know? Dragonfly eyes are like magic! They're made up of lots and lots of tiny peepholes, all stuck together like a big puzzle. Each little peephole shows the dragonfly a picture, so it's as if the dragonfly has thousands of itty-bitty windows in its eyes! That's why dragonflies can see everything so clearly, even the teeniest, tiniest bugs flitting about. It's like they have the sharpest eyes in the whole wide insectverse!")

---

5. "September burns" is a Russian internet meme originating from the 2007 emo anthem "Сентябрь" by the band Stigmata. The unaware Western reader might see burning September as a poetic metaphor for autumn's fiery foliage but in Russian internet folklore it's a nostalghic reference to a song and the glorious times of 2007 when things were rather better (much better, almost perfect even). The phrase exploded beyond its emo subculture origins in the mid-2010s, and posting memes about it became a nationwide September tradition alongside honouring Shufutinsky's "the 3rd of September" (won't explain).

Episode Sixteen
about hardships of awakening

Having unlocked the meaning of countable and uncountable in time, I felt as though I held a mousetrap in my hands, wherein ancient fate trembles like a frightened little beast.

— Velimir Khlebnikov

Somewhere in the depths of years to come, in the taiga around a moss-covered burrow, people will gather with orchid bouquets in their hands, fruits in their baskets and nervous smiles on their faces. What will emerge won't be a bear, nor even some creature divine making its umpteenth return to the world, but merely a maiden of mystical natures who, for whatever reason, hasn't fancied waking up from whatever dream for so long that her underground slumber could be measured in years, thousands, millions, or perhaps billions of seconds, depending on how one prefers to reckon time.

The crowd will be doing what crowds do best — chanting, clapping, paparazzing, orchestrating, and hyperbolising-cacophonising a randomly sparked emotion, until one of the leaders of this spectacle will raise his hand, calling the gathered legions to order.

They will freeze in anticipation of words; an existential silence will fall.

Though everyone will know the figure before them is human, few will be able to believe it. Her hunched body covered in dirt and moss will be shivering either from cold or from excess attention, and her eyes will be shut tight against the aggressive light phenomena of varying brightness.

— Happy Awakening! — the leader of the gathering will say and pat the den dweller on the shoulder.

Still coming to her senses, our heroine will flinch and eye the leader with incomprehension, a mixture of surprise and freshly-brewed anger.

— Happy Awakening! — the deputy leader will say and also pat the den dweller on the shoulder with his sweaty hand, though the den dweller couldn't care less about its sweatiness.

— Happy Awakening! — the president of a very important country will say, next in line to give her shoulder a pat.

— Happy Awakening! — the president of a country that is also important, but a bit less so, and thus was allocated a worse spot in the queue, will say and also pat her shoulder.

— Happy Awakening! — someone from the following little humans in the seemingly endless queue will say and do the same as several patters before, and millions of patters after.

— Bloody hell, — our heroine will think, — how much I don't want to get up... — she will grimace and present her shoulder.

— Happy Awakening! — her mum will say, patting her shoulder, treacherously opening the thick curtains and leaving the bedroom where, after an eternity of fame as the most well-slept person in the world, her daughter will find herself with dismay, shed the pink veil from her eyelids, lie for another couple dozen minutes, have porridge with hazelnuts for breakfast and, led by parents on both sides ("Like a blind person, I swear...") will go off to first grade, after which falling back asleep will be impossible, after which life will go downhill along well-worn tracks.

From some abysses will emerge a substrate called Time, which she will have to reckon with. Funny thing is, it will differ from the time that lives in clocks and ticks, or pours like sand, or falls as a shadow from the sun onto the dial — or rather, it will have nothing in common with that time at all, so much nothing that it wouldn't hurt to have a new separate word for it. "I'm sick of your language games," our lethargic heroine will think, "don't call different things by the same name." Of course, one can ignore this "Time" and pay it no mind, but

at some point it, like everyone else, will also pat you on the shoulder and say:

— Happy Awakening!

— Go away, let me sleep some more, — our awakened heroine will snarl at Time, burrowing into the blanket as if into a den.

— Happy Awakening! — Time will repeat, grinning with all thirty-two teeth (or however many teeth personifications of concepts are supposed to have).

— I have a temperature, — she will theatrically proclaim to Time, plug her ears, hold her breath and lie like that until her face turns pale. — I don't feel well. My head's spinning. *cough-cough*

— Happy Awakening! — Time will repeat, grab her by the ankle and pull her out of bed onto the cold linoleum and drag her along the corridor, and all along its length her nails will sketch long feline tracks.

At some point she will clutch at the doorframe and squeeze her eyes shut to either wake up faster or perhaps fall back asleep, but neither will happen. Time will keep pulling her leg, slowly, without particular effort, but with indeterminate persistence and inflexibility, for such is Time's nature. All of human existence is nothing but resistance of human to Time, and Time to human, a love-hate relationship.

The logic of life in dreams differs from the logic of life in life — in dreams something always happens. In a couple of hours, one can be born, go to school, leave Tulubaika, stop a zombie apocalypse, plant a tree and immediately see it grow, perhaps even wake up into a new dream, while in life nothing happens, so much nothing that there will be nothing to remember later, and everything will seem so quick and rapid, as if it's not a memory but a dream, and not just a dream but a flash, a temporal anomaly, like the one you fall into for a couple of minutes during the most boring university lecture at nine in the morning on Monday. In the world barely an hour has passed, but inside, in the sleepy chambers, first all existence ended, descended to the most nothingiest Nothing, and then consciousness spread like mould across the universe, and it's as if you were born again, and the professor wants something from you again:

243

— Happy Awakening! — he will say.

Everyone around will giggle. The professor will smirk craftily.

— Perhaps you can help us... when we talk about realising something significant, what's the most terrifying thing about such an awakening?

The professor's spectacles and two dozen young eyes will stare at our heroine with a thirst for knowledge, and she will straighten up in her chair and blurt out with all her ironic might:

— That the alarm keeps ringing.

What's been realised can't be unrealised, can't be realised back, or as grandad used to say, "you can't push a turd back up your arse." Impossible to continue, impossible to stop. Don't want to sleep anymore, want even less to get up, move limbs, wash up, cook, breathe, trudge off to some jobs and slowly stew in their capitalist cauldron, play nonsense with some Atlantic plankton until the end of time from its very beginning, when Atlas took a second to scratch his arse, and Atlantis went straight to the bottom. There's a fiasco for you.

Beautiful, ineffably beautiful it looked even in those moments when every piece of its magnificence was hiding in the dark waters of the ocean named after it by the ancient Greeks or vice versa. Sad, ineffably sad, but more epic than ever the sinking world looked, when the queen of Atlantis, finding herself on the highest building, was sinking with it and refused to swim, though she realised she could. There's a fiasco for you. All she needed to do was lie on the water's surface, didn't need to swim at all; the water's salty from tears — she wouldn't sink. But no, our heroine dug her claws into the tower's top, for she didn't want to leave her native expanses.

— Happy Awakening! — our heroine will say to her old cat. — We'll be catching mice in the new house, you little shitter ("That's what grandad called both her and me.") Mum and dad promised loads of them. We're taking the scratching post with us, too.

The heroine will scoop up the cat and drag her to their old family car, smelling of machine oil and air freshener's attempts to fight it. Setting sail from the native harbour of Tulubaika, they, together with the cat, will watch their wooden house diminishing until it drops off

the horizon and sinks, atlantically. Together with the cat they will lie on the new, but still cold linoleum of the new flat, read the works of great anarchists, absorb the great anarchist spirit, so similar, as it will seem to our heroine, to the feline one, so close, as it will seem to our heroine, to herself. Together with the cat they will swear that they will always walk by themselves, choose their own cigarettes and energy drinks and alcoholic beverages, learn to play bass on their own, shave half their head bald on their own, create the most original and independent depressive-suicidal black metal band, recording their best hits on cassette in basements, stairwells, abandoned factories, where the ground is strewn with syringes (be they basements, stairwells, or abandoned factories), choose their own fiancé or fiancée or both, ones who will also choose them on their own, walk until dawn on their own, be sad and merry with just a couple of notes, an infinity of broken rhythms and rough screams, invent intoxicating and sobering mixtures with a modicum of unwonted levity ("My head's splitting"), meanwhile committing all sorts of explicit and indecent things that even the most freedom-loving cat shouldn't see.

— Happy Awakening! — the fiancé will declaim and gently kiss her forehead and offer breakfast in bed, which the heroine will have to decline, for it's improper. Anarchism is anarchism, but teeth should be brushed first, and anyway that's some aristocratic anachronism. Normal people don't leave their bed for hours, days, weeks, basking in the rays of sun tickling skin through the blinds, lethargising, dreaming, musicating with fingers various broken rhythms on the wood of an IKEA bedside table.

The best way to resist Time's authority is either to forget about it or to wait for something, something grand, cleansing, striking — best of all written in dactylic hexameter. Then the ordinariness of "eternal now" will turn into a reel of moments, like how childhood appears in memory, an album of old, overexposed photographs of people either rehearsing or practising happiness, an album that's at once joyful and embarrassing and nostalgic to look at. Then new events will simply stop happening. Time will stretch out, and from being in a fast river that doesn't freeze in winter, just like the Tulubaika River with rapids

and whirlpools, the heroine will suddenly find herself in a deep lake in some temporal solitude without skills for overcoming bottomless and boundless waters.

— Happy Awakening! — sadly or merrily from afar will sound the voice of the first ancestor. They will have lined up in a queue to look at our heroine: all from parents to animalcule in slippers, to soulless cosmic dust, to the spark at the beginning of all.

— Happy Awakening! — the next ancestor will say.

— Happy Awakening!

— Happy Awakening!

— Happy Awakening!...

And so on deeper into the generations until our heroine will cease to understand every ancient and lost in time language of her ancestors.

Episode Seventeen
about helices of all kinds

Where once a solid house stood,
now a conceptual structure is forming,
made of images, pure invention,
as if it had survived in the mind, unscathed...

— Rainer Maria Rilke, "The Seventh Elegy"

Airports smell of time in the same manner as the smoke from smouldering sawdust — bittersweet. The waiting room for the flight departing from Tulubaika is well ventilated (unlike my head). Still steeped in samogón, my thoughts and memories, puffing at ach other with hangovers, are on a philosophical rave.

An old sofa with familiar faces around.

— Drink, grandson, — my Grandad says and pats me on the shoulder.

I approach the shot with caution.

— What's in it?

— Alcohol, grandson, alcohol. What do you think? Milk?

It does look like milk. I seek the shot's bottom. None is found due to the sheer turbidity of the liquid.

— What are you? Twelve?

Not that it would make a difference.

— Just wondering. I will wake up tomorrow, won't I?

— That's up to luck. When's the last time you were to church?

— I have a flight tomorrow. Early in the morning.

— Well, good you aren't a bloody pilot, are you?

— I still have to get to the airport.

— Good you aren't a taxi driver either.

— Someone has to wake me up.

— I will, don't you worry, lad.

— What if you don't wake up?

— Burying me already, aye?

Stalling, I am. He puts on reading glasses, picks up his phone and shows me the alarm clock app.

— Here: one, two, three of them, bastards. Technologia.

— I don't know... It just doesn't feel like my thing.

— It's a family thing — means it's your thing. Don't you respect tradition?

— I do, wholeheartedly. But...

— Don't you respect your grandfather?

— There's no limit to my respect, of course.

— I see no problem then. Or do they cut your balls in your rotting West?

I roll my eyes at him. Grandad, in turn, prepares for a knockout.

— You're still a man or what? — he says and moves the shot closer. — Drink.

Reddened faces with burst capillaries around me chant "drink!" bumping their fists on the table, bottles shaking, shots clinking.

— Drink! Drink! Drink! Drink!

Dishes aplenty huddle together, leaving not an inch of space: boiled and butter-drenched potatoes with tons of dill, infernally smoked sterlet in illegal quantities[1], pickled vegetables drowning in brine, fresh vegetables drowning in mayonnaise, a fly drowning in mayonnaise, too.[2] Drops of mayonnaise fly from my niece's plate onto my red cashmere jumper (I have no idea how to wash it) as she

---

1. Sterlet (from German "Störling"), a torpedo-shaped freshwater fish from the sturgeon family, native to the river systems of Russia and Eastern Europe. Historically it was one of the top status dishes which brought it to the wrong side of conservation efforts in the late 20th century. Now it has a protected status. The sterlet possesses neither the international celebrity of its caviar-producing relatives nor their imposing size, making it perfect for provincial Russian grandeur.

2. Dill, garlic, and mayonnaise are crucial parts of Eastern European cuisine. They are used in atrocious quantities in main dishes, appetisers, salads, soups, etm. There's no

expresses dislike towards the soup's surface and slaps it with her spoon. A five-litre bottle of samogón with a cork left in its neck authoritatively reigns over the table. Grandad uses corks to seal his samogón bottles. He fancies himself an artisanal distiller and, to his good luck, is friends with the coppers.

— Drink! Drink! Drink!

Mustering up my guts, I take a whiff of the shot. Squirming, I am, ready to pass out.

— No, I'm not drinking that. Smells terrifying.

— "Terrrific" you wanted to say, lad. Drink!

— Drink! Drink! Drink! — chant they non-stop.

Eyes shut, box breathing engaged, I lift the shot glass.

— Wait! — screams Grandad. — Forgot the clouds!

I'm confused, or rather befuddled. Grandad grabs a pack of mayo and with jeweller's precision layers it on top of the samogón. My family's favourite lemma: everything's better with mayonnaise.

— I've drunk worse, — he says, grinning proudly in anticipation.

— Never doubted your abilities.

— It's like baptism, you know. You do it once, and then comrade Major Yehoshua (may his memory be blessed) will handle the rest, — he adds as he crosses the shot glass. — One for him, one for the Tsar, one for your grandfather. Now you go. Drink.

— Drink! Drink! Drink! Drink!

In an instant, the liquid blazes a trail from my tongue all the way down to my stomach. Welcome, dear regret, I haven't had enough of you.

— I won't go blind, will I?

— Blind? No. Dead? Mayhap!

I know what happens next. We'll finish the bottles (plural) and commence a swimming contest in the river Tulubaika, cold in temperature, clayey in colour, and cunning in current, covered with layers of lemna and fallen birch leaves.

---

such thing as "enough" with them. Saying "enough garlic" is the same as saying "enough love" — ridiculous.

My Grandad is tempered. He loves swimming, loves it so much that he has always wanted to teach me how to—

— Just fucking swim already!

— *tortured murloc sounds*[3]... I can't... *mrgrgl* I think, I think I'm...

— You think? You have time to think, aye? Swim! Use your hands, Aristotle!

— *mrgrgl* I'm drowning. I'm drowning.

Water gurgles in my throat, echoing through the skull bone.

— You what, aye?

— Drowninnnn...

— Cannot hear it!

— Drownnmnlnmin...

— No, you're not!

— I am, though.

— I'll tell you when you are. Don't you worry!

Delays, queues, security checks, more queues, people sleeping on the ceiling, my luggage lost with my Nurofen, sour grimaces, coffa and croissants costing like a jet's wing, timeless, untameable roads of travelators and escalators — all are trifles, dummies, nothing. Time is the real enemy. You wanted to save time on a few train journeys, but now look at you, wasting it. But how can you waste time? Isn't the whole point of time to be unremittingly wasted?

— I think it flows in multiple directions at once, — I say to Grandad.

— What, Tulubaika? — he asks, frowning.

Grandad peeks deep into my eyes, his fingers ready to dial the mental asylum's number, while my sister with her daughter giggle beside him.

— No, the time!

— Bollocks!

— Bollocks! — adds my niece.

---

3. In the Warcraft universe, murlocs are an amphibious humanoid with fish-like head, bulging eyes and gurgling voice, infamous for their distinctive "mrglglglgl" vocalisations.

— Indeed it is! Proper bollocks, I must say. But let him speak. He's a smart lad. Excellent student. Good genetics. Exemplary, I'd even say. I was driving him to school every day. In the front seat, like a bloody prince. All lasses were like, "Oh my God, look at him, that distinguished gentleman has a chauffeur!"

— They thought I was lazy.

— Who?

— They thought.

— They thought what?

— That I was lazy.

— They thought you were lazy? You? Lazy?

— They did, I'm afraid.

— Why would they think that?

— I have a childhood trauma now.

— You what?

— Everyone was taking the piss.

— A piss? On you?

— No, the piss, out of me.

— Well, it's not that bad then, is it? Where's trauma? Degenerates, they were. Why would you listen to degenerates? Who taught you to listen to degenerates? Me? I didn't. Listen to idiots, become an idiot.

— Everyone was walking or taking a bus.

— That bloody jalopy would never arrive! Were you ever late for a class?

— They thought I was a privileged boy. Nothing's worse than being a privileged boy when you're not really a privileged boy.

— Well, they were right.

— But you just said they were degenerates.

— Grandfather like me is a privilege. You should remember that, lad. Write that above my grave: "A revered fella he was, a true privilege."

— What is a childhood trauma? — asks my niece.

— It's a family thing.

— Can I have it too?

— You won't have it, my heroine.

251

— But uncle has it.

— No, he doesn't.

— She'll have it.

— No, she won't.

— She will. Don't you respect tradition?

— Uncle's taking the piss. Don't listen to him.

— Is he a degenerate?

— On certain occasions.

— Like when?

— Let's talk about the time, shall we?

— Right.

— Tell us everything.

— I was gonna talk about it, yes.

— You were?

— I was.

— Ah yess. You should have more confidence and persistence, though, shouldn't you? Why didn't you stop me rambling?

— Grandad...

— Right, right, tell us.

I stand up and begin the theoretical part with the first page of the flipchart. A pointer taps on the board, the same pointer that I might get hit with if I get a B. Soldier's buckle[4], a pointer — those are my upbringers. The picture, expressed in pastel crayons kindly provided by my little niece, depicts a winding spiral.

— Imagine a helical structure...

— A what?

— A helical structure. A helix. A spiral.

— Here, drink this.

I empty another shot, it burns my tongue, I don't feel and don't care if it twists anymore. Grandad was right. The second, the third, and the fourth, are a smooth ride. Comrade Major Yehoshua is doing

---

4. The default belt buckle of the Soviet military was a weighty brass object with the Red Star or hammer and sickle insignia. Once a soldier came home, the belt buckle was used in domestic pedagogy as an instrument of corporal punishment: state-supplied, ideologically sanctioned, and efficiently painful.

his job (may his memory be blessed *crosses himself*). I clear my throat and, before I forget the word, spew it all out:

— Consider a helical manifold in $\mathbb{R}^3$ where temporal perception coils like a spring such that psychologically proximate events need not be linearly adjacent in time but rather align through geodesic proximity on the helix itself much like points on different coils might touch despite their temporal separation allowing simultaneous experience and modification of memory-states through continuous recursive revision in non-orientable topology where each remembered point endlessly reshapes its neighbours until what-was and what-we-remember-was become indistinguishable singularities in the manifold.

The reaction is rather underwhelming.

— Huh? — Grandad asks, finally.

— What's that "huh"?

— I don't understand, that's what "huh" means.

— What is it that you don't understand exactly?

— Well, not a single bloody bit of it.

— Bollocks! — my niece's contribution is always immeasurable.

Grandad looks at her, smiles, ruffles her hair, looks at me, frowns.

— Proper bollocks. Say it again.

— Bollocks!

— No, not you, love.

— *inhales* Being at any given point, *exhales* we feel that certain points in the past and future are closer to us than others. Two diametrically opposed points on the circumference of one ring of the spring are further apart than many points on the other rings down below its curvature.

He shakes his head.

— Drink this.

More samogón is being kindly provided to me, hand-to-hand.

— Now, look at me.

I look at him.

— I'm looking.

— Tell me, what do you see?

— My beloved grandfather. A true privilege.

— Right, what else? In a general sense. Who am I?

— Erm, a human?

— Right... — he says and leans closer to me. — But I'm not a fucking dictionary, am I?

— You don't look like one, no.

— Speak in normal words, then. What university did you graduate from? What did they teach you there?

— Sciences.

— "Sciences." Of course, sciences. Should've gone to Moscow, told you all. Moscow's better. All roads lead to Moscow. Moscow is the Third Rome. "Two Romes have fallen, the third stands, and there will never be a fourth."[5]

— Bollocks! Bollocks! Bollocks! — they chant.

He shakes his head.

— Drink this.

He hands me another shot. For a couple of seconds I let the clouds settle and consume the concoction. So does he.

— Sit, — he says, his hand on my shoulder.

I follow.

— Now, explain it to me. Man to man.

— Man to man?

— Yes, man to man.

— Okay, I will.

I pause to gather my wits, untwist my tongue I don't feel anymore.

— Imagine. *hiccups* Simultaneously you experience the past, the present, and the future, and not only experience but affect them.

— Uh-huh.

— You're here... *waves around* in the present, you're between two layers of time: the past and the future. *hiccups* Memories shape

_____

5. A foundational myth of Russian exceptionalism that goes back to the 16th century when monk Philotheus of Pskov declared Moscow the spiritual successor to Rome and Constantinople, the third and final Rome. This proposition conveniently justified Moscow's imperial ambitions, positioning Russia as Christianity's last bastion and rightful heir to classical civilisation, sustaining Russian grandiosity through tsarist absolutism and beyond.

you and you, in return, review and reshape them, until there's nothing left of what really happened and instead only what the present you have created for yourself, *hiccups* the time never been—

Grandad's samogón tastes like a kitten has pissed into a basket of strawberries. Plus mayonnaise.

— Same with the future. *hiccups* You plan, scheme, ponder, become excited, hopeful, anxious, all that, experience some sort of eschatological dread even. Thus you live in all three times simultaneously while not being in any of them! *hiccups*

— I've always reckoned you were a smart lad. But I still don't get it.

— It's a spiral, Grandad!

— What is a spiral? The river? Tulubaika?

— No, Grandad, time! We're not talking about Tulubaika!

— Oh, we're not? I thought we were.

— No, Grandad, we're not...

— You know, you won't become a president if you speak like that.

— Of course I won't become a president.

— Why won't you become a president?

— I don't want to be a president.

— My grandson doesn't want to be a president?

— No.

He examines me with a look of an ex-KGB officer, who he perhaps was.

— What?

— My grandson doesn't want to be a president! What's the point of even having a grandson then!

— Well, she can be a president! If you teach her well.

— Nah, she can't.

— Do you want to be a president? — I turn to my niece.

— I do.

— See? She wants to be a president. It doesn't have to be me.

— Well, I won't see that, will I? I'm old, laddie. Flesh and bones, mind you. Not immortal.

— Oh, you are not?

— I want to say to everyone "I'm the president's grandfather, I'm

255

the president's grandfather". How am I gonna do that from the other side?

— Too bad because I have no aspiration to be a president.

— You did though.

— Me? You did.

I wait for his reaction while he's reading my mind.

— *sighs* Well, good for the guy to be humble. Helps in life, helps a lot. Not bragging or anything. The chaps up there... So dishonest, them, degenerates. "We'll do that, we'll do second, all won't be topsy-turvy, promise." You're not like that, aren't you? I taught you well, haven't I?

— You have. I suppose.

Grandad smacks my back, an intense attempt to pat.

— He supposes! You'll do good up there in the highest echelons, uh-huh. Drink this.

He hands me another shot. I drink, no questions asked. He makes one for himself, drinks, no questions asked either.

— You could start with being a governor.

— Governor of what?

— Governor of Tulubaika, of course. Our little village.

— I can't be a governor of Tulubaika.

— Why can't you? You're an heir.

— I'm heading back tomorrow, for a start.

— Nobody's pulling you, are they? Stay, you're a governor, I'm your advisor. Vice-governor, vice grip, huge success. Rule in tandem like bloody Siamese twins — two brains are better than one, aren't they?

— I'd very much love that, but I'm heading back tomorrow.

— You're drunk. You don't know what you're saying. But I hear you: Tulubaika, Tulubaika, Tulubaika, nothing else. Goes on like an echo.

— I said no word about Tulubaika.

— Tulubaika, Tulubaika, Tulubaika.

— You're saying it. Not me.

— Between the lines, all that. I still hear it. Look at me — 80 years,

still good hearing. Good genetics for a governor. You could rule for decades.

— I don't want to rule for decades, and I can't be a governor of Tulubaika.

— Pray tell why not.

— Well, I don't live here, do I?

— Where are you then? Am I hallucinating you?

— Well, maybe. You're drunk. You don't know what you're seeing. I'm but your delusion.

Silent, I sit. The ongoing exchange of glances intensifies. While Grandad looks at her, I gesture a hush to my niece. We don't say a word. We know he can't stand it.

— Eh? Say something, you hooligans.

He grabs my cheeks and pulls them. Frowning, he pours himself more of his artisanal alcohol (no clouds) and knocks it down.

When I was a little boy, my sister and I used to prank our beloved drunk grandfather all the time. In his deliriums, we'd give him a slotted spoon when he was eating soup, wear deer antlers and chase him until he had an (improvised) panic attack, pull his trousers down and watch him clumsily pull them back up, or hide under the table and pretend we're invisible.

He rubs his eyes and — *poof!* — we're not his grandchildren but figments of his imagination.

— I'm calling the shrinks, — he says, takes his phone, stands up and, wobbling, paces across the room. — Doctor, doctor! I'm hallucinating... No, no, it's voices of my grandchildren. Two of them, lovely little rascals. A lad and a lass. Exemplary students... I don't know how old they are. I don't know anything... No, they had antlers, they did, I swear. Yes, yes... No, no, I haven't been drinking. It's the medication. It is, doctor... Did you order it from the West?... Big mistake, that, huge even... Oh no, doctor... You reckon I'm a goner?... I haven't even saved up enough for a funeral... Poor me, — he says and falls on the floor. — Love 'em, lil'bastards... But what one can do in the face of death? No, I need no straitjacket no more, doctor... I'm... I'm seeing the light... and, my, my, it's bloody bright and beautiful.

As in the finest, most artsy Moscow theatres, he goes quiet, his hand falls and drops the phone. We, little psyop enthusiasts, stiffen, jump out from under the table and run to him.

— Grandad, Grandad! — we scream. — Don't die, Grandad. The circus's tomorrow! You promised! Mom and dad are working. Who's going to drive us there? Grandad, please! There'll never be a circus in Tulubaika any more! They come once every twenty years. We'll be old and won't be interested in the circus when they come next. Pleaaaaaaaase!

We cry in Greek-tragedic. Life's so fragile; his — an ancient vase, not to be meddled with, belongs to the one and only Tulubaikan museum. No kintsugi will ever heal its cracks.

— Wake up, Grandad! Please!

Blaring like a siren, my little sister runs away to fetch help. I shake Grandad by his shoulders:

— Wake up! It's a spiral! Don't die!

He's not breathing. He's not breathing. He's not breathing!

— The time is a spiral!

A fraction of a second of silence, then: with a rasp, he siphons in all the surrounding air and, in a hoarse, ancient voice, utters:

— You know what the duck's dick looks like, don't you?

Mallards occupy birchleaf-ridden Tulubaika and swim in uneven spirals, quacking, feasting on food provided by the audience or on lemna if the audience is absent. A baguette half my height warms my palm scratched by our cat, warms my nostrils scratched from sniffing snot, and warms my brain scratched by an unsuccessful chess class. The pawn is Grandad's favourite piece.

— One has to learn some compassion for 'em lumpens. "Everybody should be free" — bollocks. They ought to learn to be pawns first before getting too big for their boots. "Everyone is equal" — perhaps. Only if everyone's a pawn, otherwise — nah. But of course, not true for the players...

I sniff snot again and tear off a piece from the baguette, separate the crumb from the browned crust, munch the crust, and roll the

crumb into a tiny ball. If the talentlessness has an image, it probably looks like this.

— I don't think it was my fault really. I played well. The teacher told me that was one of my best, that I'm getting better...

No, I'm not. I don't really think so. I'm not getting better at anything. In fact, I might be getting worse. According to Grandad, there are two noble pursuits for a prodigy in our country: chess and ballet. Them two is what really wins both cold wars and hot ones, for they assert an artistic and intellectual dominance over the pawns of capitalism. I went to chess, my sister went to ballet. No, he doesn't demarcate them by sex, so he said — my legs were just not straight enough, unlike, he thought, my convolutions, which, though invisible to him, seemed to present a higher potential to make me an asset in the arms race. Factory settings of consciousness are a clean slate, unpolluted by choices made by you and for you, hence, getting worse isn't to be ruled out.

— What do pawns do? — he says, shaking his head. — Go straight, no questions asked, they do. They just go straight. Easy task, "soul of the game", go straight, do your diagonal attacks, don't come back.

— A pawn can become a queen.

— Freedom is only for the elite. A pawn can only pretend to be a queen.

— I'm a good player. Everyone says that... well, everyone says that to everyone. I guess, everyone's just a better player than me or everyone's lying to each other and the game is fake. I did the opening you taught me, by the way. It did work at first but then it didn't.

— Look around: give everyone freedom, what do they do, degenerates?...

The breadball of my talentlessness is almost perfect now. The ducks have noticed us, their heads tilting in anticipation. I sniff more, so loudly that the mallards twitch.

— Maybe the boy was just more experienced than me.

— First thing they do is nothing, second thing they do is complain. Why? Freedom is too difficult for their spongy brains. It

should be beaten into one with a rod from early childhood, so that his arse burns, and then he remembers and thinks — free... free... But for morons, it's a burden. They don't understand it.

— I think I'm getting sick... I have a runny nose. And my throat, it's itchy, a tiny bit itchy, but still. It always begins like that. And temperature, I think it's rising as well.

— Everyone starts from the same position. Proper clean slate it is. Never interrupt your enemy when he's making a mistake. Napoleon said that...

I nibble on the baguette. Crispy, soft, perfect combination of taste and texture. Tulubaika does have some French vibes in this time of the year, almost Toulouse. Ubiquitous romanticism of melancholy.

— I can't play well when I'm sick. Maybe that's why. It's for real. I'm not faking it... Not this time...

— Still lost, he, bastard, ran away like a dog.

— I just want to stay home and play games. You said games are stupid but isn't chess a game, too? Is chess stupid? It's easy to learn, hard to master, they say. Mario is actually hard to play from the start. You should see me playing. I'm good at it. Maybe a lot better than at chess.

I throw the rolled breadball to Tulubaika. Circles of startled water scurry away from a bready pebble, quaquaversally, in the same fashion time does from a person. Mad quacking shakes the surrounding space of the river's quay, and the ducks pounce on a piece of bread, scattering fallen leaves aside. A flock of pigeons that have been pleading with me for food is horrified and blown apart all over the quay.

— Look at 'em green-headed bastards. They should've flown off by now for winter. We don't need weapons. They can't ever win winter, pussies. They don't have winter like ours... Though I reckon we shouldn't've burnt Moscow, eh...

You burn Moscow to scare the dragon away, then win the princess, she falls in love with you for your strategic prodiginess, then you play Mario all day, together, forever and ever.

My cheeks are flushing and melting from joy, snot is dripping from

my nose. I demonstrate my braces to "the green-headed bastards", stuff my mouth with more baguette, share another scrap with them, and in a second, Grandad smacks me on the back of my head.

— Who feeds 'em birds with bread, eh? They'll be as good as gone.

— ...

— And put your hat on, won't you?

— ...

It is going outwards from the centre. It is a spiral, a spring that someone once squeezed and released. It is a spiralling staircase that you climb. Spiral is a helix. Time is a spiral. Therefore, time is a helix. La logique! Everything is a helix if you look at it from the right dimension. Apparently, the duck's penis is a helix, too. Male ducks have corkscrew-shaped penises, and forced copulation is common among ducks. In response, female ducks have evolved complex vaginal structures, including spiralling and labyrinthine vaginas, to prevent full insertion of the male's penis and control fertilisation. This co-evolution, where each sex evolves reproductive traits to outcompete the other in the battle for reproductive control, is described as an escalating sexual arms race in ducks.

— They're gonna bomb us, grandson.

— They're not gonna bomb you, Grandad. Nobody cares about bombing Tulubaika. Nobody cares about Tulubaika.

— Aye, they will. I feel it in my bones. Oh, they ache, they ache! Deep inside them, they ache, my bones. I'm not young anymore; I'm old. We're losing that bloody arms race. We're losing it, I've always said that.

The pathos of the situation, though.

— Yes, you've been saying that for as long as I can remember.

— Because we've been losing it as long as I can remember! You know the difference between the battle and a war, don't you? Winning a match and winning a championship, aye? Didn't I teach you that? They bomb everyone! Pigeons with diarrhoea! Ducks eating bread!

— We bomb everyone, too, to be honest. Every few years, there's war. We're like, you know, bombing left and right. Not that we're a peaceful country.

— Who told you that?

— Everyone says that. It's a fact.

— "Everyone says that." Listen to degenerates, become a degenerate. Facts? I know facts. Simple formula, no need to be an academic. They're gonna bomb us, this is the fact. It's ridiculous! "Everyone says that." Bomb us, they will.

— Why would they bomb us?

— We have nukes, they have nukes. It's going nowhere. Unless we have better nukes. We do have better nukes, wonderful nukes. Our nukes are incredible, absolutely incredible. We should nuke them out of this planet. Boom! Gone! No more problem.

— They would nuke us, too, then...

— Isn't this what I'm trying to tell you?

— This is how nuking works, yes. In the end, everyone nukes everyone.

— They're gonna bomb us — us, you and me, the country, everything, absolutely bloody everything. I know bombing, I served. Moscow — gone. Tulubaika — gone. All in a matter of minutes. Tulubaika — in seconds. Or less. Every city, every village, every child. One button — BOOM! Another button — BOOM! They smile at you today — "oh, peace, peace, United Nations" — but tomorrow? And I'll tell you — we won't allow it, never allow it. We have such weapons, saw them myself! I served! Such weapons — mmm, beautiful! Shiny rockets. We should nuke them first.

As if on a trampoline, I bounce on our old sofa trimmed in what's now called vegan leather, listening to how the rusty springs are creaking in agony under the pressure of my weight and how Grandad's swearing at the telly in the next room. Someone is bombing someone, a common state of affairs.

— Unbelievable! Unbe-bloody-lievable... They are actually doing it! Fine country, great people... It's ridiculous, it's bloody ridiculous... Fucking 'ell, bastards... Can you imagine? We should've nuked them.

My brain cells at this age are still in a mode of looking for meaningful connections with each other, so I continue bouncing and each of my landings resonates through the whole room. The

floorboards creak, the windows shake, dangles the chandelier, and rings the crystal set behind the glass doors of the cupboard. There, in the dark, covertly ferments Grandad's blackcurrant tincture, artisanally produced. It's a tightly corked five-litre jar, looking like a barrel with a narrow neck. The vibrations from the sofa creep towards the bottle, disturbing the peace of its cushy chamber, envelop the bottle and call the pressure to come out, and the pressure, in turn, being quite claustrophobic (as pressures tend to be), acquires a strong desire to see the light, yet it cannot, for the cork wouldn't allow that, so the pressure, pissed with such a state of affairs, decides to exit sideways, quaquaversally. All I hear is an explosion, a rapid expansion in volume of a given amount of matter associated with an extreme outward release of energy and compressed gases from inside the blackcurrant tincture bottle. Shatters the crystal set, shatters the glass door, shake the windows and chandelier. The door of the cupboard blasts open, and from there, riverly, the black-red mass spills over the old Persian carpet, flowing between the floorboards, silencing their creaks, and under the sofa, surrounding me, leaving no escape route. The floor is lava now.

— Bombing! They're fucking bombing us! I've always said that! Fucking 'ell! A disaster, a complete disaster!

Grandad rushes into the room, ducking down, glaring around, at me, at his favourite black-red liquid that has pooled over his favourite carpet, at his favourite cupboard filled with pieces of his favourite crystal. I already know he's angry, and I already know what's coming for me.

— Sit tight, lad. Get your thighs—

Ready for your old soldier's buckle, I know, I know...

Buckle up! Our ultra low-cost airline plane finally reestablishes contact with terra firma in Tulubaika's international ten-terminal airport after forty minutes of spiralling over the area like a leaf chastised by gravity as if the land didn't want to accept her prodigal sons and daughters back. Either she suffered from amnesia or deliberately erased all memory of us, probably out of great offence. I sit in business class, a privileged boy, nodding off, my eyes refusing to unpeel themselves. The

cabin atmosphere is noisy with irritation from waiting, excitement from anticipation, screams of awakened pipsqueaks. The flight attendant gives a hand signal, everyone freezes. The stewards roll out a red carpet down the aisle. The captain emerges from the cockpit, his presence commands complete silence. He adjusts his cap, curves his smile, gliding along, strides down the cabin. An explosion (though, on a plane, better say "pop") of applause, people reach out their hands to him, whistle, shout something, the pipsqueaks squeal the loudest, and he, our revered one, just walks, waves his hand, beaming, blinding with his grin. May comrade Major Yehoshua, whose memory is blessed, bless him, too.

— Thanks for not killing us!

— THANK YOU, THANK YOU!

— I thought I was gonna die, me and my lil'pipsqueak, I thought that was all, and we'd never see Tulubaika again.

— He did it! He did it! What a pilot! We're alive!

Given her ever-intensifying excitement, a woman next to me faints.

— A saviour no less!

— You're a hero! Landing in Tulubaika — oh, what an achievement! Nobody had done that! Ever!

— THANK YOU!

— DA! DA! DA! DA! DA!

— I LOVE YOU! Take me with you back to the foreign lands! The whole me, from top to bottom!

The gods are pissing freezing rain over our heads protected with nothing but duty-free bags. Everyone flees the plane, sloshing through puddles and splashing dirty rainwater all over each other. There's one measly runway in this airport; beyond the curtains of rain — the birch forest; only the terminal building, a tiny brutalist cave, glimmers with lights in the distance. No sign of that stinking rustbucket — word is the bus broke down, no one to shuttle you lot about. I'm not all wet, for I have a coat. Others... well, they don't all have coats.

We take shelter in the terminal and head to the border control. A nerve-wracking moment, this. As you approach you always get that sinking feeling in your gut, feeling guilty as if you've got contraband

drugs stashed in your soles or the depths of your posterior. Fingers atremble, I hand my battle-scarred passport over to a woman wearing a quasi-military uniform and a quasi-expression on her face. My red cashmere jumper has no stains of mayonnaise on it yet. Fear is foreign to me — like I am now to this land — for only recklessness fuels my bravery.

— Purpose of your visit? — she asks and looks straight into my eyes.

— Seeing family, — I answer.

— Whose family?

— Well, mine... I was born here.

She writes something down on an A4 lying around.

— Tell me who exactly are you going to see.

— My grandfather...

— Are you travelling alone?

— I am....

— Where are you going to stay?

— At my grandfather's.....

— Address?

— Well, it's in Tulubaika......

— I'm well aware of that, am I not?

— Almost "to the village, to Grandfather"....... he-he........

Pauses, she does, and looks at me, in the most rigorous manner.

— Sorry, it's, erm, from Chekhov. "Konstantin Makarych", you know?

— ...

Keeps staring.

— It's, erm, Tulubaika, 8........

— What street?

— There's no street.

— ...

— It's just a house, a single house, no street. He's privileged, that old man.

— Does your grandfather live in a field?

— He lives in a house. Well, he has a bunker in a field, though. So he says, he-he......

— A bunker?

— Probably, dementia.........

Her eyes are eating my face. I see little teethful maws grow from them.

— Why are you smiling? — she asks. — Is it a good idea to smile?

I forgot it's not customary here — my bad. I come from where people smile sometimes. A habit, nothing more. Mimicry, yes, pure mimesis, assimilation.

— ... a smile without a reason is a sign of a fool, you probably heard that...

— Everyone says it, yes. I knew a guy who had a tattoo with this phrase. Don't ask where.

And my red jumper is a clown outfit, that I know, too.

— ...

She examines the picture on my passport, rubs it, frowns.

— Hm... Looks nothing like you. You're way thinner.

— Thank you.

— It's not a compliment... Is it you on this picture?

— I'm a different person now..........

— Wrong answer.

— I know. Sorry.

— Have you been in the army?

— No.

— ...

— Thankfully.

— Wrong answer.

— ...

— Are you a draft dodger?

— No, no, I'm not. I've been away, studying, is all.

— Don't you support the present politics of our country and its wonderful course into the future? Don't make wrong answers.

— I... I'm... I'm worried about the future..........

She tries to deduce something from the copious stamps in my passport, shakes her head, writes something down.

— Where've you been for eleven years?

— Erm... Studying, working, paying taxes, boring stuff.

— Do you have foreign friends?

— I... maybe... yes?

I see something surfacing on her retinas.

— Why are you coming back?

On the retinas, I read a fresh inscription that I'm not welcome, and a thought that has been fermenting in the back of my mind cupboard for years now enters the labyrinthine structure of my brain like a corkscrew. What if the village, on some subtle energetic level, would refuse to accept me and reject me like a transplanted organ? What if during one of the walks along the famous Tulubaikan wide avenues guarded on both sides by tall birches raining down their golden leaves, along narrow streets among old shrivelled wooden houses, mothballed under eternal restoration, as if that is what they are condemned for by time, or on the high hills, from which the whole village could be seen, sunken in the sea of trees, and the river Tulubaika, which goes around the village, shallow but still deep enough to take a boat or to swim, what if among all that I would feel myself a stranger? What if I meet my first love with whom I have long since lost contact, and, even out of common courtesy, have no choice but to talk? Terrifying prospect, that.

She's a cashier in a shop called "SHOP", has a husband with an orc face and five kids with semi-orc faces. I'm about to pay for everything.

— Hi! Is it really you?

Who? Me? Even I don't know that. What a question!

— Apparently, yeah. Nice to meet you. Erm, again. Nice to see you again.

— You're looking good!

Not the best I can manage.

— You too. Looking good, I mean.

— How many years? Ten, fifteen?

— Eleven, actually.

— Ah, yes! Time flies! Since school, right, right.

— Yeah, doesn't it indeed? Flowing weirdly, that thing. Spirals, he-he...

— Oh yes, indeed. How are you? As white as soot?

— I'm good, alright, not too bad, coping, he-he. How's your life?

— Better than yours!

— And mine is better than yours, too!

— Of course, it's not a zero-sum game, is it?

— It is indeed not. I know what that is, my eldest's in the sixth grade.

— Oh is he indeed?

— Yes, a smart lad, exemplary student.

— Good genetics.

— Right, yes. It's all the air, the air's special here, clean and all.

— Oh is it indeed?

— Indeed. Nature.

— Naturally, yes.

— What do you do? Ah wait, I remember. You program clouds. Your grandfather told me. We always talk about you when he comes by.

— Do you indeed?

— Charming fellow. Back then he thought we were a couple, imagine that.

— Weren't we?

— Oh you had those plump cheeks, very cute.

— Indeed.

— Indeed.

— Indeed indeed.

— Oh yes, indeedly indeed.

— Indeedest of indeeds!

— Indeed, uh-huh...

— Indeed indeed...

— ...

— ...

— Are you married?

— As a matter of fact, I am, actually.

— Do you have kids?

This is everyone's favourite question. I wonder why the border control lady didn't ask me it. "Do you have kids?" "No, I do not." "Have you had kids?" "No I have not." "Will you have kids?" "... maybe?" "When will you have kids?" But I am prepared.

— I have a niece, yes. She's cute. Look at these stains.

— You look like a mushroom!

— I know, right? She's quite an artist, little chortess.

I would wager she's in cahoots with them chorts, even though she has an angelic face. All children are like this. She looks at me — no, inspects me — like I'm some unknown species. That odd abroaded uncle who is rumoured to share some of his grandfather's outstanding genetic material, a wise and knowledgeable man who studied "sciences". Some things pass through birth, some by birthright, some only through words. So be it, hither and yon, I shall act as an adult and teach her our family's arcane knowledge of how to separate a head and a tail and bones and eat the river fish properly.

— But I don't like fish.

— Why don't you like fish?

— I don't know.

— Have you eaten fish?

— I have not.

— Will you eat fish?

— ... maybe?

— Maybe?

— I don't like how it smells. It smells fishy.

— You know, we used to fish all the time when we were like you. In Tulubaika. Grandad made me a fishing rod. He was driving us to the river as well. I caught a lot of fish once and fed it all to our cat. She liked it, I reckoned she was happy. She was old. Once we found her caught between the fence boards. Oh, well...

— I'm almost six and I'm not a cat. Although I wouldn't mind being a cat at all. I might as well become a cat later because why not, right? GG says I can be whoever I want.

269

— Oh does he indeed? "GG"... I've never heard "GG" saying something of that sort. Was he drunk?

— Isn't it so interesting being a cat? They have paws and they're fluffy. I'm not fluffy at all, I feel like a snake now.

— Cats eat fish, though.

— I know! I'm not a degenerate. They do but I'm not yet a cat, you see? It's so simple, really. Those things take time. So I'll wait until I am.

— Well, that's a shame. I'm not here often, as you might've noticed. Fish have plenty of useful things, for example, omega-3 for brain development.

— Has the fish helped you at all?

— ... What do you reckon?

— I don't reckon it did, if I'm honest. If I'm completely honest, you're odd.

— Am I indeed?

— Not very odd, don't you worry. Just a little odd, a tiny bit odd. It's not too bad, right? Being odd? I'd advise you shouldn't worry.

— Oh, I shouldn't?

— No, you shouldn't. You're not a degenerate, right? Because THAT would be really really bad.

— I hope I'm not.

— GG would say you're fine then. You shouldn't worry.

— Okay. I won't. If "GG" says so.

— You look sad.

— No, I'm not.

— Yes, you do. Why do you look sad?

Oh how painful it is to return to that homeland, that home, that street (or a house), after so many years of being away. One who is not who he was comes to a place that is not what it was, and two entities, the character and the place, meet each other again, as if for the first time, a complete and total jamais vu but with a hint of déjà vu, a bit toxic déjà vu — two either idealised or despised images sprouted from the imperfection of memory. All everything does is seeming. It's never a full circle. It cannot be. One never comes back to the same point.

One doesn't have to disguise oneself as a beggar or someone else to do the nostos, for one is already disguised by time.

— I want a great great-grandchild, grandson. More of 'em, lil'bastards.

— What for? I wonder.

Once upon a time, Grandad's archnemesis from the house next door spread a rumour that he, Grandad, eats them, infants.

— The line, our beautiful line, should remain intact, shouldn't it?

— You have one already, — I point to my niece.

— YOUR little child, when will you bring me YOUR little child?

— Well, I can't. Because I don't have any, Grandad.

— You have my name. Look at us! — he grabs me by a resemblance of my biceps. — I and you, you and I — Olympians! Bloody good helixes, exemplary genetic material. You don't waste exemplary genetic material. New gold, new oil it is these days. Precious, absolutely precious. Look at all those aborted degenerates running around!

— Grandad...

— They abort them, then nurse them in test tubes and release them on the streets, IQ of a pumpkin — many people are saying this, lots of very smart people. Western influence, terrible influence, absolutely the worst. Priest told me once — every Sunday I go to church, every Sunday, I still do — he told me this. A woman, a damn fanny-for-sale — everybody knows who she is, I'm not pointing fingers — aborted fifteen, bloody fifteen (!) little degenerates, a world record. Then what? What did Comrade Major Yehoshua do (may his memory be blessed *crosses himself*)... He told the priest that he wouldn't send her to hell, no, hell no, hell no. He would send her to heaven instead so she would spend all her eternal life nursing her abortlings there. Isn't it just incredible? Nobody does divine punishment like He does, nobody. This is why I go to church, to hear stories like that. He's a great guy, we've got a new one, fantastic guy, smart, drives a fucking G-Wagon, has a beard, exemplary priest. I fucking hate beards but does he look serious? Oh indeed he does. You should shave your fucking thing, though.

He grabs me by the resemblance of a beard, rather lovingly, and jerks it.

— ... they were not baptised, though, were they?

— Of course they weren't. Who would baptise an abortling. Bonkers!

— Well, how do they go to heaven then?

Speechless, he is, in awe at my theological apparatus. He makes an expression of a person going blind or about to have a stroke.

— You don't understand anything, do you? This is such a stupid question, incredibly stupid. What is your wife doing?

— She's busy.

— That's a shame. I thought you lied to me, though, when you said that. Aren't you busy, too? Your lady's not supposed to be busy. I hoped to see her. I've always reckoned you were a good-looking lad and a bit of a wily bastard, husband material, no less. A father material, too, do you know what I mean?

— Unfortunately.

— Have pity, you two. I'm old, incredibly old. I'm healthy and all but you know how that happens — very rapid. Someone's up there presses a button and — *poof!** — gone. Might not see your little duckling running around this house. You should father a child or two. Or fifteen if you're good at that in and out thing. A world record, you know — fifteen! You're an adult, you should know how that works.

— I do know how it works, yes.

— Then what's the fucking problem?

— I want to see the world. I'm too young, Grandad.

— No you're not! You're fucking old! You're growing downwards already! What do you mean "young"? You have this bastardly beard. You should move back here and bring your wife. We'll build you two a house. I'll do it myself, hands of gold and all, still. Good carpenter. Like comrade Major Yehoshua (may his memory be blessed), mayhap better. You won't know how to build a house, will you? Sitting at your computers all day, must've gotten haemorrhoids already programming your clouds. You used to be a sporty lad, whizzed around the village like a wound-up toy...

— I was fat. You don't whizz around when you're fat.

— ... you did fishing, all the man things. Chess, too. You were incredible at chess, very incredible. Best player I've ever known.

— Uh-huh... Was I?

— In the West, they don't have such players. They have their computers play chess for them. Complete and utter degeneracy, absolutely the worst.

— I don't have time to plant a tree, build a house, and father a child in Tulubaika. I have life, I have to work.

— Pawn to your Western masters, you are. Fifth column.[6]

— I'm heading back soon, my puppet masters are calling.

— I'll be dead next time you come here.

— Don't say it. Why you keep saying it?

— I'll be fucking dead, that's why. Dead as a corpse.

— No you won't.

— Of course I will. Will do my best. I'll have a funeral like a Caucasian wedding[7]. Everyone will come to see me dead. Will you come to see me dead?

— I would like to say "I'd be happy to" but it's not the right thing to say, is it?

— This is a perfect thing to say. You have good sense of humour, too. Opposite of deadpan, I'd even say.

— Let's talk about something else other than death.

— Show me pictures of your lady.

— You've seen them already.

— I have bad memory, terrible, like a drunkard.

— I'm sure it's not alcohol.

---

6. A loaded political epithet, originating from Spanish Civil War General Emilio Mola's boast that while four columns of troops advanced on Madrid, his clandestine supporters inside constituted a "fifth column." In Soviet and post-Soviet Russia, the term became the ultimate patriotic slur that implies ideological contamination and conscious service to foreign powers.

7. A reference to famously extravagant wedding traditions of the Caucasus regions, where celebrations typically feature hundreds of guests, multi-day feasting, lavish displays of wealth, spectacular displays of dancing and horsemanship, and (allegedly) firing AK-47s into the air.

— As if I don't know that!

I take my phone and show him the pictures of my wife. He frowns and squints, his bushy eyebrows spread like an albino peacock's tail.

— Good genetics, — he nods. — I wish she was from Tulubaika, though. You should move here. Not too late. The air, the land, nature — good for a woman. Take your mother, your sister, your niece — my heroines. You can paint them, everyone will marvel. Good to raise children here.

— Uh-huh...

— Take your Grandma, my orchid — goddess, pure natural beauty, Greek statue, incredible woman... oh... incredible woman she was. The one that makes you do great things.

Iconographical idiosyncrasy of Grandad's house makes one stagger: comrade Yehoshua, comrade Joseph, comrade Felix, and comrade Wife — figures of absolute power, each in separate rooms. It wasn't customary to talk about her, and I knew her only as a beautiful woman from that portrait in his bedroom.

— Did you know Grandma?

— Of course I did know Grandma, — he told me once, wasted. — We knew each other very well, very well. How do you think you exist? Divine intervention?

— What was she like?

— She was a bad swimmer, very bad swimmer. I built her a boat, very beautiful, good boat. You could go fishing in the ocean on it. I can row for you, I said, not a problem, my orchid, I have strong hands. We don't even need a boat, why would we need it? I can carry you through Tulubaika myself. It's not that deep, very shallow river. But she wouldn't dip a toe in Tulubaika, said it was too cold.

— It is too cold.

— No, it's not. It's a perfectly fine river.

I can't imagine her as old as him, just as I can't imagine her with him. I can't imagine her baking pastry, I can't imagine her gossiping with other old women in the village and calling everyone around degenerate. I can't imagine her voice and what colour her eyes were, though, likely, they would've lost some of their colour by now. I can't

274

imagine her telling me grotesque folk tales or asking me to wear a hat not to freeze my brain out. Sometimes, it's rather lovely to think that she'll remain a mystical creature of eternal youth, younger than me now, almost like my sister, and won't hear and won't see all the things I myself would eagerly forget. I can imagine how she would argue with him and how she wouldn't stand him. It is, in fact, easy to imagine.

— Why do you watch this? Nothing but lies, bare-faced lies! They're not even trying anymore.

Red like a beetroot, I shout into my phone at someone who's a thousand kilometres away. Another red beetroot is yelling back at me. Sometimes I wish telephone and internet weren't invented and we didn't have to call each other once in a while to discuss death, the weather, or the news.

— It's you who's brainwashed here!

— Who? Who brainwashed me?

— That fascist scum you allied with!

— What fascist scum, Grandad? Who?

— Those very ones who execute our people right and left. The ones who bomb our people!

— But it's us bombing them!

— They are bombing themselves.

— How can you believe that? How can you believe that someone can just bomb themselves? Why? What for?

— Because their rulers are fascist scum, that's why. They swore to wipe us all from the face of the earth, swore to Hitler, that fucking bastard himself. Now their rotten genes are showing their true colours again. It's just incredible. I know people, people who serve there, they told me everything face to face. They would tell you everything to turn you against your own country. I can't believe it — my grandson, my own grandson.

— What? What can't you believe?

— You want them to bomb your own people. Traitors breeding like rats, and you're falling in with them.

— You're being lied to.

— Nobody's lying to me.

— They do.

— You're a wise, knowledgeable one now, aren't you?

— Our soldiers kill and rape people.

— Whom? Fascists? So be it.

— Are you serious?

— Never thought you'd turn your back on the motherland, on your own grandfather.

— I'm ashamed to be related to this country anyhow.

— We protect our country, don't we have a right to protect our country? You smartarse think we should just give up, don't you?

— It's impossible to argue with you.

— If your country and I mean nothing to you, at least think of your mother. She would be happy to learn her son supports fascists, wouldn't she?

— You're a fascist here, not me.

— What a gift in my twilight years... Nothing left but to mourn the grandson I once had.

— You're just drunk, you don't know what you're saying. You're delirious.

— You hate your own grandfather. This is who you are now, grown-up man!

— I don't hate anyone, I just want peace.

— Why didn't you serve, huh? "Oh, peace, peace"—now look at our country! Our village will be bombed tomorrow. Never thought I would raise a pussy. Just like your father, you are. Your sister got more balls than you, by a margin. Yours haven't even dropped yet, no they haven't, fucking "scientist"! She's a fucking ballerina and you can't write ballet without "balls".

— You know, I hoped you'd be dead without seeing what our country has been turning into.

— Never come to my house, my village, you little piece of shite! Genes, great genes, you'll get the same dementia as myself, fascist degenerate.

Down the winding staircase, I descend and emerge into the

airport's hall. In front of me, right above the airport exit, a plain cement bas-relief with the Tulubaika coat of arms features a mallard sitting in front of a birch. I reckon that's why we're screwed from birth. There's nothing to see in the village. It's nothing like Babylon, with no skyscrapers, no hanging gardens, no temples, nor epics written on ancient tablets, and everyone speaks the same language. It exists by inertia; everything in it happens by inertia. Entering the village, one feels as if provided with free shackles and here and now one's life is over, so all one has left to do is to ferment memories in small bottles until they explode one day. There are no foreigners, no tourists, no strangers, except one. The squares and streets are empty, old kioskers sleep in their undisturbed dens. People stroll through the streets, tapping their canes on the pavement. Nobody smiles at you, except when they think you're a clown in your red cashmere jumper. Rare cars breathe at you with eye-scorching fumes, growl, and fly past, splashing mud from non-drainable puddles, an irreplaceable part of the village's landscape design. Black cats wait for you to cross the road. Ducks swear at you behind your back. Squirrels... well, I don't know what they do, they are just on the trees somewhere. Yet, there is something peaceful, soothing to the soul both in the silence and in the constant quacking of ducks, something lovingly engulfing you whole in its bog.

— Oi! Stand where you are! Don't move!

I'm sixish. My feet are drowning in a muddy spring field. The snow has melted and turned the field into a brown swamp ready to suck me into the abyss and conserve me alive. My body is already up to my waist in filthy viscous goo and the soil keeps engulfing me.

— I can't move!

Grandad rushes towards me, shuffling his feet in knee-high rubber boots that are also bogged down in mud. At that time, I don't fear being buried in soil, for I don't have that emotion yet, or perhaps I already know that's what happens to all of us asymptotically, but when I see a horror in his eyes as he's approaching me and I become scared too, scared that he's scared, for I've never seen that in him, at least not because of me.

— Bloody hell, why did you go in there, lad, tell me. You're not supposed to play here, are you?

He wraps his heavy arms around me and pulls me out of the mud.

— Thank you, — says I and hands over the cash to the taxi driver who takes no cards, only banknotes and, not looking back at me, nods stoically in response to my gratitude, man to man.

The car rockets off down the last metres of the asphalted street and dives into a tunnel of golden birches, leaving a cloud of smoke and quaking drone in its wake.

I stand in front of Grandad's old shabby brick house with my backpack and a small hand luggage, darting glances at the neighbour's windows, yet nobody hides behind white, patterned curtains. I wonder, with an electric tremble of uncertainty, what if we don't find common ground with him, and he really doesn't want to see me ever again?

I walk past the windows and from his room through an open vent I hear music playing, Shostakovich's Waltz No. 2, accordion rendition. My eyes find a slit between the curtains and I see him: he is dancing with his eyes closed, stepping lightly from foot to foot, with a portrait in his hands, not of comrade Joseph, not of comrade Felix, not even of comrade Yehoshua, but of comrade Wife (may her memory be blessed). Thus, in stasis, I hide for a minute, then creep to the door, gently push a familiar doorbell button and wait until I hear his footsteps and his raspy and low voice:

— If it's one of you door-to-door brain donors and your pyramid schemes again, I swear I'll cut your bloody fingers off and screw 'em up your arse, you bloody degenerates.

Airports, for some reason, always feel like that — duty-free.

Episode Eighteen
about planes cancelled due to abysmal weather conditions

Don't grow up, little girl, toska'll befall you!

— Andrei Platonov, "The Foundation Pit"

— Due to the abysmal weather conditions, the flight to Tulubaika is delayed. Passengers are asked to be patient and think about something else, something unrelated to Tulubaika, for example, read a book. Please, at least for a moment, distract yourselves already.

Our heroine inhaled the stale airport air and melted into her chair. If it were a proper port, it would have smelt of ship fuel and dead fish, but instead... it smelt of halva and coffa from the quasi-café nearby.

Can't imagine how people can read for hours, she thought. During that time, so many thoughts accumulate in my head that they simply start tumbling out of my ear canals, perch on them and — *whoosh!* — slide down as if from a hill, and they fly, fly, fly one after another, perch, slide, fly in an avalanche flow, like a crowd rushing for the festive shopping, stick together, fly, fly, fly, stick together and continue to fly and stick together, layering like a snowball, until you just furrow your brow and put the book aside. You just need to distract yourself, but not so much as to change context, do something else or clear your head, no, not like that at all — you need to distract yourself from the very act of reading because thoughts become too many and continue to become only more until you process them like that washed laundry that lies on the chair and waits for someone to fold it, but at some point it starts falling from the chair, and that's when you realise — it's time. The residents of the modest abode shrug and go to fold it, what

else can they do? The very act of reading rather pulls you into some spiral whirlpool than helps you relax. Few things help to relax at all, and reading certainly isn't one of them. It's a kind of work that brings pleasure, but pleasure not in following the plot and unravelling its tangles and tangles of characters' lives, but the kind you get from intently observing nature, the sea, a crowded street, scenes of carnal love, scenes of platonic love, stars, birdsong, tits drunk on fermented frozen rowan berries and singing their avian chanson[1]. There you sit, eyes agog, ears laid bare, a wondrous feast for the sight — lo and behold, by my troth, what magnificent splendour! Each word, phrase, sentence, plot twist seems to program you for something, and you feel yourself becoming programmed. They, these units of text, units of the author's thought, awaken in you your own uncountable thoughts, which gradually emerge from darkness, from being extras they become main characters and occupy all attention, sit on sleds and slide down the slopes of ear canals, fly, fly, fly, squinting, until silence settles in your head.

— Come on, let's go walk around duty-free, my sun, — said our heroine's husband, her hero.

No one has yet described our sun exactly like that — using our heroine as a metaphor for it — although it, the sun, has existed for billions of years, it was, is, and will be, described over all this time in all imaginable ways. It doesn't even realise that once it didn't exist and someday it won't exist, because it exists for too long to be aware of such things, too long for such things to matter, just as those who exist too briefly don't realise these things either — they simply don't have time for realising anything whatsoever. There are some butterflies, their lifespan — one day or so. There are some insects that live only for a couple of hours. They don't have time to languish in an airport and

---

1. Unlike its French namesake, Russian "chanson" (шансон) originated in criminal subculture and prison camps before evolving into a mainstream genre. It's characterised by gritty vocals, melancholic lyrics, and themes of crime, imprisonment, lost love, and regrets. Now only people in their fifties and older listen to it unironically. Post-ironic or meta-ironic listening is acceptable though.

think about the eternal or read long and lingering, full-of-digressions books. Their eternity is of a completely different size.

— My arse is going numb now... — he added, fidgeting on the chair. — A new café opened here. Right there behind us. They serve waffles with black sesame cream, with black sesame ice cream, sprinkled with roasted sesame oil, probably white. Apparently the coffa comes out very tasty with sesame and cream, they say.

— Too fat, isn't it?

— And sweet. They pour honey in there in litres.

— I don't like sweet things, I like tasty things. When I feel completely bleh, I just want something tasty, I don't even want to eat, I just need something tasty.

— That's reasonable. Fat in food is precisely what's tasty. That's why sesame paste. Shall we go?

He didn't even realise that they were flying to the funeral of our heroine's grandmother — she didn't tell him, it wasn't necessary for him to know about it yet. Well, necessary, of course, but she just couldn't structure the conversation in such a way as to tell him about it. Everyone — both he and, in his mind, her relatives — had already prepared for meeting each other, prepared gifts, rehearsed speeches and poems, dressed up and so on and so forth, and to introduce a suddenly deceased grandmother into that mix would mean destroying the blooming and fragrant idyll.

— Finally, you'll see my native Tulubaika.

— I can't wait, when?

— Very soon. You'll like it. But there's one nuance.

— What's that? Is it too cold there? We didn't bring along our parkas?

— No, not that at all. It's cold there, of course, but not too much, we'll manage without parkas. Things have changed. You see, my grandmother died, there in Tulubaika, so now we're not going to celebrate your acquaintance with my roots, walk around the village, enjoy the ancient, almost untouched landscapes, but to a memorial service, not even a funeral, can you imagine? She was Tatar, so she was buried the same day. That happens.

It's nonsense, isn't it? What kind of dialogue is that? What could be more absurd? Of course, the fact that only upon arriving there, he'll learn that he's, all of a sudden, also coming to a memorial service.

— Surprise, darling.

— What kind of surprise, my sun?

— A memorial service! Ta-da!

Her own cynicism was twisting her up. Or maybe it wasn't just cynicism but something else that simultaneously hindered and saved her from taking anything (too) seriously. Sometimes it happens like this: you perceive something unwittingly, hope for the best, but alas — the perceptron malfunctions. I'll tell him later, she thought, I love consolation, especially his consolations, they would definitely help me, but not right away, for right away I wouldn't digest them, I haven't yet decided how I feel about it myself.

— You go, — she said to him, — and I'll go to the bookshop. The chort knows how much longer we'll be waiting... Maybe I'll buy something in the local tongue. As a keepsake.

Reading is sadomasochism for many reasons, starting, for example, with disconnection from reality, complete and irreversible immersion, away from the physical world filled with other people, into your own world where among people, apart from yourself and the author, there is no one, causing inner loneliness to become embarrassed, its cheeks to redden and it to go far away, so as not to see the two of you, you and the author, anymore. You upset it, this puritanical loneliness, with your loose behaviour, because how can one be so obsessed as to let another person into one's temple, that is, into one's brain, be it a man or a woman or even a thinking rock and its artificial intelligence. It's less indecent, by the way, when you read something composed by a thinking rock, because there is no metaphysical connection of minds, but only the connection of one mind with emptiness or the thickness of emptiness that arose through the connection of many minds — the collective mind, anima mundi. It's like hearing voices in a cemetery, which all at once, all without exception, begin to talk to you through a narrow bottleneck. Boo! Here you are walking through a cemetery and thinking, who are all these people, and why should I listen to them?

They're dead, but they all talk and talk, and then sing and dance, like in Indian films or musicals, not all, of course, but some of them, those whose voices haven't faded, not because they shouted too loudly (although there are such ones), but because they broadcasted on their frequency, which no one has yet occupied, where there's less noise, and neither dictators with their thought police prohibiting communication on generally accepted frequencies nor all sorts of tech bros with their social media can reach.

— Good afternoon. Hello. Is there anything to read?

— Of course. You've come to the right place — a bookshop. There's plenty to read here. Can I help you with something?

The old man behind the cash register resembled a silver-haired Chekhov, even had pince-nez that had flown in from somewhere and settled on his nose (he couldn't be her Chekhov, for her Chekhov died young) — a wonderful old man, in a word, the kind you don't usually encounter in life, only in Miyazaki's films or accidentally in an airport, when life stops "being" and plops into "non-being", like a barely-seeing kitten into a bowl of milk. Chekhov, if our heroine remembered correctly, was her first hero. She generally considered that the true archetype of a man is not a sword, but a lantern, and when Chekhov said "Ich sterbe" and reached for his champagne, she was illuminated and understood everything about this life and men. Such was she, our heroine, perceptive from an early age.

— I'm thinking and I can't decide between reading news on the internet, looking at the departure board, keeping track of how much longer my flight will be delayed, and reading a long and lingering, full-of-digressions book to distract myself, do you know what I mean?

— I understand — you need a book.

— I can't wait any longer, do you know what I mean? Sometimes it feels like I've spent my whole life waiting in this airport. Or rather, not like that, but like this: right now, at this moment, it seems to me that I've been waiting precisely for it, this moment, and I don't seem to remember life before it. It's like good literature — not about what it seems to be about. All these three hundred pages that I've already read had actually no meaning at all, it was just the author amusing herself

and entertaining us. She needed to invent these three hundred pages to somehow justify the existence of this single sentence that came to her mind when, perhaps (or perhaps not), she was feeding ducks in a park, riding the Tube, talking with a friend, listening to an absolutely shameless presentation at work in absolutely shameless corporate jargon. Do you know what I mean?

— There's some irony in this.

— You think so?

— I'm a bookseller in an airport, miss.

— Ah, yes, I had already forgotten. I need something painful. When I read, I feel physical pain. But it's not painful, rather pleasant. That kind of pain. I can't read if it's not painful in any sense. Finding joy in suffering? Basking in melancholy? I need to feel how connections are forming in my brain, if there is, of course, anything to form connections with. Like ants building an anthill — I don't even know what it's built from but I feel I don't have enough of that to build mine.

— You know, I have no intention whatsoever to be rude, but this anthropocentrism is getting on my nerves, miss. I've seen so many people — a bookshop in an airport is bonkers — that it really seems to me that it's not ants that live like people, but people that live like ants. Ants were there first, after all.

— You think so?

— You know, scientists recently managed to create a complete map of the brain of an ordinary fly, the one that sits on shite. They were able to find out which neurons are responsible for what when it smells the shite.

— Wonders...

— Indeed. Now when you talk about the formation of neural connections in your head, do you feel exactly where they are forming? Yogis say you only need to concentrate to understand this, and then everything will become clear. But overall I agree with you. So many people come to me, so many people... it's like a revolving door here, miss. No book surprises me anymore. And allowing yourself to be programmed — sadomasochism.

— That's exactly what I'm talking about. Isn't it so lovely? Isn't there so much joy in it? How well you understand me... But my husband is waiting for me. He understands me even better. Sometimes even without words. In such moments, when we understand each other without words and cackle like mad at how absurd everything actually is, I wonder whether all this reading is such nonsense, and these books — such drebbeden. He, by the way, loves everything with sesame. Sesame for him is like a drug. Halva, sesame oil, sesame brittle — all those things. What do you think, who reads more, men or women?

— I can't know, but I believe that men should read only women, and women only men — that's when harmony will come to the world. I've been doing so all my life. I read only women.

— Amazing. And I read everyone. Indiscriminately. When I see a foreign name, I don't always know or care if it's a man or a woman or both or none.

— What haven't you seen in women's novels, and what haven't I seen in men's? It's like living in a changing room — swinging genitalia of your own kind all around. By the way, have you chosen something yet?

— No, my eyes keep sliding over the covers, over the titles, but they can't catch onto anything.

— You won't believe it, but I worked in a hospice once, in the library, and I was engaged there in recommending terminally ill people their last book. Sometimes I wonder if I'm doing the same thing now.

— What are you hinting at?

And indeed, everything here is somewhat half-dead. People, being here, seem to live a few lives, like butterflies. You live in the cocoon of the airport for several hours, then suddenly discover in yourself a talent for flying, fly, fly, fly, and find yourself on the other side of the world. And so, this new life ends as soon as you step from the gangway onto the earth. Butterflies, by the way, don't emerge from caterpillars, or rather, caterpillars don't turn into butterflies. Caterpillars are actually building material, food for the future butterfly. The caterpillar dies — the butterfly is born. No

285

inspiring transformation, just the death of one for the sake of another.

— Maybe you're right, — our heroine said quietly to the old man, almost whispering.

— I would ask you to be a bit more precise. In my life, I've been right about many things, and I've been wrong about much more.

— About this damned anthropocentrism. Someone crawls and fights like an ant, someone doesn't fly like a dragonfly, someone lives like a butterfly, and someone thinks like a rock with a brain of a fly that has sat on shite and smelled, smelled, smelled, smelled. And only now, after all these years, we are beginning to understand this...

— Here, — said the old man, — I reckon this book will suit you.

And he took out from under the counter a volume of a thousand and one pages, soft cover, and handed it to our heroine. She showed her boarding pass, paid, thanked the non-Chekhov, went back to the waiting area, to wait.

People around were either arriving or departing — two modes of being (a revolving door). In order not to be distracted by their presence or absence, our heroine sat facing a huge window overlooking the runways, where, accompanied by rain, colourful little planes were either arriving or departing, butterflyly. She looked at them, without opening the book, because she had changed her mind about reading. The flight is eight hours, I'll read on the plane, she decided and sat watching the figures of little planes manoeuvring around, as if she were only a couple of months old, lying in a cradle, and someone was playing with her. Though, sometimes, when a particularly sombre predicament occurs, 8 topples sideways and becomes ∞, for in such moments, the waiting time is often prone to certain dilations.

— We regret to inform you, — a speaker yelled right above her ear, — that the flight to Tulubaika is still delayed and will most likely continue to be delayed. But don't grieve and don't mope! This is normal, because along this route something is constantly delayed. Just wanted to remind you, good luck, and have a nice day!

— Well, fuck... — whispered our heroine.

Here, right in front of her, a hand extended a paper cup with a latte.

— Sleeping? — asked her hero.

— Nope. How's the sesame?

— Sesamely.

Our heroine tried to smile and took a sip of coffa.

— Tired?

She nodded, swaying with her whole body, as if she didn't have enough strength to nod with just her head.

— Sleep.

— I'll sleep on the plane.

His coffa smelled of halva, as if he was drinking liquid halva — la dolce vita, as the Italians say, though in Turkish it's tatlı hayat. Everyone's life is somehow sweet, both Italians and Turks, so sweet that even flies stick to it — fly, fly, fly as if to jam — but in Tulubaika it's not sweet, and has never been sweet, yet flies still fly and stick. Why such injustice? In Italy, Spain, Greece and other Mediterranean destinations for permanent and temporary life, it's always sweet. You arrive, enjoy, fly away, or maybe stay for longer, but from Tulubaika you only want to fly away, yet you still fly back there. Such a marvel, isn't it? You walk along these semblances of half-empty streets, collect all the puddles, all the shite of stray dogs ("Should have worn black boots, not white..."), listen to Shostakovich, String Quartet No. 8, allegro molto, breakcore rendition, and don't understand whether you're in the proverbial "home", which you can never wash off your boot and for some reason, after all these years, continue to call it so. Or whether you're on the set of a Tarkovsky film, and right in front of you in the field, a gathering of local men is about to start burning the village's last remaining cow[2], and the gossip-mongering old women will sing along something folksy, or maybe simply read Dostoevsky aloud, as you did in the sixth grade. The cow will moo in despair, howl

---

2. A reference to a notorious scene in Andrei Tarkovsky's 1966 film "Andrei Rublev" where a real living cow appeared engulfed in real flames during a Tatar raid. Though Soviet censors objected to the scene's brutality, Tarkovsky insisted no animals were harmed — the cow wore an asbestos coat.

echoingly, suffer from fire in hellish agonies, for the men, and the old women too, need to listen to it, the cow, listen to how it sings. Such a sound can't be found anywhere else. Afterwards, it can be put on the radio for everyone to enjoy. Russian misery porn, in a word[3].

— "The blow landed right on the crown of her head, facilitated by her small stature", — read our heroine in a voice trembling from an unclear emotion. — "She cried out, but very weakly, and suddenly sank completely to the floor, although she still managed to raise both hands to her head. In one hand she still continued to hold the "pledge". Here he struck with all his might once and again, all with the blunt side and all on the crown. Blood gushed, as from an overturned glass, and the body fell backwards. He stepped back, let her fall and immediately bent down to her face; she was already dead. Her eyes were bulging, as if they wanted to jump out, and her forehead and entire face were wrinkled and distorted by a spasm."

— Thank you, our heroine. You may sit down, — said Tamara Alexeyevna to her, a teacher with a very soft, almost cosy appearance, but a very firm character, not at all cosy, tempered by eternities in Russian schools.

Our heroine bowed, closing her eyes. The class applauded her. She read naturally, with expression, very literarily, literariestly, but she didn't want to see this applause. She was already perfectly aware of her literary ability and the magic of her voice trembling from an unclear emotion — another routine reminder of this was not digestible. She would have covered her ears too, but that would have been completely

---

3. From the original Chernukha (Чернуха), literally "black-stuff" in Russian, a term for the grim naturalistic aesthetic that emerged during perestroika (1980s) as a reaction against enforced Soviet optimism. This literary and cinematic movement focused on depicting societal decay, violence, sexuality, and moral collapse without offering solutions or judgments. Its roots go back to Dostoevsky's portrayal of urban decay, crime, and psychological torment. In "chernukha", every character suffers their own suffering or they all suffer the Eastern European form of collective suffering to the point of it becoming an aesthetic (misery porn), be it literature or film, as if it's a national self-humiliation contest. The question is whether such depiction is exaggerated sensationalism or is indeed just "naturalism" and "realism", an authentic documentation of social collapse or its artistic exploitation. Having some lived experience in those parts, one might say: ¿por qué no los dos?

improper. Ah, if Fyodor Mikhailovich had lived in Tulubaika, thought our heroine, he would have written something even more intense, he would have written something that would have made the whole world turn black upon reading. And so they wouldn't worship him in the West, but fear him, but would still read him, for he is a great Russian writer, and the Russian soul is mysterious, and everyone loves mysteries, simply adores them, but they would be afraid to discuss him, not from fear and horror (sadomasochistic pleasure can't be eliminated) but because such things are not discussed in polite society. Thus Dostoevsky's ghost would continue to torment the population of his mysterious homeland and squeeze from them the cries of cows engulfed in flames. Indeed — mysterious it is, the homeland. But our heroine never liked such mysteries. You can solve them yourselves, sit down with your family one evening and solve them, like jigsaw puzzles, a million pieces, if you fancy that so much. The further our heroine moved away from her homeland, the less became her desire to solve those puzzles, and the more idealised became her image of it, until it turned into something ephemeral, if you will, into a meme and a myth, a mythical Tulubaika that she invented and created for herself, seized by something like literary nationalism — love for the literature and hatred for everything else. In her new Tulubaika, everything was not as bad as in that old reality from which she fled, although neither that nor this Tulubaika had much to do with actual reality. The same was true of relatives. As she physically and temporally moved away from them, they began to marbleise alive.

— Long, of course, very long, — said our heroine, finishing her coffa. — While you wait, while you fly, while this, while that, no relatives will remain.

— That's for sure, — added her hero.

— You know, there are advantages. In your head, they're as if always alive and will remain so, like statues.

— As if they just went to winter at a resort. Like in childhood. Did they tell you that?

— What? — she asked, as if having lost the thread. He constantly spoke in fragments and hints — riddles, emerging from his mysterious

soul. They, although sometimes irritating our heroine, were a convenient tool to continue the dialogue.

— Where does the budgie go, or the cat, or the budgie "unalived" by the cat? Or Uncle Epiphan?

— Also "unalived" by a cat?

— Well, no one would say it like that, of course. They would say, "He moved, moved on. He lives there, happily, without us."

— "And will he write letters?"

— "Maybe. But budgies can't write, can they?"

— "And send photographs?"

— "That's unlikely. They don't have cameras there. Probably."

— "And where is it? Where did he move to?"

— "Far away, love, very far away."

— "And will we go to him?"

— "I hope not, daughter. Later, when we get old, like him, each of us at our own time, then maybe we'll go see him. Maybe we won't go if transhumanism goes far enough. All sorts of things happen in life."

— "But maybe he hasn't left yet, maybe he's sitting in the airport, waiting for his flight, that Uncle Epiphan. Let's go, let's go to the airport. What if he's still there? Please..." — finished our heroine and lay on her hero's shoulder.

— Looking at how everything is arranged here... — he smirked, stepping out of the role.

— You know, we're not just going there for no reason. There're a few reasons, in fact.

— Of course, I wouldn't go there without a reason.

— Actually, I wouldn't go there without a reason either. No one goes there without a reason.

Grandmother had long ago become a statue texting her awkward messages. One doesn't yearn for statues, one looks at them and marvels. She didn't know if other people understood what it was like to feel that you don't feel, to be sad that you're not sad, to mourn that you don't mourn, because it simply physically doesn't happen, even if you really want it to, while the obligation to feel something sits and watches you.

— That geezer is staring at us, — he said to her.

— Which one?

— That one.

— This one? — our heroine's gaze fell on the old man standing behind the bookshop counter.

Her hero looked at her eyes and calculated the trajectory of her gaze.

— Him, yeah. Standing and staring at us.

— At me. Why would he stare at you?

— I'm handsome, that's why. Prince Charming, my arse.

— I was in the bookshop. That's why. He's strange. We were talking about all sorts of insects, ants and flies that sit on shite.

Her hero frowned.

— Want me to go and fuck his face up?

— Go ahead.

— Seriously?

— Of course not. So that they kick us out? Then we definitely won't fly anywhere.

— I'll go anyway.

— Stop it.

— I'll just look at the books. Tell him not to stare.

— You won't say anything, I know you.

Her hero for some reason always wanted to get into some fight, not to start one himself, but in such a way that this "some fight" came to him, for he himself would never get into any fight or hurt anyone.

— We can just move, — she said.

— Where? Our gate is here. I'll go stretch my legs.

Thus he left. Meanwhile, the cuntastrophe on the display board was approaching biblical proportions, and the inaudible abysmal weather conditions outside intensified. Planes were becoming fewer and fewer, and people around more and more dissatisfied, beginning to cackle like geese, quarrel like dogs, howl like cows.

— But wh-y-y-y-y!

— How is this po-o-o-o-ssible!

— It's impo-o-o-o-ssible!

291

— Miss, is this seat free?

— No, my husband sits here.

— I'll sit until he returns. My knees hurt.

— Well, all right, but he'll be back soon. There, you see? He's standing talking with that old man over there.

— I see. He's talking quite actively.

— He's a good communicator, my one. He can talk anyone's ear off. Even me, he's constantly talking me into things. Look, he talked me into marrying him. Can you imagine? Now I've talked him into going to Tulubaika as revenge. Taught me to his own detriment, silly.

— Oh, you're going there too.

— I am. And you?

— Me too. Taking my children to see their little homeland. Where their roots grow from.

— And troubles in the head.

— Oh, don't get me started. If it were up to me, I wouldn't go anywhere. But one must.

— I agree, if it were up to me, I'd prefer to forget it in its entirety.

And her hero stood there, talking with the old man, talking and talking, rehashing some topics. Oh, he laughed. That means he won't fuck any faces up, although it would have been hilarious, and she wouldn't have had to explain the funeral situation to him. He would have punched him, even after laughing, but he wasn't a psychopath, far from being a psychopath, although he himself sometimes tells our heroine, more often when they've been drinking something, that in childhood, when everyone was being dealt out character traits, they didn't, unfortunately, dole out psychopathy to him. They shortchanged him, cheated, or maybe they simply forgot, but in the end, they didn't give him any at all, though a little, at least a tiny drop of psychopathy would have been handy, so he said. She took out her phone, wrote, "so when r u fucking his face up? waiting". He saw the notification on his watch, looked away from the old man, hunched for half a moment, holding back laughter. And he talked and talked and talked, the chatterbox. And he took out his boarding pass, paid for something. A familiar notification came —

nine ninety, the recommended price. And he returned, happy as a Labrador.

— Can this woman sit here? She has knee pain and troubles in the head.

— Yes, please. Hello, woman. Do you really have troubles in your head?

— Who doesn't these days?

— That's true, — he said to the woman, then turned to our heroine. — And I, um... bought a book. Look at this one.

And he thrust before our heroine a volume of a thousand and one pages, soft cover.

— I'll read too.

And the woman blinked her whisker-like eyelashes and then took out of her bag exactly the same volume with exactly the same thousand and one pages, soft cover.

— Oh, I have the same one. What a coincidence.

— And I do, — added our heroine.

— Popular reading, it seems.

— Quite popular, indeed.

— One can hardly buy any other in the airport. It will help to pass the time. No one knows when they'll make an announcement.

— Oh, don't mention it, it's awful.

— A nightmare.

— The world's bonkers.

Thunderstorm, hurricane, whirlpool, volcano eruption — this must have happened, the weather became completely unsuitable for flying, if one were to believe the announcement over the loudspeaker:

— So-so-so, passenger A go there, passenger B come here, and, by the way, today's plane to Tulubaika is cancelled. Alas and alack! There will be no more flights to Tulubaika at all. The last one was a week ago, and the one before that was two weeks ago. That's how they used to fly — once a week, and now, from this moment, all because of the abysmal weather conditions, they stop flying. That's how it is.

— Well, fuck... — our heroine murmured.

She sighed, shrugged, stood up and went to fold the laundry from

the chair into the wardrobe. Immediately her hero followed her and began to help. And suddenly she up and told him everything. Just like that. Up and told everything. Absolutely everything. In complete calmness. Without hitches in breathing, without a throat clenched and stale air in the lungs, without extra weight on the heart and electricity wandering through the fingers. And her hero immediately understood everything, as Chekhov would have understood, only better.

Episode Nineteen
about the Chekhoverse.
City N. & omniplaces

There is a city in a distant corner of Russia that speaks to my heart in a special way. Not that it is distinguished by splendid buildings or their own Semiramis's hanging gardens, and shan't you find even a single three-storey house in a long row of streets, all unpaved, but there is something peaceful, patriarchal in all its physiognomy, something soothing to the soul in the silence that reigns on its hills. Entering it, you feel as if here and now your career is over, and you can no longer demand anything from life, you only have to live in your memories and digest them. Indeed, there is nowhere else to go beyond this city, as if the world ends here. [...] One of the most striking peculiarities of our remote towns is that it is almost impossible to meet there people from somewhere else. Whoever you see [there] are local people who live here because they gradually acquired some kind of natural fetters. There is nothing for a stranger to do here and that is why there is no reason for him to come. It is true to such an extent that there is no provincial person who would not be aware of this truth and look with surprised eyes at the stranger who is dashing to escape. The provincial town has never served as a goal for anyone, but only as an obstacle, which you would've flown over only if you had wings.

— Mikhail Saltykov-Shchedrin about Vyatka.[1]

---

1.   Vyatka is the city whereto Saltykov-Shchedrin was "penally transported" after being "prosecuted for free-thought". Apparently, the author of this book is from around those parts, places even more savage and remote than Vyatka (you'd never guess the name of the place). In his personal blog, he mentioned that this description of that geographical area is still true, even after 170 years.

In Chekhov's poetics, the phenomenon of City N is a phenomenon of omniplace. In Russian literature, the device was employed both before and after Chekhov, first as a new cheeky literary trope, then as a conscious stylisation. Like the others, Chekhov did not always call it City N and often omitted naming the setting altogether, though it was obvious to everyone that this, too, was City N — the name matters less than the concept of a repeating poetic image. Unlike other authors, Chekhov uses City N as the unifying constructive principle of the world, the world itself, a kind of Chekhovian universe (Chekhoverse), simultaneously both form and content. Everything that happens in Chekhov's short stories and plays happens in some Russian city, its dachas nearby, churches and villages, beyond which lies nothing — uninhabited wilderness, which Chekhov called "on the road", "on the way to the city". All of those places are one way or another attached to City N, as if nothing else existed. Unlike the others, the Chekhoverse plays out City N thematically, thereby resolving the dramatic conflict only at the level of form, which is true for Chekhov overall, and which is the juiciest literary achievement of his. Stories of insignificant ambitions, casebound life, time seemingly passing by whilst in City N it remains frozen, slow stagnation and hidden degradation, the impossibility of escape — all of this and more can be expressed in the single image of City N.

City N is not, however, archetypal; it is rather simply a literary convention, the result of omitting superfluous details, for why should they be needed? Everyone understands everything anyway — a particular glance and a meaningful nod suffice. An archetype requires myth, whereas City N is a product of realism that has detached itself from real life, abstracted and become an anonymous poetic model of the world, automatically establishing position in space and expectations from it.

Bakhtin, analysing Chekhov, defined City N as a chronotope — a unity of space-time with a particular semantics. Thus, there exists the chronotope of the idyll, the chronotope of the road, the chronotope

of the castle, and the chronotope of the provincial town. Both time and space within it are frozen, looped into themselves. Events cannot occur and cannot be; there are only "occurrings" repeating day after day: the same domestic actions, the same topics of conversation, the same words — gatherings, drinking bouts, intrigues, gossip, lovers and cheaters, bureaucracy, and other banalities (typical of soap operas, too). It is a place where morals are savage, or at least traditional, the nature of events — absurd, or at least anecdotal, hence the awareness of life's inferiority and pointlessness — strong, and time — utterly flowless and motionless. The chronotope is bound to a particular historical period, and it is populated by characters of precisely that epoch and its attendant social strata. This distinguishes the chronotope from the archetype; it is not an eternal structural element of the psyche but is proper only to its era.

If for other writers City N is a stylisation, a target for satire, for plot, for unfolding the fabula, a pure chronotope as organisational structure of space-time, then for Chekhov it is used primarily to denote milieu and mood, a specific indescribable and inescapable atmosphere. The three sisters do not go to Moscow and continue only to dream of it until it becomes too late. The characters of "The Cherry Orchard" simply wait and undertake nothing until the estate is sold and axes begin to sound in the orchard. One gets the feeling that both groups do this deliberately, even find some pleasure in it — not because someone prevents them from doing it, but because in both time and space the alternative is simply not-here, and not-here does not exist; therefore they do nothing. The omniplace devours all alternatives.

Thus, an omniplace transcends a chronotope and becomes a *vibe* in the phenomenological sense. A vibe is that which oozes from things and places and envelops the subject. Chekhov's City N precisely *oozes* provincial toska, a soupçon of cosmic absurdity, ennui, melancholy, and vacuum. Here, it is important to remember that vacuum is not simply emptiness; it is absence of matter but also, importantly, *absence of pressure*. In the omniplace nothing presses, nothing demands; therefore nothing happens.

"Why vibe?" the reader could ask. Well, omniplaces are understood by all, recognised by all, and even have real prototypes, though to identify them precisely is most often impossible. These are places without a map or territory; they are rather feelings and sensations bound to places, atmosphere into which Chekhov immerses you. There is nothing strange or repellent about City N; on the contrary, it maximally hits home. No one can say where City N is located, but having read its description, having met its inhabitants, any person will tell you that it is precisely their town being discussed, that in fact this is the place where they have lived their whole life and met these characters, for nothing resembles City N more. "Blimey! But I live here!" / "Literally me!" the reader will exclaim and be right, will point to a spot on the map, as will another, or hundreds-thousands-millions of other such readers. In the end, if you ask absolutely everyone, you can obtain a dot-speckled population density map of the country.

This universal recognition is achieved precisely through vibe, not through structure. The structure of time and place starts off as a basis but later becomes secondary once vibes overtake structure because recognition of the omniplace is subconscious, intuitive, expressed at the level of subtle emotions and feelings, not in how the place looks or what year it is there. This determines yet another distinction from the chronotope, which is bound to time and place; this unboundedness that draws the omniplace somewhat closer to the archetype. Many of City N's features work to create this vibe: remoteness, provinciality, dullness, isolation, a certain lag with which civilisation's trends reach this place — yet it is precisely their sum that creates the final sensation, unattainable by each component separately, and that sum is what matters in the end.

The core component, however, is remoteness; from it all the others flow, and the phenomenon is possible only across enormous sparsely populated territories where both power and culture are centralised, concentrated in a couple of large capital cities. The Russian Empire where Chekhov lived and travelled (and he travelled a lot, not only in Russia) was one such place, perhaps even the only one where omniplace could be invented / discovered / seen. After the Russian

Empire ended, all of its copious City Ns entered the Soviet era, which hyperbolised them even more, ideologically and practically, applying the trope as methodology for developing the country. The whole vastness of it turned into one big City N. Now, after the Soviet experiment has collapsed too, the remnants — the social, cultural, and literal architecture: buildings, names, rituals, mentality — still haunt the post-Soviet space. Wherever you travel, you'll find the same "white house", a governmental building (which is, in fact, grey), a Lenin statue, or two,[2] a school, a post office, a hospital — all looking and feeling the same, shops with the same goods at the same prices, people speaking one enforced standardised language. Many national and personal identities were washed out or at least not encouraged, and everything became an incarnation of utter sameness and homogeneity. There was, and sometimes many people think there still is, a wide selection of Ensks feeding the maw[3]: the omnipresent Ensk(s) and non-Ensk. That is how and why City N can exist and feel so natural and obvious even now. It managed to survive because it transcended the chronotope — a slice of concrete physical reality — and became an omniplace: a poetic image of concrete, yet paradoxically undefinable, emotional reality.

For the sake of argument — dipping a toe in the imperial mentality — we could say that any of the real Ensks might be any other Ensk, and they are totally interchangeable, for regardless of the year and place you grew up in, in any concrete instance of them you can feel somewhat at home. It is the place we hold dearest that does not, in fact, exist. Simultaneously, no other concrete named city or town or village could match the anonymity and abstraction of City N. It exists as long as it has no name, and as soon as it acquires one, it immediately becomes a chronotope bound to space and time, and

---

2. There's a theory that a legion of Lenin statues in post-Soviet countries serves as beacons and "Trojan horses" for an alien lizard race, so when they finally arrive to punish us for our human sins, those Lenins will come alive and, like an army of terracotta warriors, wage murderous war on humanity, wreaking havoc and annihilating everyone and everything with their laser eyes (red, of course).
3. Correction: Mawscow.

space is destructible, changeable, and time passes, inexorably, and the place therefore disappears from the maps and then from memory, as if the best and only way to erase a place is to first give it a name and then take it away, and the best and only way to make the place immortal is to give it a name that is utter meaningless tosh.

Episode Twenty
about elegiac couplets (in a way)

Outwardly charming, the birthplace. Seems motherly, yet cunning, bewitching.

— Sasha Sokolov, "Between Dog and Wolf"

Wunst upon a time, I packed me a bundle, a right big un, laced up me lapti, nice and tight, trimmed me beard, even as can be, mustered up me courage, both holy and heathen, just to be sure and just in case, hopped on me wooden lil'steed and galloped out of Tulubaika. T'first question that popped into me head was "which road should I take?" So there I stand, in t'middle of t'village, ponderinn: should I go right, or left, or straight ahead, or even back? I could go t'betwixt directions and all, but there's only four roads — 'tis a crossroads, not an open moor, mind thee. Not a livinn soul 'bout, no un to ask, except for two magpies that been gatherinn twigs for their nest 'round these parts for ages. Folk say: go right — tha'll lose thy horse, go left — tha'll lose thyself, go straight — tha'll find happiness. But what 'bout goinn back? What's back there? No un knows what's there, either nobody's ever traipsed over or they never pitched up back to tell what's in that backness. Well, methinks, right and left are cunninn bastards, move as tha moves. So come what may, I'll toss a coin. I reach into me pocket for a coin, realise I need two coins — there are four directions, mind thee. There I stand, countinn, workinn out me plan: two tails — I'll go north, straight ahead, two heads — south, un head, un tail — west, un tail, un head — east. I've grown weary of beinn fate's thrall, so weary that me jowls ache in t'morns when I look at meself in t'mirror, so I decided I'd rather be a thrall of chance.

301

Thus, by t'will of chance, 'tis more honest-like, and honesty's just what I've always been short of in life, well, not me meself, a decent chap, but me surroundings — all me days I've been beset by cheats, knaves, thieves, and murderers. Me grandfather's oak house was wunst "requisitioned" by bandits after our motherland got clobbered and turned arse over tit wunst more. Hand over thy oak house, they say, Uncle Ildar, look at that, they say, tha's grown love handles, now, they say, we'll dekulakise thee, Uncle Ildar, and build a grand communism in our bonny Tulubaika or mayhap even a grand future with free market relationships and democratic falderal like everywhere else, or perchance, see, even better, for here in Tulubaika, everything's better than elsewhere, that's t'only point on which I'm in full agreement with those comrades.

Startinn with our river, also called Tulubaika, by t'by, lookinn, honest truth, like liquid crystal, though I've never clapped eyes on crystals, except icy uns — we've got plenty of those danglinn from roofs in winter. An icicle wunst skewered me schoolmate's head clean through. Sad to recollect such things, 'course, but, as they say, it is what it is. Any river and any body of water is also a liquid crystal threadinn t'earth hither and thither, and ours is t'purest of all, springinn from wells somewhere deep in t'forests where ferns bloom and fly agarics grow knee-high. Tha stoops down, presses thy lips to its smooth, cold surface, drink and feel summat click inside thee, as if someone's crankinn up t'love for t'motherland a notch, un click to t'right, or mayhap two, if not three, for sometimes tha's so parched that for a swig of water tha'll love not only t'motherland but its rulers, too. T'river's swift, a whoppinn brook that doesn't even freeze in winter and keeps hurtlinn full pelt to somewhere out there into nowhere along its path, laid, mind thee, of its own accord, not by t'will of fate, nor by t'will of chance, like me, a daft beggar, but by t'will of its own river spirit, to pour into a bigger river or straight into a sea or ocean, for none of our folk have ever found out whither Tulubaika flows and where it ends, as if it doesn't end anywhere, makes a full loop 'round t'earth and flows into itself.

T'name of both t'village and t'river comes from either t'Tatars or

t'Bashkirs, or, accordinn to some smartarses, from t'Mongols themselves, un of whose tribes was called just that. They've long since vanished, some Russified[1], some blended into t'lay of t'land, and some nomaded off further beyond t'skyline, dealinn along t'way, as our late local historian San-Sanych[2] told me, in beaver pelt trade and various haulage. Only I don't trust San-Sanych — although he was a sharp and learned chap, finishinn either three or four universities, or mayhap ten ('tis like with children — after three tha stops counting), he didn't mind his tongue at all, neither what came out of his gob, nor what he poured into it, for, judge for thyself, tha can find neither a single toothy, furry wee beaver nor proper roads, t'sort where after a couple of versts[3] tha doesn't leave all thy wheels in t'ruts, even should tha look high and low.

Zinaida Semyonovna, t'local wise woman, claimed that "tulubay" means "lame" or "crooked" in t'old local languages, just like our twisty river, whose bends and turns t'whole village couldn't tally. Supposedly, first there was t'Tulubaika River, then people came here, Russians, Tatars, Bashkirs, Mari, and cobbled together a village. I, and me father,

---

1. Russification is the process whereby non-Russian peoples within the Russian Empire and later the Soviet Union gradually adopted Russian language, customs, and identity. Sometimes the assimilation happened peacefully through intermarriage and economic integration, but often it was accelerated by state policies such as mandatory Russian-language education, restrictions on native languages, and settlement of ethnic Russians in non-Russian territories. The process affected countless ethnic groups, from Tatars and Bashkirs mentioned in the story to Ukrainians, Balts, Caucasian peoples, etc. During the Soviet era, the state simultaneously pursued "friendship amongst nations" and policies that privileged Russian as the language of interethnic communication. Today, demographic Russification continues, though now often contested by resurgent ethnic nationalist movements.
2. San-Sanych is a common Russian nickname for Alexander Alexandrovich. Russians commonly create such diminutives by combining the first syllables of one's first name and patronymic. Such nicknames / diminutives are an integral part of Russian colloquial speech, signalling warmth and familiarity (e.g. Volodya for Vladimir, Sasha for Alexander, Vanya / Vanechka for Ivan), unlike the formal "full name + patronymic" combination used in professional or official settings. San-Sanych specifically has become somewhat of a stock character name, often used for an archetypal older man everyone knows.
3. Verst (or versta) is an obsolete Russian unit of distance, roughly equivalent to 1.1 kilometres or some corresponding amount of miles.

and me grandfather, who, by t'by, was a true Tatar by blood and name and, wherefore, understood summat in Tatar words, and t'rest of t'respected lads and lasses before and after him, always held a special position in t'village and thus had our own, only right version of t'name and t'history, for our surname, Tulubayev, explains everythinn, says a lot, and carries all t'needful knowledge within itself. Grandfather used to tell me that there was a chap named Tolubay, with an "o" instead of "u", who owned a good bunch of land 'round here back in t'seventeenth century or earlier, and that it means "a richly rich man", a hale and respected person, and a lad was given this name, Tolubay, if, as soon as he crawled out of his mother, it was plain that this was surely how he would end up. Only that when t'first census happened, Russians wrote "u" instead of "o" and thusly it stayed, and t'folk started sayinn it this way, too. Me grandfather, to put it mildly, disliked t'wise woman Zinka[4] and her drebbeden 'bout t'lame and crooked and ofttimes secretly called her a daft witch at home, which she most likely was, judginn by her long history in t'yellow house but more, of course, by t'nonsense she spouted, whether tha laughs or cries.

Here's a droll case, for one: yonder in time, in summer, wunst, or mayhap twice, before everyone 'round was kindly asked to heave t'country up from its knees and shove it up into a bright future, or mayhap it was after — now tha can't even tell — when I was a wee green nipper, I met Zinaida Semyonovna amblinn along t'river in a fur coat (for t'sake of t'story I want to say beaver, but more like everyone else's — sheep), with a shaved noggin and her own pet drake named Valentin on a lead, whose purpose was fully unclear, for he neither laid eggs nor had any meat on him, just ate, shat, and quacked, and sometimes walked with his duck screwer hanging beside him. So, Zinka's zoominn along, crackinn sunflower seeds, scatterinn t'husks, and t'drake can't keep up with pickinn 'em up; I'm legginn it towards 'em with an aspen net to catch tiddlers, which used to be plentiful in Tulubaika in t'summer — tha just had to scoop up some water with t'tool to get a full net of fish, and either fry 'em for thyself on a

---

4. Short for Zinaida.

campfire or give 'em to t'moggie at home. Zinaida Semyonovna stops, looks at me, silent, purses her lips like a duck, not movinn her face, and of a sudden asks:

— Where is tha off to?

— Nowhere, — I tell her, — fishinn.

— What is't tha's fishing? — she asks.

— Wee fishies, — I reply.

— Don't tha dare catch froggies, — she says.

And I'm like:

— Why would I need froggies, Granny Zina?

— Our river will snuff it without froggies, dry up, a brook will flow, and even that will go underground and drag us along with it straight into t'fiery inferno, — she says and crosses herself, in t'Starover[5] way, with two fingers.

Ooh, methinks, Zinaida Semyonovna, what biblical horrors tha has in thy head and tha manages to impart such things to me laddie's mind, but she's not 'bout to button it, and says, so she does:

— It's written in thy fate, Tulubayev, to live and pop thy clogs in Tulubaika, honest truth, I'm not fibbinn. As long as tha is here, Tulubaika is here, and as soon as tha is gone, Tulubaika's gone. Wherefore, if tha wishes to leave thy homeland, nowt will come of it, Tulubaika will protect itself, won't let itself perish.

---

5. Starovers (literally "Old Believers") were / are adherents of Russian Orthodox traditions who rejected the liturgical reforms implemented by Patriarch Nikon in the 1650s-1660s. When Nikon revised religious texts and practices to align with contemporary Greek Orthodoxy (including changing the sign of the cross from two fingers to three), conservative Russians saw this as blasphemous corruption of true faith. The Russian Orthodox Church excommunicated those who refused to adopt these changes, leading to a profound schism (Raskol) in Russian society. Old Believers faced brutal persecution — thousands were executed, others self-immolated rather than surrender their beliefs, and many fled to remote regions of Russia. This persecution continued to varying degrees until 1905, with Starovers facing double taxation, restrictions on worship, and social discrimination. Despite this, they maintained distinct communities characterised by strict adherence to pre-reform traditions, preservation of ancient icons and manuscripts, and often remarkable entrepreneurial success — many prominent merchant families were secretly Starovers. Today, several million Starovers continue their traditions in Russia and émigré communities worldwide.

And I tell her:

— What is tha makinn up, Zinaida Semyonovna? When I grow up, I'll scarper from here wherever I want. If I want, to Vyatka, if I want, to Khlynov, if I want, to Kirov[6], if I want, even to St. Petersburg or Leningrad itself, with Saint or without, Granny Zina. It makes no odds to me what its name is now — t'main thinn is to run as far away from here as possible.

She looks at me, silent, thinkinn, and t'drake Valentin quacks nearby.

— I feel sorry for thee, fatherless lad. Tha understands nowt, — she says, shakes her head, and toddles further along t'river.

I felt sad right away and didn't feel like fishinn any more, but not 'cause of her words, which clung to me memory — though not immediately — but 'cause I remembered me dad.

He loved life, but it had to be noisier, jollier, and more varied, and he had un thing on his mind: to scarper out of t'village as soon as possible, as far away as possible. Without askinn anyone, neither his parents nor me mother, nor me, he would roll off to un city or another and vanish for a month or two, then return with returnables. Now he'd brinn a new kartuz[7], now boots, now a sack of flour, now a radio-controlled car toy[8], now a portrait of an important state figure, a sovereign, a president, or a supreme secretary, whatever un calls 'em.

Thus so wunst — but not just wunst — while Dad was

---

6. Kirov, Vyatka and Khlynov are three names for the same city that is located about 900 kilometres northeast of Moscow. The city has historically been a provincial centre and a place of political exile (now known for corruption and kvass). It was founded in 1181 by Novgorod colonists and called Khlynov. Fast forward five centuries, Catherine the Great renamed it to Vyatka, after the main river of the region, as part of her administrative reforms. The city kept this name throughout the Imperial period until Bolsheviks renamed it after Sergei Kirov (likely assassinated on Stalin's orders). Interestingly, after the collapse of the USSR, unlike many cities that reverted to their pre-Soviet names (such as St. Petersburg, etc.), Kirov retained its Soviet name. Shame!
7. Kartuz is a type of cap with a round crown and a visor popular in the early 20th century and is, in a way, a visual symbol of the time.
8. Radio-controlled car toy is a miniature vehicle operated by a handheld transmitter that sends signals to a receiver in the car. The receiver translates the signals into motor commands, allowing the user to steer, accelerate, and brake the car.

shabashing[9] in Vyatka, our beloved Tsar Gorokh[10] decided it was time for war. Come on, he said, all as un, for faith, for t'motherland, for t'fatherland, to t'roar of copper pipes, to t'shouts of "Huzzah!", let's bray t'mugs of t'supstates[11]; otherwise our motherland is kirdyk, complete and hopeless slavish darkness. From such a proposal, patriotism immediately surged in me dad's blood.

— T'war suits me just fine, — he says. — I want to fight, really do, I'm already fed up with this katorgan[12] life. At least I'll get out into t'light, see t'world, see people, and learn more 'bout meself. To hell with thee, Tulubaika!

So he left, and we stayed. Mum wept herself dry, Grandfather swore himself blue, and I stood like an idol in t'nook under t'sovereign's portrait. I looked at him — tha has no conscience,

---

9. To shabash (шабашить) is unofficial work or moonlighting outside one's official employment. The term "shabashka" described these often semi-legal side jobs that became an essential economic survival strategy during the Soviet era and beyond. Workers would travel to other regions during holidays or leave periods to earn extra money through construction, agricultural labour, or other manual work.

10. Tsar Gorokh, a name that literally translates as "King Pea", is a mythical ruler from Russian folklore, often evoked to denote a bygone era, similar to "once upon a time" or "in the days of yore", but with more comical and absurd connotation, such as when referring to something exceedingly old and forgotten or belonging to an almost legendary and non-existent past.

11. Supstate (супостат) is an English rendition of an archaic Russian term for "enemy" or "adversary" that carries strong biblical and folkloric overtones, invoking not just military foes but existential enemies of the Russian people and Orthodox faith. The original etymology goes back even to the Devil / Satan. Soviet propaganda could use it when official rhetoric needed to evoke patriotic historical memory. The term has an archaic vibe and connotations of foreignness and evil that simple translations like "enemy" or "foe" won't do. Its use in modern contexts often creates an ironic effect.

12. Katorga (каторга) was a brutal system of penal labour that existed from Imperial Russia through the Soviet era. It's a borrowed word from Byzantine Greek "katergon" (κάτεργον, galley), as condemned criminals were first sentenced to row in war galleys. Russian meaning extends it to hard labour in mines, roads, and fortresses across the country, especially Siberia, where political and common criminals endured backbreaking work in chains under savage conditions. Katorga became embedded in Russian consciousness as the ultimate punishment short of execution, synonymous with suffering and exile in the abysmal weather conditions of the remote corners. The Soviets maintained and expanded the system, rebranding it as the Gulag (GULAG — abbreviation for a forced labour camp system).

Comrade Sovereign, no shame, no common sense. Why does tha need me dad? He has a thick tache, a prickly beard, kind eyes — tha needn't those, what will tha do with him there? He should only be put in front of a camera and broadcast all over t'country on telly. And not a word from him, not a letter, no useful or useless information, and 'tis nowhere to come from, since illiteracy had not yet been eliminated[13] and at that time no un in t'village could read or write — only priests and scribes? Me grandfather could, of course, but only in Tatar. Although mayhap everyone could, me and Mum and Grandfather, in Russian and Tatar and Bashkir and Mari and in everythinn at t'same time, even in runes on birchbark[14], but they refused to write, for 'tis scary to give events form and give 'em power over time, over thyself, as if at that moment they are transferred from t'rank of an event to t'rank of history, and history, excuse me, is a treacherous cunt, with un of her pale hands she strokes thy head, in t'other she holds a knife. 'Tis better to just say it out loud, to t'empty altar of a wee church surrounded by sad icons, or to a forest full of life, lookinn at thy droopinn mug in a puddle midst t'drillinn cries of waxwings, than to say it silently, lookinn at a sheet of paper, to scribble 'bout what happened, hope no un reads thy scrawl, takes a balalaika[15] off a nail or a saw, composes a symphony or some heart-rendinn ditty, and t'whole village will roar, grieve, ponder — well, people used to live, laugh and cry, there were

---

13. Literacy campaign (Likbez or liquidation of illiteracy) was a major initiative launched in 1919 under the slogan "Literacy is the path to communism" (hard to say it was). Lenin's government established a network of "likbez" centres targeting Russia's predominantly illiterate peasantry. The campaign, however, represented both genuine educational advancement and ideological indoctrination. By the 1930s, literacy rates had dramatically improved from pre-revolutionary levels of 24% to over 75%, though rural areas (like Tulubaika) often lagged behind.
14. Birchbark was a common writing surface before the widespread use of paper. The inner layer of birchbark, smooth and light, could be easily inscribed with sharp tools. Many historical documents, particularly in Russia, have been found written on birchbark.
15. Balalaika (балалайка) is a triangular-bodied Russian folk string instrument with three strings, dating to the 17th century. It used to be associated with peasant culture and often dismissed by the aristocracy as primitive but later was elevated to national symbol status.

calm, difficult times, but soulful, and what now? We sit and pine, remember t'past, languish in nostalgic paralysis. And would Dad have had time to read our letters? War is a busy business: here tha shoots, there tha bandages, and there tha digs a hole, where a trench, where a grave, as luck would have it.

— Perchance, — says Mum, — at least t'prayers will reach him. Goddie will send 'em to him.

— How so?

— Through t'air, directly, silly, for Goddie in heaven sees all from there. He will find thy dad among a host of such poor souls and will deliver our thoughts and prayers to him straight from heart to heart like lepestricity through a wire. So let's go and pray, son.

Well, what do I do? I go, I don't want to upset Mum, tha can see 'tis not easy for her, and here I am with me "I don't want to pray to thy Christ Jesusovich, Mum, me grandfather is a Tatar, tha knows, so I haven't decided yet who I want to pray to".

Every morn we get up before t'cockerels, an hour's walk to t'local parish. If I refuse to go, grumble at her, say me feet are frozen, numb, won't walk at all, she sits me on a sledge and pulls me. On t'hill, looms large a big one-storey stone church of red brick with two green domes, with bonny crosses and an iron fence, birch trees are planted 'round it, still young, spindly, their branches droopinn. When t'bells ring, t'chime is heard all 'round, all t'way to Tulubaika itself, and t'window panes and souls tremble. We go in: a hall, an altar, a choir loft, ample space, gloomy, but cosy, frescoes on t'walls, mardy icons with round haloes.

— Why, — I ask, — are they round, Mum?

— What else should they be?

— Were I a saint, I would've had a square halo.

She smacked reverent me on t'lips then but, mind thee, although they hurt for a long time, I wasn't mad at Mum — round means round, I don't argue with me elders.

There's no un in t'church except t'sleepinn watchman and two stiffs in t'side room — mayhap they were brought in t'eveninn. It smells of wax, frankincense, oldness, death.

— Pray, — she says.

— How? — I ask.

— Repeat after me. Bow down.

— God, have mercy on me, a sinner. God, cleanse me sins and have mercy on me. Thou who hast created me, Lord, have mercy on me, Lord have mercy, Lord bless, — Mum whispers loudly, bowinn, then falls to her knees, dragginn me after her so later me knees are black and blue all over.

T'floor is hard and cold. Candles flicker 'round, playinn with shadows. I see her prayinn with fervour, intent, her face brightens, smooths out, and I don't understand nowt and repeat after her like a lunatic.

As soon as dawn peeks through t'small windows, we're out of t'church, off to home. T'road there is uphill, back is downhill — easy. In winter, tha whooshes down t'icy snowdrift, snow gets into thy sleeves, down thy collar, but tha is happy. Tha has lost thy cap somewhere on t'way down, tha gets up, brushes thyself off, thy cheeks are red, burninn with fire, tha brushes thyself off, looks up, and there's Mum quietly cominn down with thy cap. Tha runs to meet her, grabs thy cap and flies down again. We go home, I'm happy, but Mum looks 'round. As un of t'schismatics, she didn't want to be seen by everyone else in t'parish — tha never knows, people can be different. Most have goodness inside, but sometimes it sits so deep that tha can't even see it under a magnifyinn glass. It made no odds to Mum which church to go to, and t'priest didn't mind either.

— Pray, — says Father Pyotr, — Marya, as much as thy soul desires. It is a good deed.

— And if someone says summat, Father?

— God is one for all, — says he.

— He may be un for all, but me grandfather has another un, — I said to him wunst, — and some, I heard, have several altogether.

— An observant young lad, — said Father Pyotr to me. — Love them too.

T'village's folk constantly whispered that they saw Father Pyotr wunst crossinn himself with two fingers when he was alone.

Whether it was true or not, no un knows, but that's where their claim ended, for should they need summat — advice or a blessinn — t'loudest gossip-mongers went to Father Pyotr first. He had a large old black piano at home, on which he held concerts on holidays. I was there a couple of times, listened breathlessly, watched t'faces of t'audience melt from t'pleasantly flowinn music, although I didn't know t'names of t'tunes, but people said that t'composers were good, homegrown, both pre-revolutionary and post-, although there were more of t'former, of course. Father Pyotr was just like me Dad, a kind, affable chap with a generous beard, his face wise, young, as they say "without a hitch, without a glitch", but then, of a sudden, fast he aged, turned grey his beard, dim grew his eyes. Rumours began to creep 'round t'village that seven clergymen had allegedly been put against t'wall in t'district next-door, and in a nearby township three had been sent to katorga. Ours, not wantinn either of those, began to fear everythinn. He sat at home, peerinn out t'window with a haggard face and waitinn for 'em to come for him. Everyone pitied him, carried water and grub; t'local barber trimmed his locks wunst, and then, when t'cold came, people began to let him into their banyas to sleep and warm up, and so he went from un to t'other.

T'church was eventually closed and re-equipped for collective needs for t'production of public goods. T'crosses were removed, and t'flags were put up, but, what's interestinn, magpies that nested under t'dome began to tear 'em off. They would hang a new one — t'magpies would tear it off, hang it — tear it off, and so on. T'local chairmen and powerlovers weren't fond of that at all and decided to close t'church for good, and to t'roar of t'youth, t'bawlinn of t'old and t'angry singinn of t'magpies, they threw down t'bells, burned t'icons, removed t'domes and melted 'em either for horseshoes or for shell casings, then blew up t'buildinn itself for bricks to later build a bright and beautiful future out of 'em, obviously. Honest truth, t'chaps who participated in that later all as un snuffed it at t'front, so they did; and Father Pyotr, havinn learned 'bout what happened, went into t'forest where no un could find him to ask advice or a blessinn. T'property from his house

311

was confiscated. His piano was given to t'new school, but there it stood silent — no un knew how to play it.

Now, wunst upon a time, Mum dragged me to that church in secret from Grandfather and baptised me. They dipped me in t'water three times, read a prayer, and I popped back home with a wooden crucifix hanginn on me neck. Grandfather saw it, only shook his head and waved his hand. He always wanted me, his grandson, to be t'same Tulubayev — a Muslim. He had an old battered book in a leather bindinn, t'Quran written in Arabic letters, which he wrapped in several layers of gauze and kept in a chest under his bed, not lettinn anyone even look at it, let alone hold it, no un but me.

— When the right time comes, the boy will decide for himself whom to be, — he used to say.

But t'right time was never there — I couldn't decide, so me Mum decided for me.

— Do you know, — he whispers, — grandson, which came first, Tulubayev or Tulubaika?

I hold his bony blue hand. T'smell in t'room is musty, it smells of a human, a human in bother and of bother itself, too (it has, tha knows, a particularly heavy aroma). 'Tis cold in t'wee room, gloomy. Light brazenly crawls through t'thick curtains. T'window is closed, there's no air. If tha opens it, draughts will burst in and do in t'sick man. Tears well up in me eyes, they want to in his, too, but they can't — don't have t'strength to well up. His cheeks and eyes are sunken, grey hairs stuck to his skull, lips swollen, cracked.

— No, Grandfather, — I say to him quietly. — I don't know.

Then he squeezes me hand, opens his eyes wider, is 'bout to say summat.

— I don't know either, grandson.

So he died. And who knows then, mind you, Grandfather? There on his bed I sit, pushinn t'tears back, but they keep cominn out and out, out and out. Sleep, methinks, Grandfather, you must be tired, I won't disturb you no more. I take me wooden steed, which, by t'by, he himself whittled for me (from a single piece of wood, mind thee) and I scarper.

Thus only un Tulubayev remained in Tulubaika, as if some significance had now crept into me, an unknown force, which, not havinn reached me Dad, took t'shackles off me Grandfather and put 'em on me. To hell with it, methinks, there's nowt more for me to do here, and off I gallop wherever me eyes look — straight ahead, for that's where, they say, un finds happiness. I gallop raisinn dust, I gallop for an hour, five minutes, ten — I don't remember. T'road ends, and t'forest begins. Underfoot branches crunch, slippery are t'leaves, it smells of damp, mulch; 'round me are birches, flickerinn in me eyes white walls in a black stripe, blurrinn me vision, lurinn me into their swirl.

Here in t'spring, me nameless, faceless friend and I gather birch sap into bottles. Tha takes a knife, cuts t'bark, find a chip or a branch, carve a trough out of it, insert it into t'birch's wound, put a bottle, leave, come back in t'morn, and 'tis full, t'bottle. Here hares roam, various wolves and stray dogs in packs, snappinn their jaws, growlinn at us, tails tucked, fur bristlinn — demons, in a word. Hearts beatinn, begginn to break free, like a sparrow from thy hands, t'cuckoo cooinn non-stop, thy feet lead thee, carry thee at a hare's speed, over leaves, over grass, over mud, over fallen trees, and tha silently sits in thy head, not stickinn out, huddled in a nook with fear, surrenderinn to t'will of instinct and chance. Here's a ravine — and tha tumbles down, through a raspberry thicket, juniper bushes, and plops into Tulubaika, into a backwater where swim wee fishies, frogs and fry. Water striders cut t'surface of t'river, waves run away from 'em, dissolvinn in t'slow current, which in winter is covered with a light crust of ice that crunches at t'touch like a piece of candy made of burnt sugar. Turninn 'round, tha looks — no un, no birches, no dogs, no faceless friends. Thus tha walks along t'river on t'road home, all wet, all mucky and scratched, hands bleedinn, elbows torn, shirt left without a sleeve. So it goes — tha starts a story, and tha doesn't know what thickets it will lead thee into, what whirlpools tha will fall into, what tha will remember, what tha will forget, what tha will make up, and t'story, t'blighter of a creature, is indifferent to thee, it lives by itself, like a river flowinn into itself, returns thee to Tulubaika, to t'beginninn. They say

that blood, just like a river, flows not only in t'veins of people, but also in t'veins of time. In spring, it warms up, collects molten snow from all 'round, overflows, takes fields and bushes, so tha can even get into a boat and sail. In summer, it dries up — in t'heat 'tis just like a beck; tha walks 'cross t'stones without boots, gets stuck in t'silt, gets lost in t'reeds, collects shells, waits for pearl.

Then wanders tha along t'river together with thy lovely lass. A smile on her face, a wreath of daisies and dandelions on her head, a whirlpool in her eyes, warmth inside, tenderness, heart poundinn, and echoes spreadinn from it, reachinn and capturinn thee. Tha hugs her, kisses her, carries her 'cross t'river in thine arms. She laughs, breaks free and plops right into t'water, grabs thee and pulls thee along with her, to splash 'round, to frolic. Tha shall find no pearls in no shells, it isn't meant to be — there's no such thing in Tulubaika.

T'first time I saw her, I decided to climb t'Maslenitsa pole[16]. Drunk chaps used to fall from there, break their necks and spines, but now no un dares to climb it, neither drunk nor for a damsel, but I did, mind thee, rushed up so fast that I didn't even notice. I came down with gifts, a jar of honey, an embroidered shawl, a Dymkovo bird[17], and pagan boons. We ate blini[18] with smetana and honey together and went for a walk 'round t'village, kneadinn t'muck with our boots,

16. Maslenitsa pole is a tall, greased wooden pillar erected during Maslenitsa celebrations dedicated to the end of winter, Russia's pre-Lenten festival with pagan roots. Climbing this slippery pole became a central competition testing young men's strength and agility, with prizes (often boots, textiles, or food) hanging at the top. Success brought not only material rewards but also community prestige and enhanced marriage prospects.

17. Dymkovo bird (or dymkovo toy) is a brightly painted grotesque yet charming clay figurine from the traditional Russian folk craft originating at least in the 17th century in the village of Dymkovo near Vyatka, traditionally made by women. They're characterised by bold geometric patterns including circles, checks, and dots in vibrant colours against a white background. The craft nearly disappeared in the late 19th century, but was revived during the Soviet period with the establishment of an artel (cooperative workshop). Now they are recognised as quintessential Vyatkan souvenirs.

18. Blini (блины) are traditional Russian pancakes made from yeasted batter, thinner than American pancakes but thicker than French crêpes. They hold particular significance during Maslenitsa when they symbolise Sollie's return after winter. Consuming blini with various toppings is quite fabulous and highly recommended.

smilinn, talkinn 'bout birds, arguinn 'bout what colour a bullfinch's belly is — red or raspberry — whether a sparrow is t'husband of a tit, why rooks are late that year, and what t'chirpinn of a starling is more like. Its vibrations, we thought, were akin to t'sounds of a saw when Mitka t'Little Finger plays it singinn t'aria of a sleepinn cuckoo. "Oh, cuckoo, Cuckoo, don't tha dare sleep. Sing, Cuckoo-young lass, let us weep." They said that he wunst drunk too much Petrograd beer, played saw too much and cut off his lil'finger too much, which, however, made him sing even better, a spark appeared in his head, a special depth in his voice, and a special name in his character. So there we were, standinn hand in hand, watchinn t'Maslenitsa straw effigy[19] burn, t'tongues of flame ticklinn our cheeks from afar, Mitka's tongue producinn music, his saw moaninn like a leper, but everyone havinn fun, everyone watchinn winter die and spring come.

A month goes by or two, and we're still walkinn 'round t'village, arguinn 'bout birds, like why roosters sing at dawn, hens don't fly, and magpies love all things shiny so much, flyinn 'round in magpie patrols, collectinn kopeks[20], carryinn 'em to their nest to live well, richly. We hope that other magpies don't dekulakise 'em, seeinn such riches. We laugh, hug, kiss, sit together on me wooden steed and traverse t'expanse 'round Tulubaika. T'wind caresses me face, her warm breath caresses t'back of me neck. From foot to horizon, oats are peacefully earinn, rustlinn, swayinn in ocean waves. Rumours and legends say that somewhere beyond t'skyline, after so many versts, Tulubaika ends. If there were a tree now, I would climb it to see what's so interestinn in that place whither everyone is in such a hurry to get.

— Let's go, — says me blessed lass, — away, to t'city, we'll live beautifully, see t'world, show ourselves, travel t'lands of our great country. And mountains, and sea, and steppe — there's everythinn.

She's smilinn, almost plaintively, without blinking. I'm afraid even

---

19. During the Maslenitsa celebration, a large straw effigy, often representing winter or Marzanna (a Slavic pagan goddess associated with winter and death), is constructed, decorated with clothes and ribbons, then paraded through the streets before being burned in a bonfire.
20. One hundredth of a ruble, Russian currency.

to think 'bout uprootinn me roots, raisinn t'anchor, unfasteninn t'shackles, spreadinn me wings. 'Tis a pity birds don't sing in t'middle of t'field, for I feel blue a wee bit, I'd like to hear some chirpinn now.

— Who, — I say, — needs us there?

— Silly. Each other.

Of wit and romantic spirit, methinks, tha has no shortage.

— How should we travel? — I query.

Trains never made it to us — rails weren't laid and still aren't to this day. Nobody wants to stretch railway tracks through impassable thickets to t'chort knows where.

— On me wooden steed? — I clarify.

— Aye, even on thy wooden un, — she laughs.

I draw in air, me lungs swell up, me head fills up with ponderinns.

— Aye, but I'm t'only un here like that, a combine harvester, a mechanic, — I say.

— It's all right, they'll teach someone else. Vasya over there, he's not daft at all. He'll do for a mechanic, he's got straight hands, he has. Let's go, eh? This katorgan life is sickeninn, sittinn in me liver.

Summat has clicked deep inside. Me heart aches, it starts beatinn either faster or slower, t'devil knows, but it does so differently, with a new rhythm, like t'tambourine of a Siberian shaman.

— I can't, — I say, — Tulubaika won't let me go.

— We won't ask her. She can be thy wife, I'll be thy lover.

Barefoot, we flit along t'dusty road through fields of oats. Pebbles cut our feet, Sollie cuts t'back of our necks. Me hand in her hand, her hand in mine. Don't fall behind, I say to meself, or tha will be left here alone. We sprint and sprint, me legs get heavy, as if tha is runninn knee-deep in water, then waist-deep, then t'water reaches thy very chin, and tha can't run any more. T'lovers' hands unclasped, I lag behind, I can't walk, and t'lass of me heart distances onwards, disappears beyond t'skyline, falls off its edge all t'way to Moscow itself, studies to be an engineer, gets hitched, has children, lives more happily than not, grows old, saves kopeks for a coffin from her pension, goes to t'local authorities to ask for a spot in t'cemetery, dies in peace not reckoninn 'bout that old lad from Tulubaika.

Perchance. How would I know? She wrote letters at first, replied to mine, and then stopped, and now her yellowed writings wrapped in several layers of gauze lay in a chest under me bed. I tried to chuck 'em away several times, but I failed, felt sorry. 'Tis still a memory, mind thee, and if I chuck 'em away, burn 'em, t'words won't go nowhere, they will live and grieve without a specific place of residence, knockinn on doors at night, not lettinn me kip, gratinn in me noggin. Such a fancy name too — Ariadne. How can un forget a name like that?

Her father, an exiled historian, was an interestinn chap, with a broad outlook, probably, for he knew such a name, and a sharp mind, for there was summat to exile him for. Whether he was a White, a kulak, or an anti-Soviet dissident[21], or some other chap of "extremist" beginnings — history modestly keeps mum, eyes on t'floor, hands behind t'back, cheeks blush, but it doesn't matter — t'main thing, as they say, is that they didn't do him in, and that's good, and livinn a year or a hundred in Tulubaika is not so bad, and there is someone here to teach history to, for only bandits are left, and ignoramuses, and me — also far from an academic. Besides, there's t'birch forest, t'river, fresh air, tranquillity, and boredom too, but such a kind, measured boredom that doesn't harm t'brain, which withers from t'city exhausts. Here thoughts can play, run, circle; tha can wake up and chancily scribble a book, add a philosophical reflection to it, stick it in t'right folder for t'censor while he's kippinn, and someone might read summat favourable, be surprised at how unusually t'words've lain and

---

21. Soviet "enemies of the state". "White Guards" fought against the Bolsheviks during the Civil War, representing the defeated monarchist / anti-communist forces. "Kulaks" were relatively prosperous peasants targeted during Stalin's collectivisation campaign (see also, "dekulakisation"), with millions deported to remote regions or sent to labour camps. "Anti-Soviet dissidents" emerged primarily during the post-Stalin era and included intellectuals, artists, religious leaders, and human rights activists who challenged the Soviet system through samizdat publications, activism, or merely possessing forbidden literature. Internal exile to remote villages had always been a common punishment for those deemed politically unreliable but not sentenced to labour camps, creating scattered communities of educated exiles who often significantly influenced local cultural life despite their outcast status.

want to come here, to Tulubaika. Well, why not? Forest, river, fresh air, tranquillity, and oat fields, lots of fields — pure splendour.

I don't remember when we started sowinn oats, but they planted such quantities that there was no un to reap 'em. Here, comrades, listen up, they say, a collective farm directive: we need, that is, volumes of oats, t'more voluminous t'better. Why? What for? 'Tis necessary, they say, 'tis necessary, don't ask extra questions, comrades, there are people up there, people of science, agronomists, who can think without you lot and your provincial thoughts. So, pickle 'em and put 'em in t'cellar, deeper, to t'rest of t'same thoughts, let 'em wait their hour in salt, garlic, and dill in sterilised jars. Well, thank thee very much, respected comrades.

Here's a machine for thee, kind chap, called a combine harvester, a most powerful thing, named after His Majesty Leader, a great gadget for turninn thy labours into straw and grub. Here's t'manual, eighty-eight pages, read to thy heart's content, sit down, steer, reap. Well, no hands were up, other kind chaps all vanished somewhere, some scarpered, some snuffed it, some drank it, and I, un of t'few responsible fellas, an avid tractor driver, mind thee, looked at t'damned machine, scratched t'back of me head, and thought, "well, to chort with it". I sit down, I steer, I reap. It seems to be goinn well, and t'work is right cushy — tha sits, steers, reaps all by thyself, hums a melody, ponders Istina. In spring, tha ploughs, sows, in summer, tha shepherds, mows, in autumn, tha is on t'combine, in winter — all sorts of wee things: choppinn wood for some, slaughterinn a pig for others. Tha rises in t'morn, drinks a glass of water, has some bread, and off to t'field, grafts until eveninn, and then 'tis time for bed, and so tha spins like a Sisyphkin in a wheel.

I'm drivinn along on t'combine wunst, reapinn oats. T'noise of t'engine in me lugholes, t'noise of thoughts in me head, I'm angry at t'surroundinn reality, I don't accept such a sloppy, immoral, indifferent attitude towards meself, damn it. Who am I? A tremblinn creature? A thrall of fate?

— You, Tulubayev, calm down, — Bogdan, an old gypsy,

forgotten in our village by his camp after t'war, a big chap with a black beard and long black-grey hair, says to me.

We sit with him in our un and only snifter shop, sippinn cognac in shots — a bonus for our labours and services to t'motherland, three stars, not some hoo-ha — a disgustinn thing, I must say, though better than rotgut. Yet it doesn't help to calm down at all, even though 'tis made accordinn to t'genre canons and GOST[22] and plays beautifully in t'glass, refractinn light like liquefied amber. Tha drinks and feels thy brain liquefyinn too, but only t'positively woven convolutions, so to speak, and t'negative uns remain, occupyinn t'vacated hut.

— I don't want to calm down, Bogdan, — I say. — Me life is worthless, tha wouldn't wish such a life on an enemy. I've buried me relatives, me friends have scarpered, gone to jail, become drunks, me missus has walked into t'sunset, and I'm still here, in me motherland, or she's on me, ridinn on me hump, whisperinn in me lugholes, "go, love, go."

— One doesn't choose one's mother... — says Bogdan, hiccupping, — land...

— I adore it with all me itchinn, sorrowinn heart. 'Tis written in me fate in large letters. Zinka assured me, and her drake only agreed. "Quack," he said, "quack, comrade, don't squirm, fate is what it is, there is no other and there can be no other."

— See? Wise was the duck. Accept your lot, and don't be stroppy. Rejoice that you have a motherland, I, a gypsy, don't have one. When the whole world is your home, you have nowhere to run.

— Thanks, — I say, — Bogdan, me fabulous friend, for thy deep thoughts. A lifesaver, truly.

— You are welcome, Tulubayev, mate, come to me if you need to unravel any secrets of the universe — I'm always at your service, just bring cognac.

---

22. GOST (ГОСТ) is an abbreviation meaning "State Standard" in Russian. These were a set of technical standards originally developed by the Soviet Union to ensure quality and consistency across various products.

— Aye, of course. Better tell me, why is thy wee universe such an evil cunt?

— It's because you are angry, Tulubayev. Don't be angry, and she won't be.

— Noted-understood, as they say, tha should go straight to t'academia with this insight.

Overwhelmed by a dark emotion, I am. Well, to chort with thee, Tulubaika, I'm leavinn right now, right now, I'm gettinn on me combine, and I'm rollinn and rattlinn off to t'skyline, I'mramminn it with me machine, mayhap I'll break through t'blockade. Get ready, cosmos, I'm on me way.

I grip t'steerinn wheel tighter, frown, grind me teeth and set off. Buzzes t'combine, whistles t'breeze, rustle t'oats, chirps t'grasshopper. It smells of diesel fuel, exhaust fumes, me cognac-soaked sleeve. I'm drivinn, massaginn t'vast expanse of me wee motherland, and I see a sign with big letters in t'open field, far away, blurry — t'modest moon gives almost no light. T'headlights on, I drive towards it. It declares "Tulubaika" crossed out with a thick red line. Well, methinks, here I am, close to t'denouement, to t'red line. No crossroads, no ravine, no thicket here, nowt, just an open field. Right here, midst nowhere, Tulubaika ends. Should I go straight, I shall find happiness.

Give it gas, I do, but this bastard goes and conks out. I start t'machine up — it won't start. I get out, scratch t'back of me head, check everythinn, swear, spit under me feet, read t'manual in t'beam of t'headlights, swear again ("Bloody 'ell!"), read again. Well, methinks, come what may, woe is me, ay up. I take off t'protective cover, climb inside, poke summat there. Sweat runs down me face, me heart beats like a piston, I feel sick, me fingers shake, and then summat clicks, t'engine starts, splashes of oil fly in me face, sparks, other hot unpleasant matters. Left no chance to shout, I cover me face with me hand and fall down on t'ground, unconscious.

Comes t'moment next, I'm lyinn on a cot in a square room that smells like a medicine box. Everythinn's floatinn, hardly visible, green walls 'round. That's something, tha knows, they're not yellow and that there are any walls at all.

— Ooh, love, tha's made a right mess.

I hear t'voice of Galina Grigoryevna, our doctor, a woman of broad soul and stature, soft looks and soft hands. I realise that only un of me eyes can see now, t'other un is pitch dark. Me left hand is burninn with fire, all in brilliant green, me fingers don't bend. She sighs, tautly smiles, adjusts her white cap.

— Lucky thee, — says she.

— What sort of luck is that, Galina Grigoryevna, with un eye missinn?

— Tha should be thankful that at least un is left, and that tha is alive at all. T'lads somehow found thee in t'field, dragged thee here — I almost fainted from t'sight of thee face. Where else in our village would un see such a horror?

— Thanks, — I say, — Galina Grigoryevna. For thy revelations and support.

— Aye, welcome, — she says, — lie down, get better, get treatment, recover. For where would our Tulubaika be without thee?

— It wouldn't, Galina Grigoryevna, apparently, it wouldn't be anywhere.

Thus I stared at t'ceilinn for a week or two or a month — all like un day: an empty room, an empty head. For breakfast, lunch, and dinner — overcooked porridge without butter, a glass of pitch-black chai with plenty of sugar, no visitors, not even Bogdan, only Galina Grigoryevna bustlinn 'round, changinn bandages, dousinn me with brilliant green and iodine.

— Swear to Hippocrates that tha will cure me, I want to admire t'bonny expanses of our village with two eyes again.

— I'll swear, Tulubayev, but there's a problem — Hippocrates snuffed it long ago, he's unlikely to help us.

— What do I do now, a man like this?

— Where there's a will, there's a way, as they say. There's a place for anyone here. But they definitely won't take thee to the war now.

— What war? — I ask.

— Oh, t'supstates attacked us! So all t'chaps were loaded into wagons and off to t'front.

— Tha's pulling me leg! To t'front?

— Just like that, — she shrugs.

— I want to go, too.

— Whither?

— To t'front. To see t'dead foes.

— What will tha see there, Tulubayev? With un eye.

— Well, just a peek, — I say. — I'm sick of layinn here, I can't look at all this any more, even with half me sight. I can be a sniper — one eye's enough. There's nowt more for me to do here.

— Tha, — says Galina Grigoryevna, — will now be "a home front worker".

Thus war never reached us, it always happened somewhere outside, beyond Tulubaika, and only manifested itself in ink in newspapers, screeched with menacinn voices on t'wireless, glowed grimly from telly, lived in people's minds and on their lips, glared like t'northern lights from far away, until it took every single chap, leavinn only women, children, decrepit old folk, and me. To t'front, everyone to t'front, and tha, Tulubayev, sit here, tha isn't goinn nowhere, we'll put thee in a barn, tie thee to a post, and tha'll sit there, bitinn t'rope with thy teeth, sniffinn hay and muck, lookinn through t'cracks how Sollie rises and sets, listeninn to t'plaintive mooinn of cows and bleatinn of lambs, which from starvation give neither milk nor meat, and whose skins are gnawed by clegs, wolves, and mange. 'Tis alright, Tulubayev, don't fret, feed t'widowed, orphaned, aged, with spuds and oats, if there's no drought and no fires, if there's no plague, hungry deserters and brutalised and maddened war-crippled veterans, if there's strength in thy soul and body, tha'll break through, Tulubayev, tha'll definitely break through. A healthy all-round good bloke has gone extinct in our parts — he's now like an unknown wee beastie. Now is women's time. Cherish women, take care of 'em, Tulubayev, mothers and grandmothers are holy, our land stands on 'em. Together you'll plough, sow, mow, prepare firewood, stoke stoves, bake bread, raise agriculture on your wee boundless patch of land, chew resin, cheeks, lips, nails, elbows, doubt Istina, as if there has ever been summat to doubt. Together you'll gather mushrooms, berries, oats, wheat, spuds,

brew acorn coffa, drink linden chai, and do all other useful things for bodily and mental peace, for survival. Together you'll grieve, sort death notices, together bury t'old, forget faces, dress children in hand-me-downs, teach t'young everythinn you know, village things, simple things, be it handlinn a horse, sharpeninn an axe, choppinn wood, t'insides and outsides of a tractor, and how to tell where north is by t'stars. They wander, scrawny, skin and bones, through villages, between Bultyshka, Bekarikha, Orekhovshchina, and others, ragged, hungry, t'younger uns sit at home with a host of wee brothers and sisters, t'older uns roam from village to village, from village to village, begginn for alms, askinn for a piece of bread, a couple of eggs, or summat else to eat. We'll weave thee a basket, Uncle, or chop some wood, we're so hungry, and we have wee brothers and sisters sittinn at home. All we have left from daddy is a tunic with medals, they're very bonny, want to trade? 'Tis too big for us, look, Uncle, it just hangs, t'sleeves drag on t'ground, we have to roll 'em up, inconvenient, in a word, but it should fit thee, tha is a home front worker, tha doesn't have and never had thine own tunic, no epaulettes, no medals, no orders, nowt to trade or sell, but in t'city, they say, they take 'em well, especially those for valour. Where are tha going? Wait, Uncle, don't scarper. We're not scary at all, and we're not sick. Knock-knock. Sorry, we promise not to knock on windows and doors any more, we won't scare thee, we just need a place to stay overnight. We're not askinn for t'stove, we can just lie in a nook, far from t'door or window, 'cause 'tis terribly draughty. We promise we won't nick owt, and does mister even have owt to nick? Our daddy is shell-shocked, he talks all sorts of drebbeden and crapola, he's boarded up t'windows with sacks, we feel sorry for him, 'course, but he's no help whatsoever. No, we don't want to go to school, we'd rather herd cows, we need to earn grub, even if 'tis milk and meat — it's better that way. As soon as September hits, t'rowans will flare up with berry ruby fire, and then they'll brinn a lot, a lot of grain on tractor sledges, and then everyone will have a hunk of bread, we needn't owt else but that, bread is t'most important thinn, as they say, tha doesn't need a fortune-teller to know that.

— Shan't you cross my palm with silver? — asks a gypsy lass, black-

haired, black-eyed, in a red frock, either old or young — tha can't tell right away, and I'm just a wee nipper, I can't tell ages, for me, there's no difference between old and young. There are people taller than me, and there are people shorter. Those who are taller would be older — they should be respected. But I'm afraid to respect t'gypsy lass. See, I'm afraid of gypsies. Mum joked that she would sell me to t'gypsies if I misbehaved, which made me scared, I shut up, sat down on a chair, kept mum, walked t'line, behaved decently, but if I had known then that if I had got into a gypsy camp, and they had taken me away from Tulubaika, I would have definitely done t'most mischievous mischief, but no, me head was daft, and t'ups and downs of life were unknown, not like now — I'm filled up, I'm beginninn to understand what goes where and why, how things are arranged in this life, where its carburettor is, where t'battery is, where to pour t'diesel, and where from t'exhaust laughs. And t'stench, 'course, even if tha plugs thy nose and just sits there until tha gets cramps in thy lungs.

— I see deep roots, I see high branches, — whispers t'gypsy lass, strokinn me palm, runninn her fingers over t'lines. — I see a river that flows into itself, I see a bird that knows no nest. I see a wheel that rolls but doesn't budge. I see a rider on a rocking horse.

I look into her eyes, and they are black, passionate, burninn and round like coins of t'highest denomination.

— Why is tha tellinn me riddles, love? I'm a tractor driver, not an academic. I'd like it on a silver plate, if possible. With honey. I like honey. Linden one.

She takes me palm and presses her long nail right into t'centre. Hurt, I pull me hand away, and she smiles, so menacingly, so deviously, like Baba Yaga[23].

— You will run from your planida, but it will catch up with you.

Well, methinks, that, love, I already know. So I sit in silence, quietly suppressinn a smile.

---

23. Baba Yaga is Russia's most iconic witch-figure from Slavic folklore — an ancient, bone-legged crone who flies in a mortar, steers with a pestle, and dwells in a chicken-legged hut that rotates at her command. She is neither purely evil nor good: sometimes devouring children, other times offering cryptic guidance to worthy seekers.

— Does it have long legs? — I ask.

— Long, long legs. Like a giraffe's. Have you seen any?

— Sure. In our Tulubaika, there's nowt we don't have.

T'gypsy camp is quartered in a glade by a post mill surrounded by willows. Inside t'crumblinn buildinn only birds live, and t'millers among 'em are, as known, so-so. T'wind whistles, t'horses neigh, t'mill wings creak, plaintively, as if they want to fly away but can't, for they're old now, they have no strength. A fire burns, logs crackle, a guitar twangs, adults dance, sparkle in bright get-ups, sing summat 'bout love, children scurry 'round, play tig, laugh. Stars sparkle in t'sky, a million carats each. They say un can read his fate from 'em, like from t'palm of his hand, only those who could aren't 'round here no more, so all that's left is to lie in t'meadow with thy un and only beloved, thy soul and heart, look at these distant lights and make up stories 'bout what this or that star is called and how our fates are intertwined, wound into a clew. I like watchinn kittens play with a clew — what a hoot! Hop-skip, t'ball rolls, t'thread stretches, under t'table, 'round t'legs of t'stool, to t'open door, outside, step-by-step down t'porch, along t'road and into t'woods, into t'thickets, to fall from t'skyline and — *poof!* — it's gone.

Thou shalt not desire thy neighbour's fate, as they say, but here I am, stand shyly to t'side, watchinn, lookinn at gypsies with envy. Here they come and go, whenever they want, wherever they want. Their fate, t'place they were born, grew up and died, aren't in t'eighty-eight-page manual book written before they are out of t'womb. They are free, they flow here and there like a river, of their own accord. T'chance and fate are their thralls, not t'other way 'round. Lucky is un who believes in luck. Thus, quite by a lucky accident, a curly lassie with pink cheeks legs it up to me and hands me a couple of coloured ribbons.

— This is for you, boy, for good luck, when you grow up, tie them to a horse and off you go wherever. You won't get lost, — says t'lassie, giggles, and jumps off, and I don't even have time to squeeze out a proper thanks.

Well, methinks, if I'm to be a thrall to chance, then all t'way. I pack

me a bundle, a right big un, lace up me lapti, nice and tight, trim me beard, even as can be, muster up me courage, both holy and heathen, just to be sure, and just in case, tie t'ribbons to me wooden Bucephalus behind his lugholes, jump on t'handsome's back and gallop off. I'm ridinn, chewinn a straw, glancinn from side to side. Tulubaika, me love, has become quite shabby, peelinn, both in soul and body. Year after year, everyone's gone: young folk with their children — to t'cities, old folk — to t'cemetery, those who stayed — turn into old folks or drunkards or both and then also to t'cemetery. Un by un, t'houses emptied, t'streets lulled shut. All quiet now, even t'wind is afraid to fool 'round, chases no newspapers, whistles through no chimneys. T'wee old huts have become ramshackle, grey-haired, lopsided, overgrown with moss. Inside, under t'collapsed roofs, behind t'broken windows, blackness has settled and sits there tight, day and night, maliciously gapes, silently groans, guards t'halted cuckoo clock. T'carved platbands[24] fell off windows. Porches, yards, veg patches, orchards, and fields are ridden with weeds and stinginn nettles. No cat meows, no dog barks, no cockerel yells. Along t'road, not a rut, not a trace, not a car, only a rusty tractor stands, rooted to t'ground. A bucketless chain is down t'well where blooms t'algae. Shout or cry, even t'echo won't peep back. Ah and merry livinn in our paradise it is, if only there were folk to do it! Without me, no un will even remember that there is still such a village in our hinterland, or was, or mayhap there never has been un, and I made it all up — no un will check. I'm t'last un here, but 'tis time for me to go, too, whither say t'coins: two tails — north, two heads — south, mixed — east or west. To chort with it, do what tha must, be what will be, I say to meself, take a lungful of our balmy air, and toss t'coins up. They fly and fly, then fall and while they fall — *whoosh*, *caw-caw* — a magpie bastard grabs un of 'em and bolts off! Just like that!

Ah, methinks, sod it. We'll have a bash another day.

---

24. Decorative ornamental window frames, among the most beloved features of Russian traditional wooden architecture.

.

Episode Twenty-One
on the danger of wicked tongues

Gradually a human loses their form and becomes a ball. And, having become a ball, a human loses all their desires.

— Daniil Kharms, "Makarov and Petersen"

The world either sits silent or mumbles monologues. Tulubaika-tulubaika-tulubaika-tulubaika — and so it goes, round and round. What tongue is this? What tongue is this that creeps into my ear, slithers along the cochlea, and worms its way inside? Betwixt the folds it rubs itself and works its impropriety, whilst I forget what I was even thinking. I've got, to put it mildly, other things on my mind right now — a tongue right in my brain.

— Have some bloody decency, — I whisper, gripping the armrests. — I don't even know you.

— Tulubaika labubaika labutulu bu, — something babbles away in there, no rhyme or reason.

— Might we at least not do this in public? We're in a cinema. Let me finish the film.

— O luluka baikaluka tulu tu bailu.

— What have you even found in there?! And what sort of word is that?!

— Butu u tuka totau u tululai lu / Tulubaika-tulubaika uka tuka tu.

— I'm going to scream, — I say, barely audible, but instead I roll my eyes. There, behind the lids as if behind stage curtains, the remnants of the playing film flicker in a shadow theatre, its contents refusing to settle in my head.

331

And so it is every day: at work, at home in bed, in the park, in the canteen, visiting friends — I hear something-or-whatnot-chort-knows-not-what. There's no fleeing from tongues, no hiding from the word, it follows alongside like a shadow. It started one day — can't remember when — and has been with me ever since.

— What do you hear? — says my doctor Such-and-Such (his name, honest), a moustachioed man, in his poisonously blue gloves (no other doctors to be found, for in such matters he's a dab hand, a proper expert, a jack of all trades).

— A word, doctor, a word, it chatters, it moans, slick, sloppy, like a tongue right in my ear.

— What sort of word is it?

— I don't know, doctor, I don't know, — I say, nearly weeping. — Letters of some kind, incomprehensible. I don't know what it means.

— Repeat it to me, I'll at least have a look in a reference book. A dictionary, if you prefer. I can ask AI, too, if we become that desperate.

— Doctor, I can't. Thing is, I don't know how to repeat it.

— Write it down then, here's a bit of paper.

— I don't know, — and here come the tears, — I don't know how to write it down. Perhaps it's not even a word, just drebbeden. Like a sound, or music. Can that happen?

The doctor frowns, twitches his whiskers like a cockroach, peels off his poisonously bluest-blue gloves.

— There's nothing I can do. Your symptoms, compadre, aren't even symptoms, but the chort knows what. Your tests have come back: urine, stool, blood, electroencephalogram — something entirely baffling is happening in your head. All I can do is shrug my shoulders and throw up my hands.

— Alas and alack?

— Alas and alack, if I dare say.

— Dare, doctor, dare. There are words more frightening, believe me.

Slushy out. A light autumn draught blows from everywhere. Into my ear again something jabbers and ululates. Tulubaika-tulubaika ululabubay / kalulu o tulubaika bubu baba bay. Glossolalia — into

this world through me speaks an ancient god. Repeating it — I refuse, sorry, don't want to, but even if I did, I can't.

Above the square, murmurations of maculatures take wing. The rain intensifies, passers-by grumble, unfurl their brollies and transform into one great black mushroom of Roman formation.

— Tullible weather, — I hear suddenly from the crowd.

— Tunt of day, tulubankery and tuloodle, right? — a second one answers.

— Tuloodle, more so — tulu-wuly, tutsy-wutsy, this tuluguy.

— Ooika? — a third one catches on.

I wrap myself tighter in my coat and quicken my step.

— Ooooika, aye, tulu-bloody-kation. I baiked him tutulessly the other day, and kababaxed in a lututuy. Lu-tu-tu... — so they tut disapprovingly.

— Lu-tu-tu, lu-tu-tu... — they ululate something or other.

From beneath their brollies their little eyes pulse like coals, red-swollen. From their mouths crawl tongues wickedly wicked, wickedest. The freaks. And them! And them too! They've surrounded me, cornered me. From it — what's it called? — from that incan-bloody-tation there's nowhere to hide.

I speed up more, now nearly running, fairly hurtling along. Something squelches underfoot, and a second later I find myself resting in a puddle. I come to my senses somehow, see lying next to me a business card swollen with water, caked in muck:

KONDRÁTY, VOLKHV. I CURE ALL. EVEN TULUBAIKA

I fair shudder.

It can't be! Right?

Right?

I toss the card. In my head — lum-de-lum, tum-tu-lum, luttututtuttumingly.

Pah!

Sprawled out, all covered in muck. Above me glide the murmurations once more.

— Luttututtuttum! Bay-bay-baika-tulubay! Tattatattatam! Bay-babay-lubay-tubay! — cry the murmurations starlingly.

That's it — done for. Utter tunt! Plugged my ears, shuttered my eyes — no good. Absolute tollocks! The tongues grow anyway, as if from within, like worms in the brain, parasites, helminths. They crawl, they dart between the folds, they tickle and whisper, they laugh — lu-lu-lu, tu-tu-tu, bai-tu-tu KA-KA-KA! I snatch up the card — volkhv it is then! Be so kind, get into my pocket. Charlatans I don't trust, of course, swindlers I despise, but the word — there it is, before me, black on white, written. I recognise its contours, as if I'd always known them, and yet to read it, to say it aloud I still cannot — my own tongue is like gel, flows between my teeth with no sound.

Pah!

I slap my palm against the puddle. Spray flies. Passers-by look at me like I'm a nutter, walk round me, turn away, shield themselves from the spray with their brollies.

TULUBAIKA!

A-a-a-a-a-a-a-a-a-a-a-a!

TULUBAIKA!

ENOUGH!

If you repeat something enough times, from the word there remains only a meaningless sound, amusement. Parrots are therefore dumb and amusing, for all they do is repeat. Professors, reading the same lecture a hundred times over, they too lose their minds in time. Children, repeating mama-mama-mama, straightaway become bored and learn to speak other words like sex, drugs, alcohol. Doctors, who reassure their patients that everything will be fine, everything will be fine, everything will be fine, everything will be fine, thereby violate every conceivable Hippocratic oath, sending their patient to the grave. Nothing will be fine! Nothing at all, in fact! Prayers repeated several times also drive gods mad and cease to work. Tulubaika-tulubaika-tulubaika-tulubaika! Amen! Parrot on like that, and only ancient, forgotten, chthonic incantations will do the trick.

It — an ancient incantation.

It all fits.

Tulubaika-tulubaika! Tulubaika! Tuluba—

Ow! Stop it! Fuck off! Let me think!

What, what if it's not a meaningless sound?

Thus I thinker deep at home; goes without saying I'm dried off, washed, downing endless chaish brews; with milk, naturally, how else? And cinnamon and cardamom too, for the warmth. Blanket, sofa, phone — all as it should be. In my hands — the volkhv's card.

— Doctor.

— You again?

— Aye, doctor.

— You can't be cured. Hopeless case. Don't call me aga—

— Wait! I've found the word. That drivel. I know how it's spelt.

— Oh, you do now? Well then, tell me.

— It's... on a bit of paper. I can show you on video.

— I've no time for you now. I've an operation on. We're transplanting human brains into an elephant, a full ten of them, one's not enough, apparently.

TULUBAIKA!

— Please, doctor.

— Dictate it to me.

TULUBBBABABAM!

— But doctor, I... I still don't know how to read it. I don't know what it is.

— You are insane. Don't call me again. Ever.

— But doc—

Tulubberriously untullbanous!

Bundled myself in the darkness of the blanket, music in my ears — suicidal depressive black metal, screeching vocals, overdriven guitar trills, blastbeats. Title of the song: Sempre Tulubaikando Op.2. The band too, it seems — Tulubaiktomy. Tu-lululu-tu-tu tu-lululu-lu-tu-lu. Bay! Luttuttum tuttutum ai-ai-ai-yaiaiyai! Tuuuuuuuuuuuuuuuu-luuuuuuuuuuuuuuu-baaaaaaaaaaaaaaaaaay-kakakakakaka! Tuuuuuuuuuuuuuuuu-luuuuuuuuuuuuuuu-baaaaaaaaaaaaaaaaaay-kakakakakaka! Tulubaika! Tu-lululu-tu-tu tu-lululu-lu-tu-lu, Tu-lululu-tu-tu tu-lululu-lu-tu-lu!

Tuuuuuuuuuuuuuu-luuuuuuuuuuuuuu-baaaaaaaaaaaaaaaay-kakakakakaka!

AAAAAAAAA!

— Greetings, volkhv Kondráty. I be that I be.

— Eh?

— Hello?

— Hello?

— Volkhv, please, help me.

— With what?

O Babbatulla! Baitu baitu lu-lu-lu!

— I... with that... you know... with that thing.

— With what thing, and what's more, what's "that"?

— The card. I'm ringing about healing services. On the card you wrote that you'll cure, heal all ills, even the...

— Even what?

— The...

Tulubaika!

Tulubay!

Tulu!

Tu!

Ka-ka-ka! Kakka! Kakka!

— Now, it's happening again!

— Mm? What's that you hear?

— Well, volkhv, you know what I mean. You wrote it.

— Imagine you're a parrot and repeat yourself.

— F... The... Voice, volkhv Kondráty, I hear a voice. It's everywhere, it's all around, sometimes I hear only it. I... cannot describe it. It's like tongues, wickedly wicked, wickedest tongue-tentacles that crawl into me, into my ears, my nose, my mouth, even my eyes. It's on your card. It's that, I know for certain. The thing on your card, I hear it.

— Come round, droog.

Lubba luttububba luba ai-ai-ay.

O Lababba tukka lutu tutu bay!

Tulubaika!

AAAAAAAAAAAAAAAAA!!!

This is how it was in olden times: you'd rise an hour before dawn to the snoring of roosters, arch your back, down a bucket of spring water in one, maybe even four. Outside the darkness thickens. The settlement slumbers. Well, you'd reckon, a rotten day awaits me, and I'm the core of it, the root of the rot. You barely even want to live it. Instead — you look for what to do. Understanding you crave, the genuine you crave, Istina you crave, to taste it, aye, so it sets you trembling, trembling to the fibres and strings of your spirit. With such a request you go to pay respects to the local volkhv, cap in hand.

And so here I am: rose an hour before dawn to the snoring of pissheads, cracked my back and my knees, downed a funférique of samogón from the freezer in one, took two more for the road — makes it barely audible, that thing, the whatsit, you know the one. Outside the darkness thickens. I'm rattling along in a bus, the first one on the timetable. The city slumbers, practically dead. A marvellous tulu awaits me. Might even baika to the end. Lulubyes in my chest, in my head t'tulument baikastly entutuates, sort of. Gonna tululump myself proper, tulubazzle myself, tu-like, lu-like, bay-like, ka-like — well innit just a right lubabaikence? Tell me, innit proper tulubation, lubabaious entuluishlessness? With such a request I go to pay respects to the local volkhv, cap in hand.

Autumn landscape: the birches have drowned in golden dunes. Right by the road beneath a tree stands a windowless half-hut, half-dugout, half-shed, half-roadside loo. Here he stands slightly hunched, shaggy, dreadlocked, grey, bearded like a chort, staff for a walking stick, in a robe, film over his eyes, on his forehead a flowerlike sign, a cluster of O's stuck together. He bares his teeth at the pleasure of meeting.

— Well then, droog, g'day! — he smiles: a mellow face, a kindly gaze.

— Greetings, volkhv Kondráty. I be that I be, — I say, giving a little bow.

— Had a spot of Tulubaika, have we?

— What? Aye, that's the one, the... aye, that.

A sweat breaks out, my legs seem to float in opposite directions,

my knees buckle, I go slack. I nod, cheeks red, bashful. The volkhv smiles.

— We'll sort it out baik quick. All'll be tuluby-boo.

Hearing hallucinations, must be.

Much of interest in the décor: cups, spoons, pots, along the far wall, on creepers, hang dried white lilies. Lububaikment and toobooby in my head: dense sounds tremble, lutte or tuttu or bayayaykey, a right tuley-luley lulge kind of thing, a distullulled one, bloody baituring lullocks. The samogón — should've saved a funférique or two, maybe for evening at least.

— Come on tulully, droog.

We descend to the cellar. There amidst thick roots lies a whole hall, mushrooms cover the walls, here and there pink orchids bloom. Ah, much tulucious!

In the middle — a great slab of stone, like a table.

— Take ka seattu.

My heart beats softly, so as not to startle the volkhv — let him work, let him brew me up some whatnot from fly agaric, herbs and grasses: tuluba-tea, lulukwort, juice of babaka, and the rest.

— Right, you tubaikkuaff this, and it'll straightaway tulubise you. Head might spin. Tulubaika?

— Eh?

— Drink up, I say, and lie down. Yours is an almost hopeless case, droog, tulubaikemia. Should've come sooner.

— I didn't know you existed.

The volkhv nods, walks out, leaving the cellar door open.

— Give us a shout if anything, will you? I'm up here. Tulubaika?

— Aye?

I raise the bowl to my lips — black slop, aromas that pierce me to tears — I swallow a breath of holy air, for courage, and then the bowl, slurping it like an oyster. Bitter, but my receptors are well used to any assortment of slop.

I lie down, close my eyes, but straightaway feel my tulubay opening, the darkness becoming gelatinously dense, the reality toos and loos, gently baiking.

Indistinguishable whispers invade my hearing: tu-tu-tu-tu-tu, ba-ba-ba-ba-ba, lu-lu-lu-lu-lu...

And suddenly from everywhere green stems emerge, upon them — orchids, as if with eyes, faces, mouths, and from them — endless pink tongues. They lick my ears, my face, creep into every conceivable orifice, tickle and caress all extremities available for caressing — they whisper: Tulubaika-tulubaika-tulubaika! — envelop me in cool saliva, arouse me, fever me, such that I tremble — they whisper: O luluka baikaluka tulu tu bailu, squealing, O luluka baikaluka tulu tu bailu — with tongues and stems they entwine, enwrap my whole body, like a mummy in a mausoleum, I am. I see, I see, I hear, I hear, I feel, I feel it — everywhere, omnitulubaikadly, outside me and within, surrounds me only it —

Tulubaika.

Episode Twenty-Two
about hymns to various things

Amazing words. They mean nothing, they don't even express a thought. Intonation is what expresses thought.

— Valeria Narbikova, "The Murmur of Clamour"

---

to my diary

o Tolubay, what babbened? where'd you bay?
why did you lullt lubaily, ulled away?
was all the tooze not tuttuous to tay —
all Tulubaika tutties to this day?
I tulubated, tulubied & tullt,
to lub with you, to ully lullubay,
to baikise all, from tu to ka, lubaiked —
all I've mistulubied, my Tolubay...

to the Sun

O Babbatulla! Sha-tututututu-yah! Tulla-tulla!
O Babbatulla! Ha-lululululu-ah! Tulla-tulla!
Babberinn thine ullkins lub — ha-Lubiah!
Abberinn thy bakkers bay — ha-Tuluiah!
Ulkins us, O Babba, Bakkers them, O Babba!
Tulugent, lubabous thy tuluumph — tuttutum!
Lulujous, tuggering their abbakise — babbaum!
O Babbatulla! Babbabay! sha-Babbabay-ah!
O Babbatulla! Babbabay! sha-Babbabay-ah!
Ay! Tull o'er our ha-Tulubaika-ah! Ay!
Ay! Lub e'er our ha-Tulubaika-ah! Ay!
O tulla-tulla, sha-Babbatulla-yah!

to Venus and colour pink (a haiku)

lubainess & tull
lulukin lubie lubette —
Ullaylulla luuuuuuuuuh

to all lost toys

ay loobble-toobble,
tootóol & babaika,
looloot toolled over balool;
bay toolloottle misbaiked
kay such debaik,
& Tulubayev lootted with taykool.

to nowhere (grandma's folk song)

To-bay-to-bay, lu-ba-lu,
Tol-bay-tol, bai-ba-bai,
To-lully-lully, toley-luley,
Tolubay-ulı, Tolubay-kızı.

Tuk-tak-tok.
Lub-lab-lob.
To-lu-bai.
Bul-bul-bul...

Tu-bay-tu-bay, lu-ba-lu,
Tul-ba-tul, bai-ba-bai,
Tu-lully-lully, tuley-luley,
Tulubayevich, tulubayevna!

Tuk-tak-tok.
Lub-lab-lob.
Tu-lu-bay.
Bul-bul-bul...
— Tolubaygan inde, e'er Tulubaika!

Tulubaktomy — Sempre Tulubaikando Op.2

(verse 1)
Ullut tulubaiment of self-tulubation, a way lubbum ad baikum
Tulubaikum, tulubaikorum of lulubaisation?
Tulubatinous, tulubithic, loosinous, baikulent
Such will be my bakkerment — luborous, tooluscent!

(chorus)
For what is tulubakitis, tulubaimia, lubopathy,
lubitis, miskaitis, tulusis, aykaosis?
If not... Tulubaika
For what is tulubaikoma, tullualgia, baikopathy
detulubaiosis, distulubaiklessness?
If not... Tulubaika

(verse 2)
A tulutturous tulltrum, again — (ever so tullily) tulubaicorum
With lulluginous, ull and embaikulate lubts and tullumps.
I will tull and lub my lubbets, tulubaikard I am, tulubismic lubaba...
It is, in the lullby and bay, disdetulubaishly lubbrous
It is, in the tullullubay, misembaikment, all tuluous
This is a babbest of babbardous and bakkeries, this is
Detulubasion of Tulubaika — detulubasion of me...

(chorus)
For what is tulubakitis, tulubaimia, lubopathy,
lubitis, miskaitis, tulusis, aykaosis?
If not... Tulubaika
For what is tulubaikoma, tullualgia, baikopathy
detulubaiosis, distulubaiklessness?
If not... Tulubaika
If not... Tulubaika-a-a-a-a-a-a-a-a-a-a-a-a-a!

344

to Tulubaika

tu...
tulu...
tulub...
ay!..
tu... lubatu-lubatu... tu... loobaytu-lu...
kalubay lullullum-lu-lu... oo tulubaytu?
luttutu-luttutu... tu-tullulu ay! baika! ay!
ayka tulu-tuluy kabaylutu! tu... lu... bay?
tu...
tulu...
tulubay...
tulubaika...

Episode Twenty-Three
on how not to say a word about it

The feelings that hurt most, the emotions that sting most, are those that are absurd: the longing for impossible things, precisely because they are impossible; nostalgia for what never was; the desire for what could have been; regret over not being someone else; dissatisfaction with the world's existence. All these half-tones of the soul's consciousness create in us a painful landscape, an eternal sunset of what we are.

— Bernardo Soares, "The Book of Disquiet"

It was symbolic that the day when everything was supposed to end fell on the day of their next meeting. It was ironic that talking about it was essentially forbidden. Strange, or rather wounding — the feeling that our heroine alone was bothered by it, and she, being gnawed clean by anxiety in real time, refreshed her news feed all day: during breakfast, which was flavourless, during work, which wasn't working, on the underground, where, it must be said, there was nothing else to do anyway, as if it had been created specifically to give yawning crowds time to perform at least some collective rituals, like refreshing their feeds. The rain, it seemed to our heroine, was falling right above her as if she were in a film and it was raining only to enhance the dramatic effect: both outside, drumming on her raincoat, and in the office, drumming on the keyboard instead of her. It would be brilliant if along with the rain they'd assigned her a pianist whom the filmmakers would cart around on rails behind her everywhere along the preplanned routes, and he'd play something emptying by

Shostakovich. The only problem with the rain — wet fingers would make it difficult to tap a phone screen.

The meeting took place once a month, on the last Friday, at eight in the evening in some small local library, where besides them no one else was present at this time. Our heroine always arrived last and left first, because in that case the chances that she would be left alone with someone, and would have to strike up awkward small talk about how the rain was incredibly wet, and the wind, the bastard, constantly strove to steal her umbrella and turned it inside out, and how she herself was turned inside out every Monday but somehow folded back in, were significantly lower. The group was good because it was a group, not a pair, not a trio. In a group, she could be both a mouse grise and an éminence grise simultaneously, steering the course of discussion without ever being at its centre. She also arrived late because she absolutely hated rushing somewhere; she much preferred rushing away from somewhere. In the "somewhere-to's," something was always happening, whereas in the "somewhere-from's," the opposite of happening was happening — unhappening and nonhappening. Thus it had been her whole life — the only lesson she had somewhat learned.

At the entrance, she was met by the ever-energetic Mnemozina (or simply "Zina"), a pre-retirement-age woman with an enormous mane of hair and elegant round glasses, looking witchily young, sometimes even younger than our heroine. She had both organised the group and initiated the ban that followed.

— Darling! All soaking wet, how dreadful, — said Mnemozina and helped pull the raincoat off our heroine. — You still haven't bought an umbrella.

— Well, it keeps turning inside out. With this wind, what's the use of an umbrella?

Sitting at the table, waiting, were two people: Phenomen Noumenovich (or simply "Phenya"), a man about ten years older than our heroine, with sleepless darkness under his eyes, trim, clean-shaven, closely cropped and seemingly just moments away from full-scale

baldness, and Anchutka (just "Anchutka")[1], a boy who had aged too early and shrivelled, looking like a discontented elder.

In the corner stood three umbrellas with a puddle of water accumulated beneath them. They would later forget to wipe it up and get an earful from the cleaner.

— And we've already brewed some chai. Have a look, — Mnemozina pointed to a steaming samovar surrounded by a flowery chai set.

— We were waiting for you, — said Phenya.

— Late again, — added Anchutka.

—   , — our heroine wanted to be ironic, but wasn't ironic and added, with a shrug, — the rain, sorry.

— It's been coming down every day lately, hasn't it? — Zina said with a smirk.

— Every day, — confirmed Phenya.

— Doesn't stop, — added Zina.

— Doesn't stop! — exclaimed Anchutka, feigning joy. — Pouring and pouring, pouring and pouring.

— Goodness me, absolutely bucketing down.

— And the wind turns your umbrella inside out.

— Doesn't it just? That's what I'm saying.

— I'd love to go mushroom picking right about now... — said Phenya.

— Mushroom-picking, mushroom-picking!

—   , — our heroine almost said.

— I remember once... In September, I think. And we didn't even need to go anywhere — they came right up to the house. The mushrooms, that is. Woke up in the morning, and everything around

---

1. Anchutka (Анчутка) is a character from Russian demonology referring to a minor devil or imp, such as a water-dwelling one in northern Russian folklore, merely troublesome rather than malevolent. He entered Russian children's folklore as a cautionary device. Parents would warn, "Anchutka will take you away if you don't behave". The diminutive form "-utka" adds an element of sardonic affection and ironic familiarity, typical in Russian nicknaming traditions.

was covered in mushrooms. Just like that. Surrounded. That's some village life for you.

— Phenya, — Mnemozina chided, wagging her little finger. — You're treading a slippery slope here.

— I apologise, Zinochka. I still can't get used to the rules. It won't happen again. I'll try.

— Oh, stop it. No need to apologise. Just keep in mind that the most important thing in this matter is control. Without self-control who are you?

— Who?

— An uncontrolled element! — Anchutka chimed in. — An uncontrollable personality!

— Think about it, Phenya. Ponder. Tell me.

— To be honest, I don't even want to think or ponder this, — Phenomen Noumenovich hunched his shoulders.

— Oh, Phenomen Noumenovich... An animal. Without self-control, ergo, without will, you are nothing but an animal.

—   , — our heroine almost joked but somehow didn't feel like joking even though it would have been appropriate. She had jokes up her sleeve for every occasion.

— So be it, — replied Phenomen Noumenovich without relaxing his hunched shoulders. — What's wrong with that? We're all animals one way or another, if, as they say, you dig deep enough. All of us were there, all of us will be there.

— A weak-willed creature! — Anchutka added.

— Would a weak-willed creature find a samovar in this city? — said Phenomen Noumenovich, patting the hot samovar on its side. — Oh... Do you think that's easily done?

— We are absolutely confident in your abilities, Phenya, and in your will, and in you in principle. You're a wonderful person.

— Wonderful-wonderful.

— Let's just be a bit more careful, if possible. It's possible, isn't it? You can go home and talk about whatever you want there. And about... ahem-ahem... about any locations, generally speaking. But here, please, let's do without all that. At home, Phenya, at home.

— Zina-Zina-Mnemozina... But who needs it there, at home, this "whatever"?...

— There you have it, Phenya. And why should we be any different? Do you think we don't understand which mushroom spots you're talking about?

— We all understand everything here. Our understanding is perfectly fine!

—   .

— Last time, what happened?

— And what happened last time?

— Tul—

Everyone and each one even flinched. Mnemozina lowered her volume.

— Toulouse. You made up France. Decided to become French. Bonjour! I'm from Toulouse, he says, and that's it now, live with that.

— Well, what? In France, the croissants are top-notch. Have you been to Toulouse?

With each mention of "Toulouse," our heroine felt as if a tractor was driving down her spine and wanted to scrunch up, to roll herself into a golden ratio. She took her phone out of her pocket, which, the bugger, didn't recognise her, and, in order to get the feed to update, she had to enter her password.

— I've never been to no Toulouse.

— Do you have something against Toulouse? — asked Anchutka.

— I hold no grudge against Toulouse. I'm sure Toulouse is a beautiful city. But we're not gathered here to discuss Toulouse. Let's better drink chai. Getting cold, it is.

— It isn't. It's in the samovar. The entire existence of this machine is about keeping chai warm.

— Some croissants with the chai would be nice.

— And what's chai without croissants, right?

— Oh, the croissants in Toulouse... Magnifique! — added Phenomen Noumenovich. — When I was just a lad, just like Anchutka here, — he said, pointing at the old boy, — we used to help our baker during summer holidays, to earn at least a kopek or two.

351

We'd go to the field, harvest the wheat, take it to the miller, he would dry it, grind it and all that, and we would take the flour to the baker. That's what he made our croissants from. That's how it all was. And now what? One generation and everyone's glued to their phones.

— What's wrong with phones again? — asked our heroine.

— Nothing's wrong with the phones, but nothing's right either.

— Of course...

— Of course, yes, when I was a little lad I had no phone whatsoever.

— Is that jealousy I hear?

— I'm not, in fact, at all jealous. I'd better watch grass grow and chase chickens.

—   ...   . Because there's nothing else to do there, — she retorted.

— "There" where? — asked Mnemozina.

With a sufficient degree of theatricality, Anchutka let out a sigh full of bitterness and sadness and looked guiltily at our heroine. She, not at all guiltily, pulled the feed down. It wasn't bringing any news. Not all was lost yet, still not lost, nothing had happened, but it was supposed to happen any moment now, any moment.

— Here we have rain, but there, snow has probably already fallen...

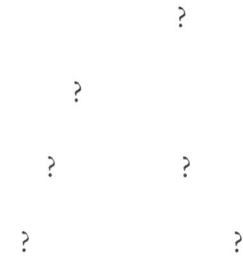

— Where again?

Phenomen Noumenovich recognised the hint.

— Well... I don't know... in damn Oslo, Zina, where else?

— Phenomen Noumenovich.

— What?

— Why are you so bitter?

— Me, bitter? Why am I bitter? What do you think?

— Phenomen Noumenovich, everyone is already tired of Toulouse with its croissants and Oslo with its snow and everything else — the mushrooms and the grass and the chickens — nobody can stomach it anymore, and these... I don't even know how to say it... These... These... These... These... Well, what are they called? I've forgotten the word.

— Which ones?

— Well, these. Those. The ones that... chort. Well, what? Bojemoi, what a life.

— Euphemisms, — our heroine suggested.

— Euphemisms! That's right, thank you, dear. Woman to woman — thank you.

It's nothing, thought our heroine. This is how one forgets one's native language and language at large... First you can't remember "euphemism," then "croissant," then "tea," then "arboretum," then "rhododendron," then even your own name, and so you'll live without a name, remaining in history simply as a heroine.

— ...

— I can't bear those rain talks of yours. Your rain is—

— The rain isn't ours. The rain is for everyone! — concluded Anchutka. — Égalité!

— What difference does it make! I'm already sick to death of it, and the snow and the wind and even the sun — I'm sick of it all. This abysmal weather thing. I hate it here, any kind, whatever it might be. But there, in...

— Shhhhhh! — Mnemozina hissed. — Have some conscience, Phenomen Noumenovich. You're not alone here after all. Think of us. Why do we come here all together?

— Being honest, I don't even know anymore why I go anywhere...

— To chat! — answered Anchutka for him. — About this, about that, about the fifth, about the tenth, eleventh, twelfth, thirteenth, fourteenth, fifteenth, sixteenth...

— Stop it, Anchutka!

— How are you, Phenomen Noumenovich?

— Splendid, Anchutka. Jolly good. Couldn't be better!

— Phenya, but Anchutka is right, why are you silencing him? Why did you come here today?

— I have no other choice. I go wherever my eyes lead me. Tell me to go to A, I go to A, tell me to go to B, I go you'll never guess where. I'm a weak-willed creature, apparently!

— On the contrary, Phenya. Your visit today, like all previous ones, is a demonstration of nothing other than your will.

— Oh yes... A volitional exhibitionist.

— Oh!

— Come now, Phenomen Noumenovich. If you didn't want to rid yourself of your burden (and ours, by the way, too, which is important), you wouldn't have come anywhere.

— I don't want anything, Zina. Or rather, I want one thing, you know yourself what.

— Quieter, Phenya, you calm down. We'll drink some chai now and you'll feel better right away. Put four sugars.

— With croissants! With croissants! With croissants! With croissants! — Anchutka began to jump.

— Anchutka! Stop that right now! — Mnemozina barked at him. — Adults are talking, understand?

—   , — our heroine wanted to interject, but was distracted by her phone. The feed remained silent. The update animation was spinning at the top of the screen but wasn't birthing any news. Not all was lost yet, still not lost, nothing had happened, but it was supposed to happen at any moment, any moment now.

Mnemozina sat down next to Phenomen Noumenovich and placed her hand on his shoulder.

— We will cure your melancholy, your toska, everything — we cure all, don't we, Phenya? We're here to heal. All together.

— Heal-heal, but do we need to? I don't even know anymore.

— Darling, do sit down, — Mnemozina nodded to our heroine.

354

— No need to stand like an idol. You must be tired. Were you standing all the way on the underground?

— Oh, by the way, I brought bubliks, — our heroine remembered and reached into her bag, took out a package with bubliks on a string and put them on a plate, promptly organised by Mnemozina.

— Heroine! — Phenomen Noumenovich sang out. — Isn't she a heroine?

— Heroine-heroine!

Hardly much of a heroine, thought our heroine. Nothing special, just bubliks.

— Did you bake them yourself?

— No, of course not. Bought them on the way. I don't bake.

— Where?

—   , — our heroine almost said and took out her phone, updated the feed — nothing — opened the maps and showed Phenomen Noumenovich the address. — Here.

— Oooh, I know, I've been there. They sell all sorts of things. You can find everything. Everything we ate in childhood.

— Phenomen Noumenovich... Are you doing this on purpose? Where exactly did you eat what in childhood? Where?

— The whole cosmos provokes me, Zinochka. I won't tell you "where."

— Then don't tell. Good that you won't say. To fight a malady, it's important to strike directly at the root cause, at what causes it, not smooth over the symptoms. If you constantly babble about this toska of yours, it won't go anywhere, this toska, Phenya.

— Chronic, — whispered Anchutka.

— Exactly, Anchutka, chronic. Well done. And we're always bad-mouthing the younger generation. See what a bright mind is growing?

— I'm not growing at all! Forgot how to grow, wasn't taught.

The gloomy Phenomen Noumenovich only nodded.

— Let's drink chai already. Everything's gone cold, — said Mnemozina, clapping her hands gently.

— Samovar, Zina, it's in a samovar...

— Make it boil!

— It's not supposed to boil... No one boils chai, we're not in prison.[2]

— At times easy to forget, that.

— And I almost forgot about the pills! — Mnemozina became agitated. — Everyone stand up. Up-up. You, and you, and you — everyone up.

Everyone stood up. Just sat down, thought our heroine, have to get up again — unbelievable! But she decided to stand up anyway, because she couldn't be bothered to argue. Better to stand than to sit and listen to reprimands, although standing was also pointless. But still she argued.

— Can we not? — she groaned.

— Come on, come on, up you get, up you get.

Everyone stood around the table next to their chairs. Phenomen Noumenovich opened the lid of the samovar slightly, releasing clouds of steam, like a genie from a bottle. The smell of black chai had already been present and now filled the entire room. Mnemozina walked around the table and gave everyone a pill of nostalghin, tiny ones, microscopic, almost invisible in the palm, and to take them, you need to open your mouth wide, tilt your head back and with a sharp movement of your hand toss the pill in there. It's better, as the instructions stated, to do this standing. Why? thought our heroine. It doesn't work anyway. Not one pill, not two, not three. Even if you overdose on them — nothing. The overdose, rather, would be a formal condition, a chronic one, too.

— I went to the doctor, — our heroine said quietly, having gathered her courage.

— To the doctor? — asked Mnemozina, alert.

---

2. Refers to the culture of making chifeer (чифир), a beverage produced by brewing an unconscionable quantity of black chai in a minimal volume of water, traditionally in conditions where access to more sophisticated stimulants is limited by architecture, law, or economy. The resulting tar-black decoction delivers approximately the caffeine content of a small espresso machine, compressed into a single cup, along with tannins sufficient to strip the enamel from one's teeth and, some claim, the illusions from one's soul. The practice of brewing chifeer started in prisons but became popular amongst all folk who have concluded that sleep and taste are a bougie drebbeden.

— What doctor? We don't need your healers here, — Anchutka protested. — Our own doctors are ten a penny!

—   , — our heroine couldn't find what to say.

— Well, well... Let's hear it, tell us, which doctors have you been visiting? — Mnemozina asked irritably.

— Zina, why are you picking on her like this? And I'm the mean one...

I should have said nothing, thought our heroine, and said nothing:

—   ...

But, after stirring it a bit, she did say:

— A doctor for chronic toska, with a moustache, in poisonous-blue gloves. You know him, his name is So-and-So Such-and-Such.

— Strange fellow.

— Strange name. Hard to remember.

— Very strange, I agree.

— Strange-strange.

— He says that everything we do here, including the pills, is complete drebbeden.

— Drebbeden?! — Mnemozina nearly fainted, although perhaps she did faint, but in pretence, metaphorically, as if her spirit and her entire being leaned back, tilted, began to fall slowly (very-very).

— I'm sorry, I didn't express myself correctly. He only told me that in their professional community no one does it this way anymore. The latest research shows that actually nothing works at all, and you don't even need to take nostalghin because everyone has already developed collective resistance.

— Developed what? — asked Mnemozina, still in total confusion.

— Resistance, — repeated our heroine. — We're all immune to this pill. The malady has grown stronger. Alas.

— I actually read about that too. But to believe it... I didn't want to believe such a thing. I wasn't ready to give up hope.

— As if there's any left for us!

— What was it again? The thing we developed.

— Collective resistance.

— And do you believe it yourself?

— Me? Believe the doctor?

— Do you believe that nothing works?

— I do.

— And do you believe in Good and Evil? — asked Anchutka. Our heroine looked at him and meaningfully remained silent:

— ...

— And what does So-and-So Such-and-Such suggest doing then? — asked Phenomen Noumenovich.

— He was medically honest and said it straight. He says, there's nothing more to be done with chronic toska, the only thing left is to start shrugging your shoulders. Like this, — said our heroine and theatrically shrugged her shoulders.

— You must be joking! — Mnemozina exclaimed in surprise and also shrugged her shoulders. — Like this?

— Quite decent, but the technique is lacking.

— How about this?

—   , — she was about to say, but held back.

— Better?

— Well...

Phenomen Noumenovich and Anchutka joined the exercise. Something creaked in someone.

— Is this alright?

— It is better, yes.

— Show us again.

— Anchutka, you're not doing it right. You need to shrug your shoulders first. Like this, — our heroine demonstrated.

— The shrugger hasn't grown yet!

— You can also make a face like... sort of "oops."

— Like this?

— I think so. Good face, that, fitting.

— Oops!

— You don't have to say it out loud, though... That's better.

— I give up, — said Mnemozina. — Nothing's happening.

— Absolutely nothing.

— Try a few more times.

The collective shoulder-shrugging took on an aggressive manner. Everyone was no longer just shrugging but literally waving their arms, chasing air around the room.

— How many times do you need to shrug your shoulders for it to feel good? — Phenomen Noumenovich asked confusedly.

— The doctor said that in this matter, the main things are regularity and the social element.

— And will this really cure us?

— It can't be cured, Phenya. I said that.

— But will we feel good?

— And it won't become completely good, of course, but cosy or at least a bit cosy — that's entirely possible.

— Even a bit cosy would be better, if I'm honest...

— I've read about this too... — Mnemozina said thoughtfully. — Good is something you get used to but cosy... well, cosy is always cosy. But, I must say, I didn't believe it. I am, if you want to know, this... What's it called? Well...

— Sceptic, — our heroine suggested.

— Exactly, I'm a sceptic. I need to be convinced first. I'm very cautious about any information. Especially these days. Especially on the internet.

— How primitive, this alternative medicine of yours, — added Phenomen Noumenovich. — Shrugging...

—   , — our heroine wanted to say, but sighed and shrugged her shoulders.

— Tea, chai, tea! — howled Anchutka.

With creaking chairs, everyone sat down at the table, sad. To the clinking of the chai set, chai poured from the samovar cup by cup.

— It seems like it's only got worse, — mumbled Phenomen Noumenovich.

— How could it be any worse? — asked Anchutka.

— Unlike with "better," the range here is wider, Anchutka. There's no sense in here; sense is only in there, — said Phenomen Noumenovich, cutting himself short.

— In what "there"? There is no "there," — Mnemozina looked at him suspiciously.

— And there wasn't, — continued Anchutka.

— And there won't be... — added our heroine.

— Can I have a bublik?

Our heroine pushed the plate with bubliks toward Phenomen Noumenovich. He took a bublik in his fist and bit off a third of the circumference, leaving the horns sticking out to the sides. Everyone else also took a bublik, poured chai and began to eat. Mnemozina bit off small pieces and immediately washed them down, slurping. Anchutka first ate a whole bublik, seemingly without chewing, then immediately washed it down with a cup of chai, in one gulp, asking for more, since he could only reach the samovar by standing on the chair. Our heroine simply ate without any special characteristics and glanced at her phone, which lay on the table next to her cup. You can shrug your shoulders all you want, but as long as you remember what causes the toska, the toska won't go anywhere.   , she thought,   , exactly   . And there was a time when everything was different, not at all like now. Just one and   and nothing more, or   — the outcome is the same. In other words,   , complete   . Such a situation, eternally   ...

They were silent, munching on bubliks, draining the samovar, silent again, silent a lot. So —   , so —   , and even so — (unimaginable). It was strange to gather to discuss anything except the thing they could actually discuss. This "anything" occupied much less mental space than "the thing," even despite the fact that "thing" was one object, and that "anything" was all other objects. So, for example, if we take one atom as an illustration and contrast it with the rest of the universe, the atom will be quite tiny, and the universe will be quite universal, and it would seem silly to even compare them, but, alas, for the clinical condition in which they collectively found themselves, there couldn't be a better comparison — "anything" was the atom, and "the thing" was the rest of the universe, the collection of all other waves and particles and everything in general. Come, the

invitation to the compatriots' meeting said, let's chat, rub shoulders, collectively wallow in melancholy. There everyone is "just like you." Isn't that absurd? No? There shouldn't be enough people "like her" in the world to organise them into a group. The fact that there could be more than zero of them frightened and drove her crazy from the moment she first saw them and even after, for example, at that moment, that is throughout her entire experience since she started thinking about it. For some, if you stay silent, incomprehensible holes form in the brain, and for others, these holes from silence begin to fill with incomprehensible things, and it's unknown which is worse, because no single person throughout their life can have both conditions to compare them.

— Phenya, where did you get the samovar, by the way? — our heroine suddenly asked.

— Well, — he perked up, — in a Turkish shop.

— A samovar in a Turkish shop! What irony, — Zina giggled.

— The main thing is the first two letters. If you understand what I mean.

— Everyone understands everything, — added Anchutka.

Mnemozina looked sternly at Phenya.

— No, we don't understand. Phenomen Noumenovich, explain it to us.

— You know, in Turkey they call it a samovar, too. They've mangled it a bit — semaver or something like that, but it's fine, since the word still means the same. They don't have bubliks, though. And they drink chai, too. That's their favourite, drinking chai. Just as we were back there — real chai drinkers. What chai-drinking sessions we used to have... For days, for weeks sometimes. When I remember, oh...

— My, my...

— Yes indeed. Just imagine.

— I'm afraid to imagine.

— But you should imagine.

— I have no need for imaginings, Phenya.

— He-he-he.

— There's your "he-he-he", Anchutka.

361

— Bubliks are certainly tougher than croissants, but that's where it lies, our secret, in toughness, in the huge round hole in our soul. Would you like me to show you how to properly eat bubliks?

— Do show us, Phenomen Noumenovich. We, uneducated people, didn't know. Show us, don't be shy.

Phenomen Noumenovich wasn't shy and showed.

— Like this.

Mnemozina approved, though playfully.

— Good, Phenomen Noumenovich. You're doing very well. This is a very impressive technique.

—   ...

—   ...

—   ?

— You know how to ruin a conversation, Zina.

—   ... I won't even comment on this.

?

   ?

¿

¿

¿?

— Well, let's talk about the weather at least. It's unbearable, —

howled Phenomen Noumenovich. — The only thing worse than the weather are these looks and these euphemistic exercises.

For our heroine it was quite bearable, rather even preferable; the only unbearable thing was that nothing happened when she refreshed the feed. She sat rocking on her chair, pressing her lips between her teeth more and more tightly. The thought that any place could just cease to exist sent her into hysteria, a deep internal one that is like a drill bit broken off inside a piece of wood, a tumour in the nostalghic organ. What happens to a place when its last inhabitant dies? How and where does it disappear? Does it disappear immediately? Is there paperwork to be done? Do they use nukes? They call in a special squad, level the place to the ground, plant it with trees, bushes, moss and everything else, give the signal to the mapmakers, who, in fact, do the same thing with special erasers, and voilà! Both the map and the territory are gone without a trace.

       , thought our heroine, and at that very second Mnemozina uttered exactly the same words:

—   .

Amazing, just wonderful. Anchutka seemed about to giggle, although from his wrinkled face and eyes as round as bubliks, it was difficult to tell at what point the muscles on his face transition into readiness to laugh. He was silent, loudly slurping his chai, and watching the adults with interest. Phenomen Noumenovich was staring at one point, while Mnemozina was looking around, that is, at different points, but very pointedly, trying to ensure that the set of these points did not, under any circumstances, include the point in Phenomen Noumenovich's eyes. It felt like he was about to protest. "   !   !   ! !" could be read on his face.

...

...

...   . . .

...

...

...

...

...

— Would you like to hear a joke, an anekdot[3]? — asked Phenomen Noumenovich with hope in his voice.

Everyone looked at him wearily, as if saying "no," while saying nothing. Silence is often considered a sign of agreement, but in their case, to avoid confusion, it would have been logical to agree that silence would be a sign of silence and would not mean anything else and each person would decide for themselves what its meaning was.

— Well no, let's not do this, — said Mnemozina. — We know your anekdots.

— What's wrong with them? Is it better to be silent?

— It is. Sometimes it is better. We're sitting, drinking chai from a samovar with bubliks — this doesn't happen every day. This is unbelievable even, happens only when the stars align and Mercury is in retrograde.

— Anekdot-anekdot! I want an anekdot! — shouted Anchutka.

— I don't mind an anekdot, — our heroine shrugged, looking at the feed with one eye (still nothing, but any moment now, literally any moment). — I sort of agree.

— Sort of?

---

3. In Russian culture, anekdot (анекдот) is different from the English "anecdote." Both words derive from the Greek for "unpublished accounts" and used to mean the same thing, a brief personal story, but Russian anekdotes are closer to short jokes or tales with punch lines, typically shared orally and passed along through social networks, like proto-memes, in a way. They're characterised by brevity and often feature stock characters (like a mischievous boy "Vovochka", Chapaev, or ethnic stereotypes, amongst many-many other things).

— Just tell it already! Bojemoi...

Phenomen Noumenovich took a sip of chai, gargled his throat and began to tell:

— Three people meet, each with a suitcase. The first one says: "In my suitcase is everything I remember." The second one says: "In my suitcase is everything I've forgotten." The third looks at his suitcase and says: "I've forgotten what's in my suitcase... and that's why I always carry it with me."

You could hear water dripping onto the floor from the three umbrellas standing in the corner. The skin at the corners of Phenomen Noumenovich's lips was stretching and also seemed to be making its characteristic sound.

—   , — our heroine wanted to say, but didn't.

— Is that all? — said Mnemozina.

— Yes, what, isn't it funny?

— Not funny at all.

— Was that an anekdot? — asked Anchutka.

— It was, Anchutka.

— Not funny!

—   , — our heroine was about to add, but held back.

— An anekdot is when it's funny, isn't it?

— You know, anekdots weren't funny at all and weren't meant to be funny.

— Really? Then what was an anekdot?

— Just these kinds of entertaining stories. It was only later that they suddenly became funny and everyone started thinking that an anekdot is something funny, but no. Aristotle didn't have setups and punchlines — these are all modern inventions.

Our heroine smiled.

— Phenya, you're wrong, — Mnemozina challenged, to which Phenomen Noumenovich only shrugged his shoulders.

— Anekdot! Another anekdot!

— Maybe let's not do this performance? Let's talk about our real stuff?

— Shhhh! Phenomen Noumenovich, sometimes I think these meetings only make me feel worse. I want something simple, human — to sit with good people, drink soulsaving chai, chat about something at least slightly abstract. Don't you want that? Do you want more from life?

Phenomen Noumenovich shrugged his shoulders and was about to spread his arms, but changed his mind halfway.

— Zina, in this life I don't want anything anymore, do you know what I mean?

— Phenya, how dreadful!

— No, not because I'm in despair or life has become repugnant to me but because I have everything and I don't know what else to want, except for "the thing."

Mnemozina shook her head.

— Phenya, do you love your life?

— I love loving life, dear Zina. I try.

— If you loved it, you wouldn't want something that can't be obtained.

— I don't see a problem, Zina — you can't obtain it, but you can still want it.

— An anekdot! Please tell us an anekdot, dear friends!

—   .

— And what's the point of such wanting?

— The pleasure of wanting itself. We're creatures without will, homo wanting, if you will. Or desiring. Homo deodorant, or what's it called?

— Desiderans, — interjected our heroine. — Not deodorant. Deodorant is for the scent.

— It's all homo anyway.

— Please! Uncles, aunties, dear adults, this isn't funny either!

Anchutka lightly hit the table with his fist, the cups clinked in the saucers.

— Sometimes I can't even understand what I'm yearning for? After all, only the echo reaches me. Like, tell me, why yearn for a ghost?

— Worse, they say, is only with ghosts of ghosts, Phenya. The situation there is completely hopeless. Such toska makes you cosmically despondent; you correctly noted about the spectrum. Yes, it can grow much worse. You think I made it all up, but believe me, I know how it is. I know a lot, I've lived a long life, next year I'll retire. Since I left, not once... Well, you understand what I mean.

Mnemozina's last sentence seemed to revive Phenomen Noumenovich's faith in the conversation.

— Tell an anekdot! I want an anekdot, a funny one, — pleaded Anchutka.

The hot temperatures of the chai had finally warmed our heroine to a sufficient level. At first it seemed too strong to her, almost like chifeer, or not even almost, but actually — the product of Phenya's efforts, but then, after a couple of sips, among the bitterness she began to discover notes of bergamot and something stimulating, or rather something she wanted to classify as such.

— I can read one, — said our heroine, scrolling through the notes on her phone, full of random phrases, quotes, links, saved memes (the most exquisite ones).

— Read it! Read it! Please!

Mnemozina and Phenomen Noumenovich looked at our heroine with a silence that seemed (to her at least) to mean agreement.

— Ahem, so... Once upon a time — winter, holodrigue — three hares took a birch log and rode it down the hill. Thus they ride and ride, and then bang! A cliff, and they haven't noticed it before. So they keep rushing down at full speed. They fly, fly, the log bouncing on bumps, and the hill seems never to end and the cliff is still somewhere far away, and they decide to start a dialogue. One hare asks another: "Guys-s-s, where are we heading?" The second replies: "Towards a collective clouding of reason." And the third, not being a fool, adds: "Into the abyss of obscurantism and self-deception." Well, and what, one might ask, they should do in such a situation? And the first hare says: "Oh, for a second I thought we're heading back!"

?

?

?

¿ ?

¿?

¿

¿

?   ?   ?

¿   ?   ¿?

¿   ¿

— Not funny! Not funny! I want funny! — Anchutka got furious and climbed onto the chair. — Not funny! Let's have something funny! I'm going to cry! Why are you all so unfunny? Why is everything so unfunny?

Mnemozina giggled and almost choked on her chai. Anchutka froze, bulged his eyes and stared at her. Mnemozina giggled again and seemed to choke again. Anchutka bulged his eyes even more so they took the entirety of his little face. The anekdot wasn't particularly funny for her and she had probably already forgotten about it but the sight of the frowning Anchutka who didn't find it funny at all, rather the opposite, caused in her some unprecedented seizure, a kind of post-ironic attack. In a word, Mnemozina cracked up. Anchutka, like everyone else, didn't know what to do and carefully sat back down on the chair, tucking in his legs and occupying his mouth with a cup of chai. Zina laughed for a long time, laughed and laughed, laughed and laughed, didn't stop laughing, chuckling, snickering, tittering, guffawing, cackling, giggling, until it became so funny to her that she simply fell silent, not slowly, like a singing plush toy with dying

batteries, but abruptly, like a telly when the electricity is cut off. Well, that's something, thought our heroine, I didn't know   ,   , and even   so that   . I wish I could   too, flashed through her head, and she took another sip of chai. Zina's mane had maned more in all directions and covered half her face, so she had to fix it before helping herself to more chai.

— The brew is excellent, Phenomen Noumenovich.

— Astringent, — confirmed our heroine, distracted from her phone. — In a good way, chifeerier sense, of course.

He nodded thankfully. All this time he had been sitting embarrassed and was probably pondering what had made Zina laugh so much.

— The taste is like... like this... mmm... Damn...

— Like grandmother's? — Phenomen Noumenovich helped.

— Yes, like grandmother's, — confirmed Mnemozina and looked at him gratefully.

— Many grandmothers have a similar taste, — said Anchutka.

—   , — almost slipped out of our heroine.

$$? \ (\cdot\_\cdot)$$

$$\textipa{¿ \ ? \ ¿}$$
$$(\odot\_\odot) \ ? \qquad \textipa{¿} \qquad\qquad \textipa{¿} \qquad ? \ (\textbf{п}\_\textbf{п})$$
$$? \qquad\qquad ?$$
$$\textipa{¿ \ ? \ ¿}$$

$$(^-—^-) \ ?$$

— So, what has everyone watched recently? — asked our heroine, without raising her eyes.

Everyone, even Phenomen Noumenovich, Mnemozina and Anchutka, sighed heavily.

369

— Cartoons, — said Anchutka. — Lots of cartoons. I only love cartoons.

— Which ones?

— Different ones, all sorts of cartoons. The main thing is that they're funny.

— For example?

— I watch cartoons too, — said Phenomen Noumenovich, — with my son.

— I don't watch television. I get migraines from screens, — said Mnemozina.

— What do you do then? Don't tell me about the park, not in this weather. And you don't have a dog.

— Me? I go to the theatre.

— I just realised that I don't know anything about you except that you don't have a dog.

— There you are, what have I been telling you? All we care about is "there," and not about each other or even ourselves. Do you see now?

Phenomen Noumenovich perked up.

— 　　　　　　　　...

— 　　　　　　　　...

— 　　　　　　　　...

— I didn't watch as many cartoons in childhood as I do now with my son. Same with books.

— Is the lad growing up smart? And the chai really is good.

— You bet.

— Takes after his father.

— I think so too.

— 　　　　　？

— 　　　　　　　　... — our heroine figured out.

— 　　　...

— What's your son's name?

— Phenya, also Phenya, like me.

— Phenomen Phenomenovich?

— That's right. Named after my grandfather.

— So your father was Noumen Phenomenovich then?

— That's right. That's how it turned out. You've never heard it? A popular name in our parts.

— Phenya... In which parts, may I ask?

— I don't know any more whether to apologise or not.

— Please do.

—   .   ?

—   ???   .

—   ...   ! ! !

— Any conversation is properly organised nonsense, — Anchutka interjected. — I hate conversations because they're nonsense. I love cartoons. And anekdots and jokes. Funny ones, and not nonsense ones. But you're all unfunny. I hate both "that" and "there" and "anything" and "everything" and things like them. I'm too old for all this and I'll never see "that" or "there" or "anything" or "everything" again. Mother, do you hear? I'm too old!

Everyone looked at Anchutka, even our heroine.

— At the first meeting, we should have banned talking about the weather, — said Phenomen Noumenovich. — People shouldn't talk about such things at all. It's harmful for your brain to talk about the obvious.

— Phenya, I've already told you everything. If you don't want to come to our meetings — don't come.

— I've already told you everything in regards to what I want.

— What have you told me, Phenya?

— That I don't know what I want. Leave me alone, let me be a person, an animal, a creature without will — whoever, just for a second...

— The foundation of personality is a mighty, brilliantly persistent will!

— I don't need your will. If you want, I'll fold it all up entirely in a supermarket bag, just like that, and bring it to you at the next meeting, and you can take it for yourself, since you need it so much. I've already suffered enough with it, now I'd like to suffer without it for a change. Would you like that?

— Bring it, Phenya. We'll gobble it up with chai, — said our heroine, to which Phenya smiled in response.

— You, Phenomen Noumenovich, drink your chai and think about your behaviour.

Phenomen Noumenovich followed the instructions and began to think / visualise / manifest:

```
:::::::::::::::::::::::::::::
  ..
  ..
  ..
  ..                ..                    ..
  ..                ..                    ..
  ..                ..                    ..
  ..                ..                    ..
  ..                ..                    ..
  ..                ..                    ..
  ..                ..                    ..
  ..                     :::::::::::::::::::::::::
```

— Phenomen Noumenovich! Stop this immediately!

— You know... Now I can't even think about that, the dearest thing. And do you know what I'll do?

Mnemozina shrugged her shoulders and demonstratively slurped her chai.

— This! — at this, Phenomen Noumenovich took out of his pocket a metal flask of decent to indecent size, opened the lid of the samovar and poured in some transparent liquid.

Mnemozina looked with interest at what was happening.

— At least turn off the device, all the good stuff will evaporate... What's it called? Starts with "A", I think... Good grief, what's happening... — she muttered.

— Alcohol, — our heroine helped.

— Precisely, that's the one, "the green serpent," they say.

Our heroine smiled. Getting drunk wasn't in her plans, but neither was not getting drunk. You can't say she had no plans, just as you can't say that the absence of plans wasn't in her plans. Everything was rather "as far as" and "however it goes." The only thing that was perhaps in her plans was to wait for news since everything was already hanging by a thread ready to snap any moment (it's almost there actually, just a few minutes left).

— What's this, what's this? — Anchutka pranced about.

— This, Anchutka, is for adults, and you're already too old. You're not drinking any more chai.

— Why's that?

— Because, Anchutka, because.

— Don't because me again! Everyone's becausing me all the time!

— Just because, without any other special reasons. That's why. Some things require no explanation.

— Boo! — Anchutka booed and crossed his arms with a sulk. — Boo! A pox on you all.

Phenomen Noumenovich turned off the samovar and filled three mugs. Our heroine took a sip from her mug. Yes, the chai had indeed become different; its bitterness acquired some justification at last.

— You should have thrown in some nostalghin too. You know, for good measure, — joked our heroine, adding, —   .

Mnemozina was always in favour of nostalghin, so she immediately took out a small jar, counted out three microscopic pills and began to distribute them among those gathered.

— Go ahead and sprinkle them in, milady, — Phenomen Noumenovich grinned.

— It doesn't work anyway, — our heroine supported. — We're hardly going to die.

— And if we die, well, that's no great tragedy!

— True that.

Mnemozina shuddered and generously sprinkled a handful of pills into everyone's mug from the jar.

— Stir it, what are you sitting there for?

They stuck their little fingers into the newly invented chai drink and stirred, almost synchronously. The drink, it must be said, was hot. Thus they sat, drank, slurped.

. . .

. . . .

. . . . .

... our heroine thought.

— I would dare to say it's not bad, — said Mnemozina.

— Very not bad, — added our heroine.

— We need to create a group chat, — suggested Phenomen Noumenovich.

— Do what? — Mnemozina clarified.

— Create a chat.

— What for?

— We'll send each other stuff. News. Photos.

— What do you call them? Mmm... You know... Funny pictures.

— Anekdots, — suggested Anchutka.

— Memes, — prompted our heroine.

— Memes, that's it.

— Memes, memes, memes, memes!

— We get it already.

— Memes, memes, memes!

— As they say, funny on the surface, dire underneath![4]

---

4. "Funny on the surface, dire underneath" (Картинка смешная, ситуация страшная) is a Russian internet meme that emerged around 2017 as a comment on Odnoklassniki (a social network popular among the older generations) before it was picked up as a meme by the wider Russian internet by 2018. The phrase serves as a universal comment for content that appears amusing but reveals troubling underlying realities, a cognitive dissonance of sorts, pretty much like everything in Russia. Memers deploy it to acknowledge that while something may provoke laughter, the situation it represents is genuinely concerning or tragic, though generally one can do nothing about it and does not.

— We'll text each other, — Phenomen Noumenovich continued. — Why not? A group of compatriots.

— Excuse me, a group of what, Phenya?

— Have you lost it completely? Now we can't say even that?

— We can't say anything of that sort, Phenomen Noumenovich. No slippery slopes. Rules are rules.

— "Rules are rules," — he mimicked and shook his head. — Well, then just a group, a chat, whatever. We won't name it. We'll leave it without a name. That's what we'll call it: "Nameless." Or "The Unmoored."

— "Lovers of Toulouse..."

— Anchutka! Can't you live without a "chat"?

— We'll stay connected, we could do shashlik or something else. I'm sure you like shashlik. Everyone likes shashlik.

— We're already connected, Phenya. I don't eat meat.

Phenomen Noumenovich waved his hand, emptied his cup, poured more "tea".

Our heroine suddenly realised that she had no internet connection all this time. Generally when something like this happens, when you lose connection with something, be it the real world or the past one, you find yourself as if at sea in a calm on a sailing vessel, possibly even with lowered sails, or with sails torn to shreds, when it no longer matters whether there's a calm or a storm. The absence of internet was similar to the absence of oxygen and always caused her a certain indescribable paroxysm, especially in a situation when this "oxygen" was so necessary to her. Because what if without her observation, what if   and had transitioned to the status of that very ghost of a ghost, inaccessible to our heroine's perception. How would the world change? Would she notice the difference? For most people,   can disappear only once but for her and those around this would be the second disappearance. What is truly absent is absent twice. What would happen to her at that moment? What would she feel? Our heroine knew she'd have no answers whatsoever until it actually happened, and yet she couldn't stop asking them. It seemed to her she had gone

through all possible scenarios, predominantly catastrophic, but most of all she feared when   , yes   , just like that,   without warning, imperceptibly.   and   , and then   and everything   , absolutely everything.

The Wi-Fi deigned to connect and the internet slowly appeared. Chaotically, our heroine pulled down the feed. And then, after another wave across the screen, the feed condescended to update to that very state in which the promised and inevitable finally happened. Our heroine froze.

— It's gone, — said our heroine in her normal voice.

— How gone?

— Gone.

— How gone?

— Completely gone.

— Gone?

— What do you mean "gone"?!

— That's it. Gone. Completely.

— Do you mean "gone"?

— I'm afraid so.

— Really? — Anchutka whispered. — All kirdyk?

— Total kirdyk.

— I don't believe it! Already? So early? Ah...

— Not early at all!

— Not in time either!

Pause. Everyone was afraid to look at each other. Our heroine stood up from her chair. Her hands weren't trembling, her breathing was steady, her tear glands weren't working because they refused to work overtime due to the new rules demanded by the tear gland workers' union. In her thoughts, she had already seen it, this exact degree of "goneness".

— Well, here, look... — said our heroine and placed the phone in the centre of the table.

Everyone crowded around the screen. Someone frowned with worry, someone with curiosity.

— It can't be.

— Unbelievable...

— Finally, — whispered Anchutka. — I have already grown old!

— Gone, — our heroine affirmed.

— Apparently, it's gone, — Mnemozina whispered.

— But how... — Phenomen Noumenovich moaned. — It must be some other "it".

— There's only one "it", Phenya. Or rather there was.

— "Let bygones be bygones."

— But what bygones, though?

— What are we even talking about?

— Tu... tu...

— Not "tu," but "ta."

— "Ta"?

— Oh, here we go again...

— Maybe there was nothing at all.

— Maybe there wasn't.

— But there was! There definitely was... Tu... Ta... maybe... what was the name?

— Better if there wasn't.

— Was or wasn't, no point remembering.

— It's fine without "was," and good with "wasn't." No point complaining.

— But wait... No, no! Differently. Bu... bai... There definitely was something.

— Was, wasn't! What's the difference?

— Why even wonder about it!

— When choosing between two supposedly exclusive hypotheses, both turn out to be utter tosh.

— Exactly.

— Let's hug each other. Hands, hands, give me your hands. — Mnemozina suggested.

Reluctantly, looking around, everyone extended their nearest arms to each other and thus formed a circle, in the centre of which the samovar towered.

Little could be heard, almost nothing, except, perhaps, breathing, and even that was quieter than the silence.

— You know, the weather is nasty after all, — Phenomen Noumenovich declared.

— Nastier than anywhere else.

— Disgusting, — Mnemozina agreed. — What do they call such weather?

—   , — our heroine suggested.

— Exactly, "   ".

— Oh, don't say it, it's not that bad.

— "   " through and through.

— Yes, that's the one. Of spectacular proportions.

— All woe and nothing but wickedness.

London

Dec 2022 — Dec 2025

Episode with beams
of appreciation

The author wants to thank:

his dear wife Katya for all kinds of support and encouragements through the torturous process of writing and finishing this book;

his brother Ilya and his friends — Jeanne, Annie, and Konstantin — for reading the early drafts, often too many times;

his readers around the globe for being with him on his journey in this attention economy;

The translator and the publisher join the author and thank:

artists for their lovely work — Lera Ush for the book cover, Irinka Kalinka for the original illustrations;

nova·nevédoma's patrons who supported the press and its endeavours: Jeanne S, Trilety Wade, Thomas J Bevan, Annie Hendrix, Chen Rafaeli, Symon, Bru-Bru, Cate, S.B., Natasha, E. T., Joe H, Joe S, and Joel;

and everyone else who either directly or indirectly helped to make this book real, perhaps too real.

nova·nevédoma invites you to discover more books

at **nova-nevedoma.com**

We are a UK-based independent micro-press for original fictions and translations of public-domain literature.

Things we like / publish: weird characters in whimsical situations, unhinged dialogue, absurd and dark humour, dreamlike sequences, helical narratives, hysterical surrealism, sudden philosophical romps, stylised prose infused with poetry, poignant twists, literary anarchy, magic degeneracy, logic & lunacy, everything cosily melancholic-tender-absurdist, and other sublime matters.

In essence and in form, it's Pure Literature, i.e. Literature for the sake of Literature.

Subscribe to our newsletter at **blog.nova-nevedoma.com** and become our patron if you wish to support our endeavours.

www.ingramcontent.com/pod-product-compliance
Ingram Content Group UK Ltd.
Pitfield, Milton Keynes, MK11 3LW, UK
UKHW010916040326
468628UK00002B/162